Stones Corner

Darkness

Volume 2

Jane Buckley

The Stones Corner Tetralogy

Volume 1: *Turmoil* (January 2021) ISBN 9781912328710
Volume 2: *Darkness* (September 2021) ISBN 9781914225598
Volume 3: *Light* (February 2022)
Volume 4: *Hope* (September 2022)

STONES CORNER, *Darkness* first published in Ireland in 2021 by

Orla Kelly Publishing.

ORLA KELLY PUBLISHING

27 Kilbrody
Mount Oval Village
Cork, IRELAND
T12 E0XT

Warning:
This book contains scenes of torture and violence and descriptions of a sexual nature. It also contains strong and graphic language depicting life in the 1970s.

This novel is a work of fiction and for personal use only, but the storyline is loosely based on actual events during "The Troubles" in Northern Ireland.
The views expressed in this book are "seen" through the eyes of the author.
While the characters are entirely fictitious, the author uses interweaving storylines to highlight how it is essential for us to try to move on from 'The Troubles'. And in doing so, it is therefore crucial for us to understand first how and why 'The Troubles' occurred and to consider the lessons, hardships and sorrows that affected our country and its inhabitants.

ISBN 978-1-914225-59-8

Printed and bound by Anglo Printers
Toberboice Ln,
Mell, Drogheda,
Co. Louth, IRELAND
A92 FFH9

For further information on the Stones Corner tetralogy please visit

www.janebuckleywrites.com or Amazon Kindle
Instagram @janebuckley_writes
Facebook jane buckley writes author
Twitter @janebuckley_sc

JANE BUCKLEY

Jane Buckley was born in Derry/ Londonderry, Northern Ireland, in the late 60s and is the author of the Stones Corner Volume 1, Turmoil. Like many of her generation, she had to leave to find work elsewhere. At the naïve age of 17, she moved to London, where she lived and worked for over twenty-five years before moving to Nice, France.

Along with her husband John (born in Cork, Ireland), they finally returned home in 2017 and live in Donegal. They love it but had forgotten how unpredictable the weather is!

Since Jane lived predominantly in London throughout the awful time that is known as "The Troubles", it was apparent then – and still is today – that not all the facts of the horrific events in Ulster – perpetrated on every side by the warring factions – were presented in an accurate and unbiased way. This was especially true in mainland Britain.

Over recent years, the couple recognised that many of the people they'd been fortunate enough to meet on their travels worldwide didn't understand why or how the conflict here in the North of Ireland began and why it continued for three decades.

Jane found this particularly frustrating and decided to take it upon herself to inform them and others by writing a historical fiction series based on her own childhood experiences and around events from this horrific period in Ireland's history.

She says writing was a frightening project at first, given she'd never written anything substantial before but, being Jane, she'd write not just one novel, but a tetralogy, hence Turmoil, Darkness, Light and Hope!

Jane believes that we need to move on from "The Troubles" as a country while never forgetting how and why they occurred. In recognition of the hardship and suffering endured by so many of our friends, family, and neighbours, we should continue to embrace the healing and reconciliation process.

STONES CORNER, Volume 1, Turmoil

Reviews 2021

March 2021: Goodreads, 5 stars***

"...Just finished reading "Stones Corner, Turmoil" by Jane Buckley. I read a lot, mostly in the Thriller Genre, & I have to say this book was absolutely enthralling from start to finish. I can't wait for the next instalment."

April 2021: Goodreads, 5 stars***

"...This book is a compelling page-turner. I did wonder about reading it - 'The Troubles' haunted decades of my life, even though I wasn't directly affected. But once I picked it up, I couldn't stop reading. The book dives into a violent scene on the first page or two, but don't let this put you off. Though it doesn't shrink from violence, the book is even-handed and shows empathy with the various sides."

C S Holmes for IndieReader, IR Rating 5 stars*** May 2021**

"...Hard-hitting, informative, richly detailed and filled with food for thought, STONES CORNER TURMOIL by Jane Buckley is a novel to get one's teeth into. Best of all, STONES CORNER DARKNESS is coming."

May 2021: Goodreads, 5 stars***

"...This book ended on a cliff-hanger leaving the reader wanting more, and the way it is composed kept me so engaged. If the next book is anything like this one, it will be money well spent. Well done, Jane, on a fantastically written book and thank you again."

May 2021: Goodreads, 5 stars***

"... Wow. From start to finish, this book was hard to put down. A genuine page-turner that had me gripped the whole way through and has me itching to get my hands on the pre-ordered Stones Corner Darkness!"

June 2021: Goodreads, 5 stars***

"...A superbly constructed thriller, written in a style that is accessible to those of us who may never really understand what it is like to live in a war zone; the backdrop for their lives, it's not extraordinary to them, it is, shockingly, their everyday lives.

A novel with a lot of backbone and an enormous depth. It keeps the reader holding his breath to see what is going to happen next."

June 2021: Goodreads, 5 stars***

"...I couldn't put it down, and I know that sounds cliche, but every page I turned, I was waiting for something to happen. This book is one of those special finds, and I can only say good things about it. Yes, it has lots of heart-breaking subjects, but it also follows a love story, which I thought was well written."

My Heart of Tears

My heart was sad that day in Court
Though I never shed a tear,
You gave me strength and made me smile
And took away my fear.

It hurt me so to say good-bye
I couldn't bear to part,
Yet a smile played upon my lips
And the tears stayed in my heart.

What power lies within your hands?
What magic spell's cast o'er me?
How can you make me smile so?
When I'm so sad and lonely?

I miss you so and long to cry
Though I promised only smiles,
I ache to hold you in my arms
And have you there a while.

But my tears are locked within my heart
And my heart's so far from me,
It's with my girl in prison
In a land that's still unfree.

My dearest love, you have my tears.
You hold them in my heart
Take gentle care of both
'til we're no more apart.

ANON

Truth, Justice, Healing, Reconciliation

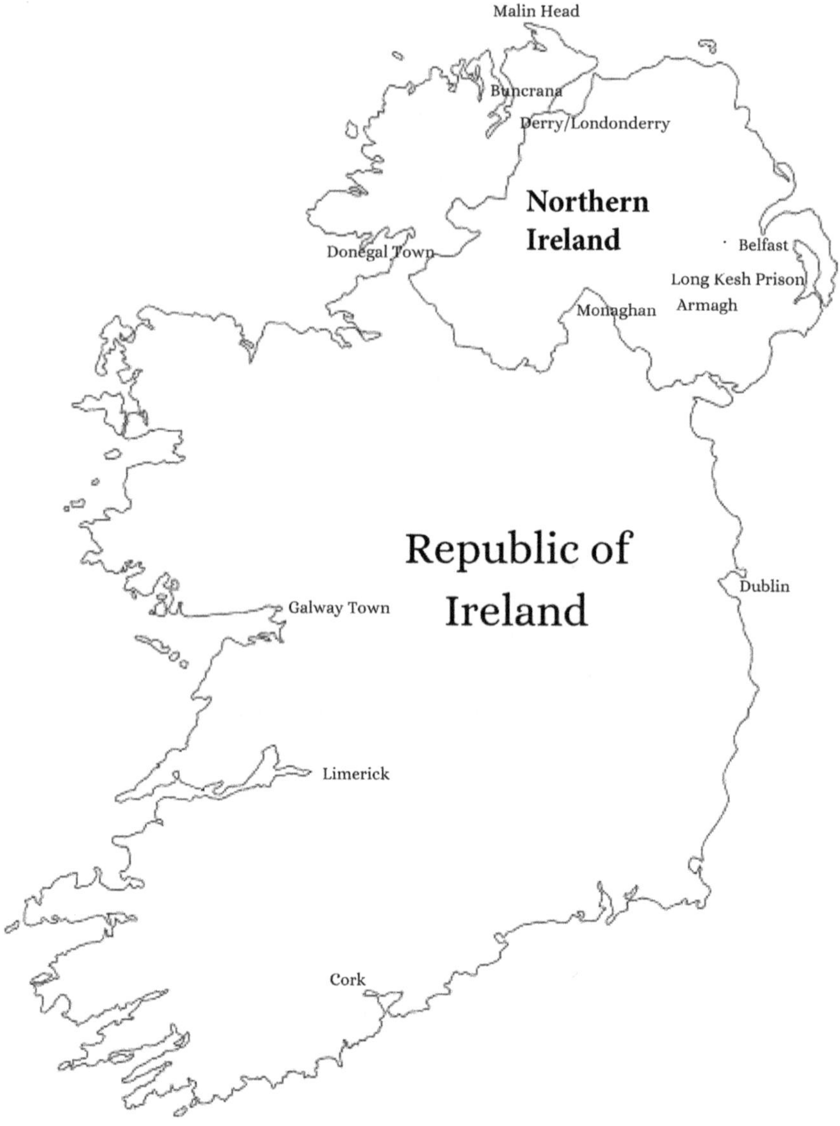
Malin Head
Buncrana
Derry/Londonderry
Northern Ireland
Donegal Town
Belfast
Long Kesh Prison
Monaghan
Armagh
Republic of Ireland
Galway Town
Dublin
Limerick
Cork

Ireland

CONTENTS

Chapter 1

Caitlin McLaughlin sat alone in the cold kitchen and wept as she read the news headlines.

THE IRISH TIMES

Dublin, 1st March 1973

Syndicated from the **Boston Globe**

CARNAGE AT DERRY CITY HOTEL!

Shoot Out and Bomb Scare as City's Bishop Hegarty Fatally Shot

By William J Barter

What began as a mission of hope involving dignitaries, businessmen and women, as well as representatives from all religious groups, unions, political parties, and industries across County Derry turned into a scene of carnage yesterday at the city's largest hotel.

Factory owner Roger Henderson and his nephew James were hosting a conference there in a bid to obtain local and government funding to safeguard thousands of jobs. Their shirt factory, Rocola, is one of the city's largest employers and much of its female workforce comes from the Nationalist Creggan area. Over the past few years, like many other shirt manufacturers in the city, the business has faced competition from the Far East. Rocola's closure would unquestionably result in economic disaster for the industrial heart of the city.

Amongst the Chamber of Commerce representatives and many others attending were SDLP member Tim Hines, RUC Chief Constable George Shalham, British Army Captain Brendan Donlan, his Eminence Bishop James Hegarty and Belfast businessman Charles Jones.

Witnesses described how during a morning refreshment break, a lone gunman, named as Kieran Kelly, 19, from Derry's Bogside – scene of the Bloody Sunday Massacre early last year – disguised himself as a waiter whilst mingling amongst the guests. He then proceeded to plant a bomb in the conference area and soon after became embroiled in a devastating gunfight.

An as-yet unidentified man fired at Bishop Hegarty, fatally wounding him. Kelly returned fire, killing the bishop's assassin, but was himself fatally injured in an exchange of fire. No one has yet been able to identify the bishop's killer, but there are rumours of his affiliation to a group of Loyalist sympathisers led by a local "Mr Big". Bishop Hegarty was well-loved and known for his role in...

* * *

Caitlin angrily threw the newspaper across the kitchen table, deciding she couldn't bear to read any more. Shivering, she stood up and walked across to the red tin tea pot on the gas hob, where she topped up her mug. She gazed out of the kitchen window into the dark early morning, seeing only her own reflection staring back. This was a nightmare. Her eyes were dry, itchy, and red from crying. Almost spellbound, she turned, sat down, and picked up the paper, automatically reading on.

...Terrified attendees were quickly ushered to safety by RUC Chief Constable George Shalham and British Army Captain Donlan. Immediately afterwards, acting on information received, both men bravely searched for an explosive device. The Bomb Squad, known here as Felix, were immediately called in. Upon its discovery, the device was defused and proved to be amateurish and unlikely to have exploded. However, the security services were not prepared to take any chances.

A young girl believed to be an accomplice of Kelly's, Martina McLaughlin, 17, from Creggan, was removed from the scene in a highly distressed state. She is currently being questioned at Strand Road Police Station. Unconfirmed reports state McLaughlin helped deliver the bomb to Kelly and is also suspected of taking part in a recent spate of beatings, torture, and murder of young British soldiers...

* * *

Many months later, Caitlin lay in her single bed, listening to the incessant rain bouncing off the slate roof. Once again, it was 5 a.m., and she was lying wide awake, bereft and in despair.

She hadn't recovered from the catastrophic events at the hotel and the horror of seeing her own sister Tina being arrested and detained on terrorism charges. But more hurtfully, Caitlin didn't believe she'd ever recover from James Henderson's, complete rejection of her after the incident. She was mentally and physically exhausted from grief and shock. Following Tina's arrest, Caitlin, Uncle Tommy, and her mother had called into the Strand Road barricaded police station several times in the hope of seeing the young girl but had been continually refused access. Brendan Doherty, their solicitor, eventually managed to get Tina transferred to the local psychiatric unit, Gransha, to be assessed and deemed fit for trial.

Caitlin's brother, Martin, remained interned in Long Kesh. She'd visited him a handful of times and could tell he wasn't exactly overwhelmed with joy to see her. He'd appeared dirty, scruffy, old, and growled with real menace when he learned about Kieran Kelly and his rogue strike against the gathering of Derry's great and good. Martin was especially furious when he was informed of Tina's involvement in the operations and her abuse at Kelly's hand in grooming her into becoming a honey-trap for British Soldiers. He'd always been extra-protective of his little sister and cursed Kelly to hell, saying it was just as well the wanker was already dead.

Although there was just her mother and Caitlin left in the house, the British Army and RUC continued to raid it. The McLaughlins were being targeted and knew it. The Brits were relentless, unforgiving, and out for retribution – no matter how petty. Raids became a weekly event, and each time the soldiers would leave their mark in a trail of wanton destruction – revenge for their mates – though Caitlin and her mother Majella had had nothing to do with Kelly's sick vigilante campaign. Cushion covers were ripped and torn open, their innards discarded, mattresses were lifted and overturned, cupboards emptied, and the contents deliberately strewn everywhere. Majella no longer fought back, and the two women would tidy up as best they could in silence after the soldiers and policemen left.

In the end, there were no more cushions to tear, the cupboards were almost empty, and the mattress in Tina's room was stripped and left unmade on the floor. Caitlin wished with all her heart that her father was still around. She missed him beyond words and morbidly wondered what was left of his body now as he rested in the city's large cemetery. Had he all but disappeared? Were his cufflinks still there? It was strange what crossed her mind in the wee hours as she lay awake. Sleep rarely visited her. The house had become a mausoleum, her life dreary and unfulfilled. She functioned, but only just.

Her mother was nothing like the fiery, strong woman she'd once been. Instead, she'd shrunk into herself with shame and guilt, aided by the powerful pills she'd been prescribed.

Cruel gossipmongers amongst their neighbours began to learn that not only had Tina helped Kelly, but it was likely she was involved somehow in the shooting and murder of Bishop Hegarty, and they secretly condemned the McLaughlins.

Majella remained quiet and dignified in public, taking it all onto her own shoulders. She didn't have the fight in her to defend anyone, not even her own family. She wished she were dead and with her beloved husband, Patrick. She prayed so hard every day they'd be together soon. She was lost, heart and soul.

When her mother disappeared to bed, either drunk, sedated to the hilt or both, Caitlin would stay downstairs alone, remembering her first kiss with James, her boss, in this very room. He'd dared visit her following the bombing on Shipquay Street when Anne, her best friend, suffered horrendous life-changing injuries and lost a leg. Caitlin had been both shocked and delighted at the tenderness and care James had shown. On reflection, she knew the precise moment she had fallen deeply in love with him: during that first kiss. She could still smell him, still feel the touch of his skin and those long, lingering kisses she'd never wanted to end. Later, they'd stolen some private time away together, a weekend of beautiful food, hot bubble baths, champagne and amazing lovemaking that now felt it'd never happened – a dream of perfect happiness. Just a few brief encounters followed late at night when they were alone in his office. He was gorgeous, and he'd made her feel so special. She knew no one would ever make her feel that way again.

During those short months together, Caitlin was ecstatic, feeling alive, fulfilled, and invincible. He'd helped her heal and given her life new purpose following the death of her father.

Laughing softly, she remembered his vibrant green eyes that morning when he'd stood up to welcome his guests at the conference. He was excited; he was buzzing and so full of confidence and belief in what they were doing. He'd been proud to pull together such a diverse group, securely and safely under one roof – or so they'd thought.

The black spectre of nightmare rose to the surface, replacing the happy memories. Wave after wave of shock and humiliation crashed over her as she recalled the last time, she'd been with him, that fateful day at the City Hotel.

George Shalham had grabbed James's elbow and taken Caitlin's wrist, pushing them both towards the stairwell at the far side of the conference room, shouting, "James, Caitlin, get out of here! Fast as you can!"

She'd instinctively reached for James's hand, but he'd pulled away from her as if burnt. There was fury in his face as he began to strike her with verbal blow after blow.

"Don't you dare touch me, Caitlin! That's your sister over there, isn't it? Your fucking sister and that murdering waiter – were you part of this too?! Did I not see what you really were all along?"

He'd given her no chance to reply before turning his back on her and running down the stairwell, leaving her behind. She'd shuddered at the venom in his words but the idea that he could believe she was part of this cruel conspiracy was unbelievable.

George Shalham, the RUC police chief who'd lent his support as a longstanding friend of the Henderson family, impatiently pushed her after James. "Go, Caitlin! We're running out of time!"

In desperation, she ran after the man she loved, crying out his name.

Eventually, she caught up with him on the ground floor and watched while he fumbled and swore in his efforts to open a fire exit. He ignored her as he furiously forced the heavy door open and quickly stepped out into a sodden delivery yard. She looked around frantically, seized his arm in a bid to lead him to safety and cried.

"This way, James, please."

Once again, he roughly pushed her hand off and looked at her, his eyes now jaded, dark and angry, and glinting with hatred and scorn. "No, you treacherous bitch. Why don't you slink back off to Creggan where you and your lying, murdering family belong? We're done...finished!"

Her whole body jolted as she remembered the unfairness of those taunts. Her mind screamed at the injustice of it when she considered her innocent father's death in police custody and then her mother's gradual decline into tablet-taking and drinking. Caitlin had no idea how her sister could've been seduced into terrorism by the likes of Kieran Kelly. She was horrified by what Tina had done, but worse still was remembering the look on James's face when his lover had admitted the schoolgirl who'd helped Kelly in his murderous plotting was her sister. The pain of his instant rejection of Caitlin was lasting and deep. Unlike the raw grief she'd felt on losing her father, this was a living thing that sucked at her heart like a leech. James was alive; he was working in the same city and yet was utterly untouchable.

After their bitter parting, she couldn't go back to Rocola and within a week received a curt, formal letter from Roger Henderson, stating "...your services are no longer required". The short letter also included a cheque for £40.00, which, in a rage, she'd torn up into what felt like a thousand pieces. She wanted nothing from any of them, she'd decided, knowing full well how vindictive and bigoted Mrs Parkes, the office manager, was. She'd always had it in for Caitlin and was probably smiling when she typed the notice letter.

By luck, she managed to find another job – working in a photographer's studio near the city centre. The proprietor, Raymond Burns, proved to be a bit of a weasel, with his dirty, chemical-smelling hands always trying to grope her. She'd put an end to it one day by grabbing them tightly, squeezing them as hard and as painfully as she could and warning him not to touch her again. Caitlin then reminded him she knew people, and all she'd have to do was make a call. It was risky to threaten him, but – like most bullies – when she stood up to him, he got the message and let her be.

Shaking her head despairingly, Caitlin tightly pulled on her father's Aran jumper, slightly tainted with faded brown bloodstains, and got up to look at the small, speckled mirror that hung on the Holly-Hobbie-postered wall. Photographs of happier days were neatly tucked in around the mirror's square frame. She studied them for a moment, particularly the one Tina had taken of the family one Christmas Day just a few years ago, using her only gift, a Kodak camera. They'd gone through the whole film in one day and never got around to buying another since processing it was so expensive. It showed them all, smiling and carefree under their paper hats, the festive turkey dinner laid out before them on the round kitchen table. This occasion was probably the last time the McLaughlins had been happy together.

Around 7 a.m. Caitlin heard banging at the front door. Please God, she thought, not another raid! She sat up too quickly from the bed and immediately felt nauseous and weak. The banging grew louder and more frantic whilst Caitlin shouted out in fury and ran down the stairs. Through the glass panel in the front door, newly replaced, she saw the silhouette of a large-framed man impatiently walking back and forth. Caitlin immediately recognised her Uncle Tommy and, with relief, cried, "Alright, alright, I'm coming! Hold your horses!"

She fumbled with the new lock and managed to open the door halfway before Tommy barged his way into the hallway.

"Jesus, Caitlin, you took your time!" he barked. He looked frozen and immediately made his way into the kitchen, calling over his shoulder, "Is your Ma up?"

Caitlin wasn't sure – she hadn't heard anything coming from her mother's room. "I don't think so. Why, Tommy? What's wrong?"

"They've brought the date forward for Tina's trial. The bastards! Apparently, she's fit to appear in court. Can you fucking believe it? They're using her as a scapegoat, Caitlin!"

She looked at Tommy, who was wearing his usual khaki fur-hooded parka jacket and jeans. Her mother's brother had aged years in the months since Tina was arrested, and his old joviality and good humour were long gone, his once calm and competent demeanour no longer in evidence. Instead, he looked like a man who carried the weight of the world on his shoulders. Someone had cut his long red hair way too short so that it accentuated the spidery, burst veins around his broken nose and upper cheeks. Somehow, he'd cracked the middle of his black-framed glasses and messily had attempted to mend them with sticky brown tape – they looked ridiculous.

His niece watched helplessly as he slumped down heavily into a chair and put his head in his hands, muttering as he referred to his only sister, "This is going to kill her. Your mother isn't fit enough to go through this shite."

Caitlin couldn't disagree but tried to soothe him. "You want some breakfast, Tommy? I think Mammy was hoping to go and see Tina this morning."

Tommy sighed, "Just tea, love, that's fine," and sat in silence, thinking.

He couldn't eat. His appetite had long gone. There'd been a time he'd have been pleased to lose a few pounds, but for now, he couldn't care less. Food was the last thing on his mind. So much had happened, so much *was happening*; he didn't have time to think straight, and the pressure of it all weighed heavily on him. Every day, every fucking single day, there was a bombing, a murder, a massacre in some shape or form – and he was close to it all, in one way or another. His days of being a straightforward community worker for Sinn Féin seemed far behind him. Recent events had pushed him into unknown territory.

So far, Brendan Doherty, their family solicitor, had proved to be a godsend. Tommy only hoped he could keep Tina in the psychiatric hospital by judicial process. It was the best place for her. Brendan had already twice renewed their appeal to extend her stay in care and won, but the most recent appeal had been summarily rejected. The thought of his youngest niece going to prison in her current mentally fragile condition was almost too much for Tommy to bear. They were charging her with murder, endangering life, and PIRA membership, though Brendan continually reassured him they'd a good argument against conviction. It was evident Tina had been groomed, bullied, and coerced into doing what she did for Kelly. The fucker had threatened her family, for Christ's sake!

Anyway, Brendan told Tommy he didn't believe the judge could impose a lengthy custodial sentence. Tina was still a minor, and the court would have to accept her medical history as a backup to any plea for leniency during sentencing. At least that was some consolation, Tommy thought, but he was still extremely worried. Tina had been in hospital for five months already, and the trial was in a month's time, 24th July, dangerously close to her eighteenth birthday on the 28th. He'd heard about the awful conditions in Armagh Women's Gaol, where he knew many local girls and women were serving life sentences. *Sweet God, not little Tina too.*

His thoughts returned to Caitlin, who'd placed his tea in front of him and was waiting for him to speak.

"Sorry, love, I was gone there." Then, raising his eyes to the ceiling, he asked after his sister, "How's she been since I was here last?"

Caitlin shook her head sadly. "Away with it. She's always away with it these days."

He said nothing. He'd asked his and Majella's mother to come and help here, but the miserly old bitch refused. She'd told him outright they were all an embarrassment, and she wanted nothing more to do with any of them.

"I wanted to tell Majella about the new court date myself… to warn her. I've already seen what the *Derry Journal* has written about it this morning. It's splashed all over the fucking front page!" he said, in between slurping at his tea.

Caitlin could imagine all too easily what had been said.

"I have to go to work, Tommy. Finish your tea, will you? I'll wake Mammy and bring her down."

He nodded. "Okay, love. How's the job, by the way?"

"Fine, Tommy. Fine."

He immediately sensed her unhappiness.

"You sure?" he asked, holding her back tenderly with his hand.

Caitlin looked at her uncle and smiled softly, an expression filled with love for him and his endless care for them. "It's fine, Tommy; it's a job. We've more important things to worry about right now. I'll go get her."

He squeezed her hand and told her comfortingly, "You know I'm here for you, for all of you. And you can tell me *anything*, anything at all."

"I know, Tommy. I know. Thanks."

Once upstairs, Caitlin stood outside her mother's bedroom door, waited for a moment, and braced herself. Her heartbeat felt too heavy and sounded too loud in the silence of the narrow landing until she heard her mother's racking cough. Caitlin drew in her breath and entered the room.

It was the smell that hit her first. *Christ*! Majella had been refusing to bathe, and the stink in the room, of her dirty clothes and body, was nauseating. Caitlin swallowed deeply as she walked to the window, drew back the light floral curtains and opened the catch to let in some fresh air. The bright light of day filled the room as she turned to look down at the curled, sorrowful figure in the bed and said, "Mammy, Tommy's here. He needs to talk to you."

The candlewick spread was immediately pulled up over Majella's greying hair. She mumbled under the covers. Caitlin couldn't make out what she was saying.

"I can't hear you," she said as she sat on the edge of the mattress and pulled the bedspread down. Majella's face looked drawn and washed-out as she smiled weakly at her eldest daughter and softly greeted her, "Hello, sunshine."

"Hey," Caitlin replied before carefully pulling the bedclothes further down, encouraging her mother to get up. "Tommy needs to talk to you."

Majella nodded and slowly manoeuvred herself to sit up on the side of the bed, revealing two emaciated, withered, and blue-veined legs. "Okay. What time is it?"

"Just after seven," Caitlin answered. "I have to get ready for work in a bit."

"Can't you come to the hospital with me, love? I don't feel I can do it on my own," Majella pleaded as she grasped Caitlin's hand.

"I can't, Mammy. I have to work. You know I do." Caitlin carefully pulled her hand away and stood up to go. She loved her mother beyond belief but couldn't stay in this pitiful and foul-smelling room. The anguish of seeing someone so crushed and broken was soul-destroying.

As Caitlin made to leave, Majella yawned and answered dejectedly, "I know, love, sorry. Someone has to keep a wage coming in. Sure, maybe Tommy will come with me? Somehow, I managed to clean some of Tina's clothes, and Mrs McFadden brought in some Wagon Wheels, Tina's favourites."

"That's nice, Mammy. You want some help downstairs?" Caitlin asked.

Majella waved her daughter away. "Don't worry about me; you get ready for work. I'll sort myself out."

"You sure?" Caitlin asked, inwardly relieved as she left her mother to sort herself out. Caitlin wasn't in any hurry to take on the responsibility of telling Majella about Tina's trial date being brought forward. She didn't have the energy and decided to leave the task to poor Tommy.

As soon as she'd chosen what to wear from her limited wardrobe, Caitlin walked back to the bathroom. She passed her mother on the landing, still not fully dressed. Majella remained in her creased, floral cotton nightdress under her husband's old navy, extra-large dressing gown. Caitlin could smell BO but saw that her mother had at least tried to wash her face and brush her hair back into a loose ponytail.

It was a start. The women smiled solemnly at each other as they each made their way in different directions, Caitlin to the bathroom and Majella downstairs to the kitchen.

Caitlin turned the hot tap on first and, as always, hoped there'd be enough water for her to have a shallow bath. Unusually, there was plenty today, and as she sank into the steaming water, goosebumps engulfed her body. She sank further, as deep as she could, relishing the heat. She thought of James Henderson and of them sharing a bubble bath in the hotel in Donegal Town. She remembered and savoured every detail while watching the steam from the water meet the cold air of the bathroom. It hovered just above the surface.

She moaned and closed her tired eyes. A few short minutes passed before she heard her mother's raucous screaming and crying from the kitchen below.

Poor Tommy.

Chapter 2

Tina McLaughlin stood in the dock, eyes unnaturally wide and clouded. Her once wild and curly red hair was now greasy and limp. Much to her annoyance, it fell aggravatingly over her itching, blotchy face. Eczema had broken out on her dry, flaky skin, and it irritated her, with colourless liquid oozing around her fading freckles. Her mouth was parched, and her lips coated in a thin white foam from the drugs she'd been prescribed. At one time, she'd liked the warm fuzzy feeling they gave her but now found she was thirsty most of the time. She couldn't see any water anywhere and looked back at two policemen, who stood upright with disinterested deadpan expressions, guarding her from behind. She hoped they'd notice her mute appeal but instead, they stared straight ahead as if she didn't exist.

Jerking and juddering uncontrollably, she flicked back the irritating locks of hair again, only for them to fall back rebelliously in front of her face. She must look like a complete nutter, she supposed vaguely. As she studied the courtroom, her frantic, convulsive movements and incoherent and soft mutterings were clearly making some people uncomfortable.

She'd been dressed that morning by her mother in the same black top and trousers she'd worn to her father's funeral months before. But this time, they hung limp and loose over her thin frame. It was evident to some of the onlookers the young girl in the dock was far from well – she made a pitiful figure.

Tina's eyes scoured the room until she found her mammy, Caitlin and Tommy. She was disappointed to see her brother Martin wasn't there, so instead gave her mother a rapid, child-like wave. Majella and Tommy had visited Gransha the night before in an attempt to explain to Tina what was going to happen in court. Through the haze of listening to them, she'd noticed they both seemed anxious and had done her best to tell them she'd be fine, saying: "Don't worry; I like it here."

She'd been sharing a room in the psychiatric hospital with a much older woman who talked constantly to her invisible child, Rosaleen. Tina sat transfixed for hours, watching as her roommate sang lullabies and whispered tender loving words to her phantom toddler. She cradled and rocked a soft pink elephant-printed baby blanket that she'd rolled up and held snugly in her arms.

"It's so sad. Turns out her little girl was killed by a bomb in a tea shop a while ago."

Tommy and his sister had heard the same story numerous times from Tina on previous visits. It appeared to be all she was capable of talking about. Trying to explain her situation and get her to listen to what would happen in court had proved futile.

One of her guards came forward, grasped Tina's shoulders and pushed her down onto the steel-framed chair in the middle of the stout oak dock. The court grew noisier and noisier as onlookers, newspaper reporters, soldiers, RUC men and women, lawyers and barristers, all crammed into the room. Some shouted to each other across the floor whilst others congregated and whispered so as not to be overheard. As with the introduction of what was known as juryless courts i.e. Diplock Courts, all verdicts were made by just a single judge.

Tina could also just about make out some of the spectators' faces, male and female, high up on one side of the public gallery. They were standing and hurling abuse at those seated below. Their curled fists were raised high in the air as they cried out in frustration and anger.

"Shame on you! No trial! No trial! Not guilty! Have pity, for Christ's sake!" They were getting angrier by the minute.

The other side of the gallery was occupied predominantly by men who waved large Union Jack flags back and forth and repeatedly sang "God Save the Queen" and other Loyalist songs. It was mayhem.

Suddenly a loud voice was heard across the din as a dark-suited, austere-looking man shouted from one side of the bench.

"Silence in Court! The Honourable Mr Justice Matthew Dodds presiding!"

Almost immediately, the chamber simmered down, and silence fell. Tina studied the man beneath the white wig.

* * *

The Honourable Mr Justice Dodds took his seat on the bench set high above the court floor and looked down at the assembled lawyers, clerks and security. His beady eyes, grey moustache, long pointed nose and jug ears gave him the well-known nickname "Dumbo", but he had a fearsome reputation for his hardline decisions despite his comical appearance.

Over days of drawn-out argument and debate, Tina found herself drifting off into her own befuddled world. For hour after hour, RUC officers, army personnel, forensic and medical experts and a host of other witnesses gave evidence against her. The prosecution aimed to build a seemingly unassailable case that would prove beyond reasonable doubt that Martina McLaughlin had been just as involved in the atrocities she stood accused of as the dead PIRA bomber and murderer, Kieran Kelly.

Throughout the proceedings, sitting in the courtroom were the parents of Valentine (Val) Holmes, the young British soldier Kieran Kelly had abducted, tortured and shot in a hillside barn above the city. Holmes's mother, Susan, was a proud and attractive woman who kept her dyed-blonde head held high and gave no obvious sign of how she was feeling or the unending pain she and her husband Tony must have been enduring.

Finally, after several long days, it was time for Tina to be unceremoniously escorted to the witness box. As she did every day, she caught her mother's eye and smiled. She noticed Caitlin smiled too and was glad. As the long days of court wore on, Tina was finding it more difficult to sleep. The lovely light feeling she'd grown used to on the medication wasn't happening anymore. Today the poor girl had woken and found herself anxious, tearful, and for the first time, really afraid. However, as she looked to the back of the courtroom, she saw – as clear as day – the love of her life, Kieran Kelly. He smiled at her reassuringly. *Don't worry, Honey; I'm here.*

A stocky, short, bespectacled man in a black gown and white wig approached her. Before opening his questioning of Martina, Geoff Wilkinson, QC, first paused for effect, surveying the spectators in the gallery. Suddenly and without warning, in a clear, posh English voice that everyone in the court could hear, he turned sharply to the witness box and addressed the accused.

"Miss McLaughlin… or Tina. May I call you Tina?"

He waited for her assent, but she was too distracted to pay him much attention, busy searching for Kieran, who'd suddenly disappeared. The QC waited a few seconds for effect before he smirked and sarcastically commented, none too softly under his breath, "*Maybe not.*" Many in the court sniggered.

He paused again before placing his next lethal dart. "Miss McLaughlin, I'd like to ask you something before we formally begin. Is there anything you wish to say to the court –especially to the parents of the young gunner, Valentine Holmes, who've had to endure and listen to all the extremely sensitive and harrowing evidence so far, day after day?" He pointed to Susan and Tony Holmes, whose heads hung pitifully low. Tina said nothing.

His voice grew louder. "Don't you have *anything* to say to this mother and father whose only son… their *only child*, I should emphasise… was heartlessly tortured, burned, beaten and shot by you and your accomplice Kieran Kelly on the night of the sixteenth of November 1972?"

The watchers in the gallery gasped in surprise, taken aback by such a harsh and direct opening.

"Order! Order!" the judge shouted.

The QC waited until silence filled the room once again. He stared coldly at the accused. Tina looked around nervously and began to pick a loose piece of skin on the side of her face. She couldn't understand why everyone in the room was looking at her in such a strange way and began to rock back and forth. She glanced to her mother for reassurance, but Majella wasn't looking at her, nor was Caitlin. They were both staring at their feet, hearts and minds full of shame and dread. Only Tommy caught her eye with a wan smile.

Suddenly Wilkinson, with one hand hovering over the witness box, banged it down hard. Tina jumped in shock, clearly terrified, and hit her arm against one of her guards, who roughly pushed her away.

"Would you like me to repeat the question, Miss McLaughlin?" the QC shouted.

Tina could only bob her head.

"Do you have *anything* to say to the parents of Valentine Holmes whom *you* tortured and murdered alongside your accomplice, Kieran Kelly?"

Tina's defence barrister, Timothy Swalding, QC, immediately stood up and shouted, "Objection, m'lord!"

"Overruled," Judge Dodds directed.

"But, m'lord, my client is still on trial and hasn't been found guilty of *anything* yet!" Swalding cried.

Once again, the exclamations from the crowd began to increase, but Judge Dodds coughed loudly, looked around in an effort to signal for quiet and mumbled audibly to himself, "*Not yet.*"

"Thank you, m'lord," Geoff Wilkinson said, eyes briefly meeting Dodds's.

"Miss McLaughlin, do you have anything you wish to say?"

Tina felt the need to say something and could only think of one word. "Sorry."

Seconds passed as the QC allowed the inadequacy of her reply to sink in. The spectators knew it'd been a mistake on Tina's part. "That's it, Miss McLaughlin, a simple '*Sorry*?"

His body language said it all as he shook his head, condemning the response. "In that case, Miss McLaughlin, let's continue."

He stepped away from the witness box and addressed the court, catching the eye of Susan Holmes, whom he'd met many times before. He smiled at her and turned again to face the accused.

"Please, Miss McLaughlin, could you tell the court how you came to be involved with Kieran Kelly?"

Almost immediately, Tina's mood lightened as she recalled their first meeting – how he'd bowed, taken her hand and kissed it, ever so gently.

"We met in Stones Corner; he kissed my hand and called me Princess. He asked me out for tea."

"I see," the QC said, pretending to be uninterested as he read a note clasped in his hand.

Tina didn't need to be pressed to continue as carefree memories of her early months with Kieran flooded back.

"He bought me beautiful clothes," she said, giggling. "He even did my make-up, bought me a wig – a proper wig with real hair an' all. He made me feel beautiful. No one ever did that for me before. I loved him." A cloud of warmth seemed to bear her up as she recalled their time together.

"He taught me stuff, history and all. He was clever and so handsome." Suddenly she became shy, wondering if she'd said too much.

Counsel could see she'd finished and immediately picked up on one point. "You said he bought you a… what was it again?" He paused, supposedly struggling to recall. "Ah, yes, a wig, *a proper wig with real hair*! I ask you, Miss McLaughlin, was this *real wig* the blonde one that you wore when you captivated young Val Holmes, when you gained his trust, when you flaunted yourself at him…only to lead him into a death trap? As the forensic evidence will show, you drugged him, kidnapped him, tortured and shot him! You and Kelly then had the audacity to throw the poor lad's pitiful remains into the middle of a road where they were run over and further desecrated by a heavy goods vehicle!"

There was a collective gasp as, with this description of her son's vicious murder, Susan Holmes couldn't contain herself any longer and screamed. She stood up and pointed to Tina in the witness box. "Murderer! You murdered my boy! How could you?"

Her shocked husband jumped up from his own seat at her outburst and pulled her back, sobbing uncontrollably, into the comfort of his arms. Dodds let the scenario play out. The QC waited until calm had settled in the court and it was appropriate for him to carry on.

"Let's move on, Miss McLaughlin. The schoolbag you willingly carried into the Londonderry City Hotel – did you know what the bag contained?"

Tina feverishly shook her head. "No, honest, I'd no idea!"

Once again, the QC's voice rose higher as he barked out his loaded questions and statements. "So tell me, and of course the court, *why* were you wearing an old school uniform when you entered the City Hotel? I mean, didn't you think it odd Mr Kelly asked you to dress up as a sweet, innocent schoolgirl, plaits and all, carrying a brown leather satchel?" He laughed scornfully, inviting the court to imagine her deliberately adding braids to her disguise in an effort to look younger.

"You're telling us, Miss McLaughlin, it never entered your mind, *not once,* that Kelly expressly wanted you to appear harmless and innocent so that you would remain unchallenged inside that well-secured environment? My goodness, whoever would expect a young schoolgirl to be carrying a *bomb* in a satchel? But I say, Miss Martina McLaughlin, YOU knew EXACTLY what you were doing and what was in that bag!"* He chuckled before driving the final nail in the coffin. "In fact, you most likely helped him to make the device!"

"No! No, I told them... Kieran frightened me. He told me if I didn't do what he wanted, he'd hurt my family!" Tina cried loudly whilst frantically looking around the courtroom for someone who'd believe her.

"I refute that! I believe you knew *exactly* what was in the bag! I believe you loved Kelly and willingly took part in the sick games you played with him! How cunning and clever you are: one night a blonde bombshell enticing young men for you and Kelly to beat up, abuse and even *murder,* and the next apparently a young pigtailed schoolgirl, making and carrying a lethal weapon into a public space that could have killed hundreds of innocents!"

QC Geoff Wilkinson was having a ball, loving his moment in the spotlight. He paused before moving closer to the accused and pointed a bony finger at her. "*I say to YOU, Miss McLaughlin, YOU knew EXACTLY what Kelly was up to from the very beginning!*"

Almost breathless, the QC studied the spectators for their reaction. He'd reached them, clearly and effectively; their horrified expressions said it all. He smiled to himself. Perfect. This was going exactly as he and Dodds had planned.

Eventually, after many hours of closely questioning Tina, the prosecution's case was over. Wilkinson had played her to perfection. He'd sensationally portrayed her to the judge and especially the onlookers as a greedy, vindictive and dangerous manipulator, who'd not only led the young soldiers on but maybe even Kieran Kelly too! There was no one who could refute what he'd implied. Kelly was dead, so the prosecutor put the rap on Tina and blamed her for everything. Wasn't she the one who'd led the first young soldier, Arnie Waters, to a brutal beating, so bad he'd spent several months in hospital? He survived but, in the end, had no choice but to leave the army on a medical discharge. The poor lad wasn't even well enough to appear in court as a key witness. Wasn't she the one who drugged Val Holmes in the restaurant, placed him in the car that Kelly was driving, took him to the barn and watched as he was tied up and tortured? Hadn't they found her fingerprints on Holmes's belongings and on the black bags in which they'd wrapped his bloodied, naked corpse? They'd even found her fingerprints and saliva on a bottle of whiskey that she and Kelly had drunk from – no doubt while celebrating the death of the young soldier. As for the attempted hotel bombing, numerous witnesses confirmed Tina's presence and swore on oath they'd seen her carrying the satchel as she entered the building. The prosecution had built a rock-solid case.

Every day, Brendan Doherty listened in horror and grew increasingly concerned about the direction the case was going in. They were losing and badly. He only hoped their QC – who, to his surprise, had made very few objections to prosecuting counsel's cross-examination – could turn it around.

It was time for the defence to begin to put their case. Timothy Swalding, QC, stood up. He was short and fat with eyes set so far apart from one another under bushy eyebrows that it was difficult to say in which direction he was looking. His gown was creased and dirty-looking, making him appear far less smart and distinguished than his opponent.

He moved slowly towards Tina, who sat drained and still on her chair, one hand propped on the witness box to keep her from falling over. She felt exhausted, confused, already defeated. All they did was ask question after question after question. She didn't want to be here anymore. She was finished. Her QC gently touched her hand and said in a kindly voice, "Miss McLaughlin, it's clear to this court that you are exhausted and unwell. Would you like some water?"

It was the first time during her protracted interrogation that someone had shown her a little kindness. She stuttered, "Yes – yes, please."

He nodded to one of the guards, who reluctantly fetched his prisoner a glass of water and passed it to her. She drank it slowly and placed the half-full glass on her lap, holding it tightly between her hands.

"Better?" her counsel asked kindly.

"Yes. Thank you."

"Miss McLaughlin, we've heard from my learned friend where and when you met Kieran Kelly. We've also heard him describe your relationship over time. If I may, I'd like to ask you a few more questions?"

Tina didn't want to answer anymore but looked to Tommy, who nodded, his blue eyes telling her it'd be fine.

"Okay," she answered sheepishly.

"Good. I'll try to keep them short. You fell deeply in love with Mr Kelly, didn't you, Miss McLaughlin?"

"Oh, yes, he was everything to me."

"And you'd have done anything for him, wouldn't you? *Absolutely anything*?"

"Objection, m'lord! Leading question!" Wilkinson cried out in fury.

"Sustained!" the judge declared.

"M'lord." Swalding smiled apologetically at him before turning back to Tina.

"Were you ever frightened of Mr Kelly?"

Tina nodded vigorously. "Yes, I was! Not at first, when he was being fun and telling me how much he cared for me, but in the end... yes."

"And when, Miss McLaughlin, did he really begin to frighten you?"

"It was about the time he made me go out with Val. Val was lovely, so funny and kind, but I think Kieran was jealous. He got really angry that night."

"The night of Val Holmes's murder. Am I right?"

"Yes."

"And tell us, Miss McLaughlin, what exactly happened that night. Take your time."

Tina didn't want to think about it and shook her head frantically. "I can't! I can't bear to remember."

Her eyes began to fill, and her mind and body recoiled as the horrific memories of that evening returned. The blood, the smell of piss, burned flesh and whiskey, Val's nakedness, then Kieran's anger, and how she'd hidden from him in the car until he'd dragged her out. Finally, Val's cold bloodied dead body being wrapped in black plastic… It was too much; she couldn't, she wouldn't think about it!

"I can't!" she cried, squeezing the glass in her hands until it shattered and water emptied onto her clothes and the floor as shards flew in every direction. She wailed when she raised her hand and saw the blood trickling from the piece of broken glass stuck deep into her finger.

"I think we ought to take a break, with your agreement, m'lord," Swalding suggested, referring to Tina's injury.

"I suppose we must," Judge Dodds agreed reluctantly. He just wanted this case done and dusted; it'd gone on too long already.

Thirty minutes later, Tina had settled a little once her finger had been tightly bandaged. It throbbed. Her QC had spoken to her briefly and told her to try and focus, to concentrate and to listen carefully to what he was asking. He needed her to emphasise how much she'd loved Kieran and that everything was his fault, not hers. She tried to remember his words as she watched him approach her in court and smile.

"Miss McLaughlin, from what you've said, I believe you loved Mr Kelly very deeply. I emphasise that, following the death of your father in police custody, your brother Martin – to whom you are very close – being interned in Long Kesh, and given the pressures of living here in these troubled times, Kelly recognised your vulnerability."

"Objection!"

Swalding ignored his colleague's protest. "He deliberately chose you because he knew you were susceptible, would be easy to manipulate and groom. To gain your trust, he spoiled you, took you shopping, did your make-up. He even taught you Irish history…"

"Objection!" Wilkinson wailed and muttered, "Ridiculous!"

Swalding wasn't finished. He hurried on, "He was your knight in shining armour, and you grew infatuated with him, loved him, wanted to please him, to do *anything* for him!"

"OBJECTION!"

"He made you feel special, Miss McLaughlin, didn't he? You'd do ANYTHING to please him!" Swalding shouted before nodding to the judge, ready to accept his reprimand.

"I really must object, m'lord. This is flagrant leading of the witness!" Wilkinson cried in fury, jumping up again from his chair.

Dodds agreed and admonished counsel for the defence. "Mr Swalding, you should know better. Don't try that line again in my court!"

"M'lord." Swalding wasn't in the least concerned about his telling off but turned back to face his client. "Please, Miss McLaughlin, in your own words, do you disagree with anything I've just suggested?"

At the thought of Kieran, Tina's heart ached. "He made me feel like the only girl in the world. I loved him...I still love him!'

It was the last straw. She broke down and cried. The horror of Kieran's death returned to her again. The memories of his bleeding body and lifeless dark eyes terrified her so much she found herself retreating into the marshmallow world inside her head, where everything was soft, rosy and safe. She was happier there. She whispered out loud to no one in particular, "He called me 'flower'."

Swalding moved closer and asked, "Excuse me?"

Tina looked up, surprised this man hadn't understood what she'd said, and repeated herself. "He called me 'flower'."

Swalding sighed dramatically and turned to face the open court, echoing her words loudly. "Mr Kelly called you 'flower'?"

Tina shook her head, remembering. "No, not Kieran, silly. Val did! He called me 'flower'." She looked at his parents across the courtroom and smiled softly, "He was lovely. Fun..."

The couple sat grief-stricken and shocked rigid. They'd never expected the girl to talk in such a way. Sarah Holmes's body quivered as she fought to contain herself.

"He... he..."

As Tina was about to continue, she was immediately interrupted by Swalding: before she did herself more damage. He asked, quickly and imploringly, "Please listen carefully to me, Miss McLaughlin." He waited until she was paying him what attention she could and asked, "In the end, did you grow to hate Mr Kelly?"

Tina shook her head, seeming outraged by such a statement. "Oh, no! I loved him!"

Swalding referred to his notes. "But you told your sister Caitlin, that day in the hotel, and I quote: '*He made me do bad things.*'" He picked up some papers. "You said *Mr Kelly* had done bad things too."

Replacing the papers on the bench, he asked, carefully and concisely, "I believe it's vital for the court to listen to and understand exactly what you meant by these statements. Let me reiterate. You said, '*He made me do bad things.*' I believe you didn't want to do the things he'd asked of you. I believe you were coerced, forced, even blackmailed, weren't you?"

Wilkinson, clearly furious, jumped up again and cried, "Objection, m'lord! This is preposterous!"

Tina began to shout and point to the back of the courtroom where Kieran had just reappeared, smiling kindly at her with his chocolate brown eyes twinkling under the courtroom's hanging lights.

"No, I never hurt anyone! I loved him! Tell them, Kieran!"

At such a lunatic retort, Swalding shook his head in despair and moaned, "*Christ*," under his breath.

* * *

"Guilty."

It was the only word Tina McLaughlin understood as she watched the grey-moustached mouth of the judge repeat his devastating verdict. Dodds sat above the court on his rosewood bench, heart fuelled with hatred and anger as he looked at the despicable accused and the tribal Fenians assembled to support her in his court. He'd lost his youngest son in an IRA bomb attack almost a year ago to the day and could barely contain himself at the recollection. He couldn't understand these people. He waited just a few short seconds for the accused's reaction to his ruling, but there was none. She hung her head low, hidden by a lank mop of red hair.

Dodds was aware of the sympathy the media and local community had shown the defendant in this case, but he didn't give a damn. Her defence had been a pitiful tissue of lies. An innocent, naïve and vulnerable young girl, who – through no fault of her own – simply fell in love and had been led into acts of savagery, was she? As if love were ever a good enough excuse.

Well, Dodds felt nothing for the stupid girl, nothing at all. If anyone thought he'd be softened into showing leniency by her sex and age, they were very wrong. He'd sent plenty of others like her down already, and for much less!

In fact, he'd already made up his mind about her sentence before the case ever began and had casually shared his views on it with the prosecutor Wilkinson over a very nice dinner a few evenings before. No matter how much the press and media squawked about McLaughlin's naïvety, age and innocence, she'd go down and for a very long time too. There was no justification for what she'd done to those young soldiers, her intention to plant a bomb in a public place or the assistance she'd given that murderer Kelly.

His Honour's manicured fingers flipped through a few legal pages he'd decided to make a show of studying. With his face averted, from under his eyelashes, he scrutinised the overflowing public gallery and the rest of the courtroom. Eventually, his gaze fell on the girl's family, who sat looking drawn, pale-faced and motionless behind the defence team – a wretched sight.

Caitlin caught the judge's eye and boldly returned his stare. He saw her bare-faced defiance and raised an eyebrow at such insolence.

She already knew her sister would get no sympathy from this man. It was clear from the beginning; he'd already made up his mind. Throughout this so-called impartial administration of justice, he'd endeavoured time after time to sway the onlookers towards a guilty verdict and had always sided with the prosecution.

His icy gaze scanned the court, moved slowly across the assembled, expectant attendees for dramatic effect and finally rested on Tina. In his public-school accent, sounding cold and indifferent, he said, "Martina Teresa McLaughlin, you have been found guilty of manslaughter, murder, membership of an illegal organisation – the PIRA – and engaging in terrorist activities. I have no hesitation in sentencing you to life imprisonment. Life meaning life, to be served in Armagh Women's Gaol. Take her down!"

White with anger, Caitlin stood up and shouted, "What the hell!"

The judge called for order as the gallery went ballistic at such a verdict. Some people cried out in anger and contempt whilst others cheered, waved their Union Jack flags and jeered as mayhem engulfed the court.

Majella screamed, pushing Caitlin aside as she hysterically tried to reach her youngest daughter, who, looking dazed, was roughly shoved down the steps to the underground cells by her guards. Tommy O'Reilly instantly wrapped his sister in his huge arms as banshee wails erupted from her soul.

Caitlin looked at him in shock. "Life, Tommy? Life! He can't do that! He can't give her life! She's only seventeen; she didn't know what she was doing! Anyone can see she's not right in the head, for Christ sake!"

Tommy shook his head, knowing Caitlin was right. He continued to hold his sister tightly until she'd calmed a little. Their solicitor walked over. Despondently, he whispered, "Listen, everyone in this courtroom knows Tina's sick. After that farce, I'm going to appeal that she stays in Gransha."

Majella's skeletal hands grabbed his. "But life, Brendan! Life!"

"I know, Mrs McLaughlin. What Dodds just did wasn't fair and wasn't even legal. We can appeal and get it overturned, I promise."

Majella nodded, placing her shattered trust in this young man. "Please, Brendan, do whatever you can, son, but just bring her home. *Please.*"

Brendan could only nod and promise he'd be in touch. He watched Majella make her away across the courtroom to their QC to plead for more help. Disappointingly, he quickly brushed aside the haggard woman and told her he was sorry, but he couldn't comment before he'd spoken to his client.

As they prepared to leave, the prosecuting barrister and his junior let out a howl of laughter whilst patting a uniformed policeman on the shoulder. Tommy stopped to look at Brendan and shared a knowing look. They were in this for themselves, like any other cabal.

Outside in the corridor, Tommy shook Brendan's hand and asked him hopefully, "Is there nothing else we can do to keep her here and away from Armagh? Nothing at all?"

Brendan shuddered. He really felt for this family, who'd been through so much already. His client was a goner, he felt, her head turned almost to mash.

"There's no chance, Tommy. None at all. We'll be lucky to get her back in the hospital, though I didn't want to say as much in front of Mrs McLaughlin. I expect they'll be taking her straight to Armagh now. We can appeal both the verdict and especially the sentence, but it's going to take time. And while we do it, Tina's going to be in gaol. I'm very sorry."

Tommy pointed angrily at the courtroom behind them.

"That was a pure miscarriage of justice, the whole débâcle. Life, for Christ's sake! Sure that Dumbo wouldn't allow us to use the medical reports in her defence, and we all know the wee girl's off her rocker!"

Brendan couldn't agree more with the big man and frowned. "I know, Tommy. I know. And Father McGuire's character reference for her was ignored too. I get it. I truly do. I won't give up, Tommy. I'll get onto that appeal as soon as I'm back."

Tommy smiled at the hardworking, compassionate young lawyer. He knew Brendan Doherty wasn't a quitter. He was still working hard on Patrick's case, death by medical neglect whilst in official custody, and knew his stuff. He needed to know it, having regularly to appeal against sentencing by kangaroo courts. The authorities were interning so many Catholic youngsters without charge. Often their only crime was being Catholic Nationalists.

As they left the courthouse, the family were met by a scrum of reporters, TV camera crews and press photographers, who indiscriminately surged at them, shouting out question after question. Flashing lights and cameras were pointed at them as they fought to get away.

"Have you spoken to your daughter, Mrs McLaughlin? What did she say? Does she feel any remorse? Will you appeal?"

Caitlin placed her arm protectively around her mother and pulled her quickly down the steps. RUC officers pushed the baying media circus back, allowing the family to climb into their neighbour Charlie McFadden's waiting car. Caitlin looked around at the feverish crowd. She saw men and women waving Union Jacks, shouting and screaming abuse at others who held large banners and posters in defence of her sister.

Eventually, they made it home. In the bathroom, Majella swallowed three of her temazepam sleepers, knowing they would guarantee her tranquillity. Peace from this nightmare world was what she wanted and needed. As she lay on her half-made bed, she welcomed the feeling of her eyelids drooping shut and soon was lost in sleep.

* * *

Later that evening, in the kitchen, Caitlin sat with Tommy drinking tepid tea. The big man sighed deeply before he said, "You can't be surprised, love. Not in this day and age." They talked for a short time longer about the injustice of the trial and the outlook for Tina until, both exhausted, they said their goodnights.

Caitlin's thoughts were scrambled as she made her way to her darkened bedroom. She swallowed down the ever-present lump in her throat and closed her eyes. Tommy was right. What else could they expect? Her sister *was* guilty. But it wasn't all her fault; Tina had been very young and clearly led astray. No one in their right mind could doubt that!

A range of emotions ran through her then, but mostly she felt guilt. *Why hadn't she noticed Tina's changing behaviour? It was obvious now – her disappearances, her roller-coaster moods, even the feckin' new red coat that Kelly evidently bought her. Caitlin should have asked where she got it. Why didn't any of them see what was going on under their noses?*

She prayed and swore to herself she would make it up to her sister. James Henderson had unexpectedly come into her life, and at that time, in the first flush of infatuation, nothing else had existed for Caitlin but her desire and love for him. He'd possessed her, gotten into her very bones.

But it was time for Tina now, and Caitlin was determined to make up for her mistakes. She had to try and erase James from her thoughts. Her mother was right, it *had* ended badly, and he *was* from a different world. He was part of the establishment that'd just sent her sister to prison for life.

She must never forget that James Henderson was a Protestant, rich and steeped in the privilege of an upper-class family. He'd had what he wanted from Caitlin, a girl from the wrong side of the tracks, and most likely would soon have moved on to his next conquest.

It was time for her to move on, to grow up and wise up. It wasn't going to be easy, but she'd bloody well do her best. Her mother and her imprisoned sister needed her, and Caitlin wasn't going to let them down. Not now, not ever.

Chapter 3

Charles Jones smiled widely and patted Judge Dodds heartily on the back. Job done. The two men were meeting in Jones's private members' club, Boodle's in London, for lunch. Previously Dodds had been to the club for Law Society black-tie events, and, my God, he loved the place. He loved its history, ambience, cuisine and proximity to the nightlife of London Town – especially after Mrs D (as he affectionately called his wife) had gone to bed! What made it even better was that on this trip they were the honoured guests of Charles Jones, Esq.

Dodds had been dying to become a member here for years and was delighted when Jones happily supported his application to join – on one simple condition. Dodds would have to agree to divert any official attention from Jones's henchman Morris, who'd been the agent provocateur and who shot the Bishop at the City Hotel before Kelly killed him in retaliation. Had Jones known the event was also to be targeted by the PIRA reject, he would've saved his powder for another day and not sacrificed his valuable enforcer Morris into the bargain. However, it'd worked out in the end with Kelly dead they'd found a very useful Catholic scapegoat. Dodds had been given his instructions. He was to make an example of the McLaughlin girl and cause an uproar by sending her down for life. That should stir things up a bit, giving Jones's Loyalist gang even more scope for reprisals.

Dodds did as he was asked by making the trial so complicated and controversial that it kept the local media and press fully occupied and diverted their attention from any putative connection between the mysterious third dead man at the scene and Mr Charles Jones. The judge wasn't quite sure of the extent of Jones's personal involvement in the shootings but certainly wasn't going to ask – not if doing as he was asked finally got him his Boodle's membership!

Mrs D loved the club's proximity to both Bond Street and Oxford Street. Dodds couldn't begin to imagine the damage she'd do to their bank account and credit cards once they were regularly staying there, but he loved her, and she deserved it. Living daily with the fear of a bomb under their car or an assassin's shot coming from nowhere wasn't easy, and the loss of Stephen, their son, had been overwhelming for them both.

Once seated, Jones quickly ordered them some drinks. The pair made small talk and studied the room until the arrival of the wine when Jones slurped his cold Sauvignon in relief and enjoyment. *Delicious.* Looking around the room again to see who was within earshot and to make sure he couldn't be overheard, he spoke quietly and cautiously. "Bravo, Dodds. Bravo. I couldn't have asked for more."

The judge, pleased as punch at such an accolade and especially coming from Charles Jones, answered impishly, "Wasn't too difficult, Charles, old boy. Closed case. Anyway, I'd already made up my mind! Of course, that young rascal Kelly was clearly insane, and as for the girl…stupid, just plain stupid, like all her kind. Shame I couldn't give her the rope! *Now that* would have caused a stir!" he sniggered, only half-joking.

Jones agreed, and a small, cruel smile crossed his face. "It'd be one less Fenian to worry about, eh, Dodds?"

He sat back comfortably in his red leather chair and lit himself a cigar. Things had gone exceptionally well at the trial, and Morris's role in the City Hotel massacre was all but overlooked. Finally, the whole affair was over, and he was free to move on with much more important tasks.

Today he was going to relax, enjoy the wine, food and company. He neither liked nor disliked Dodds, but since he'd proved himself extremely useful and likely would do again, Jones thought it best to keep him sweet – especially if his new plans bore fruit. Dodds would most definitely be needed then.

Later that same afternoon – after Dodds had long gone to meet his wife – Jones sat smoking in Boodle's dark green-panelled library reading the *Telegraph*. Glancing at his IWC watch, he noted James Henderson Snr was twenty minutes late. Jones hated tardiness; it showed a lack of respect. Tutting and sighing, he slowly folded the paper in preparation to leave; he didn't wait for anyone. However, he heard a man's voice bellow from across the entrance hall, "Sorry, Charles, bloody Victoria Line. Someone inconsiderately threw themselves in front of a train! My apologies!"

The raised voice of his guest resonated across the library so loudly that the other members in the room scowled and grumbled at such rudeness. Jones could hear one of them whisper harshly, "Bloody fool, bad behaviour."

At once, Jones shot his guest a warning look and hissed, "Keep your voice down, you eejit! Sit down. Quickly."

James Snr reddened – his host was making him feel like a naughty five-year-old. In silence, he sank deeply and comfortably into a brown leather reading chair adjacent to Jones's.

A red-coated waiter approached the pair, and drinks were soon ordered. Relaxing back into his chair, Jones updated James Snr on his meeting with Dodds and listed a number of tasks he wanted him to do. James Snr nodded enthusiastically whilst Jones thought excitedly about the coming weeks.

* * *

Earlier that day and before meeting Jones, James Snr had spoken to his brother Roger by telephone. Ever since the hotel fiasco, Roger had been extremely unwell; the whole episode had nearly destroyed him. His voice was weak, and he had sounded tired during the short call. No, there was nothing his brother could do to help, Roger had said. He was thankful that his nephew, James Jnr, had managed the fall-out from the incident so well. Everyone was talking about the outcome of the McLaughlin case. It wouldn't be long before the daily atrocities happening across the province gave more headline news stories to the many national and international journalists now residing in the hotels of Ulster, carrion crows ready to prosper from the conflict.

With the unstinting support of his friend George Shalham, Young James had finally managed to secure a loan from the Northern Ireland Office, enabling the factory to remain open. They'd also been able to pay back the huge debt owed to Charles Jones – who, upon receiving it, had appeared rather more annoyed than pleased. He'd reluctantly taken the money and even offered to change the conditions of the loan if they wanted to extend it, but Roger had declined. He'd learned by now the type of man Jones was and swore he'd never have any business or personal dealings with him again. If there had ever been a friendship between them, it was well and truly over. James Snr had omitted to mention at this point his own forthcoming meeting with Jones.

Ever since the incident at the City Hotel, it seemed James Jnr had been working relentlessly in the factory. It never became clear to either his father or uncle what James's interest in the McLaughlin girl from the office had been. He'd refused to say anything about her, and ultimately the brothers decided he would talk to them about it only when, and if, he wanted to.

There was very little James Snr could do to help at the factory. He'd no experience of the shirt manufacturing industry since his own career had been in the British Army. He was pensioned off now and as short of funds as ever, so he'd been hugely relieved when Jones asked him to get involved in his business dealings. Some of these transactions had already proved to be lucrative, and by God, he needed the cash. Still on a losing run, he hadn't had much luck with the cards lately and was under increasingly alarming pressure from some dangerous people who wanted to be paid back.

He knew he could offer Jones valuable contacts within the military and his London friends. However, after accompanying the Belfast man to a number of his sermons to Loyalist supporters, he quickly decided he didn't like this arrogant little prick with Hitler tendencies, albeit admittedly agreeing with most of what he preached about the Papists. But, needs must, whether he liked the prick or not wasn't important – he'd come across even worse forms of low life in his army days. For the time being anyway, he'd simply play along with Jones and deliver what was expected whilst reaping the financial benefits. It was a win-win.

* * *

Back at Melrose, home to James Jnr and Roger, the young man sat on the edge of his uncle's king-sized bed. His voice was filled with concern as he asked, "How are you feeling? Better for eating?"

Roger shrugged and answered half-heartedly, "I'm fine, James. Honestly. Don't fuss."

James rubbed the back of his uncle's hand, noticing how tissue-thin the skin was nowadays. "I want to fuss. We need to get you better. You're sorely missed at the factory!"

Roger hadn't been on-site for months. The factory's atmosphere was heavy with sadness. People understood how close it'd been to shutting down and still remained fearful for the future. They'd no idea what they'd do if it went down the pan. Their way of life depended on this factory. Employees' families, friends, local businesses, in fact, the whole city, needed Rocola to remain open.

Mrs Parkes, the office manager, asked daily after Roger. Given Caitlin had gone and in such a bizarre way, James had become pretty reliant on the manager's experience, tenacity and loyalty. He remembered the day after the failed meeting when he'd returned to Rocola and had been met by Mrs Parkes in his office.

"Mr Henderson, I am *so* sorry about what happened. How are you? And how is your poor Uncle? It's just horrible. I still can hardly believe it meself." Mrs Parkes was pleased to see the young man back but shocked by his appearance. He looked crushed and had aged overnight.

It was that McLaughlin girl's fault – her and that crazy family! Mrs Parkes had heard the mother was on her way out, gone all loopy. Well, she'd tried to warn him.

James could only stare at her, reflecting on the past. The old girl had been right all along about Caitlin McLaughlin. He felt a fool and prayed the woman would never refer to *that* name again or even to his erstwhile lover's existence.

Over the following weeks and months, Mrs Parkes continued to prove herself, and, thankfully, his ex-PA was never discussed again. At times, he'd come across notes written by Caitlin, and his hands would ball into fists. He hated her, yet he missed everything about her.

Now James felt his hand being patted and lightly squeezed. He looked at his uncle, who asked him gently, "And how are you, James? Are *you* okay?"

"I'm fine, Uncle. Lots to do. It's a good thing, keeps me busy and out of trouble." In an effort to cheer them both up, he added in a more animated fashion, "I did tell you Marleen was coming for the weekend, didn't I? I can't believe we haven't seen her in well over a year. It's funny, but somehow she and I always manage to pick up right where we left off. It'll be nice to see her again. Let's keep her away from Mr Jones! Remember last time they met?" he asked.

"Only too well," Roger said, remembering the dinner party at Melrose where Jones had ranted and raved so much, he'd ended up spilling red wine all over James's childhood friend's beautiful white dress.

"It'll be good to see her again, been far too long," Roger mumbled, thinking about the lovely young woman. She was the one he hoped to see James end up with since he knew his nephew had been hurt badly by that office girl. Hopefully, Marleen's visit would cheer him up. Melrose had been morgue-like for too long with very few visitors. Although Roger knew he'd soon have to pull himself together and dust himself down, physically, he wasn't ready. He felt so darn' tired. Dr Harris, the family GP, had left his practice under a cloud after a malpractice case and moved on. To Roger's disappointment, his replacement, a man called Quinn, had proved to be a particularly poor successor. Roger couldn't tolerate him; he was a clown.

"I spoke to your father today," Roger said as his nephew got up to look out of the bay window and down upon the rose garden. Pulling back the sheer, immaculate voiles, he answered curiously, "Oh, yes? How is he? I haven't spoken to him for a while. I should, but I can't bear the thought of him having any association with a bully boy like Jones."

"Hmm. Yes, one of life's surprises, that," agreed Roger. "Interesting too that he hasn't asked me for financial help lately. I suspect he's on Jones's payroll."

James laughed, "Most likely! Shame on him, really, Uncle. The best thing you ever did was to distance yourself from Jones. I never liked the man. Shalham was quite frustrated and upset about Jones when I saw him last. He told me, confidentially, of course, that our friend is on the RUC's radar. He believes Jones is heavily involved in the Ulster Volunteer Force, contributing large sums of money to pay for arms and propaganda material. They've been bombing Catholic businesses in Belfast. I read that they're likely to be banned soon."

James turned away from the window and sat on the edge of his uncle's bed once again. He enjoyed being close to Roger.

"He even suspects Jones has put his own gang together – an illegal group of Loyalist militants. It seems they've been carrying out random Catholic sectarian attacks and, in some cases, even murder. And wait for this – he strongly suspects Jones had something to do with that man Morris who killed the Bishop! Yet somehow, the snake seems to keep his head above water and his hands clean. George can't find a shred of evidence against him and suspects Jones has someone on his payroll, someone high up, protecting him from inside the force, but he can't prove that either. Poor Shalham, he was mortified. I hope Father's not getting into something he shouldn't, although I doubt he cares much if there's money involved."

Roger knew his nephew was spot on. As brothers, the two men were so different yet looked so alike. Where Roger, in the early years, worked long and hard, couldn't give a hoot about religion and became a successful businessman, James Snr was the ultimate snob and bigot. He had a chip on his shoulder about not having enough money. He'd married well and joined the British Army as an officer hoping that it would be his entrée to the upper classes. It had worked for a short time until he couldn't keep up with the expense involved and, to his peril, began to gamble – rather badly.

Roger could only recall being jealous of his brother once, when fate decreed that Joceyln, Roger's wife, couldn't carry children. Catherine, his sister-in-law, was a young, beautiful, fit and healthy girl who had given birth to James. Over the years, after his mother had left the family and James Jnr began to spend more time at Melrose, Jocelyn had come to regard the boy as the next best thing to a son of her own.

Still thinking about his nephew, Roger recalled being surprised recently to receive a strongly worded letter from Catherine, James's mother, posted from Cape Town, where she now lived. She was asking to see her son. It was the first time she'd suggested coming to Melrose since leaving his brother and choosing to make a new life abroad. This didn't seem to be the right time to mention it to the young man, though. Although the woman had written numerous times, the two brothers always destroyed her letters and ignored her calls.

Roger hadn't done anything with the latest letter as yet. Maybe it was time that he did. He'd have to think about it very carefully, given his nephew's emotional state. He knew this time he should answer Catherine; he owed her that. However, James had become far too important to him, and he didn't want anything, anything at all, to upset him – especially now. Catherine would have to wait; he'd more important things to think about.

James stood up to leave. "We'll soon know, won't we?"

"Know what?" Roger asked, slightly confused; he couldn't recall what they'd last been discussing.

James smiled. "About Father being on Jones's payroll. No doubt he'll update us next time we see him on his dealings with the odious creep!"

"Ah, yes. I expect he will."

James grabbed his blue and red Donegal tweed jacket and folded it neatly over his arm. He took a deep, deliberate breath, raising his chin and looking down at his uncle for a few moments. Soon Roger's strained expression gave way to a genuine smile as he playfully threw a book at his nephew. "What are you looking at? Off you go now! Give me some peace!"

James laughed. It was good to see his uncle with a bit of energy and banter. Long overdue. He loved him so. "Okay, okay. I'm going. I'm going. I'll come up and have dinner with you later."

"Great. Now get out of here!" Roger barked playfully.

James closed the bedroom's double doors behind him and stood still. He looked over to the winding staircase and noticed how beautiful it was, and the rest of the house too. It'd been almost two years since he'd arrived in Londonderry after his father's gambling cost them their beautiful home in Ayrshire. Cringing at the memory, he thought about how stupid, naïve and absurdly arrogant he'd been on first arriving in the city. He'd grown to love the place since then.

His uncle's friend George Shalham had kindly taken James under his wing. Indeed he'd gotten him out of a few scrapes and tried hard to educate him in the ways of the locals. Sadly, as a consequence of the security breach at the hotel conference, which they'd believed to be impenetrable, Shalham had been forced to accept responsibility for the slip-up and, given no choice, was forced to retire as Chief Constable of the RUC.

Because of his failure to keep everyone safe, he'd readily accepted the consequences. He was furious with himself and felt totally responsible for the deaths even though Kelly wasn't known to them as a threat. The man was a lone wolf, an outsider who simply operated under the radar of the security services. What really worried Shalham was how many more Kellys there could be out there. But at any rate, he had to accept it wasn't his problem anymore – professionally speaking.

As soon as Shalham was out the door, Henry Bonner had taken over as RUC Chief Constable. No surprises there. Shalham had had little or no input in Bonner's appointment. It was well known the two men had radically different ways of policing, and Shalham knew from experience that Bonner would prove to be a disastrous choice. He was an all-out Loyalist hard-liner, determined to break down and destroy the PIRA along with any other Nationalist dissident groups. Sectarian relations were about to get much worse rather than better.

Chapter 4

"Take them off!" Tina heard a woman's voice shriek in anger. "Fuckin' quick now, ye Fenian bitch!"

Confused, Tina McLaughlin did as she was told, removing her cardigan slowly, one sleeve first, then awkwardly fighting with the second, whilst another angry-looking guard joined her colleague.

Watching the skinny young prisoner with contempt and clearly irate at her sluggishness, the first gaoler PO Smyth repeated her command. "Quick, I fuckin' said, or I'll do it meself!"

Tina's thin arm was suddenly and painfully jerked back, and soon her cardigan, blouse, trousers, bra, and knickers were viciously pulled off and thrown aside until she stood frightened, shaking, naked and cold.

Next, she was forcefully pushed against the wall where her arms were splayed apart, her legs forced open, and her back pressed down as a signal for her to bend over. A gloved hand began to roughly hunt around the inside and outside of her genitals and anus. Humiliation – *it was her time of the month* – flooded the skin of her neck and chest as she watched a trickle of light crimson blood flow freely down the inside of her leg to form a misshapen pool. She was told to open her mouth, and the very same gloved hand fished inside and around, deliberately rubbing her tongue, teeth, and gums. Tina shuddered as she spat out the bitter taste, then jerked as fingers pulled and hunted through her unwashed red hair in search of lice.

Her keepers continued to examine her vibrating body, noting any distinguishing marks or tattoos. In the process, they took the piss out of the blotchy, oozing eczema sores that covered most of Tina's face, legs, and torso.

Once finished, she was forced to turn and face her aggressive and determined guards, one of whom chuckled as she gruffly pushed a heavy bar of used, strong-smelling carbolic soap into her hand. This was followed by a vicious thrust towards an old-fashioned and stained enamel bath.

Again, the same voice cried, "Wash yourself, dirty bitch. You fuckin' stink!"

Tina couldn't understand where she was. She knew one thing: this wasn't anything like the place she'd been in before. She'd felt safe there in that clean, all-white, warm building with its lovely nurses and the other patients, like Tina, who rarely spoke or bothered her. She missed the lullabies sung sweetly and lovingly to Rosaleen's ghost. This smelly, dirty, and stale place was different. It was freezing, dark and scary, and Tina didn't like it, not one bit. And for some reason, an angry, stout woman, dressed in black from top to toe, kept hitting and shouting at her! Tina wished the woman would just stop.

Sitting in rose-coloured tepid bathwater that barely reached her waist, she slowly washed her arms and body, finishing off with her feet. Subconsciously she wondered if she really did smell and washed herself a little bit more – just in case.

In a few minutes, the voice returned, screaming at her through a haze of spittle, "Out!"

A threadbare, discoloured towel was thrown at her to catch but instead fell onto the wet floor. She bent and picked it up but jumped in fright as a grating cry emanated from the other side of the wet room. To retain some form of modesty, Tina quickly wrapped her cold, emaciated body in the small damp towel, grabbed her discarded clothes and looked back over her shoulder.

She saw a young girl with wheat-blonde hair, who was clearly expecting, being pushed by the other guard towards the now-vacant bath. Tina noticed patches of reddish-brown, dried blood on the girl's hairline and at the sides of her white contorted face. She could barely make out her words between sobs as the girl pointed to the bath and cried, "I'm not taking my clothes off! Not in front of you lot! And look, there's blood in that there bath. I'm not getting in that!"

The two screws chuckled, and the short one with cruel eyes gleefully replied, "You'll do as you're told! You look like a duffed-up heifer! Doesn't she?" she asked her partner, who giggled at such an image and said nothing whilst continuing to watch gleefully.

However, the young girl wasn't having any of it. She wasn't taking her clothes off for anyone. She ran the back of her hand across her mouth and stood rigid with determination not to move.

Shivering with cold, Tina quickly put on her bra and knickers, re-fixing the used Dr White's sanitary pad within. Another uniformed woman appeared and gently steered her, half-dressed, towards an open door that gave access to a long black-and-white-tiled corridor. Her custodian closed the door tightly after them and walked on, her tapping heels making an echoing sound in the otherwise deafening silence. They came to a heavy green steel-barred gate at the end of the hallway, and the prison officer nodded for Tina to stand aside.

She waited and watched as a large key was extracted from the uniformed woman's pocket and used to open the gate. They passed through, and the screw turned to lock the gate again. For the first time, it allowed Tina time to study her. The woman wore a long-sleeved pale blue shirt with breast pockets and numbered epaulettes on her shoulders. A chain hung from the waist of her black trousers, and the keys were kept tucked away in one of their deep pockets. Her shoes, Tina noticed, were highly polished, black, flat, and looked like a man's.

Tina tried desperately to keep calm. She looked around and asked quietly, "Where am I, missus?"

Blue, surprisingly kind eyes returned her look. "You'll see, love," the woman told her. "Come now, put the rest of your clothes on, and get dressed."

In the changing room area, a trembling Tina finished putting on her only pair of jeans. Before moving from Gransha, Caitlin had given her their daddy's Aran jumper to keep her warm and cheer her up – she swore she could still smell him on it. In the distance, she could hear the ongoing maniacal cries of the pregnant girl. She looked at her warder questioningly, who turned and answered her frightened look.

"Listen, love. You've just passed through the reception area. You're now in the main gaol at Armagh. You'll be okay if you just do as you're told and follow your OC's orders. You're on Maureen Molony's wing." Tina still had no idea what the woman was talking about. Her OC? What was that?

"My name is Quirk," said the officer. "Now I'm going to take you to your cell in A- Wing, and you can settle yourself in."

Tina could only nod with a half-smile. Her head felt fuzzy as she tried to grasp what was happening. Something was very wrong here. In silence, they continued their journey through another series of corridors with interlocking gates until they finally reached their destination.

Tina stepped down into a cell through a small dark green door within a grey-painted frame. She found herself in a stone-built room with walls painted yellow below, cream above. It was a tiny space but somehow managed to contain two wrought-iron beds, two white plastic chairs and two black plastic chamber pots. In addition, there was a small, scratched table and a single battered-looking bedside locker. On top of an empty bed lay two neatly folded coarse brown blankets, a pillow, a pillowcase, and a pair of greyish sheets.

She held herself straight as she was introduced to a young, dog-tired-looking woman who sat with one leg half on and half off the other bed. Although she looked wiped out, she was still extremely pretty, with curly black shoulder-length hair and a heavy fringe over a pair of pale blue eyes. Her creamy skin was clear and perfect, her lips full. She wore a faded red Bay City Rollers T-shirt over a pair of flared black and white floral trousers.

The woman looked up as Tina entered, threw the book she was reading to one side and smiled warmly as she patted her bed, inviting the girl to join her. "Sit down, love and let's see what you're all about."

Quirk nodded gratefully and left after whispering to the OC, "She's a delicate one, Maureen, a youngin'. Not sure she's all there – keep her close."

"Will do," Maureen answered, watching as the heavy cell door was semi-closed by Quirk as she left. The seasoned guard had a reputation for being firm but fair. Quirk had been a prison officer at Armagh for many years. In her late-fifties and married, most of the long-term inmates knew she wasn't happy with the way things were changing in the prison and reckoned she wouldn't be staying around for much longer. Most likely, she'd retire soon with full benefits.

Tina took in her surroundings, noticing an arched, barred and heavily stained window that barely let any natural light through. She shook her head in confusion and said in a low voice, "I don't understand. Why am I here?"

Maureen Molony sighed. These girls seemed to be getting younger and younger. Earlier in the year, they'd had a couple of youngsters of no more than fourteen or fifteen incarcerated inside this fucking shithole. It was madness.

So far, she'd been in Armagh for eighteen months, at first interned without trial. The worst part of it was that, as an internee, they'd never tell you what they were aiming to charge you with, why they thought you were guilty or, more importantly, when you were going to be released. As an internee, she'd lived in the hope day to day of getting out. That was until she'd been set up by a super grass on the outside, who'd said she was part of a cell responsible for the bombing of a teashop in Derry. As a result, she'd been formally sentenced to fifteen years. Frustratingly, it was one crime she *hadn't* committed.

Maureen felt old, way ahead of her twenty-eight years. She sometimes wondered how long she'd be able to keep herself right.

There again, she'd no choice. She'd recently become the Officer in Command (OC) of the Republican prisoners. These women and girls, her comrades, needed her – especially some of the older ones, many of whom were grannies. She wasn't going to let them down and remained determined that this so-called prison establishment wouldn't break them – not if Maureen had anything to do with it.

They were being treated as political prisoners and allowed to wear their own clothes, as well as being granted the freedom to come back and forth between cells and across the wings. They were also allowed educational privileges but no Irish language classes – only Spanish and French. A lot of the women already spoke Irish in any case. Maureen supposed it could have been worse; it was unlikely any of them would be going on holiday to Saint Tropez any time soon!

She grabbed a blanket and wrapped it around the girl who was cadaver-thin with dark-circled eyes and appeared very young in the huge man-sized, stained Aran jumper she wore. Her legs barely filled her jeans. Her once red, corkscrew hair appeared knotted, greasy, and unwashed. It was the skin on her face that concerned Maureen most. It was red-raw and bleeding a little in places. She noticed how the girl continually scratched it using the sleeve of what looked like bloodstains on the Aran. Dr Harris would have to see her– it was clearly eczema and well out of control.

Other than her skin ailments, Tina reminded Maureen of her younger sister Lisa whom she missed like mad. She rubbed the blanket, briskly and hard, up and down the girl's bony shoulders to warm her more. Maureen sighed, looked up to the heavens and said a quick prayer. Then, speaking softly and quietly, she shared some important advice with her new cellmate. "The first two things to remember about this place, love, is never, ever ask anyone why they're here and don't tell them anything either. What's your name?"

Tina mumbled her response. "Tina. Tina McLaughlin."

Ah, shit! The OC immediately knew who Tina McLaughlin was and her *alleged* crimes. She also knew her brother, Martin. *Christ.* That was some fuck-up. She'd heard how the young girl had been groomed by that wanker Kieran Kelly. Without orders, he'd badly beaten a British soldier and then tortured and killed a second one, and as if that wasn't enough, the eejit then decided to blow up the fuckin' City Hotel in Derry. Served the bastard right, getting himself shot – he'd gone way too far! The fall-out had been horrific after poor Bishop Hegarty was shot. Night after night, there'd been awful rioting in the streets of Derry, and several blameless people had been shot dead indiscriminately by the Brits. The poor Bishop, loved by all Republicans, would be turning in his grave! He'd have hated the bloodshed and loss of innocent lives. *God love him.* They all knew it would've been catastrophic for the Cause if that bomb had gone off – there were a fair number of influential people they needed in that room!

Unusually Maureen found herself lost for words. Silence hung in the air for a minute or so until, to her relief, there came a relentless knocking on the cell door. It soon opened fully to show a small, dumpy, grey-haired woman who cried out anxiously, "Maureen! Maureen! Quick, you're needed!

The OC's eyes closed, and she took a deep breath. "What is it this time?" she asked.

The dumpy woman – truly animated by now – explained, "It's your woman again! That new one. She's fighting with Florence. You'd better get up there." Adding dramatically in an under-tone, "I think Florence's gonna kill her. You'd better hurry up!"

Shit! Maureen grabbed Tina's hand and led her through the arched door to a cell at the very end of the wing, near the Chapel and opposite the toilets. She daren't leave the young mite alone – at least not yet.

Armagh Gaol had been built in 1783 over a military barracks. Two main cell wings stemmed from the reception area, which was known as "the circle". Each wing held 140 cells, one two-storey (A-Wing) and the other three-storey (B-Wing). The year before, just over 130 male political prisoners had been transferred to the gaol from the overcrowded Crumlin Road Prison. They were long gone now, most likely to the damp and dark squalor of the make-shift men's prison, Long Kesh.

The latter was based in a former Royal Air Force station on the outskirts of Lisburn. Initially, interns were housed in their separate paramilitary groups, with the prisoners confined in Nissen huts previously used by the Air Force. The prison was not fit for purpose, resulting in continual suffering, resentment, and unrest.

A year ago, Armagh Gaol had held just two women, but today it housed just under 80, some of whom were pregnant. Seventy of the 80 inmates were sentenced, remanded, or interned political prisoners. The remaining ten were seen as "normal criminals".

Sadly, one of the young, interned women who gave birth inside had been forced to hand her young baby over to Social Services just the day before. She remained quiet, unapproachable, and lonely in her cell downstairs, staring into an empty cot. The prison officers hadn't even had the sensitivity to take it away.

Florence Sheils had been arrested after the funeral of PIRA Volunteer Jim Saunders, where she'd got caught up in rioting. There'd been no defence to her charge of "conduct likely to lead to a breach of the peace", and her mandatory sentence was at least six months in prison. Florence had accepted her fate but was struggling with the new prisoner who now shared her cell, Katherine, or Katie Davis, who clearly couldn't face being incarcerated.

Maureen understood Katie's anguish and fear. She had five children ranging from two to ten years of age, all of whom had been removed from their home and were now being looked after by their elderly grandparents on both sides of the family. Like many of the women's husbands, her John was locked up in Long Kesh too.

The screws warned all the women prisoners not to make any complaints about the conditions in the gaol. If they did, there was every prospect their children would be put into care – a nightmare for any parent. Katie was terrified as she'd just heard that both sets of grandparents were struggling and were traumatised by having to look after such young children. The agitated woman continually picked on her comrades for no apparent reason and was starting to get on everyone's nerves. Tempers were being tested, and Maureen, as the OC, would inevitably need to have a quiet but serious word with her to force her to behave. They were all struggling enough as it was.

Maureen, about to walk into the cell where the two women were viciously screaming at each other, was suddenly stopped by one of the screws. Smyth used her stocky overweight body to block Maureen's access.

Unbeknown to her, Smyth was aptly nicknamed the black widow by the prisoners. She was, however, aware she was hated not just by the prisoners but by the majority of her colleagues. Smyth wasn't bothered, not a bit. She loved and lived for this job as it gave her free access to the Papists, she so hated. Beating the fuck out of them, humiliating them when they first arrived, was what she lived for. She was short, thick-set and mannish-looking with unkempt bushy brows and bob-length dyed black greasy hair, slicked away from her face, and tied into a lifeless ponytail. It was funny how it was always the small things you noticed, Maureen thought as she stared into Smyth's eyes, noting they were yellowed, runny and bloodshot. Point to note: Smyth clearly liked to drink.

"Let me through, Smyth," Maureen said, gazing stonily at the screw. The women's faces were almost touching. Maureen's observation was borne out. Smyth's breath reeked of alcohol as Maureen repeated her request, this time with a note of annoyance.

"Let the two of them sort it out," Smyth replied with amusement. "Sure, they've been at it most of the day!"

Maureen knew Smyth was a troublemaker. With a glacial stare, she told the Green-eyed Monster firmly, "I don't think so, Smyth. If you don't let me through, I'll talk to Father McGuire. It's Tuesday tomorrow, and he'll be here. We all know what he's like, and you know what he'll do."

Father McGuire was extremely popular among the Nationalist prisoners for fighting their corner, which he did with vigour at every opportunity. He'd go between the men's prison and the women's, continually hounding both Governors. He never stopped nagging Governor Johnston, driving him crazy about the poor sanitary facilities for the women in Armagh, the inadequate food, requests for additional family visits, education classes and the many other issues the women faced. The Governor, in turn, would lash out in frustration at his staff, who then took it out on the inmates. It was a vicious circle. The gaolers were always looking to get one over on the prisoners, but even they had to tread carefully.

Father McGuire didn't know it, but most of the women panicked like fuck when they saw him entering their block and heading for a cell on any other day than a Tuesday. Most of the time, he was the bearer of bad news, such as a family illness or death. But Smyth knew the OC was right. McGuire was a troublemaker when it came to the screws' abuse of prisoners and a stubborn one at that. The Governor was rapidly losing patience with complaints from McGuire, but Smyth wasn't quite ready to give in. "I don't give a fuck," she whispered menacingly before attempting to push Maureen away from the cell door.

Maureen narrowed her eyes. A small group of women of varying ages were closing in and forming a semi-circle. Smyth barked for them to move back, but they remained still and rooted to the spot. Out of the corner of her eye, she noticed Officer Quirk moving slowly to stand next to the women and watch. Smyth knew her colleague wouldn't help her should this situation get physical. She was a weakling, a foolish Pope-lover, always trying to be nice – and anyway, Smyth wasn't afraid; she thrived on moments like this.

"Smyth. For the last time, let me in," Maureen repeated, this time with an even stronger note of annoyance in her voice.

The women's standoff lasted for as long as Smyth could count in her head to fifteen, at which point she reluctantly moved aside. During the commotion, no one noticed the cell behind her was now as quiet as a church, as the two warring inmates stood watching the altercation taking place outside their cell door.

Maureen reached for Tina, gently pushed her into the cell first and made her sit on a small wooden stool. Turning around angrily, she faced the two emotionally drained women.

"Girls, what the fuck is going on here? For pity's sake, this has to stop!"

Chapter 5

Anne Heaney sat in the "good room" of her mother's house, by the window, looking at the relentless downpour outside. Christmas was coming soon, and she dreaded it. Her mother, Liz, had done her best to decorate the place with red and white homemade paper chains, well-used pink tinsel and a plastic shiny green Christmas tree, missing a number of its lower branches. Multi-coloured flashing lights hung between school-made decorations as the tree shone out of the window into the street.

She glanced around at the room's sparse furnishings. A moth-eaten, flower-patterned, decrepit armchair sat as if on guard in the corner facing the door. She vividly remembered the day the new shiny fake leather three-piece sofa that once stood in pride of place was delivered and how excited they'd all been, including her pain in the arse father. She almost laughed at its condition now. Molly, their cat, had obviously been at it. Its stretched, pliable fabric was riddled with scratches that snaked up and down the top and edges of its worn cushions.

Anne looked out upon the street again and groaned. She was so fucking bored, she thought, as her finger traced a raindrop flowing freely down the window pane. Out of the blue and without warning, a writhing spasm shot through what remained of her right leg.

"Jesus. Jesus Christ!" she hissed to no one in particular. As instructed by the doctor, she grabbed and squeezed her thigh as forcefully as she could. The pain was intense and unrelenting. She breathed in deeply, held it and then released it into the air. She repeated to herself, "In, out, in, out, in, out" until the agony eased a little.

Over the past two weeks, she'd been making the 150-mile round trip journey regularly by bus to Musgrave Park Hospital, where they'd been endeavouring to fit her with a prosthetic lower leg. Evidently, it was a "one type fits all" monstrosity that would take some time to get used to. Her mother had insisted she take up the hospital's offer when, surprisingly, a letter offering her the prosthesis had arrived a month or so ago. The family hadn't known Anne was eligible for such treatment – naïvely, no one had even thought to ask after she'd been badly injured in the explosion.

Ever since the attack on the City Hotel ages ago, she'd hardly seen Caitlin. The hospital trips were all the social life she had these days. The more she stayed indoors, the more frightened she became about leaving the house. She didn't want anyone to feel sorry for, or stare at her, but she missed her friend. No one understood how she felt after losing her leg – apart from Caitlin. Of course, she understood: she'd been with Anne when it happened.

The one tiny, minuscule consolation – *if it could be described as such* – was the attention being paid to her by John Ballantyne, or "Porkie" as he was appropriately known! He worked in the local slaughterhouse killing pigs and began to call at her house shortly after she'd got out of hospital, asking to see her and obviously trying to court her. *Ugh*! He was short, had thinning hair, stocky arms and legs, and always carried a beer gut instead of a stomach. His face was pudgy, greasy and permanently covered in yellow-headed spots. To complete the far from pretty picture, he had tobacco-stained doorstep teeth.

At first, she'd refused to see him until it became too embarrassing for those answering the door to keep telling him to go away. So finally, and without warning, her mother started letting him in for a cup of tea. While he'd sit at the kitchen table, Anne would awkwardly drink her tea in silence, listening to his futile attempts to cheer her up. On reflection, she didn't have a chance to get a word in any way. He never stopped prattling on!

He'd been a bit friendly with her dad and was just under ten years older than Anne was. All the time she'd known him, he'd had a crush on her, though as a young teenager, she'd thought him gross. At one time, she'd never have talked to him, not to mention fancy him, but given his perseverance, she was slowly, and only very slowly, warming to him. But he came with another major drawback besides his appearance, and that was his sleazy friend Kevin Moore or "Dickie" as he was known. Dickie was a slimeball. Obese but with spindly legs, he had badly dyed light-coloured greasy hair, all plastered back with Brylcreem, a snub nose and a pair of fishlike dull grey eyes. What was worse was the sickly grin that seemed to be permanently etched on his football-shaped face. As for his breath – a rancid pile of shit smelled better!

He was an all-out worm, and her whole body shuddered at the very thought of him - a human slug. She remembered how over the years, she and Caitlin would giggle time after time at their nicknames – *Porkie and Dickie*!

Almost every day, Anne's mother would tell her religiously: *"It's a miracle you're alive. You don't realise how much blood you lost."* Or, *"You're getting better now, love, so just get on with it…"* Anne had to shut her off or walk away. It was the same conversation ad nauseam, and, God forgive her, sometimes she thought if she could make it down to the River Foyle, she'd jump in and then her pain and heartache would be gone in a matter of minutes.

She knew she was in trouble mentally and that she was becoming more and more anxious. The boredom of her daily routine didn't help. Those of her siblings who remained at home were either at work or school during the day, although, bless them, they tried their best to cheer her up on their return. She also knew she was treading a fine line with them and they were getting more and more fed up with her permanently depressed condition.

Although her mammy often nagged her, she'd been amazing, considering how tired and sad she was after losing her last baby, Emma, within weeks of her being born. Anne would never forget the tiny white coffin her eldest brother carried at the sombre, pathetic funeral. Their home didn't feel the same anymore. It was quiet in its grief.

The effect their dad had on them all was another cross to bear – particularly the way he'd frequently disappear for weeks on end, followed by the unending worry of receiving a knock at their door, either from the army to raid the house or someone bearing bad news. Bad news was everywhere – no matter where you looked.

"Ah, fuck it!" Anne said, fighting her way up from the chair. She'd make tea. Tea…Why was it that when we felt like shite or something went wrong, everyone automatically made tea?! Almost smiling at the thought, she clumsily walked into the kitchen.

It was similar to the one in Caitlin's house, with just enough space for a table in front of the usual stainless-steel kitchen sink, a white hooded gas cooker and, on the wall above the fridge, the obligatory portrait of the Pope with the customary set of rosary beads draped over it. A washing machine that continually broke down stood forlornly half-hidden in the corner.

"Alright, love?" she heard her mother ask from the sink where she was peeling what looked like a ton of potatoes.

"Grand," Anne answered languidly.

"Mr Ballantyne coming to see you today, is he?"

"Probably. Never a dull moment," Anne answered sarcastically.

"Ah, bless him, he's not that bad. Hasn't he tried to kiss you yet?!" her mother asked, teasing her with a rare twinkle in her eye.

Anne screwed up her face, cringing at the very thought. "Are you friggin' serious, Mammy? Have you seen the look and shape of him? I'd rather die!"

"Ock, he's not that bad. He's been a godsend for us, I can tell you. I know he's a bit older and all that, but he's the only one who's managed to cheer you up at least a little bit – I'll be honest, love, you're like a bear with a sore head at times."

"Suppose so." Anne agreed reluctantly, and in an attempt to change the subject, asked, "You want help with those spuds?"

"Go on then." Her mother moved aside to make room by the sink for her. Liz held the knife carefully in her hand as she watched what was once her beautiful, vibrant, and incessantly funny girl hobbling towards her.

Life had turned into a continual nightmare for them all. Liz's own baby-bearing days were well and truly over, and the lump of a man she'd married had hardly been in touch since Emma's funeral. If it wasn't for the older girls working, they'd be out on the street. Lousy, lazy feckin' bastard! As an excuse, he'd told her he was in the IRA and on the run in the Republic, but deep down, she knew he'd a woman hidden down there somewhere.

As for Anne… A different kettle of fish altogether with her moods, tears and eternal silences. At times, Liz didn't know what to do – she'd even tried to get Caitlin to call in and cheer her up. She knew Anne's friend had stuff of her own going on but was disappointed at her lack of effort – it'd been way too long since they last saw her. Though she didn't blame Caitlin for what had happened to Anne, she thought she could have stuck a bit closer to her best friend since the bombing.

Mother and daughter had finished preparing the potatoes when there was a loud whack at the front door. Quickly washing her hands and rubbing them dry with a tea towel, Liz made her way out of the kitchen, half shouting over her shoulder to Anne: "That'll be your beau!"

Anne shook her head in amused despair, placed her knife down and hobbled to the kitchen door to look down the hallway. "Jesus, Mammy. What are you like!" she cried after her mother, who quickly looked back at her with a wide grin. A glance filled with love passed between the two women as the door was opened.

And there he stood – Porkie – as proud as a drenched peacock. Liz Heaney tried her best not to laugh as he asked, through the spittle spraying from his mouth, "How you doing, Mrs Heaney? That's some downpour. The heavens have just opened!"

"It is, John. A bad night. Hurry up; you'd better get in here before you catch your death!"

"Ah, thanks, Mrs Heaney."

Liz took a final despairing look at the man on her doorstep. God, he was fat – not cuddly fat, but huge! His attempts at a shave were poor. Liz could see the small red nicks and even more milky spots on his face. He'd attempted to smooth this thick hair back before knocking, but to no avail. A stream of water ran down his face, yet tufts of hair spiked upwards from his skull. Wearing no overcoat, just a jacket and a black and white chequered shirt with a long thin purple tie, he was drenched. His flared trousers were a bit too long and covered most of his saturated shoes – the barely visible toes soaked and sodden. Liz thought he looked more like a teenager than a grown man, standing there waiting and holding a bunch of pathetically dripping carnations in a water-logged pink and white paper bag – most likely, he'd just purchased them from the local petrol station.

He really was a sight. Trying desperately not to laugh, she led him down the hallway towards the kitchen. Reaching Anne, after first wiping some of the water off his jacket, he handed her the wet through flowers.

"Alright?"

"Aye, thanks, not bad," Anne replied, nonchalantly throwing the pathetic flowers into the stainless-steel sink on top of some unwashed dishes.

"Tea, John?" Liz asked as she pushed between the standing couple, giving her daughter a look like a dagger so she'd behave.

"That'd be great. Thanks, Mrs Heaney, but I keep telling you, call me Porkie. Everyone does, and I bet you can't guess why!"

Neither of the women dared answer. Finally, embarrassed by their silence, he moved on and said jovially, "I've brought us a couple of buns." At that, he hurriedly searched his jacket pockets to produce two sodden, translucent, white paper bags containing some squashed, dampened iced buns.

As if poisonous, Anne used her index finger and thumb to take the offerings and put them on a side plate. Wanting to turn up her nose but knowing her mother was watching her closely, she'd no choice but to reply, "Thanks, Porkie, they look lovely."

Liz needed to get out of the kitchen before she burst out laughing. She suggested to Porkie, "Give us your coat, *Porkie*, I'll hang it under the stairs." She took the jacket, nodded and promptly left the two lovebirds in the kitchen, giggling to herself as she walked to the cupboard.

Porkie took a chair and sat quietly watching Anne fill the kettle, light the gas ring and put it on the boil.

"So… You're alright then?" he asked again, nervously.

"I said I was, didn't I!" Anne snapped.

"Aye. Right." Silence. Then: "Have you heard the news?" Porkie asked excitedly. His nerves were wrecked. She was a hard nut to crack.

"Not interested," was her only reply.

"You should be, Anne. There's a whole lot of them up in Belfast, Sunningdoyle or Sunnington or something. They're trying to sort things out. Them up from the Irish Government and all. End all this trouble. Could change everything for us."

She said nothing. The kettle boiled. Anne made the tea and sat down at the small table, noting her mother's long absence from the kitchen – she was obviously not coming back but leaving them to it.

What seemed like a lifetime came to an end when Porkie finished his ramblings, stood up and announced he had to go. She knew she'd been rude to him, but today she just wasn't in the mood – he'd got her at her worst. Feeling just the tiniest bit guilty, she faked disappointment and pointed to a plate.

"Are you sure? There's one bun left if you want it?" He'd already eaten the other three himself.

Touched by her concern, and to her absolute disgust, Porkie happily returned to his chair, asked for more tea and scoffed the last iced bun down in seconds – in between attempts to tell her jokes.

Later that evening, Anne sat by the TV with her mother and sisters. She couldn't believe she'd allowed the wally to stay for so long. Two hours! Two fucking hours she'd been stuck with him.

She gazed at her mother stonily and was about to speak when Liz – well aware she was in deep shite and about to get a slating from Anne – creased up laughing and cried, "I know, love! I know. Far too long! You don't have to say anything!"

"Mammy, I can't believe you! You knew he'd drive me nuts!" Anne replied bitingly. She wasn't amused but inwardly raging. She refused to look at her mother but instead stared at the TV, paying no attention to what was on.

Liz quickly stopped laughing and turned her eyes up at her other daughters, implying, "*Here we go again.*"

Anne caught the look and, getting angrier, swore at them all before hobbling up the narrow staircase to her box bedroom. Since Anne loved everything to do with the 1950s, her bedroom walls were adorned with film posters including *The Quiet Man*, *Casablanca* and *High Society*. A single wardrobe was positioned next to the window. It had once contained flamboyant, full swing-petticoat 1950s skirts but now held just a few plain everyday clothes. There were no shoes in sight – certainly no sign of her once much-loved stilettos. The space was too small for a dressing table. Instead, a small, rectangular mirror hung on the wall with coloured glass necklaces draped over the edge. Looking out of place in the corner stood an old tea chest. She hadn't paid attention to it in a very long time and exhaled a sigh of sorrow.

Sitting on her single bed, she began slowly to remove her prosthetic leg. Unbuckling the straps one by one, she felt relief as the pressure eased. She'd had a number of minor spasms during Porkie's visit but refused to give in to them or let him see her pain.

Throwing the cumbersome contraption across the room in anger, she fell onto the carpeted floor and dragged herself across to the steel-rimmed tea chest. She carefully removed the books that lay on top and put them aside before slowly raising the lid to take a peek. Tears hovered in her eyes as she looked inside. Her shoes, her beautiful coloured stilettoes that she'd worked and saved up for over the years, now lay covered in dust in the chest, destined never to be worn again. Her one joy in life was gone. Her existence now consisted only of pain, sorrow and loneliness. Her dream of meeting a rich, blond, tanned Yank, who would sweep her off her feet, marry her and take her to America, had been crushed and shattered the moment that bomb went off. That *fucking* bomb had, within a matter of seconds, robbed her of all her dreams about a long, fun-filled carefree life across the Atlantic.

Chapter 6

Father Cathal Connolly was one of six children born in Boston, USA, who, at a very young age, moved to Tipperary with his American mother and Irish father to live and work on his grandparents' farm. Not long after arriving in Ireland, his father, who had briefly led the IRA North Tipperary Brigade, was killed in action. Cathal would never forget the pain on his ma's face at the funeral, which was led by a lone piper and attended by most, if not all, of the village and many of his father's comrades. He'd watched her, his heart jagged with pity: her red, swollen and lifeless eyes, the incessant tears that fell onto her one and only threadbare black coat.

His parents had enjoyed one of those rare marriages between two soulmates who clearly lived for and loved each other. Their simple house teemed daily with laughter and love. He'd been lucky until then; all eight of them had. It'd been a very happy home.

Sadly, after his da's death, their childhoods went downhill when their mother became fixated and fanatical about religion. She'd insist they all sit together by the fire and say the Rosary "for your da's soul" at least three or four times a day. It didn't take long until he found a way out of the grieving household. He joined the Pallottine Order and became a priest – both to appease her and to gain a better education for himself.

On this particular evening, he stood staring at his reflection in an unassuming wood-framed mirror, placed above the open fireplace in the dining room of the parochial house adjacent to St Mary's Church, Creggan. He was a tall, thickset man with curly hair the colour of marmalade. He had naturally sad, light blue eyes under bushy eyebrows but was handsome in a rugged way. He had, however, the demeanour of a man who'd seen the inside of hell, and that was no overstatement – today, he'd been to a hell of sorts.

He took a deep breath, raised his chin and closed his eyes for a brief moment before relaxing. The day had begun well with the phone call he was expecting from the States. He was due to travel back to Boston soon and was expecting the call to finalise some last-minute details. The American voice had sounded excited and keen.

"So, we're all set. I've got you speaking at each of the dinners, and we've kept the numbers to a minimum. Quality over quantity, eh? We can expect to raise around five thousand dollars per night, if not more."

Father Connolly responded quietly so as not to disturb his fellow priests upstairs and said gratefully, "That's good. As long as the dollars keep rolling in."

"Oh, yes, sirreee, they're coming in alright. I've also written a piece for the *Irish People*, our new weekly newsletter. That'll give us some good coverage too."

At the beginning of The Troubles in 1969, an Irishman in New York started an organisation with the mission of "aiding the Unity of Ireland and supporting the peace process". Unexpectedly Father Connolly had been asked to help NORAID from this side of the pond. He was well respected as a natural orator and also as a staunch Republican from a hero's family.

Everything was in hand, and the caller had agreed to keep in touch as the line clicked off. It was time for the priest to visit the sick at the local hospital, Altnagelvin, on the east side of the city, known as the Waterside. As he'd been preparing to leave, a panicked and shaken Father McGuire – eldest of the three priests who resided at St Mary's – came rushing through the front door calling out for him. Upon sight of the young priest, he'd cried, "Ah, you're here! I need you, son. Quickly now, with me!"

Father Connolly had barely time to pick up his jacket and hat as he was grabbed painfully by the arm and pulled with surprising strength through the door and down the steps.

"What's going on, Father? Where are we going?" Father Connolly cried as he took two steps at a time to keep up with the older man who seemed suddenly superhuman.

"I'll explain in a second," he barked as they reached his red Ford Fiesta, where he threw his car keys across the bonnet to his bewildered novice and said, "You drive. I'll explain on the way."

Father Connolly had been relieved to drive, having recently experienced a few near-misses with his colleague – whose eye-sight was undoubtedly diminishing at a startling rate – and given the fact he'd been warned numerous times by the RUC for his haphazard driving. The car sped off as McGuire began to explain.

"It's Majella McLaughlin. I've just met Mrs McFadden, her neighbour. She told me the poor woman's hung herself! It's too much. That family's been through enough already. Quick now, Blamfield Street!"

Father Connolly knew his mentor carried an enormous weight of guilt over his own treatment of Tina McLaughlin and the way she ended up. He'd especially found the events at the City Hotel difficult to come to terms with. The girl had come to him shortly before the incident, deeply upset and asking for help, but he'd been so busy and wound up with his other problems that he'd ignored her. McGuire would never forgive himself for that; it was plain. Since then, he'd done his utmost to protect her in gaol, but so far with little success.

As they reached the pebble-dashed semi-terraced house, Father Connolly noticed a small crowd had gathered around the dilapidated front gate – likely waiting to find out if there was more news. As the two priests scrambled out of the car, Tommy O'Reilly quickly ran out to meet them. He wore a two-tone donkey jacket that was clearly too big even for his solid body and huge chest. His cheeks were flushed, and his blue eyes were brimming with tears.

He placed his hands on the old priest's arms and murmured sadly, "Father, it was too much for her. Patrick, Martin and then our Tina in Armagh. She couldn't cope!"

"I know, son," Father McGuire muttered, gently laying his hand on the big man's shoulder. "I know. Where is she?"

Tommy's heart was banging, and his throat constricted. *Christ,* he needed a very strong drink.

"I took her down off the door, Father. I had to. She was a sight just hanging there. She's on the bed. It's the worst thing I've ever seen in me life. I just… just can't understand *how* she could do it."

The men made their way into the house, taking the narrow staircase to the main bedroom – the very same room the dead woman's husband Patrick had been dragged out of, naked and broken and innocent, by the British Army.

Father Connolly looked in horrified shock at what he saw in the foul-smelling place. He'd seen his fair share of corpses, but this had to be the worst. The poor woman lay on the bed, eyes staring from her barely recognisable face, the rope mark on her neck standing out a livid purple against her tied-back, grey hair. He had to look swiftly away.

A faded flower print-covered stool stood beneath a three-drawer dressing table that held a tarnished silver hairbrush set and very few toiletries on its glass-covered top. He glanced briefly at the black-and-white photographs alongside and then saw an unopened envelope with Tommy's name written on it in neat, cursive handwriting.

The men had to leave the room. It was too much to witness the emaciated woman lying on her pathetically covered bed, so they stood respectfully outside on the landing. Father McGuire felt both deeply sad and angry as he remembered how beautiful and happy Majella had been on her wedding day. As a newly ordained priest, he'd performed his first wedding ceremony when she'd married Patrick McLaughlin. He reflected on the children's baptisms, their First Communions and Confirmations, all happy events. Patrick and Majella proved to be good and natural parents. Proud parents who'd done everything they could for their young family, only for it all to end like this. It was a tragedy, pure tragedy.

Father Connolly noticed the old priest's silent tears and, to allow him privacy, turned away and asked Tommy quietly, "Caitlin… does she know?"

Tommy shook his head. "Not yet; Mrs McFadden's just gone with Charlie to get her at work. They should be here any second. I think she's going to tell her."

His words hung in the air for a short time until Father Connolly, hearing footsteps on the stairs, rushed to the bedroom door to make sure it was securely closed. The three men stood at the top of the staircase, blocking the way. Father Connolly had only seen Caitlin McLaughlin a few times at Mass and didn't know her particularly well. To him, she always appeared sullen and remote, but he knew the poor girl shouldn't see her mother, not in that state. *No one should have to do that.*

"Mammy! Mammy!" Caitlin wailed as she rushed up the stairs and attempted to push through the human barricade. Sniffling and wiping her nose with the back of her hand, she looked wild-eyed as she cried out to her uncle, "Let me through! Tommy – tell them to let me through!"

At that, Mrs McFadden hobbled up the stairs behind her. Pulling Caitlin down and away from the bedroom that held its lifeless occupant, she openly wept as she said, "Come with me, love. *Please.*"

Caitlin screeched and, without looking at her uncle, yelled, "How could she do it, Tommy? She's gone and left me! "

Mrs McFadden was rarely lost for words, but for the first time in ages, she didn't know what to say. Although she was deeply saddened and shocked, she also felt a sense of relief. Relief at losing her best friend and neighbour– how on God's earth! Nevertheless, in her heart, she knew why - she knew *exactly* why - Majella no longer cared enough to live.

Well, maybe you'll find some peace now and be with Patrick, Mrs McFadden thought, before whispering inaudibly and blessing herself, "Rest in Peace, my friend. Rest in Peace."

Meanwhile, Tommy stared through the window on the landing to the small gathering by the front of the house. Riddled with nerves, he looked at the priest and asked crossly, "What the heck are they waiting for?"

"Pay no attention," Father McGuire answered ruefully before adding, "we need to call the police, Tommy. We need to report this and ring a doctor too."

"Aye. You're right, I suppose. I'll do it. I don't want Caitlin anywhere near here – we need to keep her downstairs."

Without hesitation, the priest agreed and bowed his head to say a silent prayer. Death had many masks, but this was one of the worst.

In the kitchen below, Father Connolly sat with Caitlin and Mrs McFadden.

He looked at the young girl, sobbing quietly as she rocked back and forth on a chair. Her neighbour lifted a packet of cigarettes from the windowsill and quickly lit one, her hands shaking at the effort. He needed to say something to fill the void.

"I'm so sorry, Caitlin, Mrs McFadden. I know it's been a terrible time for you all lately."

Too choked to respond, Caitlin said nothing as he added gently, "We'll wait for Father McGuire and Tommy and maybe say a few prayers if that's okay? Be prepared, Caitlin; it's likely the police and doctor will have to be informed." He paused, "*Given the circumstances*."

At the priest's warning, Caitlin gasped and suddenly went berserk, howling, "I'm having none of those bastards in our house! Do you hear me? You keep them away from Mammy! This is all their fault…"

She jumped up from the table and angrily marched around the kitchen, ranting and raving about how much she hated the police and anyone who had anything to do with them. Loud footsteps sounded from upstairs, followed by quick heavy thuds on the staircase as Tommy bounded down them and stood, white-faced and shaken, at the kitchen door, watching her.

"Sweet Jesus, Caitlin. What is it? Take it easy, love!"

Pointing at the priest, she shrieked, "It's him! He's just told me the police are coming! I'm not letting them anywhere near her, Tommy. I'm locking the door now."

With a warning glance at Father Connolly to say no more, Tommy ran out of the kitchen in pursuit of his niece.

Smoke filled the air as Mrs McFadden readied herself to ask the young priest the obvious but unavoidable question. In preparation, she straightened up and tipped her chin defiantly. She'd bloody well make sure her friend was laid to rest – and properly. Here goes.

"I suppose the poor woman will be condemned to hell now that she's topped herself? Will you not let her be buried next to Patrick, Father?"

Father Connolly was well briefed for such a question and answered accordingly with a sigh, "Yes, Mrs McFadden. Thankfully, times have changed, and the Church's thinking on some matters with them. You've no need to worry. We'll look after her. God rest her soul."

Chapter 7

Eighteen months. Eighteen fucking months! That's how long Iowa, aka Alice Wallace, had found herself sitting behind this lousy old desk, filling in one mind-numbing form after another. She grudgingly looked at the two tatty wooden "In" and "Out" trays on the edge of her desk, both half-full. She couldn't be arsed to get enthusiastic about anything in this godforsaken dump.

Her day had just started, and, by God, she dreaded it already – just like she did every other day spent here. She was bored, bored, bored beyond belief, and it was killing her!

She heard shouts and yells from the courtyard outside and climbed up to look through the high steel-framed window onto the scene in the yard beneath. Squads of troops were enthusiastically jumping off the back of four-tonne lorries. They mustered side by side, filling the substantial space. She studied the bustling men and women below. Not long ago, the army had raised the minimum age for service in Northern Ireland to eighteen. Without question, a few of these youngsters had slipped through the net. She knew this lot had arrived from Ballykinler Army Base after training and – like her – been told they were here in Ireland to simply "maintain law and order." *Yeah, right!*

Alone in the office, she groaned loudly as she sat down again, reflecting on how much her life had changed since the shambles in Londonderry. She supposed, on the one hand, the positive was that the hotel bomb hadn't gone off, and mercifully there'd been no fatalities or casualties other than the three shootings. But, on the other hand, her partner undercover, Kentucky – aka Robert Sallis – and she had colossally screwed up. Their cover had been well and truly blown. As a result, their particularly irate handler quickly broke the pair up and sent them off in different directions.

Now Alice found herself here in Ballymurphy, or "Murph" as it was affectionately termed. As for Sallis, he'd simply said goodbye and left her at Fort George barracks. She'd never forget the horror she'd felt after they'd both been successful in their covert ops exams and tests and been paired up with him. She'd been livid. The Provos had murdered Graham, her soldier fiancé, in cold blood, and she'd sworn revenge on them for his death. Her dream was to get back into action solo and avenge his killing, but instead, she was sitting behind this damned desk.

Feeling just the slightest twinge of remorse, she remembered how rude and unfriendly she'd been to Sallis on their first op. Still furious at having to work with him, she'd only speak or respond to him when she had to and distanced herself as much as she could. He'd accused her of being a *man-hater* and even a *lesbo*. He'd read her wrong; she just wanted to kill Provos – but on her own. After Graham's death, she'd found herself soulless, lonely and bursting at the seams with revenge and anger.

Once she'd been at Ballymurphy a while, she'd heard Sallis had been sent to West Belfast and not long after suffered some sort of head injury during a motherfucker of a riot. He'd been sent home to Newcastle and quietly discharged on health grounds. Word was he wasn't well enough to get married, and soon, like so many squaddies before him, his personality began to change. Heavy drinking didn't help his paranoia after his fiancée cleared off with a guy she'd been seeing on the side. She'd left Sallis and his shocked mother and father with a newborn baby boy. Alice shrugged. She supposed it was sad, but what the fuck? At least she only had herself to think about now.

She made her way to the kitchenette to make herself a coffee with three sugars – just how she liked it. As she waited for the kettle, she hoped there wouldn't be any more electricity strikes. There'd been a number of walk-outs by the Protestant Ulster Workers, outraged by the threat of setting up a power-sharing Northern Ireland Executive involving the Irish Government – the so-called Sunningdale Agreement. Their strikes were becoming a real pain in the ass.

She spotted a tall, tired-looking, middle-aged man, accompanied by her sergeant, purposefully making their way towards her from a distance. She recognised him immediately as her and Sallis's ex-handler. *Shit*! Remembering how angry he'd been when she last saw him, she hoped he wasn't here to cause trouble. With a cigarette dangling from his lips, the man spoke softly to her sergeant until he reached her. He removed the cigarette with nicotine-stained fingers and nodded abruptly to her.

"Iowa."

"Sir," she replied cautiously. The tension was palpable as blood pumped in her ears.

"You're needed. With me." He indicated for her to follow as he walked away. At this, Alice looked to her boyish, brown-eyed sergeant, who looked back with a slight smile. He liked her. Not once had she complained over the months though she'd obviously hated the job. She wasn't cut out to be an administrator, but she'd remained professional, and he felt she deserved a second chance.

Alice smiled in return and began to follow the handler but was soon stopped as her amused sarge prompted her to switch off the semi-boiling kettle.

"Oh, God, yes! Sorry!" Her face reddened.

"Good luck, Alice," he said and was gone.

As she ran to catch up with the Military Intelligence handler, Alice suppressed a grin. Was she back in? Didn't he just say she *was needed*? In no time, she found herself sitting in a small dark meeting room with blacked-out windows. A single light bulb dangled by a long rope-like wire hung halfway down from the ceiling.

The thin, grey-haired man lit another cigarette taken from his inside jacket pocket. Funnily enough, he looked exactly the same as the last time she saw him. He wore the same navy three-piece suit, the same red tie that hung loosely around the collar of his white shirt and, as ever, he appeared worn out. She remembered when they'd last met. To his credit, Sallis had borne the raw brunt of the man's fury, and quite rightly. It was, after all, his fault since he hadn't listened to her. They'd blown their cover while following Charles Jones and should've gone straight back to barracks instead of to the Londonderry City Hotel.

Her handler took a deep gratifying puff of the cigarette and held it for a moment while he considered the young woman who sat opposite him, still and straight. She wasn't bad-looking. The uniform helped – women in uniform turned him on. She could be doing with a bit more meat on her for his liking, but all in all, she'd do. He couldn't blame her entirely for the cock-up in Londonderry and was only interested now in her reaction to what he had to offer. He'd bet money on it that she wouldn't think twice.

"I'm led to believe you want to get out of here and back to ops?" he asked, sniffing loudly whilst rubbing his nose with the back of his cigarette-holding hand.

"Yes, sir. As soon as possible, sir," she answered determinedly. *Was it that obvious*?

"Thought so. I'm going to give you one final chance, Iowa. And this one you can't fuck up; otherwise, it could easily cost you or others their lives. Do you understand?"

Alice's eyes narrowed in suspicion as she listened to what he had to say. It didn't take long before she felt her body fill with a mixture of raging delight, excitement, fear and exasperation that hit her all at once. Engrossed, she listened carefully. This proposal was precisely what she'd hoped for!

Alice found she'd been given a few days' leave before the operation began. Apart from Sergeant Dury, she said goodbye to no one. This inglorious chapter of her life was well and truly over. Now for some real action.

Usually, personnel could fly from Aldergrove Airport near Belfast to go home. However, as time was short, Alice decided to make her way to Bangor – a local, predominantly Protestant-filled seaside resort.

The first thing she did was to get her long, brown feathered hair cut and coloured. Afterwards, she found herself admiring her reflection in shop and car windows. Her new image made her feel good. No one would recognise her. Since she'd been stuck behind a desk for so long, she'd made a point of working out regularly. Her tiny frame was now toned and taut. Back at barracks, a few of the *bean stealers* or *pads* (otherwise known as married soldiers) tried it on, but she'd firmly pushed them off.

She was staying at a pretty Victorian B&B, a townhouse that faced the shore, thankfully nothing like the decrepit place in Londonderry she and Sallis had stayed in. During the short R&R break, she read. Reading allowed her to escape her surroundings. Books helped her survive not only the loss of Graham but daily life – particularly over the last mind-numbingly boring months.

This particular night, however, Alice was to meet a close friend. After Graham's death, he'd kept in touch with her as much as he could and on the odd, very rare occasion, they would meet. He'd been delighted when he'd learned she was close by.

"Ah, it'll be lovely to see you again," he'd told her warmly on the phone earlier that afternoon.

"You too. It can't be a late night, though. I have to be back tomorrow reasonably early," she'd warned.

"Of course. I'll see you at six then."

"See you at six." She said, smiling as she replaced the receiver.

Chapter 8

Since early morning she'd been on her knees. Tina McLaughlin knelt by the entrance to the inmates' showers and baths with their red-tiled floor, situated opposite the cells on the second floor of A-Wing. Her back was killing her, but her hands hurt much worse. When she held them up to examine them, they were red-raw and chapped from scrubbing the cells and catwalks with luke-warm water topped up with harsh disinfectant.

Female prisoners lived two to a cell on A and B Wings. Sanitation was inadequate, and a slopping-out system operated. The overcrowded conditions were exacerbated by the fact that up until recently, female prisoners had to share facilities with, although segregated from, two male punishment regimes. These comprised of the overspill of internees and prisoners on remand from Belfast Prison plus those from a boys' borstal, which had been located on the premises for decades. Resources had been assigned to male prisoners as a priority, which curtailed the women's access to sanitation, exercise, and recreational facilities. They could exercise only in one muddy patch of yard and were open to verbal abuse and obscenities shouted at them by the soldiers patrolling the perimeters as well as the male prisoners. They'd been allocated one recreational room that was too small to be of any use and only contained board and card games, nothing else.

With the men now gone, there was freedom of movement for the remaining female inmates between A- and B-Wing, via a passageway running through the back of the chapel. The new C-Wing had just opened with 30 more cells built on what was once an old breakers' yard.

Tina McLaughlin had been in Armagh Gaol now for nearly six months. At first, she couldn't fathom where she was or why: her eighteenth birthday had come and gone, uncelebrated and forgotten. Some days she was okay, and then others were a complete blur, but slowly, bit by bit, she was becoming more lucid. The other women took care of her, and she liked it – they'd even nicknamed her "the youngin'".

In the early days, she took her medication, distributed daily at the top of the stairs by the medical officer. Somehow it didn't seem to affect her as much as the stuff in the hospital, and she soon found her thoughts and memories becoming much clearer. Eventually, she'd stopped taking the pills altogether – the medical officer hadn't noticed.

At the OC's morning briefing, Maureen would drill into her comrades how important it was to keep to a routine. Working was good, much better than being locked up all day. It was imperative they kept busy so as not to allow themselves too much time to think about the outside world.

Maureen allocated everyone their daily tasks, either scrubbing the floors in the bathrooms, cleaning the showers, toilets or cells, working in the laundry or sewing. In addition to allocating work, checking on each of the women and taking roll calls, the OC would read out what she could from the left-over scraps of newspapers after the "political news" had been censored by being cut out with scissors.

She grew concerned that some of the non-political prisoners were making men's prison uniforms and shared this news with a younger brother on his last visit, thereby allowing him to give the heads up to the *Boys*. As things stood, imprisoned men and women were allowed to wear their own clothes if they were deemed "political prisoners" following a hunger strike by Republican, Billy McKee. Were that to change, and she had a feeling it just might, there'd be serious consequences and trouble for everyone.

Father McGuire made a point of catching up with Tina whenever he visited the gaol. She'd half-listen to the old priest as, once again, he'd apologised for not paying attention to her on the morning of the bomb scare when she'd been so frightened and had looked for his help. It didn't matter anymore, she'd tell him reassuringly. However, what really worried her was there was still no sign of her mother. It'd been too long since she'd visited.

She'd imagine herself back in the kitchen at Blamfield with her mammy and Caitlin that night when the electric meter ran out, and they'd use candles for light. She'd been so cross at Caitlin for pinching her hidden stock of lemonade bottles and now found it pathetic and childish. She'd give anything to be back there – the three of them just sitting and talking. She found Father McGuire dismissive when she'd ask where her mammy was; he'd just say she wasn't well. She hadn't heard from Martin either, and that hurt too.

Sometimes, in the early hours of the morning and wide awake, she'd get flashbacks to the horrors of the night in the barn and Val's murder. She'd never forget the soldier's empty eyes as they wrapped him up in torn black bin bags. Kieran had been so calculating and cold, and she'd felt a fool when she realised he'd led her up the garden path. To think that *she* carried a bomb in *her* schoolbag and took it to him. The whole episode plagued her. Her body would shake uncontrollably and sweat at the thoughts that came back to haunt her. She'd been a complete idiot, a stupid, stupid bitch. *She* could have killed so many people. Such dark days that she'd rather forget and wipe from her tortured mind.

Her memory wasn't quite all there, but there were some things she clearly recalled. She'd never forget the day she'd arrived in this gaol and been stripped and forced to take a bath. Her experience the following morning wasn't much better. She'd had an introductory meeting with the Governor, a lot of which she couldn't recall. It was what happened next in the medical centre that seriously freaked her out.

There wasn't a full-time doctor on-site. Doctors were sent by agency staff for evening and weekend "consultations" and came from local GP surgeries during the day. This arrangement proved much cheaper than having a permanent, dedicated prison medic. There was also a full-time nursing sister and some screws who'd been trained in so-called basic medical care.

She'd been met by an ugly, boozy-looking man in a stained white coat, a Dr Harris. She'd never seen a man so thin and who shared her nervous habit of picking and scratching at any patch of dry skin. He'd promptly and coldly told her he didn't want her to talk to him but to strip down to her underwear quickly. She'd refused. She hadn't forgotten the episode in the bath the day before and was still having her period. Fortunately, Maureen had given her some Dr White's. She wasn't going through that again, not for a million pounds, and especially with a man *and* on her own.

Harris wasn't used to such a response. Flustered and muttering, he pretended to look for something on his steel desk. He soon left in search of the nursing sister but instead returned a few minutes later with the green-eyed, cruel guard who'd degraded and embarrassed Tina the day before.

In a frustrated, whining voice, he bawled at the guard, "I've asked this prisoner to strip to her underwear, but she refuses."

Tina looked Smyth squarely in the eye, rallying all her strength to keep calm and controlled as the guard ordered acidly, "McLaughlin. Take them off. Now."

"You do it," Tina answered resolutely.

A heavy, awkward silence hung in the air as the baffled man and woman looked at each other. "Excuse me?" they asked in chorus.

"You do it," Tina repeated cautiously. Her heart raced as she prayed for strength. *Hail Mary, full of grace.*

Smyth knew she was in a corner. She wasn't violently going to force the girl to strip down in front of Harris. He was a hateful git alright and well known for covering his back in a crisis and blame others. She'd heard he'd been warned out of the country by the Nationalists in Londonderry – something to do with the death of some Taig in custody.

She wasn't going to hit out at McLaughlin with him in the room. If McLaughlin complained to her OC and then the Governor, Smyth was convinced Harris would pin it on her. He gave her the creeps – there was something peculiar and odd about him. Unluckily for the people of Armagh, he'd ended up here.

It didn't matter for now; she'd get McLaughlin on her own another time.

"Right then," Smyth said, as she reluctantly but deliberately roughly began to remove the girl's clothes. She placed them on the floor until the bruised girl stood tall and erect in just her faded grey bra and knickers.

Harris knew it was his duty to note any evidence of mistreatment, especially in newly arrived prisoners by logging specific bruises or contusions on their bodies. With such an attitude, though, this girl could go to hell.

He mentally noted the marks on the back of her legs, torso and rear ribs but didn't record them. She'd obviously taken a bit of a beating – most likely whilst in Hastings Street barracks where the women and girls were always mistreated. His predecessor in the gaol was well known for handing out medication left, right and centre to the inmates. As he read Tina McLaughlin's notes, he noticed she'd been treated for psychosis and had been prescribed a high measure of Chlorpromazine. For revenge, he deliberately lowered the dosage and thought, that'll teach her.

Although warned by the PIRA to get out after the lack of charges over his medical negligence in the case of Patrick McLaughlin – this girl's father, had he troubled himself enough to remember the man's name and make the connection – Harris downright refused to leave Ireland. After all, it was his country too! In the end, though, it had made sense for him to leave Londonderry where it was getting too much. They'd thrown petrol bombs through the front window of his house, and the resulting fire had destroyed most of his precious books and medical papers. They'd even stolen his dog Winston, a King Charles Spaniel that never came back. He'd loved that dog.

In the end, he decided he wasn't leaving the fucking country. He'd too many particular and *special* friends here, and ultimately, when any of them got into trouble, they'd close in and help. So here he was, a GP in Armagh.

Harris looked at Smyth and nodded for her to get the girl dressed as he finally wrote in bold print on Tina's notes, *"No evidence of trauma. Fit and well."*

Smyth nodded in acknowledgement and turned to her prisoner. "Get dressed."

Tina shook her head and replied again, "You do it."

This was too much for Smyth, who instinctively reached for her baton but was forcibly pulled back by Harris, who screamed in a piercing voice, more like the wail of a teenage girl than a grown man: "No! Don't! Don't touch her! Get her dressed and out of my sight!"

At that, with a face contorted in fury, Smyth dressed Tina McLaughlin, who stood quietly and impassively staring at nothing but the wall.

Later, on her return to the cell, as she climbed up the mesh-covered stairwell, Smyth had whispered menacingly in her ear, "My time will come, miss."

Tina ignored her, too busy taking in the web-like tangle of rope that hung over each level – a suicide-prevention net. For the first time in a long while she felt proud. She'd stood her ground and stood up for herself.

Somehow Maureen had managed to get Tina political status even though she wasn't formally a member of any paramilitary group. It was important to the OC that she was put in the right category as it meant the youngin' could remain under her watchful care and be billeted permanently with someone steady who could be trusted to look out for her.

Back on the landing, making an effort to rinse the heavy wet cloth in a steel bucket full of muggy water, Tina was hit in the face by a flying rag. She screamed in rage.

"Aaggghh! Christ, that's freezing!"

Laughter filled the landing as Tina looked at her new cellmate, Bridget Barry. Bridget was in her late-fifties with wispy hair, a mixture of dark black and grey, tied back in a tight bun. Her eyes were dark, and her skin olive-coloured.

Bridget had arrived in the gaol as a remand prisoner in the early days of 1971 when there'd only been two women in the whole place. She proved to be a bit of a comedian, and Tina felt immediately drawn to her. She treated Tina like she was a grown-up, not like the others who spoke to her as if she were a child.

Bridget, whose face opened into a beautiful lazy smile as she arrived to retrieve her wet cloth, laughed loudly. "You looked like you were in one of your secret places. Come on, we need to get cracking and finish. We have to see what's on and vote!"

There was only one TV on the wing, and the women voted every night to decide which programmes to watch. There was never much contention with only two channels to choose from, and this was the main highlight of their evening before lock up at 8 p.m.

Later, over some dinner, Bridget sat next to Tina and a few other inmates in their cell. She'd been asked to look out for the girl by her OC, and Bridget, as the OC's adjutant, was more than happy to take on the role. She was a natural "Mammy" who loved to care for, nurse, and play tricks and pranks on her comrades. She was a real tonic to all of the women who had, on many occasions, needed her support to help them survive. Her laughter was contagious, and her jokes cherished.

"How you doing, youngin'?" she asked Tina, who was scoffing down Thursday's regular mashed potato and soup.

"Grand!" Tina came back at her. "This is *really* nice!"

Bridget nodded her head in agreement. The food here was bloody awful, watery and mushy. She couldn't understand how the youngin' liked it so much, watching her gobble it down at an unwavering rate.

"Listen, youngin'; I have to ask you a favour. I don't suppose you'd go to the shop for us in the morning? Liz Sweeney will meet you at the circle at seven-thirty. Me and the girls have a few things we need. Before *Crossroads* or whatever shite we're watching tonight, do you think you could go around and get their orders, and we'll sort you out with the money later?"

Tina looked at her cellmate and the others in astonishment and quickly stopped eating. It'd been so long since she'd been outdoors properly. She cried out in her excitement, "The shop! Seriously? You want me to go to the shop! Definitely, no bother, I'll go!"

At such an enthusiastic response from Tina, Bridget looked at her comrades and winked, to be met by a sea of knowing faces. The youngin' wasn't the first and wouldn't be the last to fall for that one!

Chapter 9

The word *lonely* couldn't even begin to describe how Caitlin McLaughlin felt as she sat staring into space in front of the teak-effect TV – unwatched and switched on to no particular channel. She contemplated other words she'd use to describe how she was feeling: *friendless, abandoned, deserted, alone*. Yeah, all of them. That hateful inner voice in her head just wouldn't let up as it relentlessly reminded her of everything that had happened, almost wanting to encourage her to fall deeper and deeper into a dark depression. And so it went on.

She was *friendless* – she hadn't heard a peep from Anne, nor had she turned up to mammy's funeral, which was unforgivable.

She'd been *abandoned* – her granny hadn't come to the funeral either, and Caitlin couldn't believe it. As for Tommy, bless him, she felt he'd forgotten all about her. He'd been furious too that his mother hadn't paid her respects but found he was too busy and up to his eyeballs with so many other issues to confront her about it.

She'd been *deserted* – Martin was AWOL. She'd no idea where he was. And Tina was locked up in her own hell.

She was *alone* – the house no longer felt like a home but an empty shell. She'd done her best to remain dignified in her grief at the funeral by saying nothing of her sense of isolation and disappointment in everyone – friends and family alike. But it wasn't right, and she felt like God was laughing at her.

She looked around at the once spotless, if sparse, living room and knew she'd neglected it. She'd neglected the whole house, and badly. Where once the nets had hung stark white and fresh, they were now dusty and grey. She was beyond caring as she knew she'd likely not be able to see through the windows; it'd been so long since they were cleaned. Teacups were strewn on the stained teak-effect table that was also cluttered with unread letters and bills. Bedclothes fell onto the floor from the worn brown corduroy sofa where she'd slept after being too lazy to walk upstairs to her room. The open fireplace lay barren and forgotten, along with the empty mantelpiece above it that once held photographs showing happy memories of family First Communions and Christmases.

She'd no tears left; she was hollow. Everything seemed pointless. Majella's funeral and its planning had wholly destroyed her. Even with the Catholic Church agreeing ten or so years ago to allow the burial of suicides in holy ground, there were still those seasoned hard-liners who'd fiercely opposed it. So just a few souls – mostly the younger ones – turned up to pay their respects to Majella.

Mrs McFadden from next door attended and, as always, was a rock. It'd been a much smaller affair than the huge presence at her daddy's funeral where the *Boys* had staged an illegal gun salute.

Against her better judgement, way deep down inside, she'd hoped James Henderson would appear. But, no, he hadn't, and there wasn't a single word from him, not even a card. Selfish bastard, she thought, as she heard a determined knock at her front door.

She'd no idea who it could be and cautiously pulled back the dusty net curtains and peered through the grimy window pane, making out a darkly dressed, hooded figure standing on the doorstep with their head down against a raging downpour. She felt a little frightened.

The caller was persistent, knocking the flap of the letterbox again but harder. *Shit*! Caitlin reached out to the fireplace and picked up the poker, grasping it tightly in her hand. The letterbox was rattled once again more loudly as she cried out in frustration, "Right! Okay, okay, I'm coming!" She angrily made her way down the hallway. "Who is it?" she cried, standing slightly back from the door. She quickly switched on the hallway light to see the figure silhouetted through the small, square glass panes of the door and heard a muffled response that she couldn't quite make out.

"I can't hear you! Who is it?" she cried.

The silhouette bent down, and a hand opened the postbox. A deep voice rang through it. "It's me, Caitlin. It's Seamus. Seamus Donaghy!"

Jesus, fuck! What was he doing here? Her ex! She stepped back from the door in disbelief. Her legs felt like rubber.

His voice came once more through the gap, crying, "Caitlin, for Christ's sake, let me in! I'm soaked!" She did as he asked and scrambled to open the door.

Seamus Donaghy quickly stepped inside and passed her to stand in the centre of the long hallway, shaking his coat and sending raindrops dripping onto the tattered lino.

With a broad smile and without properly looking at Caitlin, he cried, "I'd forgotten how shit the weather is here! It's like the end…" But he stopped, mid-way through his sentence, shocked as he saw her clearly for the first time.

She stood against the wall, motionless, in a worn nightdress and stained, light floral house-coat. He could see she was exceptionally thin – not healthy thin, but sickeningly thin. Her raised cheekbones were sharp and prominent against pale blemished skin. The black hair she'd once taken so much care over hung limp, long and greasy. Even her once enviably tall frame seemed to have shrunk. He couldn't get over the transformation. Jesus H Christ, she looked so gaunt.

Caitlin could see his disappointment and shock at her appearance and suddenly felt embarrassed and ashamed. She tried her best to appear unfazed as he attempted to recover from his disbelief.

He confidently walked past her towards the kitchen, where he hung his wet coat on the back of her mum's chair. He'd been very fond of Majella and she of him. He suddenly felt depressed at the sadness and desolation pervading this once-familiar house. Looking around the small kitchen, he found the kettle, filled it up and lit the gas stove, telling Caitlin to sit whilst he'd make some tea.

It was as if he'd never been away, she thought, as she watched Seamus confidently open cupboard doors to retrieve cups and teabags. Yet, he appeared altogether different. He was no longer a boy. He was tanned and had filled out in a muscular and manly way. His fair hair was longer and bleached white from the sun. He also had an air of self-assurance and composure that she'd never witnessed in him before. His dark jeans were immaculate, ironed with a sharp crease at the front and back of his legs. He wore a dark blue V-neck jumper, obviously expensive, and underneath it a floral-patterned shirt with fashionably long collar points. The smell of his aftershave was woody and alluring. Young Seamus Donaghy no longer existed, and this presentable and experienced man, had taken his place. He'd evidently been doing well for himself.

Caitlin felt gobsmacked by the way he shot out question after question about what had happened to her dad, mum, Martin, and finally Tina. She'd nodded where she could and faked the odd smile in her attempts to give monosyllabic answers. She was afraid that if she spoke too much, she'd unleash the pain that was such a tangible presence inside her. Handing her a mug of hot tea in their usual red Liverpool FC mugs, Seamus sat down and pursed his lips in concentration. He took a deep breath, stared at her and asked carefully, "And you, Caitlin? What's happening with you?"

He didn't really have to ask how she was. Her appearance spoke volumes. Christ, he'd loved her so much. She'd blown a hole in his heart when she'd refused to marry him, and he'd fled to New York first, then Boston. He'd never forget how painful it was for him, leaving his family and Derry, but the worst bit was leaving her – she'd never know how much she'd hurt him. He'd known the only way he'd get over her was to run as far away as possible. He couldn't cope with the thought of living so close and yet so far from her in his home city.

Yet – in the long run – Caitlin had been right to turn him down. Back then, he was a gobshite from Creggan, with no prospects and no ambition. He could easily have ended up like one of the many poor bastards currently being interned, left, right and centre. This train of thought was broken as she answered meekly, "Yeah, I'm working – in a photographer's in town. It's alright. I quite like it… now anyway."

"Why, did something happen?" he asked with concern.

"Ah, nothing I couldn't handle. It's fine now."

Relieved, he half-smiled before continuing, "Well, I'm only here for a week, or that's the plan anyway. I liked your mammy; you know that, Caitlin? I'm so sorry to hear what happened. She was a lovely woman and always kind to me."

Caitlin nodded. She knew her mother had wanted her to marry him, but Seamus had never brought to the surface in her what James Henderson had. The excitement, the attraction, the love. Everything!

If only, *if only* she hadn't met James and taken that stupid job with him, she wondered what her life might have been like. What *all* their lives might've been like. Martin was right: she was stuck up, she was a puke! Everything was her fault, no one else's, just Caitlin's.

Tears welled up, and Seamus looked on with concern. He grasped her hands and squeezed them reassuringly. "It'll be alright, Caitlin. You'll see. I know it feels like the end of the world now, but it'll be alright."

He opened his arms invitingly. At his kind words, Caitlin fell into them, rested her head on his chest and hung on for dear life. She allowed herself to liberate all the painful emotions and memories that she'd locked away carefully for so long and sobbed without ceasing for what felt like a long time.

* * *

The next few hours passed quickly as the couple sat, drank more tea and talked through recent events. Caitlin, feeling weary but relieved, was able to tell him everything. Seamus listened in disbelief and astonishment until, finally, feeling a little ashamed to have monopolised the conversation, she asked him about his life.

He'd been lucky – extremely lucky. After arriving in New York, he quickly decided he didn't like it and moved to Boston instead. There he found a casual job with a major construction company owned by a man from an old and wealthy Irish-American family.

His first job had been helping to clear out and tear down old buildings, during which he'd proved himself to be a hard worker.

The money was good and the *craic* even better. His work gang, like him, had all left Ireland looking for new opportunities or else heartbroken – by women or by events at home. Some of them were even on the run from the British authorities for real or trumped-up offences. The older men took time to train him as he worked, and now he was a jack of all trades, with brick-laying, plumbing and electrical skills. He'd surprised himself by taking to the building trade like a duck to water and in no time gained the attention of Mr Michael McMannus, owner of the property firm.

McMannus had a son who was no more interested in the business than he was in the Man on the Moon. In Seamus's two years in Boston, McMannus had encouraged him at work and offered to pay for him to go to night school, to study business and management, as a means of moving up in the company. Seamus turned out to be extremely good at business and finance but still wanted to keep on learning and pay back his boss for showing such faith in him.

And now he'd come home to see his family but as soon as he'd heard about Majella's death, he knew he had to see Caitlin no matter what. And so he found himself sitting and talking to this shell of a woman who was once the love of his life.

Caitlin listened and watched fondly as he spoke. His face lit up with pride as he told her of his success. What a change in him! He'd made her feel better, and she was pleased for him, really pleased.

"I'm chuffed for you, Seamus. You've done so well in such a short time. And your lot at home, I bet they're well pleased too!"

He smiled, raised his eyebrows sceptically and said, "More likely they enjoy the money I send them, don't you think?"

She understood. She, too, had shared her wages with her mum when she'd worked at Rocola as James Henderson's secretary. Quickly dismissing thoughts of him, a happy memory sprang to mind, of buying material to make skirts for work and sewing them with her mother. It was the first time she'd been able to think of Majella without wanting to weep. Cheered by this, she asked cheekily, "And what about your love life, Seamus? Do you have anyone special?"

He winced at the thought of the last few lonely years, but his eyes twinkled when he answered, "Sure, Caitlin, I'm still getting over the one that got away! What about you?" he asked cautiously – not convinced he wanted to hear her answer.

She hesitated for a fraction of a second and then lied to him. She looked him straight in the eye. Appearing surprised, she placed a finger on her chest. "Me? Jesus, Seamus, there's no one in my life. I mean, look around! How could there be with all this shite going on?"

Chapter 10

Charles Jones was red-faced, sweating and mumbling incoherently as he walked feverishly back and forth, up and down the floor of the study in his lavish townhouse – a Queen Anne building just off Victoria Street, behind one of Belfast's main thoroughfares.

The room complemented the building's history with its high-corniced ceiling, white and grey gilded wallpaper, a large solid Victorian mahogany partner desk laden with papers, a grey leather desk set, and two telephones. The desk was carefully placed between a pair of high, shuttered sash windows. Two ox-blood leather-covered Chesterfield armchairs faced it, set upon a lush dark grey carpet that allowed him to pace silently on its deep pile.

Earlier that morning, his secretary had passed him yet another hand-delivered anonymous death threat, printed in the usual bold capital letters. It was the third he'd received since the bomb scare and shootings in the City Hotel in Londonderry the previous year. Although the finger had never been *officially* pointed at him regarding his involvement in the death of the Bishop, he knew it wouldn't take too much for someone finally to put two and two together. After all, Billy Morris was known to be his henchman and had been the one to fire the first shot. Shame he didn't get a chance to shoot the other Papist cunt!

Jones certainly wasn't going to allow any Fenian guttersnipes to get away with threatening him. Replacing his deceased bodyguard had become a priority and was soon accomplished. He'd been fortunate to come upon a local man from East Belfast – a well-known Loyalist face known as Mark "Lemon" Carroll. They'd met at a recent Orange Order meeting where Jones was the guest speaker.

Lemon had the letters h-a-t-e tattooed on the fingers of his right hand. Upon meeting Jones for the first time, he was serving as a B-Special in the Ulster Volunteer Force (UVF). He left the organisation as soon as Jones offered him the job. Upon reflection, Morris had been a babe-in-arms in comparison with this miscreant! Jones had found it amusing when he'd learned Lemon had taken it upon himself to sit in the public gallery in the Belfast courthouse. The idea was that he'd learn about judicial and police procedures in an effort to avoid any mistakes while carrying out his duties for Jones. He'd proved himself to be an extremely valuable asset whilst notably neither questioning nor flinching from his boss's many requests.

What was really disturbing Jones today was the BBC News he'd just heard on the Sony FM/AM desk radio that remained constantly switched on. Two pubs. Five dead, including four soldiers. And as if that were not enough, it hadn't happened here! The fuckers, the fucking Provos, had taken their shite to the mainland and killed those poor innocent bastards whilst they'd been out having a pint in Guildford. If there was ever a time that convinced Jones of the rightness of his cause, it was now.

Without knocking, James Henderson Snr strode into Jones's study, newspaper in hand. Throwing the folded daily onto the desk, he placed his hands on the edge of it and leaned over, face twisted with fury. "Have you seen this, Charles? This is off the fucking Richter Scale!"

Jones nodded soberly at him but secretly was delighted. Finally! It'd taken him much longer than he'd hoped to ginger up this establishment figure, but it looked as if he'd snagged him at last.

Jones held back a moment before he answered acidly, "I have, James, and I'm livid. But think about it, man – it proves we're on track, morally and politically. We will avenge!"

Jones smashed his clenched fist down on the desk, causing a telephone and a pile of papers to fly up at the impact. James Snr shook his head in both despair and agreement and fell wearily into one of the chairs opposite the desk.

"So what's next?" he asked, solemn-faced.

"Well, that depends on *you*, doesn't it? I would hope that, after reading such news, you'd like to join our outfit whole-heartedly." Jones paused for effect. "How should I put it... Perhaps in addition to what you've already been doing, you could become a little more *hands-on*?"

James Snr listened and immediately knew what was meant by that. He had to admit; he'd been hugely sceptical when he first began to work for Jones. Initially, he'd thought the man almost comic with his ranting and raving about the perfidious Nationalists and Catholics. However, looking back at the numerous sermons he'd attended, James Snr began to understand better and see that, in many respects, Jones's philosophies were on the mark. A lot of them made sense in the light of this atrocity. It also helped, of course, that he had been more than generous financially.

Blood boiling, without hesitation, James Snr replied, "Absolutely. What do you want me to do?"

* * *

Roger Henderson, James Jnr and the lovely Marleen Fry were having a quiet informal dinner back home in Prehen. Lately, Marleen had found herself growing unexpectedly fond of the city. She found the people here unsophisticated but so delightfully friendly – a welcome change from her sophisticated London circle.

And then there was James – dear handsome, understanding James. Her best male friend ever since they were both knee-high. She found herself in a particularly precarious position. As the only child of rich aristocratic parents, she was under unspoken but ill-disguised pressure to choose a husband and produce an heir to the family's wealth and position. After careful deliberation, she'd set her heart on James. He knew of her bisexual tendencies from way back and hadn't seemed perturbed by them, though doubtless, he'd be surprised and shocked at any suggestion from her that the two of them should marry. She'd need to be very cautious about how she approached the subject with him – slowly, slowly, catchy monkey!

Marleen watched James sipping his wine and noticed – not for the first time – that he really was gorgeous and would definitely father beautiful children. He was tall and strongly built: perfect. He had the most intensely green eyes and eyelashes she would die for – also perfect. His face was that of an Adonis with lips that cried out for passionate kisses. *Now she was getting carried away!* His closely cropped auburn hair was thick and most likely would stay with him forever, and his accent – what an accent! She smiled at the thought of making babies with him, but more importantly, she knew James to be a good man and a true friend to her. That had to be the best basis for any marriage.

The opulent dining room where they sat was stunning, with its Adam fireplace and delicate Chinese hand-painted wallpaper. She could envisage herself running Melrose, already imagining the fabulous dinner parties they'd have. Never good at anything academically, she was rather old-fashioned and would be happy to take up the role of wife and hostess in this gracious old house.

She was aware that James and Roger were in dire straits financially, but their problems could easily be solved if James agreed to her proposal. She'd a huge trust fund to call on once she was married. They'd save Rocola, could afford to travel to the sun, wherever and whenever they pleased, and she could discreetly scoot back and forth to London to meet her special friends. She couldn't do without those friends! Ultimately it was the best course for everyone.

"And how was today?" Roger asked the young couple, who looked particularly fresh with their flushed faces and hair semi-dry from their baths.

Marleen had loved their trip to the Giant's Causeway. She'd felt as if they were the only two people on the planet; it was so quiet there.

"It was deserted, Roger. We walked from the car park right down to the edge. The light was amazing, and James managed to take some great photographs, didn't you?" she asked, looking to him for a response.

"Yeah, it was nice. Peaceful," he remarked apathetically. "Lots of fresh air."

Roger remained concerned by James's low mood. He himself enjoyed having a woman around the house again but felt for poor Marleen. James had made an effort to start with but then became distant and awkward with her, lacking his old sparkle. Roger admired the girl's savoir-faire and thought her blonde good looks splendid – she was an absolute stunner. Marleen was a classic beauty, a Grace Kelly type with bobbed white-blonde hair, expressive hazel eyes, and a beautiful open smile. She was tall for a woman, reaching James's shoulder and well proportioned with nice bosoms, he thought cheekily. James was a fool if he didn't see how magnificent this young woman was.

Following the bomb scare, Roger had insisted again that politics was not to be discussed at the dinner table, but tonight was an exception. He and James were horrified when they'd heard the news of the IRA bombing in Guildford, killing five innocents. It came as a shock to everyone that terrorists had managed to carry out such carnage on the mainland. It was undoubtedly turning the tide of The Troubles, taking them into a whole new dimension.

"I wonder if they'll catch them before they get back?" Roger said, referring to the bombers.

James knew what he meant. "I hope so, Uncle. I'd imagine the ports and airports will be well covered."

"I suppose they will, yes," Roger replied, and with a sigh added, "There'll be retaliation for this, James, and it'll be bad, no doubt about it."

The young man remained quiet. He knew what his uncle said was true but right now, all he wanted was to stay focused on Rocola and ignore divisive politics. He'd been working day in, day out to ensure the government funding was put to the best possible use, and now – finally – they were beginning to reap the reward. Morale in the factory had improved somewhat, and he found himself spending more time on the floor, listening to and watching the workers, taking into account their suggestions to reduce production costs and ultimately save jobs. It was going well. The workforce was responding positively to his suggestions. They'd visibly grown to respect James, and at last, he felt at home in the factory. Rocola was where he belonged, and he loved it.

Marleen felt the two men needed cheering up. Clapping her hands to attract their attention, she suggested in her cut-glass accent, "Roger, since I'm here, why don't we hold a very small dinner party? You needn't worry about it, leave it all to me! I think – after all this awful news – we need a teeny-weeny bit of fun, don't you?"

The mere thought made Roger inwardly cringe, but perhaps the girl was right. It'd been such a long time since they'd hosted a dinner, and he hoped it might cheer James up.

"Splendid idea, Marleen. What do you say, James? Just a select few."

Marleen was thrilled. She loved arranging dinner parties, and as she looked around the house that had been so beautifully designed for the purpose of entertaining, she knew it would be the perfect setting.

Waiting for James's decision seemed to take forever. Her heart sank as he began to say, "I'm honestly not sure I'm great company these days. I just don't know."

Such embarrassing lack of enthusiasm gave his uncle the impetus to insist. He didn't feel like partying either but knew that somehow he must get James out of his goddamn' rut and perk him up; it was all work, no play for him these days.

"James, I insist! I'm sure it'll cheer you up. And really, just look at that face." He laughed, indicating Marleen, and continued, "How on God's earth could you say no to her?"

James looked at his long-time friend and her pleading, sparkling eyes. He knew he'd been a pain in the arse lately and should make an

effort – not just for her sake but for his uncle's too. He was very fond of Marleen, and she'd done her best to cheer him up.
He narrowed his eyes at the duo and wagged his finger as he made his sole proviso. *"Under no circumstance is Charles Jones to be invited!"*

The brightly lit dining room almost sighed with relief as – for the first time in many months – it rang with the sounds of carefree laughter and conversation.

Chapter 11

Emmett McFadden couldn't believe what was happening to him. All he'd been doing was coming out of the shop by Stones Corner after finishing his paper round, with the usual loaf of white bread and pint of milk that he brought home religiously every morning. He'd just turned the corner, groceries in hand, when he'd been grabbed suddenly from behind, dragged across the footpath, and chucked into the back of an armoured police jeep. Instinctively he'd fought with all his might to get his two attackers off, losing the glass bottle of milk that fell and shattered into smithereens on the path followed by his torn-open loaf.

As he struggled to get out of the piss-stinking interior of the Land-Rover, his right knee smashed against the closing door. The pain was beyond description as he fell to the floor, and darkness momentarily engulfed him.

Squealing with pain and terror, he grasped his knee as the vehicle suddenly took off, rolling and bouncing all over the show, accompanied by the sound of screeching tyres. What the fuck! He swayed left and right as he desperately scrabbled in vain for something to hold onto but was thrown against the metal floor of the vehicle. He held his head in his hands, stinging hot tears flowing down his face as he prayed. Dear God, sweet Jesus! As if the man above heard his desperate, lone prayer, a pair of hands firmly squeezed his shoulders and pulled him up onto a bench, a soft voice telling him reassuringly, "It's alright, son. Come on, up you get. You'll be okay. Take it easy."

Emmett, terrified and bewildered, allowed his thoughts to drift – anything to stop him from dwelling on whatever ordeal lay ahead of him now.

To everyone's surprise, he'd filled out beyond belief over the past year. His formerly cherubic looks had disappeared, and almost overnight, he'd become as tall and as broad as his dad, Charlie McFadden – minus the fat. Emmett believed in keeping his mind right along with his body and loved sport and body-building exercises in the gym. He desperately wanted to play rugby but wasn't allowed to get a game in with the local predominantly Protestant team, so instead played an even tougher sport, Gaelic football. Joe, his eldest brother – who was also a big man – had been a natural Gaelic player, though sadly Emmett couldn't remember the last time he'd seen him play. Joe was still locked up after two years in Long Kesh, much to their mother's concern. She lived day by day on her nerves, having lost her job at the City Hotel when it was revealed she'd hired that murdering wanker, Kieran Kelly. She was mortified by her own mistake and nowadays rarely left the house except to attend Mass.

As he'd hoped, Emmett had done well in his exams, and his teacher, Mr McGinley, was working hard to get him to the next level. Maybe – if he were lucky – he'd go to university. He fondly remembered dreaming of taking his mother and Tina McLaughlin overseas with him one day and living together happily ever after. There was no chance of that ever happening now! Tina's involvement with the City Hotel bomb plot had shocked him beyond belief, and he was still gutted by the memory of what she'd done. As for Kieran Kelly… When Emmett thought about how many times he'd passed the shit-head in the street, it made him furious to think he didn't get the chance to knock him one.

Too late for that now and quite possibly too late for anything ever again, depending on who had seized him from the street. If it was the Brits, he was in for a kicking. RUC and it'd be all that plus maybe worse – the number of "accidents" suffered in detention was notorious. But if it was the UVF… Emmett shuddered and crossed himself.

* * *

Dear Miss Heaney.
We write to inform you that your recent loan application for £100 has been unsuccessful...

No surprise there, Anne thought as she scrunched and crumpled the letter from the city's credit union, binning it before sitting down at the kitchen table. She'd saved with that fucking union every week ever since receiving her first pay cheque and, until now, had asked for nothing. Any savings were long gone as she'd given them all to the household kitty since the bombing. She'd no idea what she was going to do for money now.

She thought long and hard about her options and, admitting defeat, realised she'd only one. To her utter shock and astonishment, Porkie – who continued to visit her almost daily – had knocked the wind out of her sails the previous evening when he'd proposed marriage.

"Anne, I know with your leg and all, it's not ideal, and I'm no spring chicken either, but I want to marry you," he began.

"What!" she'd yelled. "Are you serious!" The man had to be joking.

Nevertheless, once she'd watched his ungainly attempt to get down on one knee, she'd known he was sincere. *Sweet Mother of God!*

"I'm serious. I think we'd have a good chance for a new house. You know, one of those council ones being built in Shantallow. You have to see them. They're lovely. Everyone from Creggan's moving down that way."

She'd heard about the exciting new development just three miles or so outside the city, surrounded by lush countryside not far from Scalp Mountain overlooking Derry. It sounded nice, and the thought of getting away from Creggan definitely appealed. But she wasn't sure. The thought of the two of them, you know, *doing the business, for fuck's sake...*

Holding that thought and inwardly squirming, Anne looked up to see her mother standing at the kitchen door watching her. Liz smiled softly, her heart full of love for her daughter as she asked tenderly, "Where were you, love? Away off in a world of your own again?"

"Just thinking, Mammy," Anne whispered.

Liz Heaney knew exactly what was bothering her daughter. Porkie – who helped Liz out by discreetly handing her the odd fiver or tenner here and there – had already asked her permission a week or so ago to pop the question. He wasn't a bad sort, not really, and his wee *gifts* helped the family enormously. More so since Anne wasn't working and most likely couldn't work again. She'd already tried to find a job, but no one would touch an amputee as she made them nervous. And anyway, she still suffered bouts of extreme pain and severe depression.

Liz could understand her daughter's reluctance. Porkie wasn't Mr Perfect, very far from it, but he appeared to have a kind heart and was fond of Anne. Liz began to tidy up the kitchen and waited for her daughter to share her news. It didn't take long. Liz's busy hands were taken by her daughter, and she was led to sit down.

Anne's eyes were filled with concern as she studied her mother. She wasn't sure how she'd react when told about Porkie's proposal.

"You'll never guess what?"

"What's that, love?" Liz feigned curiosity.

Warm salty tears fell from Anne's eyes as she replied: "It's Porkie. He's asked me to marry him, and I suppose I've no choice. I mean, who else's going to take me on with this?" Awkwardly, she lifted her heavy, fake leg and stared at it. "I mean, look. It's ridiculous. I can't go anywhere without people staring, and it hurts, it feckin' hurts, *all* the time."

Liz's heart ached as once again, a cloud of misery encircled her daughter. She thought with a twinge of sadness that Anne was right. No one else would want her, not with her ever-changing moods, the pain, and her useless, clumsy leg. Only Porkie. Poor Anne had no choice; she'd have to say yes. Liz just didn't have the money or energy to look after her daughter for the rest of her days. Her expression betrayed her. Anne knew from her mother's look; she'd no options left.

"I take it you think this is my best option then?"

Liz slowly nodded her head in agreement.

* * *

They'd been travelling for what seemed like hours when in the back of the darkened jeep, Emmett and its only other occupant, Mickey Boyle, began to whisper to each other.

"I thought they'd be taking us to Strand Road barracks, but we've gone too far now," Mickey said. "Wherever it is they're taking us, son, just keep your head down and remember: say nothing. They're lifting all over the place since those bombings in England, and the bastards can hold onto us for a week or more without charging us. Be prepared, too; you might be in for a bit of a hiding."

Emmett gasped. "But I'm too young for that internment shite. I'm not sixteen yet!"

"Won't matter to them. They don't give a flying fuck. Do you have any ID on you? Anything at all?"

Emmett shook his head, clearly agitated. Fuck this. "Nothing. Sure, I was just finishing me paper round, not going on me holidays!"

The jeep suddenly jerked and bucked violently as it stopped, throwing the cursing men off their perch. Seconds later, the doors opened. Dazzling light shone into the back. The two occupants squinted and shielded their eyes to focus on their captors.

"Out!" screamed a red-faced, stick-thin RUC policeman, who waved a long black wooden baton high in the air.

"Aye, alright. We're coming. Give us a minute; we can't see properly," Mickey yelled as he leapt down from the vehicle. As soon as his feet touched the ground, the waving baton slammed across the upper back of his legs. Its power brought him crashing down.

"Don't do that!" Emmett shouted angrily, standing on the edge of the back compartment and watching Mickey with concern. "He hasn't done anything!"

"Fuck off! Now you, out!" For the second time, the baton was raised as Emmett held his injured knee tight in an effort to get out of the vehicle as fast as he could. Mickey remained bent over but gasped when he looked up and saw his young friend in daylight for the first time.

He shook his head in commiseration. There was no way on God's earth the RUC was going to believe a young bull of a boy like that was still only fifteen. By Christ, was he in for it! Mickey looked down at the asphalt beneath him and discreetly kissed the gold crucifix hanging from a long chain around his neck. He sighed, knowing they were *both* in for it.

Emmett and Mickey got themselves together and looked around as they were led into a red-brick, bullet-proof building. Emmett saw that Mickey was limping and holding his back. He wore the usual Derry boy's attire of blue jeans, a two-tone donkey jacket over a black polo neck, and the all-important pair of Doc Martens. A gold crucifix hung around his neck. He wasn't a big man, but sinewy and well fit-looking. He was bald as a coot, yet with his young, clean-shaven face, he had presence.

Emmett eyeballed Mickey, asking the question with his eyes.

Mickey was clearly troubled as he mouthed: "Fucking Castlereagh. We're in fucking Castlereagh!"

* * *

Porkie wasn't surprised by Anne's eventual agreement. He knew she'd no choice. What other man was going to take her on with a gammy leg? He'd kept the mother right, and now he had Anne like putty in his hands. Mind you, it'd cost him, handing out those fivers and tenners, but he'd finally got what he wanted. He'd had his eye on Anne for some time, more so since her da disappeared. Rumour was he'd finally settled down with his bit of stuff, some Dublin woman.

Up until Anne lost her leg when he'd frequently visited her da, she'd treated him like a piece of shit on her shoe, constantly ignoring him or, worse still, leaving the room when he walked in. He'd sworn he'd get her somehow. As for those fancy red and coloured high shoes of hers – only sluts wore the like, and he'd hated to see her in them. They'd be the first things to go on the fire once Anne was safely married to him.

What a performance he'd planned and played! Payback was due, and he could barely contain himself at the thought of what he was going to do to Anne. He'd taken note of the younger sister too, but she was a bit too fresh, and Porkie wasn't into all that kiddie porn. Anyway, it was more than likely she'd fight back, but Hopalong Annie wouldn't be able to, and he had her right where he wanted – for the time being anyway. *Sweet.*

Chapter 12

It was the anniversary of Graham's death, the young gunner being the first soldier to be murdered in The Troubles. Alice would never – 'til the day she died – forget the moment she'd been taken aside and told he was gone, shot clean through the head. He'd removed his helmet whilst on patrol, though why no one knew or ever would – it was completely against the rules.

They'd been going out since she was fifteen, but even before that, she knew him from her first year at grammar school in North London. Unbeknownst to her – *so he'd said* – he used to follow her home from school until one day he came straight out with it and asked her out. After that, he never missed a day walking her home. They were mad about each other. When they'd been together for some years, he'd asked her to marry him. For the proposal, he'd lined the path that led to their special park bench with tiny, lit-up nightlights in jars and got down on one knee – it'd been so romantic. God, she loved and missed him so much it hurt.

Today was her last day at Camp Two. Six months of gruelling special duties training over. Camp One had turned out to be the training centre where previously she'd met Kentucky/Sallis. She'd found the whole initial fitness regime gruelling, but it was a holiday camp compared with the training she'd just completed. There'd been a rigorous selection process at first, but she didn't care; she was just glad to be back and sailed through all the tests and exercises. She'd actually enjoyed the brutal training; it'd taken her mind off Graham. She'd focused herself on getting mega-fit, both mentally and physically, as well as putting the fuck-up with Sallis in Londonderry behind her.

She was now part of the Intelligence and Security Group, 14 Intelligence Company, known internally as "The Det", a covert surveillance outfit. This new unit was formed from the fallout of the Military Reaction Force (MRF) that'd recently been disbanded – they'd been told they'd gone too far and were being blamed for collusion with the RUC and several indiscriminate sectarian killings. The Det was comprised of an elite group of hardened enforcers and heavies – she being the only woman among them.

They carried out numerous overnight observation exercises in the most awful conditions as well as intense memory games to encourage them to recall those important places, faces, and myriad smaller pieces of useful intel. In addition, she'd been especially successful in the refresher training sessions on map-reading, advanced driving, unarmed combat and weapons handling. The list went on and on, and the exercises never stopped over the six months. Time flew by. As soon as it was over and she'd signed the Official Secrets Act – again – she was ready and back where she'd always wanted to be, particularly given she would now be working solo, just her and her tidy Walter PPK.

Sitting in the canteen eating some bland lunch, her mind travelled back to her dinner with Ian on her last night in Bangor. Ian Dillon was to have been her and Graham's best man. He was originally from Portadown but moved to North London as a young boy with his parents, who lived next door to Graham and his family. On holiday in Scarborough, ironically, Ian met a girl from Newtownards whom he later married. They returned to Northern Ireland, where he settled down in Bangor. They soon had a baby son, and he worked part-time as an electrician as well as a part-time member of the Ulster Defence Regiment (UDR). He obviously loved the UDR and gleefully described to her some of the antics he and his colleagues got up to.

"You'd never believe it, Alice. The lads are sound, and we're constantly giving out hammerings to the Fenians. They're cheeky wee bastards at first, throwing their bricks and petrol bombs, but once in a while, you'll catch some fucker, corner them, give them a fucking good hiding and next thing they're crying like babies for their mammies! It's great *craic*!"

She could remember Graham's funeral when Ian had gotten particularly drunk and ranted and raved about the revenge he would seek for the loss of his best friend. He'd been quickly advised to keep his mouth shut, and his mates took him home. She knew in her heart of hearts that he was the only person besides her who truly wanted to avenge Graham's murder.

The meal in the tiny Bangor restaurant had been simple but good. Alice and Ian were practically on their own, sitting at the far end of the badly painted red- and green-walled room, well hidden from the other patrons. She'd chosen the fisherman's pie, which was lovely, and ate it like it was her last meal on earth – amazing compared with army food or "*Connor*" as some called it back at barracks. Ian had done most of the talking in between drinking a bottle of Cabernet Sauvignon. She'd listened with great interest as the evening wore on and his tongue loosened, sharing more and more indiscreet stories. Alice began to devise a scheme.

Placing a cigarette in his mouth, Ian lit it up, breathed in and held it for a moment as he raised his head up and away, carefully blowing out the smoke. While attempting to keep his voice as low as possible, he'd shared another rousing escapade, whispering, "Get this, Alice.

A few of the lads were out on the town a couple of Fridays ago – a stag do, like. Anyway, four of us were in the car driving through Springfield Road, just off the Falls, on our way to the party. So… there's these two guys walking along, minding their own business when one of our lads is totally convinced they're both PIRA – he'd seen a mugshot of them or something. In any event, he was sure they were Taigs. Jesus, Alice, before I knew it, he'd only stuck a fucking SMG out the window and… wham-bam, they're both down! Well, fuck me, we took off in that car like a fucking roaring bull!"

He'd waited for her reaction, but she gave him nothing but a wiggle of her fingers in a give-me-more gesture. "Go on."

He'd caught her attention and liked the feeling.

"Talk about a high, Alice. I've never felt anything like it! I mean, they were like cannon fodder, the two of them. Gone! Both of them riddled with bullets, lying flat on the ground next to each other, blood spurting all over the place. And what's so fucking sweet, Alice, no one… I mean, no one… saw a fucking thing! They think it was the UVF!"

In his excitement, his already ruddy face had reddened further, accentuating his squinty eyes and jumbled teeth. He wasn't a looker, but she trusted him with her life, as had poor Graham.

The black-garbed waiter arrived at this point to pick up their dinner plates and offer them dessert, which they ordered. As soon as his back was turned and he was far enough away, a small smile crossed Ian's face as he gazed at Alice, thinking. He knew her too well. Fucking heck!

"Are you thinking what I'm thinking?" he asked cautiously.

She thought before answering, "I am."

Her tummy flipped. Looking at the expression on his beaming face, Ian was up for it too.

"We can't talk properly here, Ian. Let's finish our dessert and go somewhere a bit quieter. "

He'd nodded enthusiastically. Later, walking arm in arm along Bangor's high street, they'd come across an old relic of a pub that was practically empty. Alice was first to the bar and waved Ian away to encourage him to find a seat before she ordered a pint of Guinness and an orange juice. She'd an early start in the morning, but more importantly, she needed to keep a clear head given what she was contemplating.

The barman was inhospitable and grumpy and didn't speak a word as he handed Alice back her change.

"You have a good evening too," she mocked him as she walked towards Ian, who sat on a snug leather chair next to an open, blazing turf fire.

"Cheers," he said, thanking her and taking the drink.

"Cheers."

The pair of them sat in contented silence for several minutes as they stared into the fire, mesmerised by its dancing flames. Ian broke the silence after taking a quick look around. It was safe to talk.

"You want to try it too then?" he asked.

Her eyes were fixed on his face as she answered quietly, "I do. Timing could've been better, though. I'm out of sync now for six months."

She paused, considering the possibilities.

"Six months, eh? Hmm. That's quite a stint," Ian replied, disappointed.

She agreed and nodded, though she knew her updated training would prove valuable.

"I know, but we have to think through every move we make very carefully. It'll give us time to come up with other methods rather than just blasting strangers in the middle of the street. We might get away with that three or four times, but the RUC will likely come down hard after that. They're so far up the Loyalists' arses, they'll have no choice but to believe them and find someone else to blame."

He hadn't given that angle much thought but saw she was right. *Smart girl.*

Her body was tense as the flickering firelight reflected in her eyes.

"Tell me about the others, Ian. Tell me about those boys in the car, especially the one who fired the shots."

Ian Dillon, feeling merry and excited, told her everything.

Chapter 13

The noise from the incessant music and conversation was overwhelming as Father Cathal Connolly prepared himself mentally for his speech. He'd rehearsed it numerous times and had given it a great deal of thought. He knew it was good: it was fact, wasn't it? Wasn't that what these people wanted to hear? Nothing more, just the truth.

He'd seen it all himself during his time with the parish. He'd seen and witnessed the fall out from the continual RUC and British Army Gestapo-style raids and beatings. The young rioters, even children as young as ten, getting shot indiscriminately with rubber bullets; the women who worked themselves to the bone in local factories for starvation wages; and worse, much worse, the women and men who simply disappeared and then weren't heard of for days or more – interned. Well, he'd seen enough, and he was angry. Something had to be done.

Tonight's NORAID event was being held in the huge ballroom of a hotel in Yonkers, New York State. The room overflowed with white round plastic-covered tables. In chairs set around them, an unassuming, ordinary-looking crowd sat drinking and talking whilst others moved from table to table, shaking hands and greeting each other enthusiastically. It seemed to be a regular and familiar gathering where everyone knew and liked one another.

The County Cork Pipe Band, Hudson River branch, proudly played old Irish rebel songs from the centre of the wooden dance floor. They looked splendid in their plaid green tartan kilts, long green socks, black tailored jackets with embellished white shamrocks on one sleeve and bunnet-like hats, dressed with green plumes. They played their pipe music as loudly and boldly as they could. Their audience wasn't paying much attention, but the band didn't mind; they were in their element and played on.

Six huge glowing crystal chandeliers hung low from the ballroom ceiling and shone brightly against the mirrored walls – tiny diamonds of reflected light danced around the room.

All night, enthusiastic Irish-Americans continually shook the priest's hand, introducing themselves and thanking him for being there. Neither he nor NORAID's publicity director, Ken Hughes, could believe they'd sold so many tickets for just one night and were likely to surpass their target figure for donations. So far, they'd raised $7000. It was incredible; the night would be one of their best ever!

The music eventually stopped, and right in the middle of Father Connolly's conversation with the owner of the well-known Otis Elevator Factory (sadly, one of the few factories left in the area), a shrill, high-pitched squeal came from a microphone that City Council President Peter O'Callaghan was attempting to get to work. The band moved off as he took centre-stage.

"Apologies! Apologies for that, ladies and gentlemen." A little frustrated, he yanked the microphone's long black cable closer and tried again.

"Right. Okay. Is that any better?" he asked, looking around the vast room. A number of heads nodded in confirmation.

"Good. Good," he said, pausing before he began to speak in an old New York drawl. "Ladies and gentlemen, what can I say? This is simply great. It's wonderful to see you here tonight, and I'd like to thank on your behalf our familiar and much-loved County Cork Pipe Band." He clapped his hands and raised them to the band leader, who bowed in acknowledgement to the cheering crowd.

Silence gradually fell as the audience's attention was drawn back to their host. O'Callaghan spoke again, this time in a much more serious tone. There was a buzz of interest from the spectators as Father Connolly was finally introduced.

"Tonight, ladies and gentlemen, we have with us a young man who has travelled here from the heart of The Troubles, the City of Derry.

He's one of us – born here in this great country of ours – but left when he and his parents returned to Ireland. His father, ladies and gentlemen, was killed in action and died for his country, Ireland – a true Republican hero. Tonight we've asked Father Cathal Connolly to come and talk to us. Let us hear for ourselves what is really happening to our beautiful Mother Ireland."

O'Callaghan hugged the priest warmly and whispered thank you in his ear whilst offering him the microphone. Left alone on the stage, the priest surveyed the room and then solemnly began to address his waiting audience.

"Good evening, everyone. There is indeed British law and order in the North of Ireland today, but what is the nature of that law, that so-called order? Mr Harold Wilson, the British Prime Minister, didn't elaborate on that recently when he spoke out against NORAID and your mission to aid Irish people under British Occupation, but I will.

"British law in the North of Ireland has for over five hundred years contradicted and violated the laws of every civil rights charter in the world. It is a law that makes a mockery of the Magna Carta. It is a law that violates the United Nations Declaration of Human Rights and the European Convention of Human Rights. British law in the North of Ireland is the only law in Western Europe since Hitler that allows men, women and children to be imprisoned without charge or trial.

I myself have witnessed the carnage and suffering during and after Bloody Sunday. Our friends, fathers, a mother of fourteen and our sons – most of whom were shot in the back on that fateful day – were innocents! I've looked into the eyes of family members left behind, who will never, EVER forgive or forget their loss. That day that started out so full of hope ended in tragedy beyond our wildest dreams and will live on in our hearts and heads for the rest of our lives. The soul of our beautiful city has been extinguished and will take years to recover – *if ever*. And remember, we must also never forget the Ballymurphy massacre of innocents, five months before Bloody Sunday and by the ***very*** same 1st Battalion, Parachute Regiment."

He paused for a second to study the effect his words were having in the room. Bingo! The crowd were shouting and roaring in agreement to his every declaration.

"Amongst all the murder and mayhem, young schoolchildren today, ladies and gentlemen, are still being shot and killed simply for being in the wrong place at the wrong time. Their heartbroken mothers will never get them ready for school again, will never see them make their First Holy Communion, will never see them make their Confirmation or experience their wedding day or celebrate the births of their own children. All those wonderful times have been stolen and taken away, for always and ever. These men and women and their families live with a pain that none of us in this room could ever understand or bear to imagine. So many innocent lives lost, so many lives ruined, so many lives changed forever. But you can make a difference here tonight…"

And so he carried on until he couldn't guess how long he'd spoken for. There was no doubt his message had hit home hard when he stopped and thanked everyone for listening: chairs toppled as guests stood up, raised their hands and clapped and cheered. Some even whistled loudly as O'Callaghan slapped Cathal hard on the back. He congratulated the priest and told him passionately, "That was perfect, Father, just what they needed to hear."

Minutes later, he quickly made his way back to his table, where he continued to be inundated with well-wishes, handshakes, and even the odd kiss until finally, he managed to sit down and take stock of his performance. He'd been nervous, felt he might have gone too far and wasn't sure if the new Bishop of Derry, Bishop Carlin, would agree with everything he'd said. He was aware he was becoming too political in his passion and love for Derry but couldn't stop himself. Derry needed NORAID's money. The Creggan Estate needed their money. It offered the chance to alleviate some of the ongoing pressure put on the many mothers who were working all hours to pay the weekly bills. It'd give hope and opportunity to those families whose children had been orphaned or murdered and the many victims who'd been so badly injured. Their lives would never be the same again. He also knew that some of the money donated supported the IRA.

Cathal gulped down the glass of white wine that had stood untouched by his plate all evening. He looked around and smiled. This was what he lived for: to help support and encourage change in the lives of those unfortunate souls in Derry. If it meant he'd have to keep coming back to the US, then he'd do it – he'd do whatever it took.

He watched as a group of around twenty men pushed their way through the grid of tables to reach him. Their obvious leader was a red-headed, red-moustached bruiser of a man with heavy sideburns, a freckled complexion and a wide grin. He grabbed Cathal's hand and shook it eagerly.

"Ah, Father. That was just great! The boys and I, well, we're just so impressed." He indicated the group of tough-looking men standing behind him and added, "We've just this very minute decided some of us would like to come and see you in Derry for a couple of weeks. To help out in some way – just not quite sure how yet!" he bellowed, looking back at his associates who smiled and signalled their agreement.

"You see, Father, it's like this. We can do anything. We've even helped each other build our own houses, so there's gotta be something we can do in Derry!"

The group waited eagerly for his response. He thought of the many dilapidated houses in and around Creggan that could do with improvements… lots of improvements! More importantly, it would raise morale on the estate, give them a "good news" story for a change. To his amazement, these volunteer builders were all New York cops! They'd laughed and jeered when they told him they'd hold their own against the RUC if they had to.

Throughout the conversation, Cathal's eyes wandered to a young man sitting at the next table who'd been continually watching him all evening, listening intently to his speech and conversation. He looked like a military type with his number one haircut, well-shaved face and clean, perfectly pressed clothes. He wore a light taupe suit with a dark brown shirt and mustard-coloured tie – dressed to impress. Maybe he was a policeman too, maybe not, but there was something familiar about him that niggled at Cathal. Eye contact was made, and the man immediately stood up, smiled at him, moved on to the next table, and talked to a tall, attractive woman with honey-coloured hair, who quickly appeared smitten by him.

As the night wore on and the time slipped into the early hours, there was no sign of the party coming to an end. A local country band was now on-stage, and the dance floor shook in response to the boisterous and somewhat inebriated dancers. The place was awash with noise and absolutely buzzing with excitement. Cathal and his NORAID host Ken agreed they'd had enough and made their way to the lobby for – at Ken's suggestion – an Irish coffee.

Cathal hadn't touched an Irish coffee in years and smiled sadly at the thought of the last one he'd drunk. It was at home, the night before he left for the seminary, just him and his mother sitting by a peat fire. He'd made the drinks but omitted to tell her he'd sneaked an extra dollop of Jameson into hers, hoping it would help her relax. It worked, and he'd laughed as it hit her hard. He'd listened eagerly to her tales of happy memories of life with his father. He loved it when she reverted to her old self, but since then, her health had deteriorated, and he'd found her decline painful and difficult to watch.

The two men fell heavily into one of the soft settees scattered around the hotel lobby and relaxed. As soon as their drink order was taken by a youthful, green-jacketed waiter, they smiled at each other. Ken was ecstatic. This priest was a gold mine. What a find – he was a maestro of incitement! That whole ballroom had been in awe – people almost holding their breath – when the priest spoke. He was a natural, and those rousing stories, his passion… It almost made Ken want to go and join the Provos himself! *Crazy thought*. What was more important about speeches like that was that they effortlessly pulled in the dollars.

They talked and planned for the next event as their drinks arrived. The waiter had just left when the young man who'd been watching Cathal earlier made his way over. Without invitation, he sat down on an adjacent velvet chair. He smiled first at Ken and then Cathal before stretching out his hand.

At first, they looked at each other, both bemused, before accepting the man's overture of friendship. Cathal studied him as, to their surprise, he introduced himself in a strong Derry accent.

"Father, that was one hell of a speech – sorry for the language! I'm well impressed. Martin McLaughlin… Good to meet you."

Chapter 14

"Bye now. I'll see you Monday," Caitlin shouted as she opened the photographer's shop door to the jingling of its bell.

"Bye, Caitlin. Thanks now. Be careful on the way home – Friday night, likely to be trouble," Raymond Burns called out from his office at the back of the shop.

To her astonishment, he'd been amazingly supportive and considerate to her after her mother's death – he'd kindly covered her wages too when she'd taken time off for the funeral.

Seamus had gone back to the US a few weeks before. As they'd said their goodbyes, he'd made her promise she'd make a real effort to take better care of herself and try to get back to some form of normality in her life.

His visit had proved a blessing. The day after he turned up, he'd insisted on paying for her to go to the hairdresser's, after which they'd a lovely lunch and then did some shopping where he'd spoiled her. As they'd wandered around the town, she'd noticed the greetings and welcoming handshakes he received from his old friends and felt proud. They'd even gone to the Stardust, a local disco, to have a bit of fun and *craic*. For a long time, she'd thought she'd never be capable of dancing again. As he'd walked her home, Seamus made no effort to touch her, nor did she believe he expected anything from her, and so it continued for the rest of his stay. When he'd left for Boston, he'd simply kissed her lightly on the cheek before he climbed onto the bus to Dublin airport with a promise that he'd be back as soon as he could.

The night was cold, crisp and dark as she made her way home from the shop along Strand Road and towards her bus stop hoping the service would be operating. She was well wrapped up, enjoying the refreshing sensation of the cold, frosty air on her face. She normally loved this time of year and the weeks between Hallowe'en and Christmas. This year, though, the thought of Christmas was too much to bear.

An invitation had arrived the previous morning that had shaken her to her core. It was from Anne, and it seemed she was getting married to Porkie! Caitlin couldn't believe it. Jesus, the man was horrible, sleazy and, well, old. The first thing she'd done last night after work was to call at Anne's house. She'd knocked on the door, and it was opened by Anne's mum, Liz. She recalled the frosty reception.

"Yes!" she'd snapped with a fixed stare when she saw Caitlin standing there looking rather contrite.

"Mrs Heaney, is Anne about?" Caitlin asked nervously. She'd never seen Liz Heaney looking so cross.

The angry woman stepped towards her. "Ah, our Anne! You remember Anne, do you? Well, she's not up in Brooke Park playing tennis or out for a run, is she, Caitlin McLaughlin!" Liz barked.

Caitlin didn't answer. She couldn't defend herself. Instead, she stood wavering and silent on the doorstep.

Liz Heaney was livid. For months there'd been no word or contact from this young madam – no matter what troubles she'd had, it was no way to treat her friend. Anne hadn't been able to make Majella's funeral as she'd picked up a vile infection in her leg. She'd tried to call the McFaddens to pass on the message next door for her, but no one answered, and so instead, she'd posted a letter to explain. There'd been no response.

Before she'd sent the wedding invitation to Caitlin, mother and daughter had argued long and hard. Liz didn't want Caitlin to be invited, and now here she was, all of a sudden, standing on their doorstep. She huffed and puffed about whether to let the girl in but knew she'd no choice. If she didn't, her daughter would likely go off on another one of her rants. Nothing was worth that and so, reluctantly, Liz opened the door fully and said, "You'd better come in then."

"Thanks, Mrs Heaney."

Caitlin warily made her way into the long hallway and heard Anne cry out, "Who is it, Mammy?"

Liz bobbed her head, suggesting Caitlin follow her into the kitchen. Anne was eating her dinner at the table. She looked up in amazement to see Caitlin standing timidly by the doorway.

"Hello, stranger," she said kindly as her face broke into a genuine smile. She slowly placed her knife and fork down side by side on the plate and pushed it away.

"Hello, Anne," Caitlin replied, ashamed of how long it'd been since they'd spoken.

Liz grabbed Anne's dinner plate off the table and briskly threw it into the sink before making her way out of the kitchen, muttering, "Bloody cheek. What a madam!"

In silence, the two girls watched her disappear. Caitlin let out a huge sigh of relief as soon as Liz disappeared, and Anne giggled.

"Don't pay any heed to her. Sit down, Caitlin, or make yourself a cuppa. By the time I get up, it'll be Sunday!" Anne raised her stump as much as she could. She hadn't quite recovered from the infection and so wasn't wearing her plastic limb. It hurt too much, and even now, was still an awkward bugger. They'd done their utmost at the hospital to get the best fit, but it was proving more difficult than they'd thought.

"Always the joker, Anne." Caitlin smiled in spite of everything and pulled a chair back to sit down – she wasn't in the mood for tea.

"Aye, that's me. Always the joker! Mind you, I can't say I've been joking much around here lately. You've seen Mammy isn't the happiest bunny rabbit, or hadn't you noticed!" Anne asked straight-faced. "She's pretty pissed off with you."

Caitlin apologised. "I know, and I'm sorry for not being around, but it's been really fucking terrible since… well… since... you know… since Mammy."

Anne grasped her friend's hands and looked deep into her eyes, saying with genuine sadness, "I'm so sorry, Caitlin. It must've been awful for you – for all of you. I couldn't make the funeral; I'd a fucker of an infection. I tried the McFadden's with no luck, and believe it or not; I had to send a feckin' letter to explain. Didn't you get it, 'cos I never heard back?"

Caitlin envisaged the untidy coffee table at home, cluttered with unopened letters and bills. Dear God, she must have missed it – most likely at the bottom of the pile. *Shit*!

"I've not opened the post for ages, Anne. It's probably lying at the bottom somewhere. I'm sorry, but I've been totally screwed up."

An almighty weight began to lift off Caitlin's shoulders as relief cloaked her. She wasn't friendless after all, just an eejit who hadn't opened the post. She moved closer to Anne and hugged and held her tightly for a long time. Meanwhile, Anne rubbed Caitlin's head in an effort to soothe her, telling her how much she'd been missed. The girls had found each other again, and this time, they swore they'd never let go.

Standing by the closed kitchen door, Liz Heaney had secretly been listening to their conversation. A reluctant smile crossed her lips. Good. She would let go of her negative feelings towards Caitlin. She had to admit that she really was fond of the girl, and she'd certainly been through a lot herself. By heck, she'd been cross with her there for a while. Loyalty to her daughter and sadness about how her life had changed clouding everything...it was time to move on, she thought, hoping life in their hectic household might become a little calmer now that Anne had her best friend back. Maybe her erratic moods would become a thing of the past.

Caitlin sat and listened attentively as Anne told her about Porkie, explaining about his visits and why she felt she'd no choice but to marry him. Caitlin couldn't bear to listen and continually interrupted her friend with objections to his proposal.

"But, Anne… Jesus, you wanted to go to America. You had your dreams!" She screeched.

Anne shook her head, rolled her eyes and pointed to the remains of her leg. In a startled tone, she asked, "Are you fucking serious, Caitlin? I mean, look at me! Who the hell would want that!"

Once again, Caitlin didn't know what to say, so she said nothing. It was then that Anne decided to change the subject. She'd enough thinking about her forthcoming marriage, and for ages now, she'd been dying to know what'd become of the Adonis aka James Henderson.

"Tell me something – what about our Mr Henderson? Have you seen or heard anything since?"

Caitlin's heart dropped like a stone.

"Nothing. It's like I never existed. But you were right, Anne; he got what he wanted from me before he told me to get out of his life."

Didn't he just? Caitlin remembered as shame washed over her again.

Anne knew all along the relationship would go nowhere, having been totally against the two of them getting together at all. But sitting here looking at her sad, broken friend, the last thing she was going to say was, "*I told you so*." Caitlin was wise enough to know she'd been used.

When Anne thought about it, they'd both had their fair share of loss and hurt. It felt surreal, the way their lives had turned out. She remembered the blissful mornings when they'd walk to the factory together, linked arm in arm like daisy chains, laughing and sharing their stories or dreams for the future. They'd been carefree and vibrant and now look at the shape of them… Christ, how things had changed. She'd lost half her leg, she'd lost her job, and she was marrying Porkie as a last resort. And there was Caitlin, heartbroken because of that dickhead Henderson. Her lovely Mammy and Daddy dead and then her brother Martin who, as an internee, had been released early but who'd gone AWOL. Caitlin clearly didn't know he was out, and Anne wasn't going to add to her worries not tonight anyway. The right time would come to tell her but not yet.. . And then there was Tina, poor wee Tina, gone mad and locked away for life. What a complete fuck-up it all was.

Caitlin felt so much better for visiting Anne. In the end, they'd agreed to disagree over Porkie. The most important thing was that they were friends again. It might take some time to get back to where they were, but it was a bloody good start.

* * *

The bus home from work seemed to be taking forever to arrive when a middle-aged man stopped to put down two heavy Wellworth shopping bags and announced to the waiting queue: "Apparently, the Brits have closed Blighs Lane. A bomb scare. A couple of the buses have been hijacked. The black cabs can't get up either. Ye'll have to walk."

"Not again," Caitlin moaned. She couldn't remember the last time life felt ordinary, when people could go to and fro with no hassle, no searches, no rioting, no bomb scares. Other than her, not a soul in the forlorn queue complained. This wasn't unusual to them, just another day, and they dispersed, each heading in their own direction to make the long walk home.

Caitlin thought about which road to take and decided to walk past the Cathedral and make her way up to Creggan and home from there. It'd do her no harm, the walk. She'd been sitting on her arse all day.

As she made her way up Great James Street, she heard loud banging noises and screaming. She assumed there was a riot – most likely from William Street near to the Rossville flats, scene of the Bloody Sunday shootings, and quickly decided she'd better get a move on.

Barely a minute had elapsed from walking past the Cathedral to turn the corner when she felt something whizz by close to her face – so close that its passing swept a few loose strands of hair across her cheek. Thinking it was some sort of giant insect, she tried to brush whatever it was away.

It quickly dawned on her that she'd made a huge mistake: had walked right into the middle of a riot. Screaming men with white handkerchiefs masking their lower faces surged towards her, quickly followed by armed soldiers in pursuit. She felt the blood pumping in her ears as she looked around for somewhere to hide, to be safe, when without warning, her arm was grabbed, and she was forcibly yanked in at the doorway of a tall, terraced townhouse.

"For the love of God, wee girl, that was close!" a man's voice screamed in her ear. "Get in here now! Quick as you can!"

Caitlin didn't need to be told twice. She stepped inside and watched as an old man frantically closed and locked his front door, then directed her into a small living room that faced directly onto the street. A two-seater floral-covered sofa with fine white, crocheted arm covers stood against the wall to the right of the room. A black-and-white TV was positioned in the opposite corner with a V-shaped wire aerial placed on top next to an old photograph of a man and woman on their wedding day.

A well-worn chair had been placed by a roaring coal fire, with a pair of round gold-framed reading glasses placed hurriedly on the seat on top of the local paper, the *Derry Journal*.

She turned to see a well-built, white-haired man dressed in a pair of high-waisted tweed trousers, supported by a belt and a pair of old-fashioned red braces, into which was tucked a tea-stained grandfather shirt. He wore a pair of half-eaten tartan house slippers, courtesy, no doubt, of the moaning terrier dog that cowered at his feet.

Shaking his head, he looked at her in awe and disbelief. "I've never seen anything like that, love! Didn't you feel it? That rubber bullet! Jesus, it was so close to your head... If you'd moved one iota to that side, you woulda been a goner!"

A bullet, a rubber bullet! Christ Almighty! The man hurriedly ran around, turning off all the house lights before he returned to the living room. He waved her to the window to look outside, guarded and protected by the walls on either side, watching the chaos unfolding out there right in front of their eyes.

The smell of fear and tear gas was shocking as the scene outside turned into a battlefield. The clear night became even brighter as it was lit by the glow of flames from petrol bombs, constantly and randomly being thrown at the security forces. Army flares also lit up the dark sky and seconds later fell leisurely back to earth, crossing paths of red tracer-fire flying through the sky. Glass bottles smashed and splintered into thousands of pieces as they emptied and set their fiery contents erupting over the blazing ground. Stones, sticks and anything else the rioters could find flew everywhere. In the smoke-filled street, the heavily armed soldiers and police held tall clear plastic shields in front of themselves for protection, scarves wrapped around faces already half-hidden by domed, open-faced helmets. Blue lights flashed from the steel-grey armoured jeeps.

Caitlin watched in stunned silence as a soldier knelt, took aim into the crowd and fired rubber bullet after bullet into the pack of rioters, who stampeded like wild animals, dispersing in all directions. Unrelentingly, they were back within seconds as two men speedily drove a small Ford onto the pavement. As fast as they could, they jumped out, leaving the driver's door open. A lone masked man approached the car and threw a burning petrol bomb inside. Seconds later, a massive and frighteningly loud blast discharged from the vehicle as it too caught fire. It was a scene of carnage.

As the pair began to turn away from the living room window, Caitlin screamed. From the corner of her eye, she'd noticed a young child of eleven or twelve standing alone near the bonnet of the burning car. He'd a bowl shaped haircut, wore a white pointed-collar shirt under a plaid tank top and a pair of grubby black trousers that were halfway up his legs. He was too close!

"He's going to get burned!" she yelled.

In fear for the little boy's safety, she was about to run out of the house and warn him when she saw he was holding with pride in his right hand, a poorly contrived piece of mishappen wood – the poor boy's attempt of a toy rifle, along with a huge chunk of stone in the other.

"There's a wee boy there – look!" she cried to the old man, pointing through the window. They watched in horror as the child took aim with the gun. What seemed like a second later, he fell slowly to his knees, and his head hit the ground sideways. He looked to be dead.

"Oh my God! Oh my God!" she cried. Anger made her voice sound high-pitched and thin as she yelled, "He's been shot, mister! They've shot him!"

The man's eyes held hers, his breathing hard and rough. "Yeah, love, they have. They've got the child."

Silent sobs convulsed Caitlin. She clapped her hand to her mouth and indicated she was going to be sick. The dazed-looking old man led her to an upstairs toilet and left her to it. Her stomach heaved and rolled. She tasted bile and felt tremors running through her whole body as she recalled what they'd just witnessed.

Downstairs, fury radiated like heat through the old man. He was appalled. He'd just seen a young lad – a child – shot down in an act of cold, brutal murder. It was obvious to him, even from where he stood, that the wee boy had been holding a wooden gun. Jesus, Mary and Joseph, it was a toy and a very crude one; anyone could see that. Probably one the poor critter made himself. That's what these children did to play – the kids up in Creggan and the Bogside. He'd often seen with his own eyes from the bus those doleful boys and girls playing "pretend". Pretending to be soldiers, they'd stop and search each other, putting each other up against the walls, spreading arms and legs wide and then breaking into imaginary fights. That's what they saw every day with the Brits. He'd seen them play it out all the time. Why hadn't the Brits seen it? His tired heart felt overloaded with sorrow.

Chapter 15

"I'm so sorry, pet, that I haven't been to see you sooner," Tommy O'Reilly said as he looked across at his niece Tina, who sat motionless and stunned in the visitors' room of Armagh Gaol.

Mammy was dead. Dead and buried next to daddy. Tina's fragile mind was working overtime, trying to comprehend that her mother was gone, gone for good. She must've been really sick to die like that. To fall asleep and never wake up, Tina thought, as the wrenching ache of loss tore at her insides.

"It's okay," she replied in her bewilderment, "at least she's with Daddy now."

"I know, love, you're right. She's with your Da." Tommy heaved a sigh.

He and Caitlin had decided not to tell Tina about her mother's death until they felt she could cope with the news. They certainly weren't prepared to share with the poor girl the gory details of how she'd died.

He looked around the visiting room. The guards, lined up against the wall, watched every move made by prisoners and visitors. The room was cold and damp and reeked with a fetid, dirty smell. They had thirty minutes.

"You okay? Made any friends?" he asked, studying Tina with a mixture of pity and concern. He had to change the subject, not wanting to go into too much detail about his sister's death – it hurt too much.

"I'm okay, Tommy. The women here are nice. They're taking care of me, especially Bridget. They all call me the *youngin'*. I don't like it here at times, though; I'd rather be home." Nodding in the direction of the screws, she told him cautiously, "Those women there, most of them anyway; they're horrible."

"How love? Tell me, you know you can tell me, and I'll have a word," Tommy said apprehensively.

Her eyes briefly met his. She didn't want him to worry and so reassured him, forcing back her tears, "It's nothing. It's okay. Honest."

Tommy shook his head sombrely and asked again, "Are you sure? You just tell me and, I swear to Jesus, I'll sort it."

Tina's deadpan expression was answer enough. Subject closed. She didn't look great but was a bit more coherent than the last time he'd seen her. He'd never forget the state she'd been in by the end of the court case. They'd thought she'd gone completely la-la. It appeared this place was actually doing her some good even though it looked and felt like a shithole.

Tina could see his concern and, in an effort to cheer him up, told him, "We were jiving last night, Tommy; the *craic* was great." She smiled. "Some of the other girls were useless, but I did alright. I even gave them lessons!"

"Is that right? Good *craic*, eh?" he answered, slightly surprised. Jiving! How on God's earth could they be jiving in this place?

"It was, Tommy, a real laugh, and they played a joke on me too – made me look like a right eejit. The girls only asked me to go to the shop one morning, and there's me ready to take all their orders, get up mega early like a stupo and actually ask the screw to let me out, me with me list an' all!"

He hadn't heard her talk so much in ages and was pleased as punch. He understood humour was likely one of the ways the poor critters in this place coped.

"You were well caught there," he chuckled.

Tina half-smiled at the memory.

"Tommy," she said softly, "how's Caitlin? Is she speaking to me?"

He groaned inwardly. By not telling Tina all the facts about Majella's death, he'd left her wondering why her sister hadn't visited. The truth was, Caitlin was too badly shaken – by their mother's death and after getting caught up in a riot and witnessing the young boy being shot. "She's not great, love, but doing her best. And of course, she's speaking to you. I've asked her to come and see you next time. Would you like that?"

"Ah, I would, Tommy. I'd love to see her. I miss her."

Tommy talked some more, updating Tina on any other news, and soon the visit came to a close. As he rose to leave, the big man opened his arms wide, inviting a hug from his niece, who disappeared into his embrace as he held her close. His moustache tickled the side of her face as he whispered, "We miss you, Tina, and we love you. Take care of yourself, love, and I'll see you very soon. 'Bye now."

Before Tommy could be warned by the screws to back off, Tina quickly returned his hug and smiled as her brimming eyes looked up into his. "Thanks, Tommy. Thanks for coming." He smiled tenderly at her.

As they walked out of the room in opposite directions, Tina looked back to catch his eye again and said goodbye with a small wave.

Back in their cell, Bridget lay reading one of the many books the inmates shared. Once Tina arrived and sat on her bed, instinctively, Bridget knew something was wrong.

"What's up, youngin'?" she asked, sitting upright and alert.

Tina's bottled up tears finally escaped, streaming down her face as she sank down on her bed. She gulped, trying to control herself. The older woman quickly came to her side and held her.

"Ah, love. What is it? Tell me."

"It's Mammy, Bridget. She's gone. Fell asleep and didn't wake up," Tina cried into the woman's large, warm and lavender-scented bosom.

"Ah, no, hen. I'm so sorry," she said, sharing the young girl's pain – she'd never recovered from her own mother dying all those years ago.

This was one of the cruellest things about being inside. The missed birthdays, the missed weddings, even the missed funerals – all the usual family occasions. Her eyes clouded over at the recollection of her own losses.

Bridget was proud that under her wing, the youngin' had come on in leaps and bounds but was now desperately worried Tina would zone herself out and retreat into her own world again.

She hugged the girl as tightly as she could and stated firmly, "Listen to me, youngin'; you'll be alright. Do you hear? You'll hurt like fuck at first, but we've got you. Remember that, all of us, we're here for you and promise we'll get you through this."

Nodding, Tina back-handed away her warm, salty tears and sobbed quietly, "I know, Bridget, I know. It's just so sad after me Daddy going suddenly, but thank God Mammy wasn't in pain or anything. Tommy said she just fell asleep and didn't wake up."

Some consolation at least, Bridget supposed. She pulled Tina back into the refuge of her arms and held her tight. Although she tried her best to be as upbeat as she could, sometimes Bridget Barry felt she was living her life in nothing but a rotten pit of cruel pain.

The following morning everyone got up as usual. Tina and Bridget made toast using a Kosangas fire and waited for their post under the arched windows at the end of their wing. They'd finished their chores and were feeling too lazy to exercise in the yard. Together they sat quietly as they attempted to get their bread toasted just right, but soon the atmosphere swiftly changed as the wing began to buzz with low whispers.

Long Kesh had been set on fire! The men there were living in brutal conditions. Similar to a World War II camp, there were sometimes up to 80 or 90 of them living in each ramshackle hut. For months the internees had been protesting against such conditions by refusing meals and only accepting bread whilst throwing bed linen up onto the cage perimeter wire and not cooperating with the camp authorities and screws. There were no formal hospital facilities, only a tiny and dirty treatment shed, and like Armagh gaol, no resident doctor.

Recently, one of the young men had complained of shocking pain for a week but was ignored. His unheeded cries for help led to an agonising death from the virus he'd picked up.

Now the men had set their "cages" on fire. Inevitably the rioting prisoners would be on the end of terrible beatings by the British Army, maybe even worse. A lot of the women in Armagh had husbands, brothers and fathers there. The OC heard some of the men had been taken to hospital. No one from the Kesh ever got to the hospital unless they were seriously injured.

Maureen Molony was resolute in her plan. Enough was enough. It was time to show the men of Long Kesh they had their women's support. She called a staff meeting where the women from the three wings put forward their ideas for a suitable protest.

They decided they'd wait until the Governor did his next morning round at 11 a.m. when they'd kidnap him, his chief and any other screws who were on the wing. The OCs from each wing were given their separate responsibilities and told to inform their girls of the plan.

As they waited, Maureen asked the OC of the Ulster Defence Association (UDA), who wasn't sure if their men had taken part in the Long Kesh fire, to join them in the protest, and she agreed. The Ulster Volunteer Force (UVF) women wouldn't join in. They didn't want to mess up their remissions.

The tallest and strongest women were appointed to carry out the kidnapping, and when he arrived, with little resistance, Governor Johnston, his chief screw and another prison officer were immediately taken to a cell in B-Wing.

The women decided to keep everyone there as they needed to barricade the entrances to all the other wings. To stop the screws from locking them up, they'd taken the cell doors off. Not an easy task, but they did it anyway.

They were soon in charge and, over the next few hours, systematically wrecked the gaol. Some screws who'd escaped from A-Wing had pressed the alarm bell that set off a high pitched, shrill sound. Meanwhile, beds were broken up, sheets torn apart, bolts from the beds gathered and laid out as ammunition to shoot at the Brits. They fired them from homemade slingshots using knicker elastic and anything else they could find. Water puddled on the ground from broken pipes as the women, laughing nervously, ran about splashing like children. The stairs to the wings were gridlocked with beds, cupboards, tables and chairs – anything they could find. Bathrooms, toilets and sinks were broken or destroyed.

Governor Johnston and his staff, including a prisoner who'd been injured, remained calm and dignified in their cell with only a plastic *po* to use as a toilet. The women wondered who'd give in first! Maureen spoke a number of times to Father McGuire, who'd made a mad dash from Derry once he'd heard the news.

Rumours began that the British Army was outside and likely to try and get in through the roof. Looking out of the windows, the women and girls could see the commotion below with blue, flashing lights, police holding back barking, drooling German Shepherd dogs and British soldiers everywhere. News reporters and TV vans scrambled to see and film as much as they could. The women grabbed their sheets and wrote: *Prison wrecked – end internment* in large letters, hanging them from the windows for the media and outside world to see. Someone suggested they turn off the lights as a means of stopping the Brits from operating inside.

The heating had already been switched off, and soon the women were freezing.

Bridget, who by now was exhausted and needed a break from her duties, found Tina shivering with cold on a striped mattress at the end of the catwalk opposite two remand prisoners, Roisin Murray and her sister Eileen. Bridget took Tina in her arms and cocked her ears to hear what the other girls were saying.

"Sure, I nearly died! I mean, there he was, this big lump of a fella with a spanner in his hand and me, for Jesus' sake, look at the size of me! I just hit him a whack on the knee with a bar, and he fell down, right in front of us! And him still holding the fucking spanner in his hand! I wasn't going to wait, so I made a run for it; I ran like fuck."

Roisin saw that she'd Bridget Barry's full attention and, attempting to impress her, spoke up enthusiastically.

"Turns out they were two chippies doing work here, so the OC locked them up with the Gov!"

She stopped talking when she saw the OC come striding towards them with a serious expression on her face. Maureen cocked her head at Bridget, instructing her to follow. Bridget carefully detached herself from Tina, who'd balled up into a foetal position and was fast asleep. Bridget followed her friend into a doorless cell at the other end of the wing.

It was clear the stress of the day had taken its toll on Maureen. Her eyes were red and puffy. She looked and felt exhausted.

"Bridget, we have to stop now. Father McGuire says the Kesh men appreciate what we've done, but we're to stand down. Go and spread the word, please. Let's get everyone back into their cells – doors or no doors. I'll release the Governor and the others."

Chapter 16

Lemon sat outside Charles Jones's office, waiting for him to arrive and smiling to himself. He was pleased as punch with the last job he'd carried out and couldn't wait to tell the boss. He loved working for Jones, who, like him, was a relentless, hard-nosed bastard. Jones clearly hated the Fenian fuckers as much as his bodyguard did.

It'd been a textbook hit, and Lemon knew his boss would be well pleased. The whole thing had been over in seconds. Seeing the two men chatting and laughing together as they walked out of the Catholic church, he'd simply aimed, fired and… wham-bam. It was the expressions on their faces he'd never forget. They literally didn't know what hit them – two fewer Pope-loving bastards to worry about. Jones had told him in so many words: he didn't much care who was killed or where the hit was made. Just keep things clean, swift, with no trace *or* witnesses to be left behind. Job done.

Lemon made every effort to chat up Jones's posh secretary, but she was having none of it. Completely appalled, she looked at him with obvious distaste, taking in his nonsensical clothes, body odour that made her want to gag, and fingernails that were long, discoloured and dirty. She couldn't understand why her boss kept the massive oaf around. She wasn't interested in any of that – *thank you*. Pointing to a chair placed outside Jones's study, in a schoolmistress's clipped tone, she instructed Lemon to sit down, be quiet and wait. He half expected her to tell him to put his fingers on his lips. *Bossy bitch*. She needed a good fuck to lighten her up!

Minutes later, Jones arrived, well-dressed and dapper in his usual dark suit, white shirt and bright orange tie. Seeing him, Lemon rose to his feet and waited. Jones shook his head in dismay as he looked at the sight in front of him. *What the fuck*!

Unlike Morris, who'd made a huge effort with his personal hygiene and appearance and who always looked professional – most likely drilled in it from his military training – Lemon looked beyond ridiculous. The moron wore an orange polyester bomber jacket with red topstitching. The thing was garish enough on its own. Worn with tight, creased, stained blue jeans and black waxed hobnailed boots, it made Lemon stand out like a spare prick at a wedding!

Forcing himself to keep his voice calm, Jones nodded to Lemon and suggested he follow him. Lemon trailed behind and watched as his boss walked to his desk, emptied his briefcase of its papers and finally sat down. In a voice that could have frozen peas, he made a suggestion.

"Lemon, don't you think it's time you smartened yourself up?" At which he threw a wad of £10 notes across his desk. "Go and get yourself a bloody decent suit, some clean, plain shirts and ties. I can't have you hanging around me looking like an orange clown."

Lemon felt blood pumping in his ears, and his face went white with anger. No one ever spoke to him like that and survived. *No one!*

Jones could see he'd hit a sore point and, in a deceptively friendly tone, told him, "I'm only doing this for your sake, Lemon. You're working for me, and I have my standards, that's all. Let's say nothing more about it. Now, tell me what last night felt like!"

He was referring to the shooting of the two Catholics. Lemon smirked and said wickedly, "A very satisfactory outcome and, as we thought, the UVF will take the credit!"

Lemon's fury at his boss's comments continued to dissipate as he proudly reported in detail on his success and how he'd handled the assignment.

* * *

Later that afternoon, Jones sat back at his desk and spoke quietly on the phone to Judge Dobbs, reassuring him that his Boodle's Club membership was in the bag. Even though the club had just been bombed by the IRA, it wouldn't be closed for too long, and it was still accepting the "right" kind of Irish.

"Dodds, it's all fine. There hasn't been much damage – the stupid thugs threw a bomb into an empty dining room, that's all. They'll have it up and right as rain in no time."

Jones listened as Dobbs continued his moaning in a voice laced with annoyance.
"That's all very well, Charles, but the place is obviously a target. It's bad enough having this mayhem here in Belfast, but to bring it to the centre of London… It's barbaric."

Jones couldn't disagree with him there. Over the past month, there'd been a huge increase in the number of IRA bombings in London and Manchester following the end of an IRA ceasefire. They'd been on a rampage all over London and the South-East, attacking a military outfitters in Old Bond Street, a number of four-star hotels, a chemical plant, a gasworks and even a waterworks in North London. It'd been a bloodbath with several civilians killed, many more injured and millions of pounds worth of damage inflicted on property.

"Couldn't agree more. Now, my apologies but I have to go. I'll talk to you soon."

Judge Dobbs didn't get a chance to respond as Jones quickly replaced the black receiver in its cradle and, through his open door, glimpsed Henderson stamping towards him, looking extremely angry.

His eyes flashed, and Jones swallowed a little nervously. He'd never seen the man in such a state. Henderson entered the room before forcefully slamming the wooden-framed door shut behind him. The frame shook in protest.

"I've just heard!" he screamed at Jones, who cowered away slightly from his very agitated employee.

"Heard what? What!" Jones answered as confidently as he could but was inwardly quaking as he spoke.

"You utter bastard. It was you all along! You were behind that hooligan who shot the Bishop and fucked everything up for my son and brother!"

James Henderson Snr had been quietly taken aside by a loyal army friend who'd warned him about Jones's antics with Morris and the rumours that the Belfast businessman was behind the Bishop's murder.

Jones stood up, attempted to walk around his desk and out of the room, but James Snr met him halfway and forcibly pushed the small pug-like man back into his chair.

"You've made a complete fool of me, Charles. A complete fucking fool! All this time, I've listened to your rantings about the Queen, the Union and Ulster… and for what? I trusted you. Believed in you. Have you *any* idea what you've done? You've literally killed my brother and devastated my son. They tried…they worked so hard… to make that conference a success and save the factory, save all those jobs. Rocola is in my blood as much as it is in theirs, and I was sickened by what happened at that hotel."

Jones wasn't having it. Attempting to get up from his chair, he snarled, "Oh, don't be such a bloody hypocrite, James. *Save those jobs?* That's the last thing I wanted! I planned for those Fenian bitches to lose their jobs – every single one of them. I practically owned that factory! Your brother borrowed up to the hilt from me. And you… *You* knew exactly what my plans were and what I needed you for. You took my money, didn't you? Everyone has a price, including you, so don't stand there and preach to me. You're right; you're a fool! Now get the fuck out of my house; I never want to see your pathetic, sorry face again."
Time stood still as James Snr took a final glance at Jones and hissed in a threatening tone, "You know, you're right. I do know what you've done. I do know what you plan to do… and I also know what I'm going to do with that information, so help me, God. You'd be surprised, Jones, but I still have contacts in *very* high places." He turned around, opened

the office door and stormed out, leaving Jones's posh secretary open-mouthed with shock at her desk.

* * *

Young James Henderson climbed the stone staircase to the fifth and top floor of the administration block at the factory. He'd just held another successful meeting downstairs, adjacent to the machining room, with a number of the shop stewards and a few key staff. The most experienced of the stewards was Paul Doherty, who appeared reasonable and fair, and James enjoyed working with him. Doherty was happy to challenge the management but also willing to listen and compromise where necessary. McScott, Rocola's accountant, had finally received the last six-monthly instalment of government cash, and the feedback was that overall the Secretary of State's office was content so far with how it'd been utilised. *Good news.*

One of James's greatest concerns, however, was that there had been a significant increase in the daily riots around the factory, especially stemming from Stones Corner. Every day, it felt like, there was at least one fatality somewhere in the city from either shootings or bombings. People were beginning to accept it all as normal and becoming immune to the grisly sights and scenes on the streets and television news. Abnormal had become normal.

Opening the glazed office door that finally had his name etched on it, James quickly took his seat. Mrs Parkes saw him arrive and promptly followed him through into the office. Her voice, with its broad East Belfast accent, sounded decidedly worried as she said, "Mr Henderson, your father's been trying to get you two or three times on the phone. He's on his way back from Belfast and will be home in time for dinner. He told me to tell you that he needs to talk to you urgently."

James had no idea what it could be about since he'd last spoken to his father months ago and wondered what could be so urgent that it justified him driving the whole way from Belfast – where he now spent practically all his time – to Londonderry. Feeling a little unnerved, he thanked Mrs Parkes and told her he'd kill for a cup of coffee. She hurriedly left.

Staring at the desk that lay empty just outside his office, Caitlin McLaughlin again entered his thoughts and was abruptly dismissed. He kept meaning to ask Mrs Parkes to get that desk removed but always forgot. Writing in his notebook, he added the task to his "to do" list. Mrs Parkes remained in her own office at the end of the corridor with her two young assistants. James had asked her to find him another personal secretary, but she'd been deliberately slow in her search – she wanted to keep close to what was going on in Rocola.

He was feeling so much better these days. Marleen had been amazing and was now a regular visitor to Melrose. Her good humour and bottomless energy had certainly helped his uncle's mood too. She'd even managed to acquire a small terrier for his uncle, who now rarely left the house for either work or pleasure, and to everyone's surprise, he'd taken to his new little friend with enormous enthusiasm. Personally, James didn't like the mutt but kept schtum to keep the peace.

The office door opened, and Mrs Parkes returned with a cup of piping hot coffee and a chocolate digestive.

James laughed. "You spoil me, Mrs Parkes. Thank you."

She smiled and quietly left the office. The aftermath of Caitlin McLaughlin's departure in disgrace, the current bomb scares and her fear of the factory closing had left her mentally exhausted but content enough to be top dog in the office again.

James sipped his coffee and began to go through the post. He separated letters addressed to himself from those for his uncle. Most, if not all, of the letters, were business-related – until he came across a handwritten airmail letter addressed to him. Intrigued, he examined the South African postmark and turned it over to read the elegant cursive writing at the top. His stomach turned – his mother's writing.

* * *

At the same time as James realised who had written to him after a gap of many years, Marleen answered the phone in Melrose's kitchen to hear James Snr speaking urgently down the line. "Marleen, it's me – James. Is my son there?!"

Tutting at such directness and the total absence of any polite greeting, she answered curtly, "No, he isn't."

She listened unfazed as James Snr insisted he must talk to his son as soon as possible. With a marked absence of any thank you or goodbye, the line suddenly died.

How rude, she thought as she made her way back into the warm kitchen. Mrs McGinty, the housekeeper, had become quite fond of Marleen and was teaching her the tricks of the cooking trade in her well-run kitchen. Marleen especially loved baking Irish soda bread or even making homemade sausages.

Upstairs in his study, Roger attempted to read the *Derry Journal* but found himself persistently being interrupted by small painful bites on his feet. The culprit – Ned, his pup. He'd taken to the little brute and particularly enjoyed it when Ned would quietly curl up at his feet and place his tiny head on his slippers.

His phone rang in the corner of the study. Roger was recuperating by the heat of a roaring fire. He climbed awkwardly from his chair, stretched his arms up long and tall, and yawned. Ned watched and mirrored his master's actions, making Roger laugh as he patted the animal's head.

Slowly making his way to the phone, its ringing becoming more and more impatient by the second, Roger cried, "Okay, okay. I'm coming!" He picked up the receiver and answered promptly, "Henderson."

Upon hearing his nephew's soft Scottish lilt, Roger smiled. "Hi, can you talk?" James asked.

"I can. Everything okay?"

"Hope so," James replied.

Before mentioning the airmail letter to Roger, he said that his father had been trying to contact him at the factory, was currently on his way to Melrose and was most insistent he should see them both there as soon as possible.

Roger was perturbed and a little offended. Normally James Snr would call him first to tell him he was coming to Melrose, and yet he'd heard nothing from his younger brother for weeks.

"Have you any idea what's going on, Uncle?" James asked, sounding concerned.

"None, James, I haven't a clue."

"Well, I guess we'll know as soon as he arrives, won't we?" James mumbled, unsure now if he should mention the airmail letter or not.

He held back for a second as his uncle, sounding particularly jovial, told him,

"Wee Ned here is keeping me company. Those girls have been in the kitchen most of the day, and they're spoiling him rotten with their cakes and the like!"

James half-smiled and decided he'd tell him about the letter later. Instead, they talked about the shop steward Paul Doherty and the successful outcome of the meeting with him.

* * *

Dinner was long over and had been taken without James Snr, who'd failed to appear. The two men were beginning to worry since it was getting extremely late when the headlights of a car, entering Melrose's gravelled courtyard, shone into the living room where they were waiting anxiously. James ran straight to the front entrance and opened the door, giving the caller no chance to knock.

George Shalham stood white-faced and silent before him, dressed in a heavy black winter coat over what looked like a pair of pyjamas. Silence stretched between them, and James felt he needed to fill it quickly. The skin on his arms and neck tingled and crawled in anticipation. "George, what is it? Come in."

Shalham remained where he was and looked into the young man's tired eyes. He shook his head in sympathy as he said, "I'm so sorry, James. It's your Father."

The airmail letter remained on the half-moon table in Melrose's hallway, soon to be forgotten.

Chapter 17

The man's heavy boot hit out hard between his legs, and the pain was beyond excruciating. Emmett McFadden couldn't believe this was happening to him. He and Mickey had been separated once they'd walked through the underground corridors lined with numbered interview rooms in the RUC's Castlereagh holding station, East Belfast.

Emmett had no idea what time it was or how long he'd been here, but he was shitting himself. They'd torn some of his hair out and kept hitting him on the left side of his face. It felt like it was twice the size of the other. He was so tired and dazed.

A heavy boot caught him again, and he screamed like a wild cat as the red-headed policeman's face came in closer. Spitting out his words angrily, he shouted, "We know you did it, Emmett! We've got witnesses. Now before I kick your balls off, are you going to fucking sign or not?"

Emmett didn't know what the man was talking about, and his hammering head hung low as he cried, "I don't know what you're on about, mister. I haven't done anything!" He looked at his assailant, pleading for him to stop. "Please, please, mister, no more!"

But Detective Jonathan Black had no intention of terminating this interview. He was far from finished with this one. He laughed as he pulled down his white shirtsleeves, stretched them out and carefully pulled them up again, one fold after the other. He was well known for getting the job done. He liked it that he'd such a reputation for being a hard man. There wasn't any formal training for this line of questioning, and, surprisingly, he'd found he was a natural at it and enjoyed the challenge of breaking Papist men and women.

The Diplock courts were proving to be immensely successful. It allowed judges to make faster rulings, "supported" by either a confession or witness statements. Conviction rates rocketed as they locked away more and more of the Republican fanatics. So far, very few Loyalists had been charged under these new powers.

As a result, Chief Constable Bonner was happy, the press was happy, everyone was happy. Black laughed as he thought of the four men they'd brought in today, charging them all with the same offence. One of them would eventually give in and sign a confession. He'd gone from room to room individually interrogating them. The mick who'd come in with the youngster McFadden was proving a hard nut to crack, but it was still early days.

Finally fixing his shirt, Black looked at the boy who sat naked from the waist down, his tracksuit bottoms crumpled and lying around his ankles. He was a big fucker for his age, although Black couldn't care less what his birth certificate said. These Fenian terrorists were getting younger and younger every day.

"Mr McFadden, I'm going to explain it to you one more time. We have two witnesses who say they saw you holding a certain handgun, and that very same handgun was used to murder a young, recently married colleague of mine in Londonderry. On his first day there too. Poor bugger. So listen, lad, you're totally fucked. You're going down. If you really want me to stop all this, it's simple: just sign the fucking statement, and we'll get you some food and a nice cup of tea. I think that's reasonable, don't you?"

Emmett could barely shake his head in refusal. He wasn't going to sign anything. He knew what that meant, and there was no way he was going to gaol. No fucking way.

Black sighed heavily and sat back in his chair, thinking. He knew the boy had a brother, Joe McFadden, in Long Kesh, and so, leaning forward, he asked his prisoner with faked concern, "How many brothers did you say you had, son?"

At the sudden change of tone, Emmett became confused. He'd never mentioned he'd brothers. "Brothers?" he muttered.

"Aye, brothers. How many do you have?" Black asked. He'd used this tactic before, and it always worked well in breaking down their resolve. Emmett remained quiet, wondering where this question was leading.

"Come on, son, how many?" Black repeated, less patiently.

Emmett looked up. His bruised and damaged face was a real sight. Blood from his ear had trickled and dried along his jawline, leaving a dark brown, paint-like streak. Tufts of hair were missing from the side of his head where Black had pulled them from their roots. His head hurt like hell as he answered woozily, "One."

Black snorted. "One, eh? Well, you don't anymore, son. We got your Joe trying to escape. He's a goner."

No way! Emmett thought as a deep surging well of anger and frustration engulfed his beaten body. He lifted himself up, chair included, and lunged at Black like a rabid dog.

Black jumped back to the far corner of the room, laughing heartily. He held up his hand to placate the prisoner. "Okay. Okay. Take it easy, son. I'll let you ponder that piece of news – but don't worry, I'll be back."

The detective quickly opened the door and closed it behind him. He looked left to right in the lighted corridor and found himself alone. He clenched one fist and brandished it over his head. Not long now. The lad wasn't far from signing – one down.

* * *

A few rooms along the corridor, CID Detective Adrian Walsh was having much less success than his colleague as he sat staring into the bloodshot eyes of his detainee, Mickey Boyle. He was a tough bugger this one. Walsh was never comfortable beating the shite out of these men and women, who were continuously interrogated for hour after hour over a period of days. Every Monday morning, CID officers held a conference call with their boss where they had to report the number of arrests and convictions they'd carried out over the previous week. It'd become a fucking conveyor belt, bodies in, bodies out, and he was sick and tired of it. This wasn't why he'd joined the police service.

He'd watched Black sporadically visit this interview room and each time give Boyle a bashing – even holding a lighter near the poor man, scorching his face and then doing the same to his testicles. Walsh couldn't do or say anything – he'd be blackballed – so he had no choice but to turn a blind eye and let Black do his work.

Boyle certainly hadn't done himself any favours when he'd first arrived at the custody desk staffed by a tall, bald, sharp-featured sergeant. Handcuffed, he'd stood straight and proud, next to his baton-wielding guard, who watched and listened intently as he was processed.

"Name?" the sergeant asked hurriedly, looking down and writing.

"Michael Sean Boyle"

"Address?"

"Twenty-nine Rosecommons Gardens, Creggan, Derry."

"Date of birth?"

"Under thirty-five."

The sergeant looked up at him and frowned. He knew the eejit's date of birth from the driver's licence they'd taken when he'd been searched. The custody sergeant sighed and moved on.

"Occupation?"

"Freelancer."

"Freelance what?"

"Undertaker."

"You're a smartarse, do you know that, Boyle?" the tired policeman commented. It'd been a hell of a day and he – like many others – hated manning the custody desk.

Boyle grinned mischievously and quipped, "I do. Oh, and by the way, I've got a special on – two for the price of one. If you or any of your esteemed colleagues need my services in the *hopefully* not too distant future, just say the word." He winked.

Seconds later, he was the recipient of a quick and painful crack over the back of his neck with a baton.

Hours later, Emmett sat in the same awkward position, hands tied to the back of a soaked metal-framed chair. He couldn't stop himself from falling asleep, even with an agonising headache, and had woken to find he'd peed himself. He was horrified. No one came near him for what felt like hours, and he needed the toilet again; he needed to shit. There was a knot in his stomach as he thought about his brother Joe. He hoped to God it wasn't true and half wished his tormentor would return so he could get to a toilet. On the flip side, if he came back, the hiding would continue, toilet or no toilet.

The door opened, and Jonathan Black stood there studying him. Eyeing the pool of liquid the boy sat in, he smirked and mocked, "Dear, dear me, Mr McFadden. What *have* you been up to?"

Emmett stared boldly at him and replied as calmly as he could, "I need the toilet."

"I think you're a bit late for that, don't you?" Black responded sarcastically.

"I need to go to the toilet," Emmett repeated, getting annoyed.

Black nodded. He didn't want to take the risk of the boy shitting in here anyway. The windowless, hospital green-painted room was small with no air-conditioning, and it already stank. Black opened the door and shouted down the void of the corridor, "Help needed here!"

Returning to the room, he waited until he heard footsteps running speedily down the corridor. A young fair-haired police constable stood at the doorway and nodded at Black, who barked and pointed to Emmett.

"Get him sorted! He needs the bog!"

The policeman looked in disgust at Emmett's half-naked, bloodied hulk, wondering why the fuck was it that he and the other PCs always had to pick up after CID's mess.

* * *

Mickey Boyle watched Black retreat from the room. He'd been at the policeman's mercy for the last two hours with a continual barrage of questioning about a policeman being shot in Derry. Even after Black's threats to his family and close friends, Boyle knew he had nothing on him. Ultimately, of course, it didn't even matter as the DC could easily get one of his many grasses to act as a witness and set him up. However, Mickey knew one thing: he wasn't signing anything.

He was twenty-five years old, and this wasn't the first thumping he'd taken, although it was probably the worst so far. He'd seen the delight in the DC's eyes as he and the other fucker lifted him up and began to batter his pulsating feet with their batons. His loathing for these men had no limit, and his heart was filled with an ardent raw hatred that seemed to give him neverending courage – over his dead body would he break.

He heard Black's voice shouting down the corridor for help, and his heart dropped like a fucking brick. Jesus, they must have given the lad some beating if that red-headed, gobshite was asking for help. He prayed the kid, who by now was probably terrified, confused and desperate to get out, hadn't signed anything.

* * *

Emmett would never forget his relief at getting to the toilet and the feeling of fresh cold water splashing his bruised hands and face. He looked in the glass mirror and barely recognised himself. Dismissing the unsightly image that returned his stare, he shuffled towards the waiting policeman with his hands outstretched, ready to be cuffed.

Black waited patiently for Emmett's return. He'd moved a small desk from the back of the room to the centre and laid out some papers neatly on top. He carefully positioned Emmet's puddled chair next to the desk and his own on the opposite side. He pointed at Emmett to sit and silently pushed a sheet of paper across the desktop towards him, placing a pen by its side.

Black nodded to the waiting policeman, asked him to remove Emmett's handcuffs. "You can go now," he said. The relieved young constable left the stinking piss-laden room.

Black sighed and spoke earnestly. "Emmett, I have no problem with real men, but I do with dickheads, and *you're being* a dickhead. Now sign the fucking document."

Chapter 18

Somehow – and she'd likely never know the way it was done – they'd found Alice a job working in an off-licence in West Belfast, supported by an Irish passport and other viable documentation. Her background and history were that her parents were Irish, killed along with her younger sister in a tragic car accident in Hertfordshire. As a result, she'd decided to move to Belfast from London, where she was born, to be near her remaining family. When she related such a tragedy, she found people became embarrassed and quickly changed the subject.

She'd completely changed her image, nowadays wearing short skirts, high-heeled black shoes, low-cut jumpers and tops – the tighter, the better. She had her pixie haircut coloured auburn red and, to her surprise, really liked it. A complete metamorphosis. She'd reinvented herself top to toe and was now known as Brona Doyle.

Home was a small bedsit just above the off-licence that was comfy and easy to keep. It wasn't a surprise to her that it didn't take long for people to begin to trust her. Most of them wouldn't suspect a woman working for Det – especially one with the slutty image Brona had.

Depending on how successful she was, they'd told her it was likely she'd be undercover for anything up to two years. And so, almost four months in, she was finding herself settling into a routine and getting to know the locals well.

In the interim, she'd called Ian a number of times, and together they'd put their plan into place. It wouldn't happen for a few months yet, but with the support of one or two of his close UDR colleagues, they'd thought carefully about everything, and the outcome would definitely upset the Provos.

Standing behind the glass-topped counter on a particularly wet, quiet and dark Friday evening, while she was filing her scarlet fingernails, the loud, penetrating buzzer on the off-licence door vibrated and made her jump. Looking at the camera, she saw a figure peering back. It was almost impossible to make out a clear image of the person under the wide-brimmed hat they wore. Reluctantly, she pressed the button to let the customer, or whoever it was, in.

She held the sharp steel nail file tightly in one hand as she watched the stranger enter. She'd never seen him before. He was a tall, powerfully built, broad-shouldered man of about thirty-five, with the saddest eyes she'd ever seen. They appeared weighed down with lack of sleep, and numerous deep-set lines bracketed his brows and cheekbones. He was clean-shaven and handsome in a weird way with thick, shoulder-length, curling dark hair, a heavy fringe and trimmed but bushy sideburns.

"Hello," he said quietly.

"Hi. Can I help you?"

"A forty-ounce bottle of vodka," he ordered, studying the shelves laden with alcohol behind her, "and two bottles of Coke."

"No bother," Alice replied. "Haven't seen you here before," she commented.

"Nah, just visiting. Up at a wake."

"Sorry to hear that. Anyone close?" she enquired, faking sympathy.

"Cousin. Shot," the man answered bluntly.

"Bastards," Alice said, carefully placing the three bottles in a large brown paper bag.

"Aye, I know." The man sighed as he took his wares and paid. Waiting a few moments, he looked at her as if trying to suss her out.

"You're not from around here either with that accent?"

"Who, me? No, my mum and dad were, though. They died along with my sister in England. Car accident it was, so I came home," she answered, encouraging her eyes to well up.

"Ah, Jesus, sorry for your loss," he replied, shocked.

Alice smiled. *It worked every time.*

Faking a broken voice, she told him, "A while ago now, not to worry. But the pain, it never seems to go away."

The man smiled softly and whispered, "You're right there, love; it never leaves ye."

An awkward silence hung over them until he looked at her to say something else but thought better of it and, with a small wave, was out the door. He'd surprised her with his aura of sadness, but soon she'd forgotten all about him as another customer arrived to be served.

The following week he came back, but this time had a lighter air about him. His order remained the same. She enquired, "Another wake?"

"Nah. Not this week. I had to stay around a bit. Got a bit of a job on."

"Ah, that's good. What do you do?" Alice asked, now interested.

"Joiner," he replied, almost too quickly.

"There's always work for a joiner." She decided to flirt and put out her hand to introduce herself.

"Brona – Brona Doyle."

He smiled warmly and took it. "Patrick Gillispie."

"Nice to meet you, Patrick," Alice said invitingly.

He didn't get a chance to say another word as the shop's buzzer was pressed loudly and continuously. *Jesus Christ, she hated that noise!* She looked at the security screen to see a couple of teenagers dressed in dark donkey jackets and jeans. She buzzed the door to let them in.

Around sixteen years of age, the two boys were moving jerkily and were obviously agitated, walking back and forth around the small shop, muttering over the displays to each other. One of them appeared to tower over his friend, who was all of five foot two. They had pockmarked skin with red, erupting spots poking through unshaven, grubby stubble. The taller of the two twitched like a rabbit. They were dressed like vagabonds, with their ill-fitting dirty jackets and jeans.

Circling the small shop, and almost bumping into each other, the comical duo hadn't noticed Patrick standing behind them in the far corner by the window. He watched as the tallest boy pulled out a small handgun and pointed it straight at the girl.

"Empty the fucking till *now*!" he snarled, attempting to frighten the shit out of the redhead.

Alice smiled, looked at him with contempt, folded her arms and was clearly unimpressed. "Keep cool," she said, slowly and evenly.

He hadn't expected her to be so calm and unafraid. Clearly frustrated, he cried out hysterically, "*I said,* empty the fucking till now, bitch! Before I do you in. I'm telling ye, I'll do you in! The money… I want the money NOW!" He shook the gun in his hand for added effect.

His partner in crime watched on proudly, smiling with glee and excitement until he turned around and noticed Patrick. The colour quickly drained from his spotty face, and the next second, he'd frantically grabbed his crony's arm and was attempting to get them both away and out of the shop.

"Max!" he whispered urgently as he tugged manically at his brother's sleeve.

Pissed off at the interruption, he tugged his arm away angrily and cocked the gun.

At this, Patrick slowly and deliberately walked up behind the youngster and smacked him hard across the back of the head. At the same time, he grabbed the gun.

It happened so fast, Max couldn't understand what the fuck was going on. That was until he looked at his bruv, Damian, who shot him a warning glance to draw his attention to Patrick. It was Max's turn to turn white. *Shit! Shit. Shit*!

The two brothers locked eyes. As one, they turned on their heel and ran like wildfire as fast as they could from the off-licence and Patrick.

Alice threw back her head and laughed. What a pair of eejits! She hadn't laughed so hard for yonks. Patrick's face broke into a genuine smile, too; her laughter was infectious.

"What a pair!" she said between giggles.

"I'm saying nothing." He tutted as he inspected the handgun. Immediately he knew where it'd come from. He'd deal with those two wallies later.

Alice went quiet as she watched the way he held the gun comfortably, how he opened it and looked at her, telling her to no great surprise, "No bullets. Empty."

"Small mercies. What are we going to do with it?" she asked carefully.

"Leave it with me," he replied confidently, "I'll sort it."

Bingo! She'd noticed how the two boys had reacted when they first saw him. They were terrified. Instinctively, she knew he had to be involved with the Boys and was obviously well known on the local scene. It was perfect, exactly what Det had hoped she'd bring in. She'd bagged it!

"Well, I, for one, am glad you were here," she said as she watched him place the handgun into his deep pocket.

"Me too," he answered, "although you handled that well. Kept calm. Good on you."

Alice smiled but said nothing until, almost shyly, he asked, "I'm going to be working like mad over the next week or so. You don't fancy a quick bite to eat one night, do you?"

"Love to," she said, her heart racing like crazy.

* * *

Patrick walked out of the 7–11 off-licence feeling pleased. He'd liked the girl from the first time he'd met her. Normally he wouldn't go for that type, but there was something about Brona that interested him. Naturally, he'd checked her out and found her story to be true. She'd lost her parents and sister in a freak car accident north of London.

The pressure had been on over the past few weeks and would likely be getting worse. As such, he had to be very careful, keeping people, known and unknown, at a safe distance. Everywhere you looked, someone was grassing someone or other.

Command had finally come to the conclusion that they needed to make structural changes to the organisation; their security was being breached. The first thing to do was to reduce the numbers in each cell and, importantly, keep them totally separate from one another. They'd lost too many good men and women thanks to snitches.

He hadn't planned to spend so much time in Belfast but knew he'd no choice. The last week had been a nightmare, with the funeral of one of his comrades and the double-dealing British propaganda that followed. The poor bastard was shot from a passing car while innocently standing on a street corner. The British Army quickly told journalists that he'd fired at an undercover patrol, and they'd had no choice but to return fire. No doubt the inquest, *if any*, would be a farce. Christ, he was tired, but he looked forward to seeing Brona again, thinking he might just try his luck too if he was clever.

The days passed until Brona Doyle, and Patrick Gillispie sat opposite each other at a table in the local fish and chip shop, which was just off St James's Crescent in the Falls district of Belfast. He'd managed to pop into the off-licence earlier in the week to arrange a time and place to meet. There wasn't anywhere particularly good to eat around the area, so they'd gone for simple fish and chips.

Alice looked at Patrick, who'd clearly made an effort to smarten himself up. He wore a pair of grey, flared corduroy trousers with a white shirt under a black and white, diamond-patterned tank top. His black Chelsea boots shone brightly from a recent polishing. She noticed his callused hands were red and dry from the cold.

She'd been right. Eureka! Det informed her that Patrick Gillispie was a member of the Provisional Irish Republican Army – and not just any member, a pretty senior member. He was well up on their wanted list.

She was told he normally spent most of his time in Monaghan, a county town near the border in the Irish Republic. It meant he was close enough to watch, prepare, plan and carry out cross-border, high-risk solo missions. Det knew there'd been some discord between the PIRA and old IRA and that big changes were coming. It appeared Gillispie was pro these changes. They'd been after him for months and were pleased she had got talking to him. Now he needed reining in.

Over dinner, their conversation was easy and relaxed as Patrick asked about her childhood and parents. She knew her brief like the back of her hand, and so her narrative fell easily into place. It was easy for her to reminisce about her own childhood experiences, topped and tailed to suit her cover.

He watched her carefully as she spoke, deliberately asking her open questions whilst revealing very little about himself. She was good fun and looked particularly sexy tonight in a black V-neck jumper, matching short leather skirt and white knee-length boots. Her cropped red hair was a bit much, but he found her rather pretty, especially her eyes when they shone with the buzz of conversation. He was looking forward to getting her into bed.

Chapter 19

Martin McLaughlin had never imagined he could feel so ill. The small well-travelled freighter fought to climb up and over the swell of the gigantic Atlantic waves. He almost laughed as he remembered his misplaced confidence when they'd left in a calm sea from Port Gloucester, North East Boston, to begin their 3,000-mile journey to County Kerry. As soon as they'd passed the breakwater, though, all hell had broken loose. He'd thought at first he'd never survive the journey.

It'd taken them a couple of hours to load the ship with its seven tonnes of munitions consisting of rifles, light/heavy sub-machine guns, grenades and much-needed ammunition. They were to meet an Irish dragger off the coast of Kerry and transfer their cargo.

It'd been a particularly successful year so far. He'd been surprised when he was suddenly released from the Kesh. After he'd moved across the border to Malin Head, he'd been even more surprised when one day his Uncle Tommy turned up out of the blue in Farren's Bar – it'd become a regular drink-fuelled haunt for Martin. Their conversation was blunt, to say the least. His uncle had quickly grabbed him and taken him over to the empty snug where they sat by a burning stove.

"We've got to get you out of here, son. You're killing yourself. For Christ's sake, look at the shape of ye. Your mother would turn in her grave. Don't fucking bother to ask, but I've called in a couple of favours. We're going to get you over to New York. I've got a contact there, a good friend from way back. There's one condition, mind. You've got to pack in the drinking, Martin. It's got to stop!"

He grunted as he helped Martin get up, said their goodbyes and pushed his nephew out of the snug and into one of the nearby cottages that Martin had rented and that just happened to be adjacent to the main bar. As they entered the cottage, Tommy continued,

"If anyone can get you back on track, this guy in New York will. He's in AA."

Martin raged at such a suggestion and tried to defend his actions, denying he was an alcoholic – he just liked a drink.

Tommy simply ignored his excuses until they sat down on the blanket-covered sofa where Martin had slept the night before. The big man looked around at the chaos of the small cottage and hissed in frustration, "Listen to me. Now our Majella's gone, and your father too, neither me, Caitlin, nor, God love her, your Tina, can take any more death in this family! You're on the road to self-destruction, Martin, and if you keep going the way you're going, you'll soon be with your Ma' and Da'! So, whether you like it or not, you're off to America, son. Subject closed!"

In the end, Martin had no choice. Deep down, he was relieved beyond belief. The biggest problem he had was coming off the sauce – it was far from easy with the withdrawal symptoms of tremors, shivering and sweating, the infamous DTs. He knew they'd only last a week or so, though. He'd been there before, so would stick with it this time since he wasn't for letting the big man down. This was a golden opportunity to get out of Derry – at least for a while – and sort himself out.

As soon as a travel date was agreed, he grew more and more excited. Soon after that, a newly presentable Martin McLaughlin arrived in New York.

Tommy's contact turned out to be the number one PIRA man in America, Brian Meenan. On the way from New York's JFK airport, Meenan had been as blunt as Tommy and warned Martin he wouldn't take any shite. No alcohol, and Martin should remember his host knew every trick in the book and would be watching him closely. Meenan was a man in his mid-sixties who'd never married, lived with his sister, and lived and breathed purely for the Cause. Martin knew he'd been lucky to get into the US unnoticed, but it hadn't proved to be too difficult.

Most of the New Yorkers were of Irish descent anyway and directly or indirectly supported the Cause. Going through Immigration, his passport had warranted just a brief glance and a smile.

He knew he was a car wreck when he'd been in Malin. As he'd thought, the DTs eventually subsided, and he was feeling so much better. He was sleeping better, eating better, and his energy levels had increased. Being interned for so long, missing his ma's and da's funerals and deserting Caitlin and Tina had nearly destroyed him. But with his own determination and the help of Brian and his sister Sinead, he quickly began to get his act together. He'd lived with them for a while at the start. Sinead was a terrific cook, and he ate well. She had a slight soft spot for him and helped him smarten up by getting him a set of new clothes and making him tidy his hair and general appearance. He'd never forget Brian and Sinead's kindness. They'd even found him a job as a bartender in a local Irish pub, The Galtee. Meenan believed in throwing him in at the deep end and said working in a pub would test his resilience. It had worked. Martin couldn't think of touching the stuff again.

Cathal Connolly, the priest he'd met at the NORAID dance in Yonkers, NY, proved to be a great help too. It was uncanny and a pure stroke of fate that he turned out to be one of the three serving priests in Martin's own Parish, St Mary's, Derry. He'd updated Martin on how his sisters were keeping. He grew concerned and felt even more guilty as he listened to the priest.

"Caitlin took your Ma's suicide really badly after you left, and Tina only found out a short while ago. Everyone was worried about her state of mind and if she could handle it. She wasn't told everything, only that Majella fell asleep and didn't wake up. She took it badly too, but the surprising news is that Father McGuire tells me she's doing better in gaol than in hospital. She's under the protection of the women there, especially one called Bridget Barry."

Listening to the priest, Martin had felt wretched. As yet, he still hadn't been in touch with his sisters. There wasn't any *real* excuse for his lack of contact; it was just as time went on he'd found himself working closely with Brian Meenan, and soon, once again, Martin McLaughlin returned to duties and became an active PIRA Volunteer.

* * *

Now, sitting opposite him on the lower deck of the ship, was a new comrade, Seamus Donaghy, Caitlin's ex-boyfriend. Along with his boss, Seamus had attended a few of the black-tie events that the Derry priest Father Connolly spoke at in Boston and got riled up when he heard what the priest had to say. So, as soon as he got back to Derry, he too became a PIRA Volunteer and, in due course, found himself sitting next to Martin McLaughlin on an arms-smuggling mission.

Martin had been shocked at the alteration in the youngster, not recognising him at first as he'd changed and matured so much.

"Seamus Donaghy? Seamus Donaghy, who went out with our Caitlin?" he'd asked in surprise when meeting up with him.

Seamus laughed too when he realised who Martin was.

"Aye, that's me. I was in Derry recently, and I saw her. She's doing alright, Martin. She wasn't great at first, but I gave her a bit of a talking to and took her out a few times – she promised she'd keep herself right."

Martin nodded and smiled. "Ah, that's good. Be careful with our Caitlin; she's a hot-head!"

"Don't I know it!" Seamus recollected. "I've seen her at her worst."

But talking about his sister had made Martin sad and his heart heavy. The only consolation he could think of was that he was doing something she and Tina could be proud of. It was a huge risk for him and a massive responsibility – getting this precious cargo of armaments successfully back to Ireland. But it was worth it. The risk was worth it. It could result in absolute victory for the Cause, an end to this bloody war and, finally, after hundreds of years, a United Ireland.

* * *

Father Connolly had travelled back and forth several times to the US, becoming a bit of a celebrity there. After his debut NORAID fundraising speech, where he'd first met Martin McLaughlin, it appeared the New Yorkers and Bostonians couldn't get enough of him. Time after time, invitations landed on the hall floor of the parochial house – much to Father McGuire's chagrin. The old priest was furious with him for being away so much from his duties and well aware of his high-profile activities in the States. He also hated the fact that Bishop Carlin – who'd surprisingly commended Cathal on his New York speech, having read about it – had given his full approval for the young priest to continue his US excursions. It meant more toil for the remaining two overworked and weary priests.

"I can't understand it, Father. How can you go off again? We've got so much to do here already and especially now with those New York policemen arriving next month. How are we going to manage it all?" Father McGuire asked, clearly frustrated. "It's not fair on me, and it's not fair on Father Moore."

Father Connolly took the time to reassure him that everything had been already sorted for his US visitors with a planned schedule, all agreed by Father Moore. But McGuire wasn't giving up.

"I know what you're doing over there, son. Fund-raising events for prisoners' wives and families, my arse! It's not for those people; it's for the bombers! We've both seen too many victims and families with their hearts broken in this city – you can't call this helping the needy! There has to be another way." Father McGuire, although a Republican through and through, was weary and sickened by the conflict. He just wanted the violence to end.

Cathal remained tight-lipped – if the old man only knew the half of it. Since he'd met Martin McLaughlin alongside Brian Meenan, they'd put a series of plans together for how they could really help finish the war by providing arms for the Cause back home. The priest had always been a Republican at heart, especially after his father's death. Listening to the passionate and resolute after-dinner speakers and others, who'd continually cried out for a United Ireland, he found they'd opened his eyes wider to the victimisation of the Irish by the British.

Meenan had somehow arranged for a cache of arms to come from Libya. He'd actually been there and met Gaddafi and, to his astonishment, the big man himself swore "*to help the IRA eradicate British Imperialism and its allies*" by providing them with arms. Meenan then chartered a US DC3 plane – completely stripped down inside – and filled it with everything from rockets to guns and thousands of rounds of ammunition. It'd transformed their arsenal and immeasurably boosted the Volunteers spirits when it arrived safely at Shannon for onward distribution up North.

* * *

On board the *Claudette*, Seamus and Martin sat in the trawler's galley, quietly playing cards as a means of distracting themselves from their churning stomachs. They'd not been able to eat since they knew where it would end up – most likely on their shoes. Outside, the wind was howling, and the battling rain smashed angrily against the ship's portholes like rocks hitting a barn door.

Attempting not to throw up and remain calm in front of Martin, Seamus tried to hide his seasickness as he looked at his fellow sailor and asked hopefully, "How long do you think now, Martin? We've got to be close."

Martin removed a cigarette from his mouth and told the boy reassuringly, "Not long, Seamus; we should be coming in soon. They're due to meet us at midnight. Another few hours, that's all."

Seamus sighed and watched Martin as he studied his hand of cards. He wasn't anything like Caitlin had described him when they'd first gone out together. At that time, she'd told Seamus her brother was a drunk – a filthy, nasty piece of work. Yet Seamus was finding him very different from the man she'd described.

He'd obviously changed over the years since his early days in Derry. His appearance nowadays was spotless under his short-cropped Marine haircut. His black jacket had been brushed, with not a speck of fuzz on it, and underneath was a brown knitted scarf, knotted smartly and tucked neatly into his jacket. He looked immaculate. Seamus wondered why he hadn't stayed in Derry after getting out of gaol. "Can I ask you something?" he said cautiously. Martin nodded.

"Why didn't you stay home after you got out?"

Martin carefully placed his playing cards face down and looked at Seamus. His eyebrows lifted as he remembered the black days after he received word of his mother's death. His expression made Seamus wonder if he'd gone too far.

"I couldn't stay," he replied reflectively. "So I ran. Too much had happened. I couldn't face the Kesh again. I took the cowardly way and drank to drown my sorrows, headed up to Kate Farren's in Malin Head and drank myself into oblivion. I don't remember half of it, only that I was given a chance to go to the States, and I grabbed that chance. It was Tommy who got me here. Good old Tommy. He warned me, you know! Told me I was drinking meself to death. And you know what? At first, I was *so* angry at him." Martin sighed. "But of course, he was right. I haven't touched a drop since."

Seamus wasn't sure how to answer that but sat stone-faced until he asked, "What was it like?"

"What was what like – the drink or gaol?" Martin laughed.

"Gaol."

"Long Kesh is a living hell, pure hell, but the interrogations before in the cop stations were worse, much worse. They'd hood you, make you stand with your legs wide, your arms up and open, your hands and fingers spread out… *and* if you moved just one inch, Seamus, they'd batter you. They hammered the inside of my feet so bad; mine were twice their normal size when they'd finished. They'd scream and yell in your ears, question after question. No wonder so many poor fuckers signed confessions. Nine days they had me in, but I wasn't going to tell them anything."

"Jesus," Seamus whispered. He wasn't sure if he could be so strong. "What happened then?"

Martin could feel his eyes well up as he thought about it. "When I got to the Kesh, a guard asked me where I'd been. I couldn't tell him. He didn't know I'd been hooded for nine whole fucking days. When I told him, he showed me the first act of human kindness in days. He told me I'd be okay; I was amongst men now. I'll never forget him."

* * *

Father Connolly sat in a popular café, The Rainbow, across the street from the Strand Road police barracks. Its interior was designed like an American diner with stainless steel-based stools fixed to a long metallic bar that started as you came through the door and stretched to the far end of the room.

On the opposite side were high-backed, red vinyl-lined booths, each fitted with matching stainless-steel tables. Pictures of iconic New York sites, including the Empire State Building, were displayed around the red-painted walls.

A Bible lay open next to a pot of tea and a small jotter where he'd made a number of notes. People would assume he was preparing for Mass, but only he knew he was noting down car registrations as they drove in and out of the barracks. He was trying to identify covert civilian vehicles against a list hidden in his Bible. There'd been a number of fatal sectarian shootings from the vehicles, and their registrations numbers had to be confirmed.

They knew that covert army and police vehicles had a number of special built-in features, including hidden radios and speakers, microphones to record conversations and video cameras to surreptitiously film suspects. Some cars even had Kevlar armour-plating with gaps that the operators could shoot through, as well as many other unseen additions. Today, he'd had no luck in identifying any.

For the past four Friday mornings, he'd made a point of sitting in the same café and writing in the same notebook. No one paid any attention to him other than the odd parishioner who recognised him from Mass. As he sat and watched, he noticed a splendid white Rover park outside the police station. A man and a woman were visible inside. The man stepped out and ran round to the entrance of the fortified barracks.

The woman took her time, first gathering her bag, opening it to search for something and then pouting to touch up her lipstick in a hand-held mirror before climbing out of the car.

Father Connolly noticed the man had disappeared into the station. He recognised him from the *Derry Journal* and thought it unusual to see him dressed so casually. The woman had gotten out of the car by now and was making her way across the street towards the café. He took a look at her as she approached, noting she had a kindly air about her. For no particular reason, he half-smiled and decided it was time to move on.

He started packing up his belongings. She approached him and asked if he was going.

"Yes. All yours," he replied politely.

"Ah., wonderful. Thank you! Sometimes it's so difficult to get a table here on a Friday morning. My husband will be joining me soon."

She smiled and thanked him again. He thought her charming. Saying a polite goodbye. Father Connolly paid his bill and left.

* * *

At Strand Road barracks, ex-RUC Chief Constable George Shalham couldn't find anyone of consequence to approach. He'd hoped to get a chance to talk to Bonner but found he wasn't on-site, and so, despondent and frustrated, he left to meet Hilda for their usual Friday morning tea and cake.

All in all, Shalham was beginning to enjoy his retirement and was secretly pleased his golf handicap had shown a steady improvement. He remembered he'd bought a little something for Hilda and so made his way over to his latest acquisition, a bit of Rover luxury and a dream to drive. His lump-sum pension had come in particularly handy. He was happy and feeling good when he looked across the street to see Hilda sitting patiently at the café's window, waving to him. Delighted that she'd got a table so quickly, he looked to his right and was already crossing the road when out of the blue, a saloon car raced menacingly towards him with its rear window wide open.

Within seconds his body danced like a puppet as bullets from an automatic rifle tore into his skull and shredded his torso. Lying on the ground, George Shalham looked up and found a young priest praying over him as he stuttered on his dying breath.

"J-J-Jo-Jo..."

Chapter 20

The job was done and dusted in literally minutes. She'd closed her eyes as tightly as humanly possible and held her breath as mentally she took herself off to America: diners and burgers, boys in football shirts, girls in cardigans, rock 'n' roll. Anything to get her mind away from what he was doing to her.

Anne, the recently married wife of John "Porkie" Ballantyne, had at one time dreamed of having it all, the whole American package. Now here she was, lying in a sweaty, double bed that was much too small for the lumpy, heavy man on top and inside her, drooling and rubbing himself against her like a dog.

He whined and rolled his sweating, saggy body onto its side. As the smell of whiskey wafted through the air, she coughed lightly. She'd been dreading this moment and knew it wouldn't be enjoyable. There'd been nothing pleasant about it; it'd been grotesque! *What the fuck had she done?!*

Before the wedding, she'd half-heartedly joked with Caitlin about sleeping with Porkie to try and make herself feel less concerned. However, Anne had never dreamed her first night as a bride would be so fuckin' awful, even after the large vodkas and Cokes she'd gulped down during the reception to blur the edges. As soon as she and an inebriated Porkie got inside the small double room of the B&B in the seaside resort of Buncrana that was to be their one-night honeymoon destination, he'd grabbed her roughly, slobbering in his drunken state while he attempted to kiss her. His coarse, stubby hands had hurriedly torn off her simple white wedding dress that now lay on the cigarette-singed carpet, ripped and forlorn.

She'd taken such great care when she'd made it – what a waste! She wasn't even sure if he'd come. She certainly hadn't; she felt nothing but revulsion.

The church wedding at St Mary's had been simple, and Father McGuire looked almost sad as he watched her slowly and carefully walk down the aisle escorted by her eldest brother. Her father was nowhere to be seen – they'd put the call out – but no one knew where he was.

The wedding reception had been held on the top floor of a local pub in Creggan. Dickie's speech as best man had made her almost ill. He'd been a total embarrassment and cruel in his drunken state, holding a brimming pint of Guinness high up in the air. It spilt onto the white paper tablecloth as he leered and winked at the groom.

"Well, well, well. I never thought he had it in him! What a catch… Anne Heaney, eh? Sure the woman wouldn't even look at him a while back! But let's be honest, she's not *the whole* Anne Heaney we all knew. It's what's left of her that he's marrying, with her missing a leg and all!"

He laughed – as did the groom – but the remaining five tables in the room sat in stunned silence, hoping someone would stop such an inept speech. Caitlin groaned as if she'd been hit in the pit of her stomach – *what a wanker*! She looked at the bride's shaken expression and the fury of her mother, Liz.

Porkie said nothing but egged Dickie on, waving his hands frantically for his friend to keep going.

"He's had his fair share of women has our Porkie; you wouldn't believe the half of it! Never, ever underestimate a *Ballantyne*."

To prove his point, Dickie looked to Porkie's father, who sat, pissed as a fart, at the end of the table. The man had clearly made no effort to get dressed up. He wore a crumpled black shirt with no tie and a dark green pair of trousers with no belt. His face was alcohol- flushed and hot, his beard long and untrimmed and adorned with food that had stuck to it as he attempted to eat.

"I mean, let's be honest, Mr B, you've had your fair share of tits, pussy and ass too!"

The groom's father smiled drunkenly and, trying to focus, screwed up his eyes and laughed. Dickie was right. At one time, he'd been a bit of a Casanova, but no more; age and the demon drink had finally caught up with him. He looked at his mousy, temazepam-fuelled wife sitting stonily next to him in a hazed, tablet-induced calm. *Ah, the good old days.*

And so the tirade continued until the mother of the bride couldn't take anymore. She'd pleaded with her eldest son to stop Dickie's cruel rant, but even he was too pissed to stand. Liz stood up and cursed at the best man as she hadn't cursed in years.

"Right, fuck-head, that'll do! Fuck off away with ye, ye eejit! You're nothing but a no-good wanker!"

The spectators burst into a round of jeers and applause, booing Dickie off.

Porkie stood up, waving his arms to settle his guests as he roared, clearly smashed but trying his best to act sober: "Okay… okay… everyone! Sure he was just having a laugh! Take it easy!"

He looked down at his bride, who sat white-faced, her earnest eyes beseeching Caitlin for help. Porkie turned to the wedding guests and apologised for his best man's antics.

"He's an eejit, I know. Apologies, everyone, sure he means no harm!" the groom cried as the room dutifully began to quieten down and listen.

"Thanks for coming to celebrate our wedding." He looked at Anne again and smiled with pride. "She's a picture, and I couldn't be happier."

The wedding party murmured their agreement as he carried on, "As most of youse know, we're moving into a new house t'morrow, the start of our new life together. So thanks for the wedding presents; they'll come in right handy."

Porkie caught Caitlin's eye and conceded, "And thanks to Caitlin too for being a bridesmaid and a good friend to my *wife*." He laughed. "You look lovely."

But Caitlin felt ridiculous. The wedding budget had been meagre, and consequently, her bridesmaid's dress was second-hand, made from a cheap, light peach satin-like fabric. She and Anne had attempted to make some improvements, but it was still pretty horrible. It was all Anne could afford. Caitlin couldn't believe her friend was marrying such a fuck-head twunt of a man and wasn't going to complain over a stupid dress. All she had to do was look at her friend's sad face to realise what a travesty of a match this was.

The groom closed down his speech, and the guests politely applauded, secretly relieved it was over. What a palaver, they thought, as the smoke-filled room began to buzz with their murmurs and whispers. *Did you see how the bride was? Poor thing, she looked lovely too but so miserable, certainly not your usual smiling bride! And that best man's speech, how embarrassing for her. Awful… just awful!*

The music began, prompting Porkie to lead Anne onto the empty dance floor while everyone clapped. Their engagement had been so speedy that they'd not had time to find a special song for their first dance. Instead, Porkie had decided Phil Coulter's '*The Town I Love So Well*' would do.

In a lewd tone and holding his wife tight, he whispered in her ear, "Just wait 'til I get you later. I'm going to fuck the life out of ye."

She looked up at him with contempt. *Sweet Jesus.*

The song seemed to go on forever until finally, the DJ put on a Bee Gees hit. Within seconds the dance floor sprang to life as the guests' bodies swayed and moved in every direction to the upbeat music. Anne got off the floor as quickly as she could and back to the top table, where she drank another vodka down in one and headed for the ladies.

As best man, Dickie decided to take it upon himself to grab the bridesmaid and pull her towards the dance floor, but angry and repulsed, Caitlin told him haughtily to leave her alone. Far from happy at such a snooty rejection, he pulled her roughly by the arm again until Seamus – who'd accompanied her to the wedding – pushed him away. Even more pissed off now, Dickie raised a clenched fist and pummelled Seamus right between the eyes. A crack was heard as his nose exploded, the pain excruciating. In fury, he leapt back up and made for Dickie.

They tried to beat the living daylights out of each other until a number of male guests, with difficulty, managed to pull Dickie off and away. Caitlin anxiously led a dishevelled and bloodied Seamus down the narrow staircase to the bar below, which was relatively empty. The blonde, bee-hived barmaid, upon seeing his condition, quickly made her way over and passed Caitlin a wet towel.

"Christ, Seamus! Are you okay?" Caitlin asked in shock, her heart racing. He looked dreadful. She'd thought Dickie was going to kill him. The side of her own face hurt like hell as she'd accidentally caught a fist in full flight when she'd intervened. Seamus gently pushed her off and said, "I'm fine, Caitlin. Just give me a minute."

His head was reeling. *Fuck*! He'd thought the bastard was going to do him in. The man had been like a wild dog: biting, pulling his hair, throwing punch after punch. The low-life had even kicked him in the balls. Seamus wasn't a fighter and knew he'd been lucky to get away relatively unscathed. His whole body shivered, vibrated and trembled. He'd never been in a scrap like that and knew if he hadn't drunk those last few Irish whiskies – Irish whiskey never agreed with him – he wouldn't have dreamed of jumping the ugly hairy bastard.

The only consolation was that Caitlin looked so worried. He took her hand, raised it to his lips and kissed it. It was the first time he'd touched her so lovingly. Caitlin squeezed his hand in return and smiled softly as she continued to wipe his face with the towelling cloth.

Meanwhile, upstairs, returning from the bathroom and completely unaware of the fight, Anne was searching for Caitlin but couldn't see her. Liz, on the dance floor, saw her daughter's anxious expression. She rushed over, cupped her hands around her mouth and asked over the ear-splitting music if she was okay.

"Where's Caitlin?" Anne shouted back, eyes still searching the flashing, multi-coloured lighting over the dance floor.

Liz touched her daughter's hand and took her aside. She told her briefly about the brawl but said she was not to worry. Pointing, she told her that she'd seen Caitlin take Seamus downstairs.

Anne nodded and was about to make her way to the staircase when, infuriatingly, she walked straight into Porkie and Dickie, swaying with their arms wrapped around each other's shoulders. Porkie's newly bought white shirt was ruined with dark bloodstains from his friend's crimson and bloodied face. They were both three sheets to the wind, and each held a naggin of whiskey. Porkie yelled unintelligibly, gesturing to Dickie.

"There she is, me wee wummin! Wher've ye bin?"

Anne rushed by without answering and made her way downstairs to the bar, to the strains of the distant yelling and slurring of her new husband: "Anne, me love, where'd ye go? Dik'ee, where'd she go?"

As she reached the bottom step and looked into the lower bar room, she saw Caitlin tenderly washing the blood off Seamus's face with a cloth. Something like envy overwhelmed Anne then but disappeared as quickly as it had come when she saw the bruised man take her best friend's hand to his lips and kiss it. Unspoken words seemed to pass between them until Caitlin squeezed his hand and smiled. Anne smiled too. She was glad to see her friend happy and away from that dickhead Henderson. And so, wearily, the lonely bride turned to walk back up the stairs to Porkie and Dickie – her heart sinking at the very thought of what was to come.

* * *

Caitlin did the best she could to get the blood off Seamus's face. His nose continued to bleed even with the icy cloth the barmaid had just handed her.

"You'll have to go to A&E," she told him fearfully, "I can't get the bleeding to stop."

Seamus shook his head. He wasn't going anywhere; he was going to take full advantage of Caitlin's concern.

"I'm fine. Just give me a second, and we'll go back up. It's still early."

Caitlin was grateful. She'd been worried about having to leave Anne so early in the evening. She looked fondly at Seamus and, once again, thought about how mature and grown-up he'd become.

Despite his injuries, Seamus felt happier than he had for ages. He kissed Caitlin's hand again and thanked her for taking such good care of him. Upstairs the music slowed, and their eyes locked as he whispered invitingly, "Fancy a dance?" Her smile said it all as they made their way back upstairs.

* * *

When Seamus last left for the States, she'd promised him she'd get better and had kept that promise. Work had been going well, and she'd been asked to do some photographic modelling, which at first had been daunting, but soon she began to truly enjoy it. She was also doing some catalogue and magazine work, in addition to her day job, and the extra money helped. She'd given a witness statement along with the old man who'd saved her from the rubber bullet to Brendan Doherty, the solicitor, about the murder of the young boy with the toy gun, but had heard nothing nor had any officials come near them for a statement. Brendan told them later the only response he got from the security services was that "*their eyewitness evidence wouldn't be accepted at face value*".

At the inquest, the formal response of the authorities was, "*The boy was one of many dangerous rioters posing a serious threat to life and property.*" No surprise then when the Coroner accepted the police's story. Night after night, Caitlin revisited the tragic scene. She remembered everything about it, but although she'd described it in detail to Brendan, it made no difference. Case closed.

* * *

She'd been to see Tina with Tommy, and the visit had gone well, although she was sorry to see her sister looking so unwell. The siege at the gaol had taken a heavy toll on her, but she'd been so glad and relieved to see Caitlin that the siege was soon forgotten.

"Ah, Caitlin, it's lovely to see you again. I have to say sorry to you… I'm so, so sorry for everything that happened. Everything I did. Honest." After her apology, she'd broken down and wept uncontrollably. Caitlin rose to embrace her but was rudely told to step back by an ugly screw with short, gelled-back dark hair. Grasping her sister's frail hands, Caitlin shook them to make her look up.

"Look at me, Tina, and listen, please. It was *not* your fault! Do you hear me? I know now that Kelly took advantage of you. I'm the one who should be sorry. I was too busy falling in love with James feckin' Henderson to pay attention to anything or anyone else. I was the one who deserted you."

Caitlin's confession about James Henderson took her sister and Tommy completely by surprise. Tina choked up and cried harder in between her words, saying, "I've screwed that up too with him, I mean, haven't I? I'm so sorry!"

Caitlin saw the pain in Tina's face and attempted to reassure her. "It doesn't matter, love. It really doesn't matter anymore. What matters is getting *you out* of this place – and soon!"

Tommy couldn't agree more, so they updated Tina on her appeal and their last meeting with Brendan Doherty.

Rumour had it Martin was in America, though Caitlin couldn't believe it. She couldn't believe he'd go so far without at least telling Tommy. She'd asked her uncle, but he'd quickly told her he didn't know either. His answer was sharp and to the point, and she thought maybe he too was cross with Martin for the lack of contact. She assumed he was hiding out somewhere in the Republic – most likely Malin Head. He loved the peace and safety there, especially Farren's Bar.

Luckily, Seamus had had to return to Ireland at the request of his boss in the Boston construction company, which had allowed them to spend more time together. There was something up, though, something a little odd about the way he'd disappear for a couple of days and be coy about where he'd been when he returned. She prayed he hadn't got himself involved in anything political. So many of the lads now were, but she thought it highly unlikely he would bother, given he lived in America. She'd been nervous about asking him to the wedding but didn't want to go on her own, so she had plucked up the courage anyway. He hadn't hesitated to accept, secretly delighted given that he wanted to get closer to her.

Caitlin was still cautious and wary about their relationship. Whenever she found herself growing too close to him, she couldn't help but retreat and become aloof. She knew why.

She'd spotted James Henderson's Jaguar a few times in and around town, and whenever she saw it, her heart dropped to her stomach. She was sure he'd seen her once and had stopped to look, but he'd driven on. The effect he still had on her was undeniable. She tried to pretend the memories of their times together were becoming more distant, but at times, they were still able to make her catch her breath in longing.

Chapter 21

Without warning and just before lights out, Smyth and another screw, that neither Tina nor Bridget recognised, unlocked their cell door as the woman and girl were harmlessly singing and laughing over their efforts with the David Essex song '*Hold Me Close*'.

Bridget, in her favourite flowered nightie, sat comfortably on top of her bed and was about to finish off a baby blanket she was crocheting. She wanted it ready for the following morning so she could add it to the pile of arts and crafts the inmates sold to the outside world. The women prisoners, unlike the men, weren't allowed wood or leather for crafts, so embroidery and crocheting were commonplace. This was a means of raising money and adding a small amount to their much-needed prisoners' defence fund. It also helped top up their spending money and enabled them to add to their sparse food parcels.

Bridget laughed contentedly, watching the youngin' dancing in the tiny space between the two beds. She was doing so well, way beyond the OC's and Bridget's expectations. Finally, recovering from the shock of the siege, she'd made a huge improvement both mentally and physically and was in nothing like the bad condition she'd arrived in. The women on her wing looked out for her and loved her being around. They took great joy in seeing her blossom from a fucked-up, drug-deadened child to what she'd now become – a funny and happy young woman. She especially adored their games at night when they'd each take a turn and pretend to invite famous Hollywood actors or singers for dinner, dreaming up delicious menus and imagining stunning venues, clothes and conversation. The youngin's improvement was a miracle that gave every one of them a new sense of purpose and hope.

Tina, who'd talked to Bridget about Kieran, began to understand that what she'd done for him was not her fault. He'd taken advantage of her, primed and blackmailed her. Nevertheless, she'd made an awful mistake and deserved to be punished – so many people could have died. Over the months, she'd accepted her fate. Life in this place gave her strength, surrounded by the love of all these wonderful women – they gave her a reason to survive, a reason to get better. She didn't need those tablets anymore and felt her mammy had sent these women to help her. She missed her so much but could feel her everywhere. As for Caitlin, Tina missed her too and hoped that she'd forgiven her for everything she'd done. If she ever got home, she'd make it up to her sister. Somehow.

"McLaughlin, you're being moved!" ordered Smyth, looking delighted. The idea of separating these two devoted women was sheer joy to the screw! She'd been waiting for her moment to get the little bitch back after her pig-headedness with Dr Harris. And this was it, she thought, as she watched McLaughlin's face go pale and her eyes widen in fear.

Smyth threw what few possessions Tina had into a small brown cardboard box whilst her recently recruited, like-minded colleague, Gladys Drake, watched and smiled approvingly at her partner. Determined to make a mess, cause a nuisance and impress her new lover, Drake tossed Tina's narrow, thin mattress and blankets onto the ground. She giggled as she spotted the shared, half-filled *po*. Mimicking a penalty shot, she took aim and kicked it hard across the floor, waiting until it slammed against the stone and its contents splattered against the postered wall. She nodded at Smyth in satisfaction – *goal!*

Throwing her wool work aside, Bridget stood up angrily and faced the pair. Her face was flushed with rage as she remained protectively in front of the youngin'. Tina peeped over her shoulder as Bridget demanded to know why she was about to lose her cellmate.

"What the fuck are you on about, Smyth! She's not going anywhere; you can't move her!"

Smyth didn't rise to the woman's anger but remained cold and calm, lying through her teeth.

"The Gov wants all sentenced prisoners together in one wing." Bridget didn't believe a word of it.

"She's a Republican political prisoner! She can't go in with that lot; she's still a wee girl who's been with us for months. Sure, look at her; you know she's not right in the head. For Christ's sake, leave her be!"

Tina made a point of looking dazed and confused, but Smyth was adamant there was fuck all wrong with the girl, and she was putting it on. Anyway – she was out of this cell.

* * *

When the Governor had been ordered to accept Tina McLaughlin and take her under his care after she was transferred from Gransha Psychiatric Hospital in Londonderry, he'd been livid. He didn't need any nut-jobs or psychos in his prison! He'd enough to deal with already.

He'd fought the order and lost. Given little choice, as soon as McLaughlin arrived, he immediately put her under the care of the A-Wing OC Maureen Molony. He knew the vulnerable girl would be well cared for, and the other women would look out for her, thereby taking the onus and responsibility off his skeleton staff. All the women in this gaol needed to be approved by their respective political groups in order to obtain political status. The PIRA command knew Tina's family and background, and they were convinced she hadn't colluded with the security services or broken any orders. Although she wasn't a Volunteer, they ruled that she should be given political status. So Martina McLaughlin fell safely under the command of OC Maureen Molony alongside the rest of the Republican political prisoners.

Maureen Molony ran a tight and orderly ship, but the PIRA ordered her and many other Republican women not to co-operate or recognise the British Commission, nor would they accept the prison's procedures. The British believed these commissions were an opportunity for internees to ask for their right to freedom. Those who recognised the commission were most likely to be sent home.

The internees who refused to acknowledge the commissions adhered to their own rules – organised and disciplined both inside and outside prison. They felt they had a reputation to uphold, and although Governor Johnston found this particular OC difficult and stubborn at times, he quietly respected her ability to command.

The vast majority of Republican women Volunteers in Armagh would never consider defying her orders. They believed they should not have been jailed in the first place and were determined and proud not to acknowledge or accept the Commission's charade and petty rules. Most of them knew if they bowed to British Rule, it meant they could likely go home. But as a matter of principle and under orders, they couldn't recognise the political establishment.

The gaol was now filling up fast. They'd just built a new wing, and the pressure to keep costs down was phenomenal. Governor Johnston tried his best to be fair – especially after the siege. He'd never admit it, but he knew the difference between good and bad, and most of the women in his prison were fundamentally law-abiding and straight. They should never have seen the inside of a cell. However, he had a job to do and was paralysed by the system. And now came even worse news. He'd learned of the upcoming change to government legislation around what was termed a "political prisoner vs a criminal prisoner" and their respective rights. He knew instinctively that this change would lead to a dangerous and violent outcome – not just for him but for everyone here.

* * *

Bridget Barry was livid when she was held back, her neck and face pushed tight against the cell wall by one huge hand of the tall, butch-looking screw. Without warning, Bridget's clean granny-style floral nightie was bunched and held up as the screw's baton was pushed up rigidly between her legs and deep inside her vagina. She fought as hard as she could for what felt like hours, but the intrusive device and its constant movement tore at her tender tissue.

Totally shocked and too wounded to fight anymore, she'd no choice but to stop struggling. She was truly mortified as a swell of shame, embarrassment, and humiliation consumed her. She couldn't believe what was happening to her; it was too much!

Tina was pinned up hard against the postered cell wall by Smyth, her head locked by a baton held tightly under her chin. She screamed hysterically as she watched her friend's violation. She clawed at Smyth to get to Bridget and save her from such wicked abuse.

Eventually, Gladys Drake's arm grew tired, and she withdrew her baton from Bridget. She smiled knowingly at Smyth, who yanked Tina, squealing, out of the cell and onto the catwalk.

Left alone with Bridget, Drake continued to play with her prey, taunting her with the baton and allowing the old bat to think she was finished with her. However, as soon as Bridget began to pull her nightie back down, Drake smiled menacingly. She wasn't quite finished. Once again, her baton pulled the bloodied nightie back up, and this time, the baton was driven into Bridget's backside.

It wasn't so much fun the second time, and Drake quickly grew bored and stopped – her arm hurt too much anyway, and she decided the show was over. Glancing at her watch, she noticed it was nearly home-time.

Helpless, humiliated beyond belief, and in agonising pain, Bridget's guttural screams were heard across the wings and beyond. Her confined comrades called out in terror, wanting to know what was going on. Between her cries, Bridget heard the youngin' calling for her and reached out in vain. The noise began to penetrate Drake's head, and so, to find solace and silence, she raised her baton and finished Bridget off with a heavy crack on the back of the head. She'd suddenly remembered it was her turn to cook and they had to get home!

Meanwhile, yanked by the hair, Tina was cruelly dragged and kicked down the catwalk by Smyth. She yowled and squealed in fury at Bridget's abuse and molestation. On all fours, she was dragged along painfully until Smyth – who was having a ball and ignoring the screams emanating from the locked cells all around – made her stand and walk to the wing's exit.

The sound of the prisoners' baying screams and pounding on their cell doors in answer to their comrades pleading reverberated against every brick of the building. Tina yelled her heart out in response and sobbed loudly, "It's Bridget! She's doing awful, awful things to Bridget!"

The noise of the women's cries began to fade as Tina was forcefully pushed through the exit and onto another wing. She was terrified and wasn't sure if she was imagining it as she heard singing coming from one of the dank, dark cells on the ground floor below. The cells that only held newly arrived internees. It was a lone, beautiful high-pitched voice that grew louder and stronger as the other Republican women quickly recognised the song and joined in. The chorus became deep-seated and powerful as the women, united in music, sang their hearts out. The atmosphere grew thick with defiance and pride whilst Tina's body suddenly slumped and fell heavily against the tiled floor.

Terror became the victor as she returned to her safe marshmallow world, her sheltered place. She was singing with her daddy in front of their open fire in Blamfield Street. They were singing loudly and proudly, their eyes filled with love. The song was '*Four Green Fields*' – her daddy's party piece.

Smyth cursed and pushed and kicked Tina's slumped body towards a cell door. Pushing her prisoner against the wall outside, in an attempt to keep her upright, she fought to open the door with one hand. Eventually, it gave way. Smyth led Tina down a step and into the cell where two young women sat upright in their beds, clearly annoyed by the intrusion.

The girls were in their early twenties and wore identical black Iron Maiden T-shirts and black trousers. One of them had a small black crucifix tattooed on her right cheek and the other girl a red one on her left cheek. Both of them sported midnight-black hair that was long and straight. Their features were fine under translucent, pale skin. They were bizarre – obviously headbangers.

The one with the black crucifix asked Smyth, in bewilderment and annoyance, "What the fuck's going on?"

"You've got a new cellmate, love," she answered with disdain. She, too, was getting fed up and needed to be off home. It was Drake's turn to cook, and they were running late. She threw Tina carelessly towards the girl's single bed. Tina landed on top – just.

"But we've no room!" the girl shrieked in frustration, pointing at the cell's sparse furniture – there was barely enough room for two people in here, let alone three!

"Make room!" Smyth barked angrily as she left the cell, locking its door with a sense of great satisfaction.

She quickly made her way back to Tina's old cell to catch up with her partner. She'd watched Gladys in awe as she'd enjoyed herself raping and sexually abusing old Bridget. Smyth'd never seen anything like it – not for real! Her tummy swirled with a mixture of fear and excitement – a new feeling – a feeling she liked.

Fortunately, it was a bank holiday. With only a skeleton staff on duty, Smyth and Drake knew they could do as they pleased. She heard Gladys call to her, "Hey, Olive, come and see this! Quick!"

Increasing her pace, Smyth stood outside the cell and looked in. On the floor lay Bridget Barry, face down and out cold. Her torn nightdress remained high up around her waist, exposing a craggy, wrinkled flat bottom that oozed a fine stream of dark, red blood.

Chapter 22

The Coroner's verdict was Accidental Death. Driving too fast across a notorious stretch of road through the Sperrin Mountains, it was deemed James Henderson Snr had lost control of his Austin Allegro. Crashing down an embankment, his car immediately caught fire with him unconscious and trapped inside. Neither Roger nor James got to find out what he'd been so desperate to tell them. It had to have been something important, but now it was lost to them, and they'd never know.

Ned, the pup, was being particularly energetic, and his shrill barks were getting on both Roger's and James's nerves. The young dog sensed unhappiness and was trying desperately to get some form of attention from the two men. Eventually, he nipped and barked loudly at James, who immediately picked him up and called out to his uncle as he swiftly made his way out of the house to the garden, "I'm sorry, I just don't have it in me today to take that noise! I'll put the little bugger out."

Roger nodded. He understood that James was devastated by his father's untimely death. His nephew had withdrawn from everyone, including his uncle and Marleen but especially the poor girl. Just days after the funeral, Roger came across an unopened airmail letter on the hallway table and recognised the writing. He'd quickly thrown it in the fire – that was the last thing any of them needed right now.

Outside Melrose, James set the moaning pup down on the gravelled driveway and looked at him. His heart sank as the innocent mutt stared back with his brown, doll-like eyes asking: *What did I do*?

"I'll be back for you in a while, Ned. Just play around the garden a bit." James closed the door on the whining pup and swiftly made his way across the hallway and back to the study.

Roger sat at his well-worn desk surrounded by papers and binders. It was Friday morning, and Roger and James had got into the habit of spending Fridays together at Melrose to review work at the factory and plan for the following week. They were both engrossed in reading papers when Roger's grey telephone shrilled loudly, making them jump. They chortled, and Roger answered with his usual greeting: "Henderson."

James heard a buzz of excited chatter at the other end. He watched the colour of his uncle's face turn grey and then pale white as the old man removed his wire-framed glasses and carefully placed them on top of some papers. James waved at him, desperate to know what was wrong, but Roger gestured for him to be quiet and still as he continued with the call. James waited. Forcing his voice not to break with emotion, Roger asked the caller, "And where is Mrs Shalham now?"

He listened, nodded and said he understood. The voice babbled on as the handset shook in Roger's hand.

"I see. And no witnesses you say?" he enquired.

His uncle's words sent a chill up James's spine. Whatever had happened, it wasn't good, and he questioned whether, in his delicate state of health, Roger could handle any more nasty shocks.

* * *

Charles Jones had recently arrived back in Belfast when he heard a newsflash announcing the assassination of ex-RUC Chief Constable George Shalham. Ding-dong! Job done. The man was weak, and Jones had had little or no respect for him. Shalham's replacement, Bonner, didn't take shit from anyone and had been a fellow member of Jones's Orange Lodge for a number of years before moving to Londonderry. Their developing relationship was working out just fine, and it was coincidental but timely that they were due to meet for dinner later that week.

A loud knock on the door made Jones look up to see Lemon. The burly man had done as ordered and gone shopping. There he stood, dressed in black from top to toe – most likely a cheap C&A suit – with a black tie and white shirt. He looked like an undertaker, but it was still a huge improvement. Jones waved him in.

"Come in."

Lemon smiled as he approached the desk, nodded in the direction of Jones's radio and asked gleefully, "S'ppose you've heard the news, boss?"

"I have, Lemon. Yes indeed."

"Bet you're relieved," he answered matter-of-factly.

"I am."

Jones mulled over his success at getting rid of not just Henderson but Shalham too. To the outside world, Henderson's death was a tragic, fatal car crash and Commander Shalham's murder most likely carried out by the Provos.

Henderson had to die after he'd had the temerity to threaten Jones. Shalham's death had been the result of sheer mischance after a terrified lone witness had approached the ex-RUC man directly, telling him they'd seen another car driving Henderson's off the road and down the embankment at Glenshane Pass. Shalham's determination to find out the truth about the death of his best friend's brother had led to his own downfall when he'd started to ask the wrong questions of the wrong people. Once again, Lemon had proved himself more than capable. He was, however, still looking for the witness.

For now, though, Jones suggested Lemon should sit down and discuss with him – amongst other things – the route to the Orange Hall at Newtownhamilton where Jones was due to speak that night.

* * *

Paul Doherty, Rocola's shop steward, watched his boss with concern, noting the man's sagging, glazed eyes. Unusually for him, he was slumped over his desk and looked exhausted. Paul knew he hadn't taken in a word of what had just been said. He waited for some kind of response, but nothing was forthcoming, so he patted his boss lightly on the arm.

"Mr Henderson, sir. Are you okay?"

James jumped at the touch, jerked upright and fell back in his chair. Shit. He'd almost fallen asleep!

Unsurprisingly, following his best friend's horrific murder, Roger had retreated to his bedroom. James had called Marleen, who was holidaying with a girlfriend in Paris, and upon hearing the news, she'd promised to get back to Melrose as soon as she could. Much to her delight, James told her they needed her and to hurry. She knew Penelope, her latest amour, wouldn't be too happy to cut their trip short, but the Hendersons came first.

In the meantime, James had lain awake all weekend on the sofa in Roger's bedroom, nursing and caring for his uncle. Now, embarrassed by his unprofessional behaviour, James was mortified and apologised to Paul.

"I'm so sorry. My uncle hasn't been well this weekend, and I've been sitting up with him. He received some bad news and hasn't taken it too well."

Paul understood, knowing Roger Henderson was a long-time friend of the cop who'd been wiped out near the Strand Road barracks. He'd never met Shalham but had heard he hadn't been a bad 'un, not like that fucker who'd recently replaced him, Bonner. Paul knew what loss was and wouldn't wish it on his worst enemy – he'd lost his only daughter, shot by the Brits on her way home from school, and felt enormous empathy with James and the old man.

"Ah, sure, I know, Mr Henderson. Why don't you call it a day and go home? Get some sleep, and we'll pick this up again tomorrow. Nothing urgent."

The man's suggestion he should go home was like honey to a bee. Paul shook James's hand, sent his condolences to Roger Henderson and left the office. It didn't take long for James to pack up, finish what he had to with Mrs Parkes and make his way back across the bridge and home to Melrose.

* * *

Charles Jones was livid as he waited in his parked car outside an L-shaped, yellow-brick, one-storey building with a Union Jack hoisted and lit up above its red door. They were in the arse end of nowhere, somewhere called Tullyvallen, not Newtownhamilton itself. Jones didn't like the look of it. This place was too exposed against the dark surrounding countryside. He'd assumed the meeting would take place in a Protestant area and was furious to find himself here. The place was minuscule, a fuckin' shed, *and* a total waste of his time. He was used to the grandeur of the seventeenth-century First Derry Presbyterian Church and the like. Who did they think he was?

"Turn back!" he shouted angrily at Lemon. "Take me home. I'm not going anywhere near that place!"

Lemon was confused. He'd assumed his boss knew about the Tullyvallen Orange Lodge – who didn't? They were one of the most dedicated lodges in the Order and well known for their ardent espousal of no surrender or giving up their Queen and country.

Lemon smiled as he recalled their claim to fame. During the Irish War of Independence in 1920, some 200 IRA Volunteers had surrounded and attacked the Royal Irish Constabulary barracks in Newtownhamilton. After a two-hour firefight, the IRA breached the barrack's walls with explosives and stormed the building. But the men inside, all of whom were members of the Tullyvallen Lodge, refused to surrender until the building was set alight with petrol from a potato-spraying machine. A fuckin' potato-spraying machine. Imagine! Lemon laughed.

"What the fuck are you laughing at?" Jones snapped from the back seat.

"Boss, this is one of the most devoted and loyal lodges in the land. Look."

Lemon directed his gaze to the red door that was opening up. A stream of animated-looking men emerged, dressed in dark trousers, smart black jackets, white gloves and wide orange sashes covered in insignia. All of them were wearing black bowler hats. They talked excitedly as they made their way over to the car to welcome Charles Jones. They'd been looking forward to his arrival for weeks.

Fuck! Jones thought. He'd no choice now but to stay. He quickly looked at his watch: 8.30 p.m. Perhaps if he got it right, he'd be home and in bed by 10.30.

* * *

Deep in the trees behind the lodge and not far from Jones's car, two armed men and a woman in camouflage waited for the celebrations to end. They patiently watched Jones and his henchman being welcomed, led up the steps and entering through the unassuming front door of the lodge.

In silence, they waited another ten minutes, making sure the coast was clear. The woman who led the gun party then nodded, and immediately one of the men ran to the side of the building where he'd planted and set a four-pound bomb. Looking left and right, he ran back as low and as fast as he could across the exposed yard to jump and land next to his comrades, well hidden in the shrubbery.

The masked woman looked at her watch and whispered, "Good job. Let's give them half an hour to clap their way into Eternity!"

* * *

George Shalham's funeral took place three days after Marleen arrived at Melrose. It was a suitably solemn affair, but what surprised many was the number of Nationalists who quietly and respectfully stood outside the Protestant Church to mourn the RUC man. Shalham had clearly had more of a unifying effect on Derry than Chief Constable Bonner, and his cronies would ever acknowledge. James had been proud of knowing a man of Shalham's stature. Proud too of his widow Hilda, who held her head high and acted throughout with great dignity.

The pain of her loss was clearly evident afterwards in her red, tear-filled eyes when he and Marleen slowly approached her, along with his uncle, after standing with the long file of mourners queueing to pay their respects to the widow.

"Hilda, our deepest condolences," Roger said sadly.

"Thank you, Roger, James," she answered quietly and nodded to Marleen. She touched Roger's arm lightly and told him, "If you'll wait for me a while, I've something I want you to see."

It was almost an hour before she was able to break free from the well-wishers and find the Hendersons in the press of funeral-goers. She stood very close to them and glanced over her shoulder before sliding her hand into her handbag and pulling out an A5 brown envelope.

"I wanted to give you this, Roger. George was concerned about your brother's accident and took notes of a meeting he had about it with an eyewitness on the scene the night the crash happened. That was the purpose of his visit to Strand Road barracks the day he died – he wanted to share this new information. He was told no one senior was available to talk to him.

"Can you believe that? A proud man and none more loyal to the RUC, but they cut him loose. Completely dismissed his line of enquiry into your brother's death. George didn't tell me everything, he always said it was safer that way, but I thought you should have the notes he made since the police seem determined not to read them."

At her words, Roger's and James's hearts dropped. They looked at each other in confusion but said nothing.

Hilda Shalham was flagging now, grief and the high emotion of the past few hours threatening to overwhelm her. She was dead tired and just wanted to go home.

But before moving on, she looked at the younger man, who closely resembled his dead father as he'd looked thirty years before, and warned: "Be careful, James. I believe whatever George found out, it cost him his life."

James, Roger and Marleen didn't mention the envelope or its contents until they were safely inside James's Jaguar. Marleen was the first to speak, attempting to dismiss the incident. "That was all a bit cloak and dagger, don't you think? I mean, it was a car accident pure and simple."

To her embarrassment, the two men, caught up in their thoughts, didn't respond. By the time they'd driven back to Melrose, Roger was feeling particularly tired and retired to his room.

The men agreed they'd go through the contents of the envelope together before dinner. In the meantime, Marleen poured James a stiff drink, and they sat down in the wood-panelled library.

James was nervously tapping his toes and twisting his hands together. He couldn't wait until Roger woke up to find out what Shalham had discovered and possibly died for. He swigged down his drink hard and fast and rushed to retrieve the envelope from the pocket of his uncle's coat in the hallway.

Marleen raced behind and watched him prise open the envelope.

"I really think you should wait for your Uncle, James. It's what he wanted."

James ignored her. He *had* to know if his father had been murdered. They hadn't always seen eye to eye, but it was his duty as a son to find out all he could about the circumstances of James Snr's death. Shaking with nervous tension, he read through the handwritten notes. Marleen waited, hoping he'd tell her something.

He replaced the notes carefully in the envelope and sealed it as best he could before looking at her. She was dressed in black with her blonde hair pulled into a chignon. She was simply gorgeous, classic chic. Interrupting his thoughts, she tugged on his arm.

"What, James? What does it say!"

Even though they were safe in their own house, he lowered his voice before replying. This was dangerous knowledge.

"That someone saw everything that happened the night father died. A witness. They didn't want to report it since they recognised the person driving a second car present at the scene. Marleen, they saw father being deliberately driven off the road. He was murdered all right."

She gasped. "You can't be serious! Who is this witness?"

"It doesn't say. Just the initials *MG*, and the notes are dated a month ago – that's it."

Marleen slid her arms around him and held him, resting her head on his shoulder.

"Thanks for being here today," he told her. "It meant a lot to us."

She'd have preferred that "us" to have been "me", but James did not pull free from her embrace, she noticed.

"Just try and keep me away," she told him. "I'll have to pop back to London and to see my parents occasionally, but while your uncle's so down, I'm happy to stay for as long as you want me."

James kissed her on the forehead. She's have preferred a proper kiss but… softly, softly.

When he woke up, Roger accepted James's apology for jumping the gun and reading Shalham's notes without him. Over the following weeks, they thought long and hard about what to do until, eventually, Roger came up with an idea. It was risky to some extent, but they'd no choice. He'd never met the man face to face but had heard he was fair and extremely well connected on both sides of the sectarian divide. If anyone could find out what really happened to his brother, Tommy O'Reilly could, Roger said.

He seemed not to know that O'Reilly was Caitlin McLaughlin's beloved uncle, and James decided not to enlighten him. They needed help and, to get it, James was prepared to sup with the Devil himself –

so long as he need never speak to Caitlin again. Paul Doherty at Rocola was tasked with contacting O'Reilly on their behalf and setting up a meeting at the factory.

It proved harder than expected to get O'Reilly's attention. Frustrated at a delay of some months, Roger told Doherty, who had called to fill him in on their current lack of progress: "Well, it's not to be wondered at, I suppose." Meaning that the affairs of Protestant business owners would naturally not be at the top of O'Reilly's "to do" list.

"No indeed," Doherty sighed. "He's taken his sister's death awful hard, and his young niece in Armagh… well, they say her mind's gone. And maybe that's a blessing with a life sentence hanging over her."

Roger felt ashamed. Theirs was far from the only family left to carry a burden of grief, unable to see any glimmer of brightness ahead. O'Reilly had his own troubles; it was plain.

"I'll keep on reminding him for ye," the shop steward promised.

Roger decided not to pin his hopes on it, but while he had this bright and eager young fellow with him, he took the opportunity to question him about the state of Rocola's order book. Not good at all, it seemed, with the Far East encroaching more and more on their traditional markets. But Doherty and James had identified some interesting new prospects…

Roger surprised his nephew over dinner that night by suggesting he recruit an assistant manager to specialise in expanding overseas markets. When James replied that he really didn't have time to place an advert and conduct interviews, Roger told him there was no need. Time for Doherty to come off the shop floor and into the top office. They wouldn't find a smarter candidate.

Chapter 23

It was over a year since Emmett McFadden had been interrogated and beaten by DC Black in Castlereagh – and what a year it'd been!

The policeman had been unsuccessful in compelling Emmett or Mickey to sign anything. Mickey found out later that one of the other poor buggers, arrested the very same day, had given in and signed a confession. Black reluctantly released the remaining three days later in the dead of night, when they were ungraciously thrown from the back of a police jeep somewhere in West Belfast.

Much to Emmett's surprise, Mickey knew exactly where to go, leading him to a tiny corner bar complete with grilled windows, a heavy steel-reinforced front door and security gate – it couldn't exactly be described as inviting. The dive was called The Shamrock Bar. Mickey pressed a loud buzzer and looked up into an outside camera placed high above the door. Within seconds the gate was released, and they entered.

There were very few people in the smoke-filled space as the men made their way to the bar. A well-built, middle-aged barman, who looked fit for his age and wore blue jeans and a red and white Arsenal shirt, watched them. A cigarette hung loosely from his mouth as he nodded to Mickey, indicating for him to go through to a back room.

Obediently Emmett followed, knowing he needed to find a phone and call his mother straight away. She'd be worried sick. They entered a lounge area where, sitting at a small table, were two men. The first was Brian Monaghan and the second Patrick Gillispie. The elder of the two half-smiled at Mickey as he told them to sit down and, in a harsh West Belfast accent, began to question them.

"What happened to ye?"

Mickey coughed and looked at Emmett, nodding his head. "Both of us in Castlereagh, five days. That fucker Black got at us."

The other man shook his head in commiseration. Black was well known by most, if not all, the Volunteers.

"You obviously didn't sign anything then?"

"Nah, and this wee man here didn't either." The cloth-capped man looked at Emmett. There was nothing "wee" about him; he was a hulk of a figure, but on closer inspection, had the face of an angel, albeit he'd clearly been through the mill at the hands of Black. His left eye was swollen and cut, with traces of dried blood. Brian Monaghan could smell the poor critter from where he sat.

"How old are you?" he asked delicately.

Emmett looked at Mickey before answering. Mickey nodded for him to respond.

"Fifteen, nearly sixteen, though."

Jesus, Monaghan thought. "Nearly sixteen, eh? You from Derry too?"

"Aye," Emmett responded. "I need to get to a phone, mister. Me Mammy'll be going off her head, and I need to find out about my brother. Black told me our Joe's been shot trying to escape from the Kesh."

Monaghan knew this to be false straight away; Black was a manipulative bastard. No one'd been shot trying to escape, at least not for a while.

"He's a lying cunt, lad. No one's been shot."

Relief flooded Emmett and replaced his long-suppressed fear. He sat still and silent, staring at the two men as his eyes welled. A single tear quickly ran down his stinging cheek and onto his chest. None of the men said a word but waited respectfully for the young man to regain his composure. Emmett was embarrassed but couldn't help himself. His relief was so huge, more so for his ma – he knew she couldn't handle much more. Monaghan dug in his pocket for some change and told him there was a phone out the back. After that, they could go upstairs to have a wash, find some fresh clothes and a bite to eat.

Emmett didn't hesitate but reached for the coins, mumbling his thanks. He ran through the door in search of the payphone.

Once he was out of the room, Mickey filled the two men in on what had occurred. He was the one who'd shot the young policeman, and they were all behind what he'd done. They talked about the learnings of the operation for a while until Mickey shared an idea with them regarding how they could utilise Emmett – if he were willing to eventually become a fully committed Volunteer.

Mrs McFadden couldn't contain herself when she heard her youngest son's voice. "Ah, Jesus, Emmett, I'd no idea where you were. All I heard was someone saw you being lifted. I've tortured them down in the Strand barracks, but no one would tell me anything! Where are you love?" she cried.

"I'm somewhere in Belfast, Mammy. Mickey, the man they lifted with me, says he'll get me home soon. I'm okay. Don't worry; I'll be back before you know it."

Mother and son continued to reassure each other until the money ran out, and Emmett made his way back to the waiting men.

* * *

Kevin Moore, aka Dickie, opened the brown envelope and looked inside. Happy days! He'd hardly told them anything, just a few names, and *voilà*. Enough to put down a deposit on a beaut of a car he'd seen in Desmond Motors. He quickly put the stuffed envelope into his jacket pocket and made his way to the front door of Porkie's new house in Shantallow. The bus service was slow from the city centre and even more of a reason why Dickie looked forward to having his own set of wheels.

He knocked on the front door and looked back onto the street. He envied his friend this house, everything so new and clean, and begrudged him, even more, the fact that he had Anne for his wife – even with her crummy leg. Dickie had made a few passes at her, but she'd roughly pushed him away and told him to fuck away off. She'd hardly spoken to him since the wedding and always appeared listless and miserable whenever he was about. If he walked into a room, she'd walk out. However, there was something about her rejection that turned him on, and he wasn't giving up.

As for Porkie, since he'd lost his job, he'd become a lazy bastard. The slaughterhouse where he'd worked had to close, given its unfortunate location right in the middle of the Bogside with its continual rioting. The large refrigerated container trucks were constantly being hijacked and looted, so the family owners finally had had no choice but to close. Dickie knew the only way to keep Porkie sweet was to pass him the odd fiver. He'd the upper hand now with extra cash coming in and hoped his new wheels would impress even the cold bitch his pal had married. He'd taken the opportunity this morning to try and get Anne to himself, knowing his friend was in town signing on.

Dickie knocked on the door hard, but still, no one answered. He wasn't going to give up. He'd seen Anne's outline in the window as she'd pulled back the net curtain. He bent down and yelled through the letterbox.

"For Jesus' sake, Anne, let me in! I know you're there!"

She stood rigid with revulsion in the kitchen. She wasn't going to let that repugnant shit into her house, especially when she was on her own. She'd pushed him off numerous times, but Dickie kept on trying to touch her up and was beginning to really frighten her now.

"Anne, let me in!" she heard him cry again impatiently.

* * *

Emmett and Mickey finally made it back to Derry, and the two men continued to cement their friendship once they had settled back home. Since they'd been in Castlereagh, Mickey had been arrested several more times, but fortunately only taken to the Strand Road barracks and – with the help of Brendan Doherty, his solicitor – had been out again relatively quickly.

Mickey always believed in taking things slowly and thinking them through until, finally, after enough time had passed, he'd arranged to catch up with Emmett at his aunt's house in Greencastle in the Republic.

As for Emmett, he'd hardened beyond recognition. He'd never forget Black and his interrogation. He'd lost both his brother and first love Tina McLaughlin to gaol, never knowing when they'd be home, and he missed them both. Tina's uncle Tommy always had time for him, and when they met in town, he would update him on how she was. Emmett had written a couple of letters for him to pass on but never got a reply. It'd been ages since he'd last seen her. His mother wouldn't allow him to go to the trial. His dreams of university were well out the window now as he'd had to leave school to work – his family needed the money. He was working in a garage as an apprentice and had already applied for his provisional licence, hoping to get his full licence as soon as he could.

Mickey had proved to be a good friend, and although Emmett knew he was deeply involved with the Provos, the boy was okay with that. They'd come through a nightmare together, and a special bond had been formed. He was looking forward to catching up and was glad when Mickey took the time to come and see him one day.

"It's good you came down, Mickey. I love this place," Emmett said as they walked together past a derelict Anglo-Norman fort, used on Derry City's crest, that stood on the edge of clear blue Lough Foyle in the Republic of Ireland. On the other side of the shore just three kilometres away was a British Army barracks, Magilligan, not long ago a temporary male internee camp.

Mickey looked around and inhaled the clean air. It was a beautiful evening, alright, and still bright, even at nine o'clock. The sea glistened, and the red sky continually changed colour as the sun began to set. Appreciating the view, he agreed, "It is lovely."

The men walked on a while in silence until Mickey stopped and touched his friend's sleeve.

"There's something I need to ask you, Emmett, and I want you to listen very carefully."

Judging by Mickey's tone, Emmett who'd a feeling for some time that something was up, was about to find out. He noticed Mickey studying him and lifted his chin, encouraging his friend to continue.

"You know I'm involved. Right?"

Emmett nodded, remaining quiet.

"I'd like you to think about becoming a Volunteer, Emmett, fully committed to the Cause. Willing to do whatever we ask."

Mickey waited as his young friend thought about it. Not that long ago, Emmett wouldn't have dreamed of getting involved, but, lately, he'd been so disheartened with what was happening to his city, his family and his friends – not to mention himself – it had made him think. It was only going to get worse. He was tempted but knew he couldn't kill or hurt anybody. He just didn't have it in him.

"Mickey. I… I... I don't know," he stuttered. "I honestly can't imagine me hurting, or worse still, killing someone."

Mickey understood. "I don't want you to kill or hurt anyone, Emmett. Listen to me. I want you to be part of a special unit that very few people know about. You don't ask questions, you don't disobey orders for any reason. You'll be chosen to do very specific jobs, not often, but when asked, you must do them by the book. And that's it! No violence involved, just fetching and carrying for us. You'll need to get that driver's licence of yours as soon as you can."

Emmett was listening intently. His excitement mounted. He wouldn't have to hurt anyone, but by agreeing to drive for the Boys, he could maybe make a difference in this long war. With his comrade beside and looking out for him, he knew he'd be okay.

* * *

Within weeks Emmett McFadden was sworn in as an IRA Volunteer in a secret ceremony in a barn near Sherriff's Mountain. Someone whispered that this was the place where a Brit had been tortured by Kieran Kelly, the nut-job who'd tried to blow up the City Hotel.

As soon as the ceremony was over, Mickey winked and patted him on the shoulder, shaking his hand and welcoming him. "*Fáilte*, Emmett. *Tá fáilte romhat*."

Emmett inhaled sharply, his heart racing. This was it. He was in, and there was no going back. He was now a member of a highly secret Republican unit: the Unknowns.

Chapter 24

Time passed swiftly as the woman known as Brona Doyle continued to work in the 7–11 off-licence. On her rare days off, she made a point of meeting up with Ian to finalise their plans.

Her routine was safe and secure, and she appeared to be well-liked by the customers. She'd even helped the prisoners' defence fund as they went from pub to pub, sticking their collection boxes in people's faces, collecting money. These encounters often proved fruitful, and she shared the intel she gathered with Det, identifying particular faces, their cars and local haunts.

Patrick Gillispie would come and then go for weeks on end. Not once did she ask where he was or what he was doing, and, as a result, he began to trust her more. They'd been out a few times together, to a couple of dance halls and to see some of the showbands that were brave enough to come to the North. She'd even met his twin, Dolores, four minutes younger than him. From the outset, she experienced distrust and animosity from the woman who was unbelievably overprotective of her elder brother. She could be a problem.

Tonight Alice and Patrick were sitting together having drinks in The Shamrock, Patrick's local. It was a dive but a valuable place for Alice as she scanned the room filled with a stream of lively chatter. She was able to identify at least three of the men as active Provos. They'd gathered at the bar, laughing while they discussed the latest Gaelic result.

Patrick took her hand and squeezed it. "You okay, love?"

She squeezed back. "I'm fine. Bit hungry, that's all."

Pointing to his remaining pint of Guinness, Patrick told her he'd finish it soon, and they'd be off, but he needed the toilet first.

Her eyes followed him as he moved confidently across the bar dressed in a dark green duffel coat and flat Donegal tweed cap. He nodded to the barman and headed in the opposite direction from the toilets. What was he up to?

About to rise and follow, she was suddenly pushed back into her seat and held down by Patrick's twin. Dolores was slim, medium height, and much younger-looking than her twin with long, straight brown hair. Her brown eyes and high cheekbones complemented her oval face and wide mouth.

"Where you off to then?" she asked sharply.

"Toilet," Alice replied, yanking her arm free from the woman's grasp.

Dolores waved to the back of the bar. "Ladies is that way."

She sat down and moved in close to Alice's face, whispering maliciously,

"There's something about you, Brona Doyle, something I don't like. And I swear to Jesus, I... will... find... out."

Unusually for Alice, she felt frightened and exposed. She wasn't prepared to show her fear, though. Instead, her eyebrows went up, and she sat back, assuming a listening position as she asked calmly: "What the fuck are you on about, Dolores?"

In response, Patrick's twin gave her a look of contempt. Pretending to aim a gun, she pointed one finger at the side of Brona's head as she whispered, slowly and intimidatingly, "*Bang. Bang.*"

Nothing more was said, but Dolores's eyes remained firmly fixed on the other woman's until she was grabbed and taken away by a young drunk, singing loud rebel songs and pleading for her to join him.

Alice couldn't move. She sat frozen to the spot. She was sure she could hear her heart thumping. Her eyes were jumping all over the bar, wondering if these people knew, if they really knew, who she was. She could hear her ragged breath rising and falling, unaware that Patrick had returned and was standing by the doorway staring at her uneasily.

"Jesus, Brona, you look like you've seen a ghost! You alright?"

She shook her head and pulled herself together. "Course, yes, just hungry like I said. Let's go."

Within seconds she'd her faux-fur leopard jacket on. She shivered as they stood outside the pub in the rain. She couldn't get warm; the cheap thin nylon fabric of her coat was keeping her neither warm nor dry.

Patrick took her by the arm and led her down the street. They both walked fast with their heads bowed against the rain. Soon they were in their favourite fish and chip shop. He instructed her to sit down at a table by the window and warm up whilst he went to the counter and ordered their usual.

* * *

Ian Dillon and his four UDR-uniformed accomplices were ready and waiting for the mini-bus to make its way towards them. It was 1 a.m., and they'd set up a checkpoint on one of the main roads, inside the Northern Irish border, that connected Newry to the Dublin road. The plan had been laid carefully and meticulously by Ian and Alice. The target was a young and successful Gaelic Football team, who regularly travelled back and forth across the border playing the Nationalist game. Up to now, given the late hour, the uniformed men had only come across a few cars and quickly waved them through.

Ian listened in silence as he thought he heard a vehicle approach and warned his men,

"I think this is it, gents. Get ready." He so wished that Alice was with them all; she'd have loved it but understood she couldn't, given that she was otherwise occupied!

On his order, men armed with machine guns stood in the middle of the road and watched a set of headlights making their way closer and closer. In the silence of the country road, they heard loud singing and laughter emanating from the vehicle, whose registration number they already knew.

Ian nodded to his men, stood out front and flagged the old mini-van down with his torch.

The vehicle slowly came to a halt, and the driver's window was sluggishly and awkwardly rolled down. Ian raised his torch to see a black-haired, square-faced man with twinkling pale blue eyes, who was smiling and clearly thinking: *It'll be okay, I've only had a half-pint, nowhere over the limit.*

"Mornin'," he said jovially over the giggles and laughter of the young players in the back.

"Morning, sir," Ian answered. "Can I ask you and your passengers to get out of the van, please?"

The driver sighed; they just wanted to get home. The *craic* had been great and to win the game even better. One of the young men protested from the back at the request to get out, but the driver shushed him.

"Come on, lads. Let's do this quickly, and we'll get home sooner!"

Ian watched the driver and the tired but merry youngsters climb out. He told them to step aside from the vehicle. Pointing to the top of an embankment at the edge of the road, he ordered them to wait there, allowing his colleagues to search the small bus, including its contents.

One of the young men, slightly inebriated because he'd sneaked a few quick ones whilst Dermott, their trainer and driver, wasn't looking, attempted to make eye contact with Ian. He proudly sang, "Tell them, tell them, we've just won The Cup!"

Dermott and the remainder of the team yelped and jeered, some whistling up into the clear night sky.

Ian's uniformed men briefly caught his knowing smile when the team's world turned searing red hot. An almighty explosion raged as their van disintegrated into a million pieces. In slow motion, Dermott found himself flying high into the air and landing hard and fast at the bottom of the embankment. His eyeballs pounded, blood exploded from his head, and a blazing heat wrapped itself around him.

Mayhem ensued as wild, random white tracer shots cut through the air. Voices screamed and screeched as bodies danced under the impact of the dum-dum bullets that came scything in from all directions and riddled the young men. Soon they fell to the ground, carpeting it in bloodied bodies.

Dermot ran screaming up the embankment, dodging the bullets, attempting to get to his boys. The shooting suddenly stopped and the air filled with cries for mercy. He couldn't move as he watched Liam Murphy, the drunken lad who'd been so proud only moments earlier, his upraised palms a horrifying crimson red, pleading with the black shadow that was slowly approaching him.

"Please, please, don't shoot!"

A single shot rang out against the crackling and sizzling sounds of the burning bus.

At the top of the embankment, Dermot ducked down to hide from the assassins and, in sorrow, placed his face on the rough grass and cried. Hearing voices, he slowly and carefully raised his head to watch as the leader of the murderous uniformed squad strode confidently over to another man to ask: "Are you sure we got all the bastards?"

* * *

The following morning, the newspapers and TV channels were full of images and interviews about the bloodbath. Six young men, all seventeen years or under, murdered, shot to pieces, and no one had as yet claimed responsibility. Although the mission hadn't been one hundred per cent successful, Ian thought it wasn't a bad result even with the loss of two of their own men: the bomb they were planting in the van going off prematurely. Other than that, they'd made their point and had learned valuable lessons for the next time.

Back in Belfast, Alice was leaning over the counter reading the *Belfast Telegraph*. Not bad, Ian. Not bad at all, she thought. She'd agreed with him that they wouldn't make contact for a number of weeks after the hit. Given Dolores's behaviour the other evening, Det had advised Alice to lie low and not to report in unless she was in fear of her life. Patrick had gone off again but said he'd be back at the weekend. He had a surprise for her.

She made some tea, sat down and reopened the paper. Earlier that morning, she'd seen the driver's TV interview, constantly repeated over and over on all of the channels, detailing his horrific experience. His curly black hair was singed, and blood caked his blistered, charred face and stuck to his beard. He couldn't stop shuddering and sobbing as he told his rambling tale.

"I heard them! I'm telling ye, I heard them making sure they were dead! I heard my boys screaming for help!"

Alice felt nothing but contempt. Mission almost accomplished. Next time they'd be more careful about their mopping up.

* * *

Later that day, the buzzer in the shop went, and she looked over to see Dolores waiting impatiently outside. Here goes, Alice thought as she reluctantly let the woman in.

"How are you doing, Dolores?" she asked, not that she gave a flying fuck.

Dolores ignored the question but appeared agitated and tense as she asked, "Is Patrick here?"

"You mean, for once, you don't know where your Patrick is!" Alice answered in surprise.

Dolores smiled – a smile that was too wide – making her way round to the back of the counter as if to assault Alice. She was so ready for Dolores but knew she mustn't make a move. She'd spent too many months building up the trust of these people. She wasn't going to throw in the towel now, not for this weirdo.

Dolores planted herself menacingly full in Alice's face and mouthed, "Fuck off." And then she was gone.

Alice sighed with relief as the door closed behind her. It was the first time Dolores had ever come to the shop, and it *was* rare for her not to know Patrick's whereabouts. She paused, considering the possibilities. Something was up, and she was going to find out what it was.

Chapter 25

"Forgive me, Father, for I have sinned. It's been a *very, very* long time since my last confession…" Martin McLaughlin said, smirking as he sat in the darkened confessional in St Mary's.

On the other side of the grille sat Father Connolly. He didn't find it funny when McLaughlin took the piss. "Not amusing. And put that cigarette out!" he told him sharply.

Martin had forgotten the fag was still lit and burning as he held it between his lips. He knew he shouldn't take liberties and quickly put it out, whispering an apology. "Sorry, Father. Just a joke."

Father Connolly remained silent and annoyed. Martin chuckled softly at the priest's lack of humour and began to update him on the latest cache of arms on the way from the US.

"The boat got stopped by three Irish Navy patrol vessels just outside County Waterford, Father. All of them lifted, including Brian Meenan, and taken to Dublin. At least the last three loads got through, including one with a couple of those RPG7 rockets – we've only had a few of them to date, and they're lethal. It's likely that'll be the last shipment for a while now that the authorities have cottoned on."

The priest was miffed, knowing McLaughlin was right. It'd be some time before they'd try again, and it made sense to wait. The only blessing was some crew members on the *QEII* were still managing to get some small consignments of Armalite rifles from the US to the UK. The arms were picked up and driven from Southampton to Belfast without any problems – but there were too few of them.

"You're right, Martin. We need to lie low. I'm due to go to Boston the week after next. We'll have to rethink. By the way, did we find out who killed that policeman, Shalham?"

Since being present at the man's death, Father Connolly had kept tabs on the investigation surrounding Shalham's death. He'd been told there'd been a quiet but unspoken respect for the Chief Constable amongst the Nationalist community. Shalham had done his best for the city, including issuing a formal warning to his superiors that the Parachute Regiment shouldn't come near Derry – *full stop*. His advice was ignored, and Bloody Sunday was the result. He'd been blamed for the mess of the failed bomb attempt on the City Hotel and had been put out to retire. Those in the know were well aware it'd been his idea to apply for government funding to keep Rocola open, thereby saving thousands of Catholic jobs.

Following the shooting, Connolly kept revisiting the scene in his dreams. The man's shattered body, his blood-streaked face as he'd gazed fixedly at the Catholic priest who'd tried to bring him consolation in his dying moments. He'd been intent on saying something with his failing breath. If only it'd been a little clearer. Connolly could see it was something important. He'd even visited Shalham's widow later on and told her what her husband had said, but she too had no idea or little clue who "Jo" could be.

Martin was quick to dismiss any connection to Shalham's murder. "We don't know anything about that. He wasn't on our radar. Not us, Padre."

They spoke a while longer until Father Moore arrived in the church, calling out for his colleague. At the disruption, Martin quickly left the confessional and slipped into a pew with his back to the flustered young priest who was stomping down the aisle in search of Father Connolly.

Martin still hadn't gone home or contacted any of his family after successfully completing the delivery of the arms cache in Kerry. Instead, he'd spent weeks hiding out, going back and forth between a number of safe houses in the city and just over the border. No one recognised him, and fortunately, the US donations ensured he had enough cash to keep himself smart and clean. He'd also promised Sinead, Brian

Meenan's sister of whom he'd grown fond, that he'd keep well away from the booze. Drink made him vulnerable, he knew, and he couldn't afford to make any mistakes.

For some time, and from a distance, he'd kept an eye on Caitlin. When he'd initially seen her coming out of the photographer's shop where she worked, he'd been pleasantly surprised. There was nothing left now of the skinny girl he remembered. She was a striking-looking woman, turning heads in the street wherever she passed by. He'd noticed, though, that she escaped the usual banter and deliberately crude remarks often thrown at good-looking women by men who wouldn't stand a chance with them. There was something about Caitlin – the sense that she'd been touched by tragedy – that kept the gobshites at bay.

On the boat to Kerry, Seamus had told him he was keen for the two of them to get back together but was taking things slowly. Caitlin remained fragile, and he didn't want to rush her.

* * *

Earlier that day, Martin had visited his parents' grave in the city cemetery. Standing over the neatly trimmed grave and reading its headstone in the dull September light, he could barely believe they were both gone, the twin pillars of his early life, now just a tangle of bones in the boggy soil.

As for his younger sister, he'd been told by a woman who kept a safe house and had been released from Armagh earlier that year that Tina was doing okay, better than when she'd first arrived in gaol. She'd told him that the poor girl was damaged by her experiences at the hands of Kelly and then by the justice system but that the women in Armagh looked out for her. Martin knew Tina had always hero-worshipped him and recalled the many times he'd played jokes on her to wind her up. She always fell for them and still adored him like a puppy. There were times when he'd deliberately taken advantage of her soft spot for him, sending her out in all weathers for his cigarettes and beer, and he felt piercing regret for that now as well as for the many tales of Republican exploits he'd raised her on. He'd never meant for her to follow in his footsteps. His little sister, sentenced to life imprisonment… Christ, but it was a cruel place their small world had become.

And tonight was the night Seamus had suggested he should finally visit Blamfield Street. Martin couldn't describe the way he felt at that prospect. It was a muddle of emotions: shame, excitement, fear. He was early but knocked on his old front door anyway and stepped back, holding a box of Quality Street before him like a shield. The door opened, and there she was, transfixed by astonishment.

"Hello, Caitlin," he said contritely.

She stood motionless at the door until Seamus came up behind her and impatiently peered over her shoulder. As soon as he saw Martin, he pulled Caitlin back and reached forward eagerly to shake his hand.

"Ah, Martin, there you are!" he said enthusiastically. "Good to see you – sure it's been a while." And then, with a wink of collusion while Caitlin's attention was still fixed on the caller, "Jesus, Caitlin, let your brother in!"

Her heart was racing. Like Seamus, her brother looked very different these days. He was immaculate and well-groomed and, like a ninny, stood on their doorstep holding a box of chocolates, waiting to be allowed in. *He wouldn't have done that before.* She'd heard rumours he was back. Dazed, she opened the door wider.

"You'd better come in then."

Martin exhaled sharply and sniffed. He wiped his nose using a white handkerchief he dug from deep within his pocket.

"Sorry. Thanks."

He walked along the familiar hallway straight to the kitchen and looked around. It was exactly the same; nothing had changed: the round table, the six cushioned chairs, the red Liverpool FC mugs that he and his dad got one Christmas, the holy picture of the Pope on the wall. It looked exactly the same but wasn't. This place felt soulless and steeped in sadness.

He half expected his mother or father to walk in or to hear them shout from upstairs. His heart sank like lead as the reality of losing them hit him again. What a selfish bastard he'd been! What a completely selfish bastard, leaving Caitlin on her own in this tomb!

He sat down in his usual chair and waited in silence while she put the kettle on, and Seamus helped her make the tea. Finally, all three of them sat at the table in awkward silence. It was up to Martin to start.

"I'm sorry you had to deal with Mammy, you know what I mean, the funeral an' all. I'm especially sorry for not being in touch since…"

Here Caitlin interrupted, asking crossly, "But where were you, Martin? Where *were* you!"

"In America. I couldn't stay here, Caitlin. The police and that lot have it in for me. I had to get far away."

"And they've no post or phones in America?" she asked sarcastically. Seamus, in his determination to bring together what was left of the McLaughlin family, quickly intervened.

"Sure, Caitlin, the most important thing is that Martin's here now. Isn't it?"

She looked at him and wondered. Why was Seamus so all of a sudden friendly with Martin? Had he seen him before tonight? America, eh? They'd both been in America…

She considered her choices. She could tell her brother to fuck off or choose to let it go. Finally, after thinking long and hard, she gave a nod. She was genuinely pleased to see her brother looking so cleaned up and, after all, other than poor Tina, he was all the family she had left.

She stood up and opened her arms to him. Martin, wet-eyed at such an act of forgiveness, hugged and held her tight.

Seamus watched the scene in delight. He'd been shitting himself all day, unsure of how he was going to tell Caitlin her brother was back. *Thank God.*

The tea was soon served and Martin, never taking his eyes off Caitlin, asked her question after question about how she'd been doing.

Once she'd finished her tale, he gently took her hand and squeezed it in an effort to reassure her he was here, he would protect her – and over his dead body would he let her down again.

Chapter 26

The two men sat in Porkie's new kitchen finishing off a large bottle of Jameson. Neither of them was drunk – as yet.

Anne, pregnant and miserable, had left them to it hours earlier and disappeared upstairs for some peace. She could hear Dickie's voice getting louder and louder below as the night wore on and her husband's sycophantic laughter in response.

Over the months, Porkie had gone from bad to worse. At first, his demands in bed had been outrageous, and she'd got to the stage where she'd just give in, to get it over with, in the hope he'd soon fall asleep. He couldn't find work, and they were living on the breadline. She'd tried to talk to him about Dickie's visits and how he'd continually bang on the door, insisting on being let in. But Porkie was having none of it, shrugging off her complaints and telling her his friend was harmless and to stop being so dramatic. She'd loved her new house when they'd first arrived, but now she felt like a bird in a cage.

Looking around, she took in their sparse bedroom. The cotton curtains barely kept in the heat, and the thin carpet was worn. Everything, including the furniture, was second-hand – even the bedclothes. They were still stained no matter how many times she'd bleached them. Everything here was horrible; the whole place was horrible. And Shantallow had meant to be the start of a new life for them.

That morning Anne had been refused credit in the local mobile shop. Although she paid the bill every Friday when they got Porkie's Giro, they'd end up using credit for the week ahead, and so it became a vicious circle. She looked at the small red exercise book on her bedside table. The owner of the shop would list what Anne bought and tally it up at the end of the week to be paid. Up until today, she had relied totally on that credit to buy the necessities of life, and now the old bat had stopped it. Mrs Divine gave no reason, just said that she wouldn't do it anymore. Of course, she'd told her that just after Anne had paid last week's bill, and now she was left with exactly £3.22 to get them through the week ahead. She had to pay to top up the electric meter, the TV meter, pay the *Pru man* as the local insurance man was called and who called like clock-work every Monday tea-time plus of course pay for their food – it was daunting.

At first, she'd been afraid to tell Porkie she was pregnant when they were so short of money and had imagined the prospect of a baby would send him through the roof. However, to her absolute surprise, he was delighted by the news and left her to get on with it. He was old fashioned when it came to "women's stuff", so he moved into the small box bedroom once her body started to change shape. He told her he didn't want to harm the baby and his sexual demands decreased.

The relief had been overwhelming; she even felt a small flicker of gratitude. Now she had just over two months to go. Two months when she could feel safe from his physical proximity and unwelcome attentions. But tonight, the noise in the kitchen below was growing so loud she couldn't take it anymore. The neighbours, who'd at first been so lovely and friendly, ignored her these days. They'd enough of Dickie's shouting and banging on her door and his foul language whenever they'd asked him politely to go away.

Anne awkwardly made her way down the stairs. For some unexplained reason, instead of going straight into the kitchen to remonstrate with them, she stood outside the closed door and listened carefully. It was Porkie's voice she heard first. He sounded upset.

"I can't, Dickie, have you *any* idea, *any idea at all,* what they'd do to you if they found out?" Anne stood frozen and fixed to the spot. What on earth…!

"But it's easy money, man, money that you could be doing with now you've a wain on the way. Think about it. Just watch and listen, then tell them what you see and hear. No one'll ever find out. Easy cash."

Porkie was silent for a moment. His friend was right in a way. They desperately needed money, but to do what Dickie was suggesting… It was a seriously dangerous game, and Porkie knew he was too much of a coward to grass anyone up. They'd all heard about the punishment beatings and shootings of anyone found colluding with the authorities.

He poured himself another long, straight whiskey, greedily gulping it down until it took effect, and he began to feel more cocky. Why not find out more and fuck the risk? He needed the cash, and it *was* a way out of his pressing difficulties with the local bookies as well as providing for his wife and child.

"Tell me then, Dickie. How does this game work?" he slurred.

Dickie knew he'd snared his friend beautifully *and* earned himself a bonus. He'd been encouraged to recruit at least three people willing to pass on information, a cash sum to be paid for each new grass. But Porkie was the first and only person Dickie would take on. He wasn't that stupid; Porkie as his sole associate would do just fine.

"All you do is, like, sit in a bar, listen and watch what's going on. Everywhere you go, just watch and listen. We both know who's involved and who isn't. Simple as that. I tell you what; you won't even have to deal with the Brits. I'll do it. You tell me what you've seen or heard, and I'll pass it on. Jesus, Porkie, I've made a small fortune already. I mean, look at what's parked outside!"

Porkie had been well jealous when Dickie bought the car – maybe he could get one too… Dickie laughed, knowing exactly what his friend was thinking. He had him now, caught hook, line and sinker.

When Dickie finally got the car from Desmond Motors, he'd been thrilled to bits, telling everyone he'd won a wee bit on the football pools. People believed him and were happy for him. They knew he was a bit thick, but never in a million years would they think he'd be dumb enough to be a grass. He grew up in the same streets as them, and they'd all gone to the same schools; he was a Creggan man through and through.

Nudging Porkie along, Dickie continued, "Think about it! You'd be mad not to!"

Outside, Anne hesitated, with her hand on the doorhandle. Should she go in and tell the two thick morons what she'd heard, or should she leave it? All she knew was that she could never be a part of this. Grassing to the Brits was for the lowest of the low. Over her dead body, would she taint herself like that. She crept upstairs to her bed and started to think hard.

Meanwhile, in the kitchen, another large Jameson was poured into Porkie's glass. Dickie had caught his friend and now needed to reel him in until he was fully committed. He moved closer, and Porkie tensed, his head spinning. He didn't know what to do. Ah, fuck it. They needed the money, and he was sure Anne would understand – she'd have to. He'd tell her in the morning. He looked at Dickie and saw a flicker of anticipation in his expression. Porkie shrugged his assent, though it was barely perceptible.

"Okay," he whispered.

Dickie immediately raised his glass to seal the deal, and as the glasses clinked, they toasted each other: "*Sláinte*!"

Upstairs in bed, the baby kicked hard in Anne's stomach, and she smiled. The thought of a new arrival gave her a sense of purpose, the need to keep herself safe and well. Anne concluded she'd no choice but to tell someone. It was perfect, a way out of this hell hole. If Porkie joined Dickie and became a grass for the British, she could get rid of them both.

* * *

The following morning, the large bottle of Jameson still stood prominently in the middle of the kitchen table, empty now. The sight of the two smeared glasses beside it made Porkie feel even worse than he did already. His head ached, his stomach churned and cramped. He carefully shook his tender head and asked no one in particular, "Jesus… why?"

His wife failed to answer but sat down opposite him, staring stonily at his useless hulk.

Porkie stared back defiantly and asked, "*What*!"

He leaned back in his chair, closing his eyes for a moment and praying she wasn't going to start. Anne moved her chair a little closer to his and continued to stare straight into his eyes before asking, "Porkie, what were you and Dickie talking about last night?"

His eyes widened as he wondered what she was referring to until a flash of memory hit him like a train. *Fuck*!

Anne waited. It was his choice. He could come clean and tell her, and she could tell him to wise up. Or he could dig his own grave.

He lied to her through his teeth. "It was nothing, Anne, honest. Just the usual rubbish." He swallowed loudly. It was too late to change his mind. He couldn't go back on his word, or Dickie would never forgive him.

Anne shook her head in disappointment. She got up and was about to go towards the sink when suddenly he grabbed her hand and pulled her back to him. In a rare, loving moment, Porkie touched her stomach with the palm of his hand, pulled her closer and placed a gentle kiss on their unborn child.

* * *

Later that day, Anne visited her mum. Liz was thrilled her daughter was pregnant even though she knew Anne was unhappy to be dealing not just with Porkie but his creepy sidekick too. A baby would give her daughter the chance to focus on something else, Liz told herself.

The Heaneys' house had grown more and more quiet as Anne's siblings grew up and left Derry to find work. A few of the younger children were still about and loved playing in the streets. The girls would swing around lamp posts on ropes until their little bottoms became too sore. They'd skip or play hopscotch whilst the boys pretended to be soldiers with sticks or wooden guns or went speeding up and down hills in their homemade go-carts.

Later, on her way back to Shantallow, Anne passed St Mary's Church and remembered her wedding day. It felt a lifetime ago.

It was nearly five o'clock, and suddenly she felt the urgent need to go to Confession. What if she were to tell a priest what she'd overheard last night? At least that way, she'd be able to rid herself of this heavy, dreadful weight of guilt. Grassing on their own community… She knew sooner or later a grass was always caught and punished. Porkie had been so sweet this morning, but he'd clearly decided to join his mate working for the British and that put her and their child in danger too. Everyone would think she was involved or else knew about it. She had to tell someone. She had to protect her unborn baby.

For ten or fifteen minutes, Anne sat forlornly on a wooden bench just inside the churchyard until she'd made her decision. Yes, she'd tell a priest. He'd likely give her good advice, and, most importantly, he couldn't tell anyone else since the secrets of the confessional were sacrosanct.

Feeling relieved to have made up her mind, Anne went into the church and queued up for Confession. She noticed it was Father Connolly's turn to hear it. She'd never met him but had heard about him from Caitlin, who'd said he'd been a rock when Majella died. Not being able to kneel in her condition, Anne sat back, lowered her head and sought the intercession of Saint Bernadette, her favourite saint, soon becoming lost in prayer.

Inside the confessional box, Father Connolly had just finished instructing a parishioner to say three Hail Marys and three Our Fathers. It was the same old stuff: stealing someone's milk from the doorstep, hiding away the drink and swearing on all the angels and saints that they were staying sober, or else the kids dobbing school or bullying.

No major sins, just the usual day-to-day offences against God. He was tired today as it'd been a particularly tough week. Someone out there was grassing, and there'd been a number of failed, low-key missions.

He exited the box and saw a young pregnant woman waiting. She was so deep in prayer he almost didn't want to disturb her, but she looked up and caught his eye. He smiled at her and watched as she stood up awkwardly and limped her way towards him. For a brief second, he was taken aback when he saw her artificial limb but quickly smiled again, his eyes filled with warmth and understanding.

"Hello there," he said, welcoming her. Anne noticed the moment of sympathy for the loss of her leg. She was used to seeing that, and it didn't bother her anymore. What she did like were his eyes. They were honest eyes. She knew she'd found a confessor she could trust.

Chapter 27

Following the savage assault on Bridget and their separation, life changed dramatically for Tina McLaughlin.

Her two new cellmates proved to be resentful of her and continually found fault with her for impinging on their precious space. They weren't political prisoners but two sisters who'd been sentenced to a life stretch. No one knew yet what they were in for, except they didn't come under the protection and authority of any OC. They thought it ridiculous the way they'd been forced to find space to put another bed in the tiny cell. It was a blessing Tina had so few possessions.

* * *

Late the morning after Bridget was attacked, the OC had been to see Governor Johnston and had then escorted Bridget to the medical room. Dr Harris had unceremoniously and without a shred of empathy checked the woman's wounds. There was severe internal damage, and he recorded in her notes: "*... gashing and ripping, likely internal penetration of an appliance of sorts causing severe bruising, bleeding and damage to genitalia. Cause unknown. Query self-inflicted?*"

He admitted – if only to himself – that the woman had been badly hurt, but nothing that wouldn't heal in the long term. And so he'd simply handed her a few paracetamols and told her she'd be okay in a week or two. Bridget remained silent throughout the examination as the OC watched on. Harris was a worm; everyone knew it. There was no point in harassing him and causing a scene at his lack of compassion. More importantly, Maureen didn't want to distress Bridget further. She looked at her poor violated friend and felt overwhelmed with sadness. She couldn't grasp how, in God's name, one woman could do such a merciless thing to another. It was beyond comprehension.

Governor Johnston, though well aware that someone had been seriously injured, refused to investigate the circumstances. A female prison officer committing an act of sexual violence on an inmate? Such things were impossible surely; the mere thought of it made him sick. *Nothing like that could ever happen in Armagh*! Just the thought of the story passing beyond the prison's stone walls caused his stomach to churn, wringing his burning ulcers. *Over his dead body!*

Ultimately, like Harris, he'd been of no use to the woman treated so cruelly while under his care, stonewalling anything Maureen Molony said and fobbing her off with platitudes. "I've already seen Father McGuire and assured him there'll be a full investigation into these claims." *He'd no intention of doing anything of the sort.* "I've got to warn you; however, I've been assured by my staff that Mrs Barry had been particularly violent and assaulted one of our new recruits. I won't have it, Mrs Molony, fact."

But Maureen wouldn't take no for an answer.

"With respect, I won't have it either, sir. Let me talk to Martina McLaughlin. She was there when it happened. She'll confirm what Bridget said, I've no doubt, and let's be honest: we both know any investigation wouldn't be an independent one. Leave it to me to investigate the facts. Let me deal with this, please."

She'd watched as he consulted his watch impatiently. Most likely due on the golf course. "You can't expect me to believe anything McLaughlin says, Mrs Molony. The girl's not all there."

Maureen could only shake her head sadly and again try to reason with him. "Have you seen Bridget for yourself, Mr Johnston? She's like a broken rag-doll! Refusing to speak, refusing to eat. She's all but lifeless – and she was one of the strongest women here before this happened."

Johnston's patience was running out. He was late for his next meeting and tapped the table with his index finger whilst considering her words. He knew from experience the woman sitting opposite wouldn't let this go. Throwing up his hands, he gave in and said,

"Okay, have it your way. Talk to McLaughlin. See what she's got to say. You sort it and report back to me. Now leave me in peace!"

The OC smiled victoriously and left his office before he'd the chance to change his mind.

* * *

Although Johnston had agreed that Maureen could talk to Tina, it took a frustrating three weeks before she had the opportunity. Tina hadn't been well since the attack on her friend and had refused to leave her cell. Every time the OC tried to see her or talk to the Governor again, she'd been stopped from coming off her wing.

That was until one day Tina was forcibly thrown out of her new cell by her two uncaring cellmates, who refused to put up with her presence anymore. They'd slung her bedclothes and meagre belongings after her onto the walkway. And so, in desperation, Tina retreated to the warmth of the laundry carrying just a few possessions that fell carelessly and unnoticed along the catwalk.

To Maureen Molony's relief, she looked up and noticed Tina wandering around looking lost. She'd been hard at work in the hot and steamy room, and when she saw the youngin', she pulled her swiftly into a corner so they could have a private talk. Tina looked every bit as bad as Bridget. Her eyes were red and raw-looking. She'd lost all the weight she'd managed to gain when she was settled and looked after, the results of months of Bridget's loving care now lost. The youngin' had mentally retreated back into her safe place. The OC wasn't even sure she was fully aware of where she was. Treading carefully, she began to question Tina about the night of Bridget's assault.

"How are you feeling, love?"

Tina looked at the woman next to her and thought how pretty she was. She had kind eyes and was holding her hand. Tina liked that. It made her feel safe. Sweat ran down the woman's brow, and Tina gently lifted a hand and wiped it away with one finger.

Maureen smiled at the childlike gesture and repeated, "Tina. Are you okay?"

She smiled, stared down at the floor and answered, in a voice barely above a whisper, "I'm okay."

This was going to take longer and be more difficult than Maureen had thought. She took the girl's hand and asked in an encouraging tone, "You remember me, Tina, don't you?"

She looked at the pretty woman, considering.

"I'm not sure."

"Tina, you're with me and the other girls in Armagh Gaol. We've been looking after you, all the girls but especially me and Bridget. You remember Bridget, don't you?"

A terrifying memory returned as soon as the girl heard that name. Bridget… poor, poor Bridget! She leaned forward, crossed her arms tightly around herself and began to sway back and forth.

Maureen could see she was remembering what had happened and quickly pursued it. "That's it, youngin' – Bridget. I need you to tell me what happened to her. Can you do that for me, honey?"

Tina's face contorted as tears ran freely down her cheek. She stared vacantly ahead of her as the horrible scene played out again in front of her staring eyes.

* * *

On his usual Tuesday visit following the Bank Holiday, Father McGuire was briefed by the OC. He was distraught when he heard what had happened and visited Bridget once she'd returned from the medical centre. He could make out her huddled outline wrapped tightly round with coarse brown blankets. *What a pitiful sight.* He nodded at the women who sat with her and asked them politely to leave. Sitting down at the bottom of the iron-framed bed, he took out his Bible from his briefcase and held it close to his chest as he whispered, "Bridget. It's Father McGuire."

From childhood, it'd been instilled in Bridget and her siblings always to respect the Church. She couldn't ignore the elderly priest and so, slowly and carefully, raised herself to a seated position. It took a second or two for her to focus, her face screwing up at the pain deep inside her. A flicker of a smile crossed her face as she noticed the tear-filled eyes of her confessor – poor creature; he'd a soft heart for a priest.

She glanced down at her hands, unable to look him in the eye since he'd know everything, and she was ashamed. Her hands shook slightly as she said, "Hello, Father."

"Hello, Bridget. I'm so sorry about what has happened," the old man replied sadly. He swallowed, not sure what else to say or do.

Bridget shrugged. "Nothing to be said, Father. What's done is done."

"I've seen Governor Johnston. He's told me there'll be an investigation. You know he's a good man. He'll see it through."

Bridget admired the old priest's blind trust in the establishment. She knew there'd never be an independent investigation into the violent abuse she'd suffered. It'd likely fall back on her. They'd blame her, say she'd been obstreperous and had been injured while trying to stop them from taking the youngin' away.

She made no comment about the investigation but asked in a worried tone, "The youngin', Father. Tina, is she okay?"

He hadn't seen her yet but imagined what he'd find now. At times, his faith was well and truly tested, and this was one of those times. He'd seen such an improvement in the wee girl, and it was all down to this damaged woman and the others. A buried memory of Tina at her First Communion suddenly sprang into his mind, and he could picture her hair, that glorious long thick curling red hair that Majella McLaughlin had struggled so hard to control. His throat contracted with the pity of it all.

"I haven't seen Tina yet, but she's next on my list. Meanwhile, is there anything at all I can do for you, Bridget?"

He was struck to his soul when in a faint voice, she told him, “Yes, Father, you can. Just get me out of here, will you? I can’t do this anymore.”

* * *

Back in the laundry room, Maureen continued to interview Tina. Officer Quirk saw them deep in conversation and made her way over to stand nearby – not so close as to intrude but enough to hear what was being said. The OC and screw acknowledged each other with a quick nod.

Quirk already knew what had occurred in the cell. She was mortified at the way Smyth and her collaborator Gladys Drake openly joked about it in the locker room. Quirk had had enough of their sick behaviour and wanted to help but had to be careful to watch her own back as well. She knew any officer who snitched on her workmates would live to regret it.

Chapter 28

Charles Jones stared at his reflection. What was left of his face was now hideously patchworked by the first series of skin grafts. In places, his raw new flesh shimmered in the light. His right eye was red and bloodshot and drooping, clear fluid continually flowing from it. The shattered cheekbone beneath had been reconstructed but looked odd and out of line with the other. The distinctive pointed tip of his nose had been lost, and it was now flat-ended.

At times, he felt it would've been better if he'd been blown to smithereens or shot to pieces like others in the Orange Hall on that November evening.

He'd been coming to the end of his speech and, surprisingly after his early misgivings, enjoying himself before the rapt audience when two masked gunmen burst in carrying assault rifles and began to spray the hall with bullets. In addition, a side window was smashed in by another rifle, followed by a torrent of random gunfire.

Out of nowhere, Lemon appeared to grab his boss, frantically pulling him towards the back of the hall in search of a fire exit. An off-duty RUC man, as Jones was to find out later, was angrily shouting and brandishing a pistol, shooting back at their assailants. He thought he might have hit one of the attackers and ran to the back of the hall for cover, falling down breathless next to Jones and Lemon. Over the relentless gunfire, he'd shouted to ask if they were okay. They'd nodded.

The RUC hero rose to a crouch, took aim and fired once more, but this time failed to hit his target. He hunkered down and waited. After what felt like an eternity, the shooting finally stopped. Smoke filled the air. They could hear screaming, moaning and hysterical cries from the body of the hall. Jones and Lemon carefully got up from the floor and surveyed the apocalyptic scene. Jones counted one, two, three, four, five men – definitely dead, and several others severely wounded.

As Lemon offered Jones his arm to lead him out, a blazing white light and an indescribable scorching sensation engulfed them. The air around them seemed to gather together, compressing them, then releasing itself violently, throwing them high against the wall behind. An inferno engulfed the already ravaged hall, and then the fireball imploded around them.

Jones couldn't remember anything much after that, only waking dazed and confused in hospital three days later, bandaged extensively and in unspeakable and unending pain. Lemon, for some ungodly reason, hadn't been as badly injured as he was. His arms and legs were burned, but his ugly face remained untouched. The doctor told Jones it was likely that a large piece of melting nylon-like fabric – likely from the hall's curtains or a Union flag – had landed on his face, red-hot and burning, liquefying and searing into his skin.

The whole experience was terrifying and, at times, tested even Jones's resolve. However, in the end, the experience had made him more determined than ever to get his revenge on the Nationalist bastards. He'd never give up. *No surrender!*

* * *

A few days later, Charles Jones, Lemon and three beefy hooligans were sitting at Jones's kitchen table. They looked like hooligans because they *were* hooligans. Lemon had assured his boss he'd trust these men with his life, and anyway, Jones owned them. But Jones wasn't too sure he could trust them so carefully ran through their plan on a need-to-know basis.

"Just remember, gentlemen, you owe me money, all of you. I know where you live, I know where your mother and father live, even better, I know where your grandparents live. If *any* of you grass or let me down in any way, you can guarantee my lieutenant here, Lemon, will pay you and them a visit. That…you… do… not… want! Do you understand?"

The three goons nodded fervently. They were aware of the risks, and one or two of them had already seen Lemon operate when he was raging. But worst of all, they knew Charles Jones meant every word he said.

"This supposed truce with the IRA has ended," he told them cynically. "The whole thing has been a farce! Nothing more." Jones coughed deeply and cringed as pain ran through his head. He'd have to take some more painkillers and soon.

"Gentlemen, you and Lemon have done a magnificent job so far. However, I want us to *really* make our mark this time. No more guns or baseball bats. No more chains or batons. I want knives. I want you to use knives. I want you to slaughter those Papist bastards like pigs!"

Chapter 29

Emmett had been working in the garage for months and was relishing it. His boss was a good and patient man who taught him well.

Once he'd passed his driving test the very first time, he'd been given a few assignments as part of the Unknowns. It'd been easy really, just picking up a few guys and taking them over the border where they were met by local Volunteers. He'd been ordered not to speak to them, not a word, just to keep his mouth shut and drop them off. It made sense that he knew nothing about them or why they were on the run – he didn't want to know. All he had to do was drive, drop them off and turn back to Derry again. It suited him. At least he felt he was doing something.

He'd not seen too much of Mickey since the swearing-in ceremony and when he had his friend looked stressed and worn out. Day after day, there were numerous attacks on both Catholics and Protestants. Tit for tat, especially in Belfast. Three people from the same family were killed when their drapery business was bombed by the IRA, and then two Catholics shot dead in retaliation by the Loyalists. There seemed to be no end to it.

His mother was even more stressed when the Civil Rights Association called off its "rent and rates" strike. It meant that any arrears on the house were being deducted from her benefits, taking a good chunk out of what little income they had. His own pay packet wasn't great since he was just an apprentice, but he tried his best. He knew she was trying to hide her money worries from him, but she needn't have bothered. He knew her too well. As for his father, there was no point in going there. The man was getting bigger and bigger, lazier and lazier.

That morning, the boy had seen Tommy O'Reilly passing in the street and run over to say hello and to find out how Tina was. Emmett liked Tommy. He was a good soul and always happy-go-lucky. But at the mention of Tina, his face had clouded.

"She's not good, son. They moved her a while back to another wing. Took her away from the women who were looking after her. She's gone back into her own world. Worse than ever."

Emmett's heart almost stopped. "Ah, shit, Tommy. I'm sorry to hear that. Can't you get her home or even to Gransha?"

Tommy and Caitlin had spent months pestering their local MP and writing numerous letters to everyone and their dog, highlighting Tina's case and her vulnerability in the prison system. Few were answered, and those people who did respond proved useless, passing the buck to another department or person. He'd seen Tina just the previous week and been shocked by her deterioration. He might as well not have been there for all the attention she'd paid him. After that, he'd suggested to Caitlin she'd better come with him on his next visit. She immediately agreed. But no need to further burden the young fellow with their family's problems. Tommy knew he'd always been sweet on Tina.

The two men talked briefly about football and soon said their goodbyes.

* * *

Mickey Boyle sat at the wake of his nineteen-year-old cousin, the youngster's smashed head held tightly together with bandages allowing him to lie in his open pine coffin. His aunt sat beside him, white rosary beads in her shivering, shaking hands, crying and saying over and over again, "They didn't have to run over him, Mickey, like a dog. They didn't have to run over him or Paul."

She wore a small silver cross in the hollow of her throat. Below it, her pulse beat, hard and rapid. Mickey's cousin Brendan wasn't involved in the Cause but had sadly happened to be in the wrong place at the wrong time. He and his best friend Paul Kennedy had been rioting, like all the youngsters, when one of the British Saracens knocked Brendan over. Paul had gone to help his friend, and he too was badly injured when the armoured car reversed, killing Brendan outright.

Mickey sat stone-faced with fury. Today was a dark day.

He got up to leave and reached out to hug his aunt. Holding her tight, he couldn't find the words to comfort her. As he released her, she whispered in his ear, harshly and desperately: "You find out who did this, Mickey Boyle, and deal with it. Will you do that for me?"

He looked at her, seeking confirmation from her that she knew what she was asking. Her eyes met his and did not flinch. Without his saying a word, she knew he'd see it done.

"Thank you, Mickey. Thank you."

His aunt wiped away her tears, breathed deeply and shook her head slightly to regain her self-control. Brendan's death would be avenged. Mickey never had, nor ever would, let her down. The burden of such a promise added to the neverending responsibilities he was already struggling to carry.

* * *

Martin McLaughlin sat with Father Connolly having a coffee in the priest's usual haunt on a Friday morning, across from the Strand Road police barracks where George Shalham had been shot. He'd not seen the priest for a while and was surprised when, out of the blue, Connolly had contacted him via his uncle Tommy and asked to meet. The arms caches from the US had come to a complete halt, although Martin knew the priest was still involved with NORAID. Other than that, they'd little contact.

Martin had given up on God years ago, but he admired the priest's loyalty to the Cause and knew he risked losing everything if it became known he was involved. The Catholic Church could be unforgiving. Martin grew concerned as he supped his tea and watched the priest, who appeared agitated and was clearly worried about something.

"Are you alright, Father?" he asked.

"I don't know, Martin, to be honest. A lot on my mind is all," he answered ruefully. Martin waited. He knew there was more to come. "Can I ask you something?"

Martin nodded.

"Anything, Father."

"You probably know there's been a serious breach of intelligence about operations and such like. Someone, somewhere, is snitching."

Martin nodded again. There'd been too many leaks of late, and concern had been growing in the local brigade. A high-level internal investigation had been set up to identify the source of the leaks.

"If I were to tell you, *hypothetically*, that I know who it is, could you use that to your advantage?"

Wow! Martin hated snitches. He'd no problem with them being severely punished – even killed. They were the scourge of the Cause. Always had been, always would be. Containing his excitement so as not to deter the priest from saying more, he answered in a subdued tone.

"Well, Father, *hypothetically*, yes, we could."

The priest nodded. Exactly as he'd thought. Of course, he could never outright share the specific information that Anne Ballantyne had given him in the confessional. That would be breaking his sacred duty as a priest. He could, however, *hypothetically* trap the snitching culprits and thereby benefit the Cause.

"Okay. For a number of reasons, I can't tell you exactly who it is, Martin, so don't ask. But I strongly suggest you set them up, somehow for as long as you need. Make it worthwhile. Use them if you can. I'm going against everything the Church has taught me by sharing even this much with you. Listen carefully. Have you noticed a certain individual driving a brand new car and flashing his cash around the estate lately with his corpulent friend sitting alongside him?"

Martin was ecstatic. He knew exactly who the priest was referring to. If he took this information to senior command, it would be greenlighted with orders to make a public example of *any* grass.

The two men continued to talk until it was time for Father Connolly to leave. They both stood up and shook hands. The information had been passed on.

Martin sat back down as Siobhan, his favourite waitress, offered him more tea. He thought back to the last time he was in this café. It had been with Kieran Kelly when Martin had tried to warn him they knew of his hidden homosexuality. It had left Kelly vulnerable to blackmail by the authorities, and the Provos didn't like that. And all the time, the dickhead had hoodwinked Tina into believing he loved her… Martin shook his head. He couldn't go there again.

He paid and thanked Siobhan, who beamed with pleasure to see the change in him. She was pleased to see the lad had finally caught himself on. He looked so much better, smarter, neater, well-mannered. Martin took his change gratefully and looked for the nearest pay-phone. He had an important call to make.

Chapter 30

Alice told her boss she was going back to England to see some friends for a break. She was due a holiday from the off-licence and was feeling tired.

Instead, and at the last minute, she'd been given an assignment to join an SAS team who'd been instructed to go over the border to the Irish Republic. Their sole purpose was to grab a senior IRA member that only Alice could identify. It was one of the three men she'd recognised from The Shamrock the night Dolores, Patrick's twin, had accosted her.

From the very moment they'd crossed the border, the eight-man mission proved to be an unmitigated disaster as the team were quickly spotted and arrested by the Republic's police, the Garda Siochana. The only explanation they could come up with was that they'd made a map-reading error and accidentally crossed the border. Alice had been due to join them the following morning and was relieved beyond belief to have avoided arrest.

Patrick Gillispie, however, had simply disappeared. When Dolores came looking for him that night months ago, she'd seemed perplexed not to know where her brother was. Alice knew he was up to something big. There hadn't been a peep from him since then, and she was annoyed. Although she'd gained valuable, solid information whilst they'd been together, and also when working in the off-licence, it wasn't enough. The only consolation was that she and Ian had managed to coordinate a few more attacks on Nationalists following their success with the Gaelic team. The RUC couldn't prove a thing about who'd been responsible for that, and no one had been charged.

Instead, Alice kept working, kept collecting for the prisoners' fund, kept listening to conversations all around her in search of useful information as well as trying to find out where Patrick was. She'd teased his friends, asking if they knew of his whereabouts so she could cut his balls off for not being in touch with her. They'd simply laughed and joked back: *perhaps good old Patrick has a bit on the side.* It was evident they weren't going to tell her anything. She was becoming more and more frustrated.

* * *

Dolores Gillispie, meanwhile, kept a close eye on Brona Doyle. She'd finally managed to find out where Patrick was, but something deep inside told her she couldn't share his whereabouts with this woman who'd appeared from nowhere. Dolores had shared her concerns with her brother, who'd dismissed them at first, telling her she was being paranoid – again. He'd tried to reassure her by double-checking Brona Doyle's background, and once more, she'd come back clean. Dolores wondered whether it was because the bitch was English that she was unconvinced but somehow knew she was hiding something. She hated the English or anything to do with them. No matter what Brona said, Dolores wouldn't believe a word of it. And so she watched from a distance, keeping a close eye out.

One day when Brona was away, Dolores called into the off-licence and was told the woman was in England – that in itself fuelled her suspicions. *England.* She'd lied to the off-licence owner and told him Brona had borrowed a book that she desperately needed back. She asked if she could go upstairs to look for it in the flat – it'd only take a minute.

The faint-hearted owner knew exactly who Dolores Gillispie was and that there'd be repercussions if he said no – such was her reputation. He just wanted her out and away from his shop, and so he quickly handed over the key.

Upstairs, Dolores looked around. The place was filled with books. They were everywhere, methodically placed in neat piles. She recognised a few as she read the titles and authors: Dickens, Austen and Orwell, to name but a few. Dolores quickly searched the cupboards, drawers and shelves and found nothing that could incriminate or tell her anything about Brona. There were no family photographs, letters or anything personal and this in itself was suspicious.

Returning downstairs to the shop, she handed the key back to the short, bespectacled owner, who with relief placed it back in the till. Thanking him, Dolores asked casually, "When's she back?"

The man answered quickly, "Monday."

"Okay. Thanks." Dolores stood staring at him for a while, thinking. She made him feel very uncomfortable.

"Anything else?" he asked, attempting to look busy.

"No. That's it. Thanks." At last, she was gone.

* * *

Patrick Gillispie wondered how Brona was doing. Most likely, he'd burned his bridges there, he thought, with a twinge of sadness. She'd got to him. He'd had no choice but to go down South, and for months his time had been taken up with carefully planning a number of missions so secret that he couldn't even tell his twin. He knew Dolores would be livid that she hadn't been asked to accompany him – especially after her successful attack on the Orange Hall in Newtownhamilton.

He was sitting by a blazing peat fire in a small, intimate pub in Clonakilty, far from the North of Ireland. Wielding a large poker, he played with the fire, sending sparks spiralling around like tiny red stars carried on a whirlwind. His thoughts were interrupted when he saw his trusted comrade Brian Monaghan arriving with two pints of Guinness. He passed a pint to Patrick and supped at his before taking a chair. Patrick looked at him and pointed at the man's lip, crowned with the cream of his pint. Brian's eyes twinkled as he ran the back of his Aran sleeve across his mouth.

"That's some night out there," he commented, looking out of a window made up of six tiny squares of glass set in the thick white-washed wall. The rain appeared to be bent on battling through it to reach them.

"It is that. Glad we're in here," Patrick answered and nodded thoughtfully. They'd been outside all day training in the ditches and dunes of Dunmore beach, and he'd never been so cold in his life. By the end, he couldn't feel his hands and feet, believing he'd never get warm again. In addition, they were both starving and had just wolfed down a huge bowl of Irish stew.

The two men were exhausted. This particular assignment would involve just the two of them, the rest of their comrades having left weeks ago. The two men had grown close as they planned their mission. Silence – a familiar friend – engulfed them as they both relaxed and watched the dancing flames of the open fire, breathing in its peaty aroma.

* * *

Alice was back at work. After the failure of the SAS mission, she hadn't gone anywhere near England but instead contacted Ian, who immediately invited her to Bangor. She wasn't too sure but then decided, fuck it; she'd earned some respite. She needed to be herself again; she needed to be Alice Wallace once more. And anyway, she liked Ian. He'd done everything she'd asked, by the book, and so once again, they sat in the same bar, having the same drinks. Ian was buzzing, hoping Alice had a new scheme in mind.

"Well. How've you been doing?" he asked quickly.

"Jesus, Ian, I'm so tired. Being Brona Doyle is killing me! It's gone too quiet. That guy Gillispie I told you about; he's done a fuckin' runner and disappeared, and no one is saying *anything*. Can you imagine? I'm running round half of West Belfast collecting money for the fucking Republican prisoners' defence fund!"

Ian nodded his acknowledgement of the shame of it. She was powerful, this woman, and he admired her for it. He couldn't do what she did.

Alice huddled herself closer. "Look, Ian, I've been thinking. How about we target The Shamrock? I'm convinced they've a back room that's used as a Provo HQ of some kind. Every time I've tried to get near it, some big fucker is permanently standing by the door guarding it. And listen, the outer and inner doors are reinforced steel! It's like Fort Knox in there."

Ian slapped the palm of his hand on the table in delight. A wipe out! It could be a complete wipe out of some Provo honchos. This woman never ceased to amaze him.

"Nice one, Alice! You know the place, and you know the movements in and out of it. What are you talking about: shots or a motherfucker of a blast?"

It was one of many ideas that'd come to her on her way to Bangor. She'd wipe out Dolores! Blow her and the others to smithereens. Well, it was one way of guaranteeing Gillispie would return from whatever rock he'd crawled under.

Ian chuckled softly as his mind raced too, reeling out questions and thoughts on how they'd do it.

"When? How? Shooting won't work…It's likely they've got a camera at the main door, eh? We wouldn't be able to just walk in and strike."

All the likely scenarios ran through his head as he continued to think out loud.

"I think it should be you, don't you? They'd be wary of me, a stranger. It wouldn't make sense. Yeah, you'll have to do it! Brilliant idea. Just brilliant!"

Alice knew Ian was right. It'd have to be her. A timed bomb.

Ian noticed her silence and ran a hand over his mouth, realising for the first time the implications if she went solo. Of course, there was an element of risk in her handling a bomb, but ultimately it would cost her her job. He knew how much the job meant to her – but worse still, if caught, she'd likely be sent to prison for a *very* long time. Her arrest could implicate him and his lads. They'd go to gaol, all of them – maybe it wasn't such a good idea, after all, he thought.

He quickly offered to re-fill their drinks so as to get away and think. When he returned, she told him, "Ian, I know you're worried about me being caught. Trust me; if I am, I won't tell them about you or the lads. My mind's made up: I'm going to wipe out The Shamrock."

Then she surprised him even more.

"I'm going to down this drink, and then I'm off. There is just one thing I need from you – a quartermaster to help me. Someone to provide the explosive. After that, I think it's better you and me never see each other again."

Chapter 31

Father Connolly had just finished conducting a baptism. His conscience had been screaming out all weekend after his meeting with Martin McLaughlin. Anne Ballantyne had trusted him when she'd asked for his advice in Confession all those weeks ago. He was torn between his duty as a priest and his duty as a member of the Provos. He'd chosen his earthly associates, and now the men he had indirectly identified were living on borrowed time. The blood of both of them would be on his hands. Sooner or later, he'd have to face that fact.

Today was the day the New York policemen were finally arriving for a two-week stint. A lot of effort had gone into planning and replanning their trip. He'd thought they were having it on at first and weren't serious about their commitment to helping. However, not long after he'd returned from his trip, he'd received a phone call to set a date and work out a draft itinerary and work schedule. Fifteen of them were due to arrive later that afternoon, most likely jet-lagged, and so he'd planned an early dinner for them and then to bed. He looked forward to their visit – it'd be a distraction.

So far, he'd raised over £50,000 from his visits and speeches in the US and was delighted. As part of the fundraising effort, the Yankee cops also raised a substantial sum to buy much-needed timber, paint and decorating supplies for the houses they planned to repair or redecorate. To ensure fairness, anyone who wanted work done had to buy a fifty-pence raffle ticket with the twenty lucky winners having renovations done to their homes. Unfortunately, a number of houses most desperately in need of repair hadn't been selected.

* * *

Later that afternoon, Father Connolly drank tepid tea made by John McMonagle, a seventy-five-year-old man who'd been diagnosed with prostate cancer. He'd ignored the usual symptoms for months, too embarrassed to visit the doctor, and of course, now it was too late. He didn't have much time left. Father Connolly was particularly fond of the WW2 veteran who'd served in the British Army but had been captured not long after the war started. John was a fund of good-humoured stories, including the one about how, upon release from the POW camp, he had been the only prisoner who'd put weight on! His mother had been African-American and his father Italian. His wife had died years before in childbirth, along with the baby, and John had never remarried. He was a popular man who – along with Tommy O'Reilly – fought tooth and nail to ensure local people received all the help they were entitled to, in particular when it came to assigning new housing. Up to then, most new tenants were single, Protestant and ready to vote for the Unionist Council. Gerrymandering had to stop, and John had been vocal on the subject.

Father Connolly knew he'd miss the gent and his quirky sense of humour. When they'd first met, they'd hit it off immediately – unlike Father McGuire and John, who disliked each other intensely. Something had happened between the two of them when John's wife passed away, though Father Connolly had not been able to find out what.

Thinking of poor Father McGuire, who seemed to wake up every day snappier and in a worse mood, Father Connolly asked John how he was feeling and if there was anything he could do.

"You could have a word with your man above," John joked, raising his eyes to the heavens. "See if he could fast-track me – get me through those pearly gates quick."

The priest laughed and answered, "I'll see what I can do. Seriously, do you want to talk about what's going to happen?"

John closed his eyes and shook his head. "Father, we both know there's nothing to be said or done. I just feel so sad. All those years wasted in that bloody camp and then losing my Elizabeth and the babe. I can't help thinking I should have done more with me life."

Father Connolly dismissed the thought with a wave of his hand and added pointedly, "Don't you dare say that, John McMonagle. What happened in wartime wasn't your fault. Liz dying was cruel but not your fault either. And for all the hard work you and Tommy have done over the years for your neighbours, you should be getting the Nobel Peace Prize!"

At that, John laughed. He supposed the priest was partly right, not *all* of it was his fault, but he was bloody terrified at the thought of dying and not knowing where he was going. His faith had deserted him in the camp after what he'd witnessed. He'd only let the priest in for a cup of tea because he liked the young fella and, since he could no longer work, had been lonely as hell.

"I'm not sure about the Nobel Peace Prize, but I admit I've enjoyed working with big Tommy. He's a good man."

The priest nodded in agreement before asking, "How's Mrs Kennedy next door? Any news?"

It was John's neighbour's youngest son Paul who had been tragically run over by the Saracen and was still in a critical condition.

He shook his head. "I haven't seen her, Father, these past few days. I think she's spending all her time by the wee lad's bedside. Awful. It'd break your heart. Just pitiful."

Father Connolly agreed. It was a ruthless, pitiless way for a young man to die.

* * *

Later that evening, waiting under the dry porch of the City Hotel and watching his American guests climbing down from their airport bus, Father Connolly laughed at their obvious enthusiasm. They were waving and shouting their hellos as soon as they saw him.

Next to him stood an American journalist who'd arrived in Derry some time ago and had grown to love the city and especially its people. To his delight, he'd become a bit of a celeb after winning several prestigious journalistic awards for his unbiased coverage of The Troubles. He was well regarded by both communities as a fair-minded and professional reporter. He'd heard about the revamp project and the arrival of his compatriots and agreed to cover it. It would be a refreshing change to report good news rather than more of the sickening violence he usually witnessed day after day.

The reporter suppressed a smile as he watched the noisy procession and, in a lazy Midwestern drawl, teased the priest, "Jeez, Father, will you look at the state of them? You're sure this was a good idea!"

The priest could only agree: the off-duty cops did look ridiculous, every single one of them. Most of the broad-shouldered men wore plaid, open-necked shirts on top of three-quarter-length shorts worn with socks and open-toed sandals as if they were expecting a heatwave! The heavens had opened all afternoon, and the car park had partially flooded. However, it seemed nothing was going to deter their enthusiasm or dampen their spirits as they patted each other on the back and laughed whole-heartedly, pointing to their wet socks and feet.

The weary bus driver, who'd listened to the busload of loud blabbing Yanks the whole way from Belfast airport, couldn't get away quick enough. His head ached. As fast as was humanly possible, he grabbed their luggage out of the side of the bus and jettisoned it on the semi-flooded ground.

One of the tourists broke away from the group and made his way over to the two watching men, offering them his hand. His grip was firm.

"Father Connolly. Good to see you again!" he barked before looking at the reporter and introducing himself.

"Officer James Halloran, New York Police Department at your service."

"William Barter, The Boston Globe. At *your* service!"

The man whooped and turned to look at his colleagues, crying, "Listen, guys, we got us a real live reporter from The Boston Globe!"

The men whistled and catcalled at the news as they plodded to the hotel entrance carrying their sodden suitcases.

* * *

Later, when everyone was checked in and preparing for dinner, the priest, reporter and Officer Halloran sat in the reception area drinking beer. Barter immediately took to Halloran. The policeman appeared genuinely interested in what was happening in the city. It turned out his grandfather had sailed from Derry Quay with his wife many years before, and he'd managed to identify some distant relatives still living here. He'd even arranged for his wife to join him for a few weeks after the project finished.

"I'm due to retire soon, guys, and I thought, why not! Why not bring Colette over and make a real holiday of it? She's a bit nervous, mind you, with The Troubles an' all, but what the heck – life's too short!"

The priest looked at him and nodded sympathetically. The police officer was probably one of the smallest men in his group but very solid. His bright brown eyes glistened as he talked.

"You're not to worry, Officer. I'll put the word out. You and Colette will be absolutely fine!" The priest smiled mischievously, followed by a slow, theatrical wink.

Chapter 32

"Ah, Anne, he's so gorgeous. You'd never think that Porkie could produce something so beautiful," Caitlin laughed as she looked down at baby Sean.

Anne knew her friend was right. The baby, her baby, was perfect. His skin was smooth as velvet, not a mark on him. His eyes were huge and bright. When she'd first held him and looked into those eyes, they'd all but told her, *Don't worry, I'm here, we'll look after each other.* The love she felt for this bundle of joy never ceased to amaze her.

The two women were sitting in Anne's kitchen on a wet April afternoon. Porkie had barely greeted Caitlin when she'd arrived with a few bits for the baby. He'd simply grunted as he'd answered the door and saw her standing there. Porkie no longer looked like himself. He'd lost a power of weight. The flesh on his jowls hung loose and wobbled when he wagged his head, indicating Anne was in the kitchen.

He appeared deflated and miserable, and Caitlin wondered what was up with him.

She had been with Anne when she'd given birth. Porkie had gone AWOL and only turned up the next day. He'd refused to tell Anne where he'd been when she asked. She didn't really care. The birth had been long and difficult, but baby Sean made it all worthwhile.

"He is gorgeous, isn't he?" Anne crowed before exclaiming excitedly, "I want you to be Godmother. You and Seamus, Godmother and Godfather."

Caitlin was delighted and, of course, agreed, hugging her friend, then blushed and suddenly winced with guilt and shame, remembering her last encounter with poor Seamus.

"What's going on in that head of yours?" Anne asked with a twinkle in her eye. She knew her friend so well and had noticed her blush.

"Nothing," Cailin answered unconvincingly.

Anne knew then. "You've done it! You and big Seamus have done it, haven't you?" She laughed as a deep red blush suffused Caitlin's face.

"OH MY GOD, thank you! It's about fucking time! I thought you'd never get over that Henderson twat!" Anne chuckled, then blessed herself.

It hurt Caitlin when her friend referred to James in such a way, but she knew Anne was just being protective of her.

Seamus had finally made a move unexpectedly the night Sean was born when they were celebrating his arrival with some wine. They'd been sitting comfortably on the sofa in Caitlin's front room watching his favourite sitcom, *Fawlty Towers,* when he began to rub the inside of her palm with his index finger. It tickled, so she looked at him and giggled. He held her gaze and moved in for a kiss – a gentle one she found hard not to respond to. It grew more and more urgent as their tongues wove together.

Breathless, he stopped kissing her and murmured, "Christ, Caitlin, I've been wanting to do that for ages. You've no idea."

She was surprised by the urgency of her own response. She got up and pulled the living-room curtains shut to darken the room and give them some privacy before turning to him and asking: "Do you want to do it again?"

He smiled, of course he did, and quickly got up to turn off the television. As they sat in the darkened room, he leaned over and asked quietly, "Are you sure, Caitlin? I don't want to mess this up."

"I'm sure," she said, delivering the words softly, half in a whisper.

Caitlin was lonely, he was lonely, and one thing led to another as they kissed deeply and rushed to remove their clothes. Their hearts raced. They wanted each other, needed each other. Caitlin let herself go as she pulled at his belt awkwardly, struggling to remove it. He had to stop kissing her and unbuckle the thing himself. She placed her hand on the front of his trousers. He felt hard and was clearly excited. They stood face to face and removed their clothes until they were as naked as the day they were born.

She was everything he'd ever hoped for and imagined. Her small breasts were perfect, complemented with dark brown coloured nipples that stood out pertly. Her waist was neat, her skin milky and smooth, with discreet light golden hair between her legs. He smiled as he noticed a small birthmark on her hip. She'd never told him she'd a birthmark. He couldn't believe his luck but was still anxious.

Caitlin saw the uncertainty in his eyes and fondly touched his face. She felt his erection, stroked it gently and pushed herself against him, assuring him it was okay. He understood the small movement and kissed her again, this time much deeper with longing, and pulled her gently down onto the sofa.

His fingers explored her nipples, her breasts, her navel, until they sought and found the wetness between her legs. She shook as he expertly found her spot and caressed her. He was making her feel so good, so very good, as she gave in to his touch. Nothing else existed. All the heartache and pain was forgotten as her breathing became more rapid, and she responded to his exploring fingers. She was climbing up and up, high into an exhilarating paradise, not wanting it to end until finally she had no choice but to let go or it would kill her. She released all her tension, all the pain and grief. Gasping and crying out, she found her freedom and screamed, *"James!"*

Seamus sprang off her as if electrocuted. Naked and more vulnerable than she'd ever felt, Caitlin gasped and reached out for his hand. Like James Henderson before him, he shook her off in fury. In a steely voice, he told her, "I don't fucking believe this, Caitlin. Who the fuck is James?"

In brooding silence, he hastily picked up his clothes and ran into the long, narrow hallway to dress.

Caitlin rushed around to find hers in the semi-darkness of the living room. She cried out after him, but he'd already gone, the front door still shuddering from his exit. Lying back, she groaned. She couldn't believe it herself. Christ Almighty, would she never be free from James Henderson!?

After that, Seamus literally cut her off. She hadn't seen or heard from him since and missed him desperately.

* * *

In the kitchen with her friend still smiling and joshing with her, Caitlin nervously told her, "We didn't, Anne, at least not the whole way. I've screwed up – again."

Anne grew worried as she watched a veil of sadness fall over Caitlin's face. For that brief moment, she'd actually believed something good had happened to her friend.

"Why – what happened?"

Caitlin wasn't going to go into every detail. She was still too ashamed and embarrassed. She puffed out her cheeks, shook her head and said regretfully, "I called him James."

"Ah, Jesus, Caitlin. In the middle of it?"

Caitlin nodded sorrowfully.

"That's bad. That's really bad!" Anne said, whistling softly. She knew Seamus was mad about Caitlin and, being the proud man he was, would be badly hurt. He thought she'd been on her own since he'd been away when of course, there'd briefly been James Henderson.

"I know, Anne. I don't think he'll ever forgive me," Caitlin sighed.

Anne couldn't respond. She didn't know what to say but knew it was unlikely, especially after being hurt by Caitlin so badly before.

For once, Porkie was on cue, and Anne was glad of the interruption when he entered the kitchen. Sensing the tension, he looked at his wife and her friend and asked, "What's up?"

He gently took his son from Caitlin and placed him over his shoulder, rubbing the child's back expertly. The two women looked at each other but remained quiet.

"You're not going to tell me?"

Anne spoke first. "Just girlie stuff, Porkie, nothing for you to worry about. You want a cup of tea?"

The man looked sceptical but muttered, "Aye, I'll have a cup."

Caitlin looked at him once more with concern. Although she'd no great affection for him, he really didn't look well. "Are you alright, Porkie? You've lost some major weight."

Porkie was in torment and shitting himself. Every time there was a knock at the front door, his heart would jump as he wondered if this was it. They'd come for him. He'd tried to keep his distance from Dickie, but his friend was determined and shadowed him most of the time. Porkie had overheard some useful titbits of information in his local. They'd proved enough to earn him some welcome cash and at just the right time, too, before the baby was born. Anne asked where it came from. He'd told her it was winnings from a lucky streak on the dogs when he backed several winners. He wasn't sure she believed him, but she reluctantly took the money anyway.

"I'm alright, Caitlin. Just a few things on my mind," he answered with a heavy heart.

Holding baby Sean tightly, he walked out of the kitchen before he was asked any more awkward questions.

The women watched his retreat. Caitlin looked at Anne and asked, "Is he really alright? He looks like shit. What's up?"

"I can't tell you, Caitlin. I just can't," Anne answered with a sigh.

Caitlin tried again. "It must be serious if you're not telling me. Come on, Anne, we tell each other everything, don't we?"

Anne looked at her friend for a few seconds without a response, then stood to put the kettle on. In their comfortless living room, Porkie played with his son and wondered if he'd survive long enough to see him grow up. He'd warned Dickie that people were beginning to suspect where his money was really coming from. Not only had his friend bought a car, but he was buying new clothes and flashing wads of cash around in their local. All they'd have to do was put two and two together, and most likely, they'd tar Porkie with the same brush if it got out Dickie was a grass.

"Jesus H. Christ, what have I got myself into, son?" he asked sadly, looking deep into the eyes of his newborn.

Anne took him some tea and heard him talk to baby Sean. Her husband had lost well over a stone by now, and it was obvious the pressure of what he was doing was taking its toll. Porkie had proved to be a good dad and was treating them both with kindness nowadays. Even though she knew where the money came from, she'd no choice but to accept it to buy the pram and other bits for the baby. Since Sean had been born, she'd recognised Porkie wasn't altogether bad. He was just too easily led by that creepy fuck Dickie. Thank God she'd only spoken to the priest! He'd been sympathetic but had warned her not to tell anyone else; otherwise, Porkie and Dickie were both dead men walking.

Chapter 33

"You're out of here this morning." Quirk smiled as she shared the good news with Bridget Barry, who lay tightly tucked under her worn brown blanket on the bed in her shared cell.

After listening to the conversation between the young McLaughlin girl and Maureen Molony, the prison officer had known she had to do something. It wasn't often she saw the OC so frustrated, and Quirk felt she had to help. Although she would never in a million years voice it, she respected the way Maureen led the other women, allocating them tasks and roles and giving them a sense of purpose. She encouraged them to educate themselves where possible and always remain disciplined.

The OC and her Republican comrades were recognised as political prisoners, allowing them free association and educational opportunities that now included Irish history, language and literature classes. But Quirk and her Armagh colleagues had received a written warning only this morning that these special-category privileges were to stop for new internees, and they should be prepared for repercussions. In all probability, their political status would eventually be removed altogether from the others, and that would most likely lead to serious trouble among the prison population.

Quirk was thankful she only had a month of service to go, and then she was out of the job. She couldn't stand this place any longer. The strip-searching, the abuse, the punishments, the mind-games, were all getting too much. This prison was standing on the edge of a precipice, and Quirk didn't want to be here when all hell was let loose.

"What do you mean?" Bridget asked her warily.

"Like I said, you're out of here today. Get your things together," Quirk answered, smiling.

But Bridget couldn't believe her. "I've heard that before, Quirk. I'm not going anywhere. They're just trying to get me fuckin' hopes up *again*."

Bridget tightened the thin blanket around her as much as she could before pulling it over her head. She didn't need to hear any more of this shite.

Quirk frantically shook the woman's shoulder and whispered urgently, "For Jesus' sake, woman, I'm telling you the truth. Now get up before they *do* change their minds!"

Bridget could tell Quirk was telling the truth and pulled the blanket down again. "You're serious, aren't you?"

She nodded and watched the woman's tired eyes fill up.

"I'm very serious, Bridget. Now hurry up, please. Sort yourself out." Quirk looked at Bridget's cellmate and ordered her to help.

Quirk hadn't felt so good in a very long time. She made her way out of the small cell and walked along the gangway. She stopped and looked over the iron rail, thinking back to the previous days and the risks she'd taken.

* * *

It had all started with a simple stroke of luck.

Minding her own business, Quirk had been walking past the half-open door of the small medical room when she'd heard Smyth and Dr Harris talking together animatedly.

"I can't let you see her notes, Smyth. I don't have them!"

Smyth knew they were all up shit creek, including Gladys if Bridget Barry's medical notes were shown to Mr Yeaman, the new stand-in Gov. Governor Johnston had put himself on sick leave. As far as she was concerned, the incident was over, swept under the carpet. Yet, worryingly, she'd heard from a source in the Governor's office that Yeaman had asked for Barry's medical records within days of his arrival.

Obviously, Maureen Molony and Father McGuire had got to him, insisting he review the case.

Governor Johnston was off for the foreseeable future. Unbeknown to most, he wasn't prepared to face the barrage of hatred and fury from the inmates once the proposed removal of their special political status was brought in. The only difference between the treatment given to the women here and the men in Long Kesh was that women could continue to wear their own clothes. Like Quirk, Johnston was getting out as quickly as he could before he was forced to deal with the backlash.

Quirk stepped back against the wall and listened carefully to the heated discussion between Smyth and the duty doctor. "Where are those notes now, you fuckin' eejit?"

"Governor Johnston had them, I don't know!" the doctor replied in exasperation.

"Shit!" Smyth answered, obviously rattled.

"I… I panicked. I went to his office to change them," Harris stuttered.

Smyth screeched, "Why! Why on God's earth would you change them?"

Harris had been half-cut when he'd decided to amend Bridget Barry's notes. From what he'd first written, anyone could see he'd been anything but professional when he examined her. He'd stupidly implied the woman's injuries were *self-inflicted.* The likelihood of her doing harm like that to herself was vanishingly small.

He desperately needed this job and so had decided to take advantage of Johnston's absence. In the Governor's office, he'd easily found Barry's file. To his annoyance, in his drunken stupor, he'd fucked up when he'd altered it. His handiwork was as clear as day, the amendments making it clear the notes had been tampered with. And now he faced Smyth, who frightened the bejesus out of him – more than most men did.

"I-I-It's okay, though," he told her. "I p-pushed the file inside another. They won't find it in a hurry."

"So long as you remember which one?' Smyth queried threateningly.

She had to get into that office and retrieve it. She didn't know Yeaman or what he was like. He could be cut from the same self-serving cloth as Johnston, but if he was the whistle-blowing type, that file could open up a can of worms.

"I'm going to get that file, Harris, so help me, God! And you can get off your arse and come along too. We need to make that fucking thing disappear – for good this time."

Quirk knew then she had to speak up and had prayed the new Governor was the type to listen to his female staff.

* * *

Back in her cell a few days later, Bridget Barry continued her preparations to leave. Her heart raced as she hugged her comrade and OC, holding her as tightly as she possibly could. Whispering in Maureen's ear, she told her, "I'll never forget your kindness. You're a credit to A-Company and all the women here. Take care of yourself and them. We'll see each other again, I promise."

Maureen hugged her back. She'd miss Bridget but felt nothing but relief that the wounded woman was getting home. Handing Maureen a few belongings she wouldn't be needing, including a homemade radio and some books, Bridget looked around at the small room that'd been her "home" for such a long time. She was torn. The women within these walls were more than friends and comrades; they were her sisters. They had put down loving roots in her heart. She wondered sadly whether she'd feel such companionship again but knew it was time to let go. Time for her to be a mother and granny again to her own kin. She'd given these girls and women her all. It was time for Bridget Barry to move on now. Time to put herself first.

Quirk entered the cell and was pleased to see Bridget ready. Outside on the landing, she could see all the other women on the wing lined up in silence. They were happy for Bridget, but no one said a word until the OC began to clap loudly. One after another, the women joined in. The sound of their applause reverberated against the high ceiling and enveloped the cavernous Victorian gaol. It rang against the roof and the arched windows, and echoed around the stone-walled cells as more and more women joined in. It was always a good day when one of the long-termers got out – it gave them all hope.

Tina McLaughlin could hear clapping, and it made her happy. She liked clapping, and so she joined in, dropping her mop as she did so. She was standing in the circle downstairs outside the Governor's office, washing the floor. What was going on? she wondered. About to ask, she saw a dark-haired woman walking towards her. Tina knew her but couldn't remember how or from where.

There was something familiar about the woman's eyes. They glowed as she rushed over and grabbed Tina, smothering her in a deep embrace. She smelled of lavender.

"Ah, youngin', it's lovely to see you."

Bridget hadn't had a chance to take in Tina's appearance, too delighted at first by this last-minute encounter before she left. But finally, she released the girl and held her at arm's length. There was nothing left of the Tina McLaughlin she remembered but skin and bone. Her sunken face had aged well beyond her years, and her skin was pallid and clammy. Tufts of her beautiful red hair had fallen out, and bald patches showed beneath. Sweet Jesus, Bridget thought. Sweet Jesus. There was nothing she could do to help the youngin' now, though, and so she hugged her once more and told her she loved her before quickly walking away. She couldn't bring herself to look back as her eyes filled with tears.

Tina felt sad as the sweet-smelling woman let her go and left. She tried her best to remember who this was. Why would she say that she loved Tina? The clapping had stopped, and she soon forgot about the woman as she picked up her mop and began quietly singing to herself.

Quirk watched the scene with immense sadness. She escorted Bridget Barry to the spiked security gates, where the two women shook hands before Bridget walked off towards the bus stop. Watching her go, Quirk thought back to that crucial moment just days before when she'd knocked on Governor Yeaman's door.

* * *

"Come!" she could just hear through the thick wood.

She'd only seen the man from a distance so far and was surprised when he turned around from searching a filing cabinet to see that he was young. In his mid-thirties, of medium height, white-faced and clean-shaven. He wore a dark blue suit, a white shirt but no tie. He appeared flustered and frustrated, searching the cabinet for a particular file.

"Yes. What is it?" he asked in a Northern English accent before shouting snappishly at his secretary who sat outside: "Pot of tea, now!"

Quirk was slightly taken back. She hadn't expected an Englishman.

"Sir. My name is Quirk."

Before she could continue, he interrupted, "Ah, yes. I've heard good things about you."

"Thank you, sir," she answered, feeling baffled.

"In his absence, Governor Johnston kindly left me notes on each member of his staff. I'm sorry to see you've decided to leave us. May I ask why?"

This was her chance. Finally, she'd nothing to lose, and so she told him everything: about the humiliating strip searches, the physical and mental abuse, the random cell searches… but most importantly, about Smyth and Drake's involvement in the sexual abuse of Bridget Barry. She told him about the conversation overheard between Harris and Smyth in the medical room and how Barry's notes had been tampered with. How she was sickened by the continual bragging in the locker room between Smyth and Drake about what they'd done to Barry.

He listened and asked clear and detached-sounding questions about the incidents. He then waited as his tea was delivered and the office door shut before he spoke once more. His voice was neutral and determined, but his eyes told a different story.

"I will look into it, and depending on Barry's response, I'll recommend that she be sent to Musgrave Park Hospital for medical treatment. After that, it's likely – given the time she's done and her age – I'll see her released on medical grounds." Quirk couldn't believe what she was hearing as he stood and whispered harshly, "Off the record, Quirk, if ***she or any*** of her so-called comrades whisper a single word about these accusations, I will have her straight back here in solitary for the remainder of her term! I've got the Press on my back as it is with Rees's announcement on the 'criminalisation' of political prisoners. And I certainly don't want any of your claims to get out, nor do I have the time or resources to investigate them! Especially as her damn' file seems to have disappeared into thin air. Do I make myself clear?"

Quirk felt irritated by his directness. So, he wasn't going to do anything more about the wider problems in this place, about poor Tina? But getting Barry released was something at least. Finally, the poor woman could go home.

"Yes, sir. That's it. Thank you, sir."

"Off you go then, Quirk. Good luck."

He abruptly dismissed her with a wave of his hand and supped his tea before crying out angrily, "Christ, can't I even get a decent cup of tea around here?"

Making a hasty exit, Quirk was more convinced than ever she'd made the right decision to get the hell out of the prison service.

Chapter 34

James Henderson groggily opened his eyes and groaned inwardly when he saw he was in an unfamiliar bed and sharing it with Marleen. He looked under the covers and found himself naked. Marleen clearly was, too, as she lay on her stomach with her bare bottom half covered by a white cotton sheet. *Oh, no*! He sighed and lay back and ran his hands through his short-cropped hair. At Roger's insistence, last night, the young couple had gone to dinner at a local hotel, just the two of them, to celebrate her return to Belfast after another trip to London. As it happened, they'd drunk more than they'd eaten.

He barely remembered getting home but could recall them giggling together in the library while they retold stories of the wild parties and fun they'd had in their younger days. The last thing he remembered was opening another bottle of champagne… He groaned as he saw the empty bottle standing on the bedside table. It was his uncle's favourite Dom Perignon – the one kept for special occasions. *Shit*!
He couldn't remember getting into bed at all, let alone with Marleen! He groaned in despair and hoped nothing had happened. He daren't ask. James got up slowly, picked up his clothes and tiptoed out of the guest bedroom.

* * *

Marleen knew she'd taken unconscionable advantage of James last night. She'd pretended to be asleep in the morning but had seen his shock and surprise when he'd woken up next to her, clearly struggling to remember what had happened.

It never occurred to her to tell him nothing had, that they'd "slept" together only in the sense of sharing her bed. Everything was going to plan, albeit much too slowly for her liking, and on this trip, she was determined to get what she wanted. James Henderson must finally be made to propose to her.

* * *

Roger Henderson sat upright in his bed, struggling to breathe. It hurt like hell, and he knew this was more than a lung infection. He was dying. He felt frustrated and humiliated that he still hadn't been able to find out who'd murdered his brother and knew these emotions were taking a deadly toll on his body. Pain raged through his bones, but he didn't want to complain and be a drag on the young people.

He was pleased to see Marleen return time and again to Melrose. She worked hard to laugh and joke with him and keep his spirits up, perching on the side of his bed, looking, and smelling delightful. One thing he was certain of now that she was back again: he'd get his nephew to make an honest woman of her once and for all. Roger knew he didn't have much time left to achieve that.

* * *

Late that afternoon, James had just left Rocola and was making his way back through the city to Melrose. He was finally going home with some good news for his uncle and was looking forward to seeing Marleen too. He'd had an unexpected visitor to the factory earlier when Tommy O'Reilly turned up out of the blue. Mrs Parkes's face was a picture when she saw the big, hefty man in his usual donkey jacket walk unannounced into the office and insist on seeing James.

This wasn't the first time he'd called in to update James on the progress – or rather, lack of it to date – of his enquiries on their behalf and over their meetings, James had developed a healthy respect for Caitlin's bluff, straight-speaking uncle.

Mrs Parkes had stomped off when O'Reilly asked for three sugars in his tea, which hadn't yet been offered. He'd looked after the departing woman, laughed and joked: "Not the greatest looker for a secretary, eh, James? Bit of a hard act to follow, our Caitlin!"

"Don't start, Tommy, and don't go there!" It was the first time either of them had openly referred to James's previous connection with Tommy's niece, and for a moment, there was an uneasy silence.

"Fair enough, James. Fair enough," O'Reilly said finally. He shrugged and sat down, his bulk overflowing from the seat of the leather visitor's chair. James sat too and leaned forward, ready to listen to what the big man had to share.

"So, Tommy. What do you have?" he asked hopefully. He could tell this time it was more than just a polite summary of failed leads.

"It's not everything, but… I think it could really be something," Tommy O'Reilly replied.

James waited in silence as Tommy went on. "You understand, what I tell you now is in the strictest confidence? It must be. I must try and be as neutral as I can in everything I say and do. Otherwise, this bloody conflict may never end!"

James knew from Paul Doherty, Rocola's shop steward, that given Tommy O'Reilly's role in the community, it was highly likely he'd be involved in various covert negotiations between several political parties. O'Reilly somehow managed to keep everything close to his chest without offending anyone. The man was likely to be up to all sorts, and James understood the need for confidentiality.

"I do, Tommy. I understand," he confirmed. They waited in silence as Mrs Parkes brought in the tea on a tray and almost dumped it on the desk. Annoyed, James told her he'd pour. She grunted and left, slamming the door behind her.

Tommy couldn't help laughing. "Jesus, she's something that one, James! What's her problem?"

He laughed too and replied, "She's angry at the world, Tommy, and everyone in it! She's nothing like Caitlin."

Hearing her name for the second time that afternoon, a wave of sadness overcame the two men, each for their own reasons. Over time, James had found his anger towards her fading. He'd found himself thinking back over the weeks leading up to the doomed City Hotel conference and had realised Caitlin couldn't have tipped off Kelly or her sister. She would never have involved herself in any plot to take human life, and he was wrong to have believed she had. He bitterly regretted now how much he'd hurt her. He knew where she worked in the photographer's shop on the Strand Road and found himself driving past it more than he needed to. But too much time had passed for him to contact her now, too much water under the bridge. She deserved a kinder lover than he had turned out to be.

Tommy sat up straight, ready to talk. "Well, James, I'm convinced we know who your witness is and where she is," he announced.

"She?" James asked in shock.

"*She*," Tommy replied. He, too, had been surprised when he'd heard the witness was a woman. It was a brave thing for anyone to do, risk their own life by giving evidence against a murderer – that said, there was something powerful and determined about this one. He'd never understand the ways of women – why and how so many of them were now involved in the conflict surprised him. Ironically, at one time, the old IRA didn't want women to participate, seeing them as more of a hindrance than a help. They'd initially believed the "weaker sex" should stay at home instead, looking after the house and family, though from what he'd heard, that was changing recently.

Tommy drank from his cup and continued, "Aye, a woman. I've spoken to her."

James was elated. "But how? How did you find her?" he asked hurriedly.

Tommy wasn't going to tell him how. This man didn't need to know. The Provos weren't stupid or naïve. If anything, they were protective of Rocola, and of the Henderson's too, did they but know it. The Boys knew that uncle and nephew had done their best to keep the women of Creggan in work, and so they'd put the feelers out and come back with some solid information.

"It doesn't matter how, James. All I know is that the man driving the car that steered your father off the road is employed by Charles Jones."

James had always disliked and distrusted the Belfast man. So, Jones was behind it all, was he? But why? James's father had been working for him… Unless whatever he'd urgently wanted to tell them on that last night had also been about Jones? That must be it! And maybe Jones didn't want them to find out… O'Reilly could sense the young man's brain working like clockwork.

Finally, James said: "So… Charles Jones."

"You know him then?" O'Reilly asked, gulping down his tea. He grabbed a Mikado biscuit off the plate and ate it in one.

"I do, Tommy. He's… he was a friend of my uncle's. We haven't seen him since the City Hotel meeting."

At that, the two men looked at each other and saw they were each thinking the same thing.

After swallowing another biscuit whole, Tommy commented, "I remember hearing some rumours about Jones. He was there when Bishop Hegarty was shot, wasn't he? And the third man, Morris… We haven't heard a whole lot about him since then. But there was talk of Loyalist sympathies."

James nodded. It was all beginning to make sense now, the pieces falling into place. He was finally going home with some news for his uncle and found himself looking forward to seeing Marleen this evening too.

* * *

Meanwhile, on the other side of the Province, Charles Jones and Lemon were sitting in the foyer of the Europa Hotel, Belfast. The hotel was well-known and used by journalists from all over the world, who thronged its corridors, sharing and catching up on the news as it happened. Not only was the place popular with them, but it was also frequently visited by the Provos and had become the most bombed hotel in Europe – thirty-six times!

Jones pointed at an American journalist who stood at the reception desk, checking in. "You see that Yank over there, Lemon? Put him on our list. He's been asking too many people the wrong questions."

Lemon was surprised at such a request since he'd no idea who the man was. Afraid to ask, he waited until Jones told him.

"His name is William Barter, and I don't trust him. He's a fucking Republican sympathiser, and the shit he writes for the US papers makes us all look like wankers. I want him gone."

Lemon didn't need to write the man's name down. He had it in his head already and was dreaming up a suitable departure for the pressman.

He thought about their last assignment in Belfast when they'd used an axe on another Fenian. The bugger never knew what hit him. Jones had asked for knives, but Lemon and "the kids", as he now called his punishment squad, enjoyed seeing the expressions of shock and terror on the faces of their targets just before the axes fell. And for the Yank, he'd think of something even more creative.

Jones was in constant pain. He'd noticed some of the hotel guests and staff staring at his scarred face, some sympathetically acknowledging he must have been a victim of some serious incident, whilst others quickly looked away for fear of staring too long. He didn't give a rat's arse. The painkillers he'd been prescribed were strong and incredibly effective. The only problem was he popped them like sweeties and was continually running out and needing to use street sources to acquire more. He'd been warned they were highly addictive and likely to cause major changes in his personality and behaviour if abused. He'd never given much thought to his personality – let alone his behaviour – and decided he couldn't care less.

"You got that?" he asked Lemon gruffly, eyes still fixed on Barter. Lemon was like a big stupid dog: the more you kicked it, the more it wanted to please you. "Just don't do it here; wait till he gets back to Londonderry. I'll be there myself in a few days."

Lemon liked going to Londonderry. He'd a bit on the side there who was never up to saying no. Happy days. He smiled in anticipation.

* * *

Back at Melrose, James and Marleen sat at a table set for dinner next to the fire in Roger's bedroom. Roger had just been bathed by a local nurse they'd hired and was feeling fresh but subdued.

"I just can't believe it," he murmured after a long silence. "Charles Jones. The bastard. But why?" It was incredibly rare for him to swear and almost unheard of in the presence of a lady.

James answered, "Well, O'Reilly seemed to think there might be a connection with the events at the City Hotel."

"But that was a bombing, James," Roger said, sounding confused. "And some rogue Provo was behind that – a young girl went to prison."

"No, Uncle, Jones had nothing to do with the bomb. It was the shooting of Bishop Hegarty he'd arranged. The guy who shot him was one of Jones's henchmen. Because Kelly took him out of the picture straight away, it turns out the RUC were able to concentrate their enquiries solely on the bomb plot. O'Reilly thinks it highly likely Commander Bonner covered up Morris's link to Jones, and Shalham was asking too many questions about why. You and I both know Bonner is in Jones's pocket.

"I think that's what father found out. He came to realise Jones set out to ruin the conference and us with it. We owed him money he thought we couldn't repay, and that suited him down to the ground. Think about it! He never wanted to help us by investing in the business – he wanted to close it down and cause the maximum hardship he could because most of our workers are Catholic. That's it in a nutshell!

The death of the bishop was the icing on the cake. We all know Jones abhors Catholics! Father was going to tell us what he'd somehow discovered, and Jones had him stopped."

By now, James was choking with fury. Marleen topped up his glass with wine and moved it towards him, encouraging him to drink.

Roger felt a complete fool when he thought of the number of times that fat creep Jones had eaten at his table and drunk his best wine. His brother had driven back to the city that night to warn them. At the thought, Roger began to silently weep.

James quickly ran to comfort him and looked helplessly at Marleen. She embraced them both, gave Roger a handkerchief and poured him a glass of water.

There was a light knock on the bedroom door, and Mrs McGinty walked in, asking if they'd finished dinner. All three sat in silence and nodded, watching the housekeeper pick up the used plates and glasses, placing them carefully on a tray. She asked if anyone wanted coffee or tea.

To pull himself together, Roger smiled at his nephew and suggested she bring another bottle of red Burgundy instead. Mrs McGinty tutted but was secretly pleased. Her employer was always better when the young couple were with him in Melrose.

As if sensing her thoughts, Roger looked at James Jnr and Marleen. He could only describe them as beautiful. They looked like they'd wandered off the set of a magazine shoot. Marleen wore a long white silk dress with a faint blue floral pattern. She'd thrown off her shoes to reveal crimson-painted toenails. Her blonde hair was loose and fell softly around her perfectly made-up face. James wore his blue and red Donegal tweed suit with matching waistcoat and an open-necked white shirt beneath.

A while later, cheeks flushed with wine, Roger asked them, "And what have you two been up to all day?"

The young couple laughed. “I’ve been working, Uncle, as you well know!” James exclaimed. Marleen joined in, “And I’ve been taking some more cooking lessons with Mrs McGinty.”

They both laughed when he suggested they should go out for the rest of the evening.

“Why don’t you two lovebirds have some fun instead of being stuck in here with an old invalid? I need to think about what we do next about Jones. So go on! Go! Take what’s left of that bottle and find somewhere beautiful to sit while you enjoy it.”

The couple knew this wasn’t a request but an order, and so they said their goodnights and made their way downstairs. Marleen was elated. This was going to go to plan; she just knew it.

Chapter 35

Emmett wasn't too pleased that his mother wanted to get involved with Women for Peace. The movement was started after the death of three children who'd been walking to school when they were knocked down and killed by a wounded IRA man. While trying to escape from a British Army patrol, he'd been shot and had lost control of the car that then ploughed into the innocent children. Peace rallies followed all over the Province, organised by the children's aunt in protest against violence conducted by all sides in the conflict.

Most of Emmett's friends thought it a waste of time and that the movement was pro-British. Surprisingly, though, a rally in Belfast brought out 25,000 protesters from the two communities and passed through both Catholic and Protestant areas. They walked from the Shankill Road to Woodvale Park in Belfast. A rally had been arranged in Derry too, and he'd pleaded with his mother not to go. There was a chance she could get hurt. Some of the women from Derry who'd gone to the Belfast protest had been injured and, on their return, were still being intimidated. She wasn't going to give in to his pleas, though, and determinedly joined the 2,500 brave Derry protesters. More and more peace rallies were happening all over Ireland and even in England.

As for his work with the Unknowns, Emmett continued to bring people back and forth across the border. He'd been assigned a female partner on whom he secretly had a major crush. Her name was Elizabeth McKenna, or Liz as she liked to be called. She was a pretty thing, not an out and out classic beauty but attractive in her own way. She wore her blonde hair short and straight. She had a delicate face with bright, light grey eyes and full lips. It was her smile and humour that he liked the most, the way she lit up the room wherever she went. She was also notably clever and quick-thinking.

For a short time, he'd felt guilty about his feelings for her when for ages, he'd thought himself devoted to Tina McLaughlin, but he'd grown to realise that had just been a first crush, a naïve young boy infatuated with the girl next door who barely noticed him. Anyway, poor Tina was long gone now, mentally and physically, and he was a man with needs!

* * *

One Saturday morning, Emmett and Liz were charged with delivering a package to a cottage in Malin Head, the most northerly tip of Ireland in the Republic County of Donegal. Emmett loved Malin with its wild Atlantic breakers, rugged landscapes and spectacular views. It was Ireland at its best. The package had been carefully hidden deep inside the driver's door panelling of their brown Austin Maxi. They were slowly approaching the border checkpoint at Coshquin just outside Derry when Emmett stalled the car as a British soldier raised his hand for them to stop. He walked over to the Austin whilst Emmett rolled down the window, the handle stiff and awkward.

"Morning," the soldier said, smiling.

"Morning," Emmett replied quietly, passing his newly issued licence across for inspection. He didn't look at the soldier when he spoke but instead stared straight out of the car window.

"Where're you off to today?" the soldier asked pleasantly as he read the licence, checking the picture of Emmett and then bending down to look at his female passenger.

Emmett's heart was beating like a drum, and he hoped and prayed he wasn't blushing or appearing nervous.

"Out for a run in my new car. I just got her, and we're thinking of Kate Farren's in Malin."

The soldier hadn't heard of Kate Farren's but stood back and raised one eyebrow when he surveyed the car. "I'm not going to ask how much you paid for her."

Laughing, he said, "Whatever it was, it was way too much! But away you go and enjoy your day."

With one hand, Emmett rolled the car window back up and drove off using the other. The pair said nothing for a couple of hundred metres until Liz giggled and screamed, "Sweet Jesus! Me heart's racing!"

"Mine too!" cried Emmett. "I thought I was going to shit me pants!"

* * *

Mickey promised he'd avenge his nephew Brendan's death, and here he was, lying low on an embankment on one of the unapproved and rarely used border crossings, at the top of Sherriff's Mountain on the outskirts of Derry. He wasn't alone but accompanied by the new man Seamus Donaghey who'd been assigned to him. Mickey had heard about Seamus and the work he'd done bringing arms over from America. He was obviously a true comrade.

Seamus was due to go back to the States soon. After his humiliation with Caitlin, he'd purposely kept away from her. Before it happened, he'd been travelling all over trying to get business from the country's largest building suppliers. Mr McMannus, his boss back in Boston, had hinted he'd help him set up a franchise here if he wanted. But now his romantic hopes were dashed, Seamus had given up on the idea. He'd only returned so as to be near Caitlin, but it seemed there was no future for him here.

Seamus looked at his comrade and whispered, "Any minute now, Mickey."

They were waiting for a British Army patrol to arrive. It monitored the border area every evening at random times. Much to Mickey's frustration, he hadn't been able to identify the soldiers who'd been driving the Saracen that killed his nephew and injured his friend.

Their names had been kept secret by the Brits, although a formal statement said the soldiers involved were charged with "reckless driving". There wasn't any police investigation, and so, unsurprisingly, both men were disciplined but remained out of military gaol and in the service. For the time being, this target was the next best thing.

The army tried daily to close or monitor 200 unapproved roads that enabled cars or lorries to travel back and forth freely between the Republic and Northern Ireland. Most of these roads had no fixed police or army checkpoints, so they were a nightmare to safeguard. The security services continually blew up the small bridges and either dug up or laid tonnes of cement or barbed wire to block access to possible escape routes. However, it was an impossible task to seal a border that ran for 360 miles from Derry around to Newry. The army ceaselessly monitored and investigated these roads, on foot or in jeeps or Saracens, often with helicopters hovering overhead to scan the ground seeking "bandits".

Mickey and Seamus, dressed in dark green camouflage, had set a number of landmines hours earlier and, from a relatively safe distance of 800 yards or so, kept a close eye out, making sure no innocent persons or animals strayed too close to the hidden devices. They'd had a close call with some roaming sheep earlier, but Seamus had sensibly scared them off by clapping his hands within reason and hissing at the confused animals. They'd both laughed at the spectacle that had unfolded – two camouflaged bombers chasing sheep!

Normally they would have left by now, but Mickey wanted to make sure the assault was a success.

"Do you hear that?" he whispered harshly as the sound of whirring blades grew louder and louder, closer and closer. Seamus nodded.

Both men tucked themselves deeper into the rise of the embankment, covering themselves with brambles and branches they'd cut earlier. With faces almost touching, they knew this was it and stared at each other, waiting. The only sound seemed to be the beating of their hearts as the seconds and minutes dragged.

Ten minutes and still nothing. Shit! Mickey thought. Something must have gone wrong. But as he shifted slightly, several almighty blasts were heard, and the ground literally shook beneath them.

* * *

Mickey and Seamus could hear screams and frightened voices coming from the smoking vehicles. They looked up to see the helicopter whirring low over the scene and knew they had to get away fast. They became soaked and frozen as the heavens suddenly opened and the sky went dark. But darkness and rain helped cover their retreat. It was all downhill from here, and the country lanes were lined with old oaks and mile after mile of gorse. Having carefully hidden two black-framed bikes on the roadside the night before, they crawled their way towards them. They just had to get the mile or so to the bottom of Coshquin, where a safe house waited to shelter them.

"Quick, Seamus!" Mickey exclaimed through the driving rain, frantically grabbing one of the bikes.

They could barely see for the water pouring and streaming down their faces. The sky was becoming blacker. Behind them, over the hill, the mist was tinted red and white by the helicopter's lights. They heard the far-off wailing sirens but focused on keeping their heads low as they flew down the hill, bumping and scraping over the muddy, stone-clogged laneways. They were frozen and aching in every limb but borne on the wings of vengeance.

Chapter 36

Martin McLaughlin sat in the local pub next to Jackson's shop in the Creggan estate, the only shopping parade in the area. He looked around the smoke-filled room and took in all the faces. Some people caught his eye and smiled in acknowledgement. It was Friday evening, and the bar was relatively full. A lone Country and Western singer in a star-spangled bright blue and silver shirt stood in one corner of the bar, blasting out mournful songs. No one other than a drunken elderly woman, who cried as he sang, paid any attention. Martin knew her face and recalled that Debbie was well-known locally. A sad case since she'd lost her only child to a British soldier's bullet during a riot. Another investigation that would never happen.

Martin was weary, but then who wasn't? War was tiring. He nodded to the barman to top up his lemonade. The door opened, and in came their target in all his glory. What a complete twat, Martin thought as he watched the fleshy man walk towards the bar, order a large Paddy whiskey and produce a wad of cash from his back pocket. His Celtic green and white football shirt had slid upward and partially showed the hairy gut that hung heavily over tight-belted jeans.

Here goes, Martin thought as he walked over to the empty barstool beside him.

"Alright?" he asked.

"Grand," Dickie answered, looking at Martin McLaughlin and wondering why he was even talking to him. They'd never spoken a word to each other before this. With one gulp Dickie emptied his glass and clicked his tongue for another.

Martin nodded to the barman and asked for a large Bushmill's for himself and another drink for Dickie.

"Christ, what a day!" Martin exclaimed as he grabbed the glass from the bartender and appeared to drink the liquor down hard and fast until he began to choke. He coughed and coughed until Dickie hit him hard on the back. Martin raised his hand and moved away. His eyes filled and streamed as he tried to catch his breath. Finally, he laughed and looked at Dickie, crying, "Jesus fuckin' Christ! I thought I was a goner there!"

Dickie joined in. Picking up his drink, he joked, "Me too! If you thought I'd be giving ye mouth to mouth, you'd another think coming!"

At his flippancy, Martin laughed, and Dickie quickly ordered another round, suggesting Martin take it easier this time. He'd already achieved what he'd sought – Dickie's trust. The barman was in on it too. There wasn't any whiskey in Martin's glass but flat Coke, and he was pleased as punch with his performance so far.

The music appeared to grow louder and louder as the night wore on. Dickie was soon inebriated and really enjoying himself. Martin McLaughlin wasn't as bad as some made out, and boy, could he drink. Unlike Dickie's lightweight pal Porkie, McLaughlin matched him drink for drink – and that took some doing. He believed he'd found himself a new drinking buddy.

Sticking his wrist out and drunkenly pulling up his left sleeve, Dickie showed Martin his latest purchase, a shining gold Longines watch. Pointing at it and swerving to stay on the barstool, he slurred, "See this, Martin? I won some money on the pools, and look what I got meself!" He leaned back, waiting for praise. It came loud and clear over the din of the music and shouting drinkers.

"I'd heard, Dickie. I meant to say, good for you!" *Yeah, right!*

Dickie didn't say anything but bobbed his head up and down and sluggishly saluted. It was time to play his next card, thought Martin, as he made a show of looking around the bar in case someone could be listening. He crept in closer to his drinking partner.

"Actually Dickie. I've been meaning to ask you… I don't suppose you'd like to make some extra cash? That's if you need more, given all your winnings! But seriously, you know what I'm talking about? Just a few small-time jobs and stuff to help us out. Nothing major."

Martin eyeballed him and winked to check that he understood the nature of the jobs.

Dickie knew immediately and nodded enthusiastically. What a night this had turned out to be! If he got in with McLaughlin and Co, think how much the Brits would pay him! Like a winning line on the slots, he could see the pound notes stacking up and hear the money pouring in. *Jackpot*!

"Anything I can do to help the Cause, Marty. You ask anyone around here. I'm a tip-top, tip-top dog!" he garbled.

Martin sighed with relief. He'd the two-faced bastard right where he wanted him. "That's great, Dickie, that's just great! I knew we could trust you."

And so Martin McLaughlin told Dickie what he wanted and, more importantly, how much they'd pay him to do it.

* * *

Dickie woke the following morning. His head hurt like hell, and his stomach heaved as he ran to the tiny cold bathroom, where he puked his guts up. Sweat gathered on his brow, and his hands shook. *Christ*. He couldn't do this anymore. It felt like the lining of his stomach had decided it'd had enough and was getting out of Dodge. He shivered, and his whole body wobbled like a blancmange. Placing his hands on the wall, he guided himself back to bed, where he sank back under the bedclothes. No sooner had he closed his eyes than he felt the wetness beneath him. Fuck, he'd pissed himself again. He'd no idea how he got home. Racking his alcohol-sodden brain in an effort to remember, he shut his pained eyes until, finally, he recalled himself singing with Debbie the barmaid and the feckin' star-spangled singer on the bar.

"*Come on, ye young rebels, and listen while I sing, for the love of one's country is a beautiful thing…*"

He cringed at the memory and looked at his gold watch. It was only 10.30. It was going to be a long, agonising day. He felt like he was dying.

* * *

A week or so later, Martin knocked on Dickie's front door and looked around the street. Dickie lived in one of the small terraced houses along the Lone Moor Road in the heart of the Bogside. The street was dark and quiet, given it was just before midnight. Standing next to Martin was a Volunteer called Eamonn Doherty, whom he'd known from their school days.

Knocking on the door again, not too loudly, they waited until there was a sign of life. A light went on in the hallway, and Dickie half-opened the door, surprised to see Martin McLaughlin.

"I thought you'd given up on me," he said quickly, opening the door wider to allow the two men to enter.

"Busy, busy, Dickie." Martin laughed as he looked at the dishevelled man in his dirty striped pyjama bottoms and string vest, his hair tousled from sleep and face covered in several days of unshaven stubble. He looked and smelled like shit.

"Sorry to get you up, but we need to be extra careful. Someone out there's grassing."

Dickie said he understood and played shocked with his hammering heart beating wildly. He coughed forcefully and answered, "Bastards."

Martin looked at him but said nothing.

Dickie had already passed on the good news to his handler: McLaughlin wanted him in. He could still see the way the man's eyes had lit up in delight, although he'd warned Dickie to be vigilant.

"Be very careful. Don't ask too many questions. Just play along. And keep in touch."

Dickie noticed there'd been more cash than usual in the brown envelope that was slid across the table to him in a quiet country bar well away from the city.

"Any chance of a cuppa, Dickie?" Martin asked as they made their way along the hallway into the kitchen at the back.

As the two men entered the room, they were hit by an overwhelmingly sweet putrid smell. They looked at each other in disgust. No woman, no man even, had cleaned this place in a very, very long time – it was a pit. The black bin in the corner overflowed with empty tins of Heinz beans, empty crushed beer cans were covered with cigarette ash and finished butts. Dishes of all sizes and cutlery hardened with food lay dry and unwashed in a black-stained Belfast sink. It looked like the man had used and left dirty every utensil in the place.

"Bit of a tip in here, Dickie, don't you ever clean up?" Martin asked, bitterly regretting his request for tea.

"I know, I know. I keep meaning to get round to it, but you know how it is, Martin," Dickie answered, taking a proper look himself around the kitchen. His visitor was right; the place *was* a tip.

"Do you wanna sit down?" he asked the two men. Martin and Eamonn looked at each other and together said, "No, thanks."

Martin decided he'd get the deed done and get the hell out. He was beginning to struggle for breath in this rank, foul place.

"You remember what we talked about? The night you ended up singing with Debbie and the star-spangled banner!"

"I do, aye," Dickie retorted defensively. He remembered only too well, and every time he went back to that bar, the piss was continually taken out of him.

"Well, we've got a wee job for ye. Some *goods* need moving. It's like this..."

Martin began to give Dickie his orders, and once again, pound signs flashed before his eyes.

* * *

It was 2 a.m., and Dickie found himself parked in a side lane not far from a large barn at the top of Sherriff's Mountain. He sat in the driving seat of a hijacked bread van with its engine running, waiting for the return of the four men he'd dropped off – what seemed like hours ago – a mile or so back.

He'd been given directions and told to wait. They'd come back with the *goods,* and he'd drive them to a safe house. He was disappointed McLaughlin wouldn't tell him where exactly. Dickie knew once he'd the address, the information would be worth more.

Anyway, he was dying for a piss and a fag but daren't move. He'd been told by McLaughlin, who'd scared the fuck out of him when he'd turned up dressed top to toe in his balaclava and Provo gear, that he shouldn't get out or leave the van *under any circumstances.*
McLaughlin also told him as he climbed out of the van, "Trust me, Dickie, we'll make it worth your while."

"It'd better be!" he'd cried back. Martin nodded briefly at his comrades unobserved by their target.

"They're taking their fuckin' time!" Dickie found himself saying to no one in particular. He continued to wait, not knowing that Martin and his colleagues were long gone and wouldn't be returning.

He was ignorant of the men's drop-off point and couldn't know that he'd left the group just five minutes from a safe house that only Martin and his comrades knew about. They'd quickly run through the fields to the back of the house, opened the door and changed into clothes left out for them. After that, they'd hidden their uniforms and split up into two cars, driving off in different directions.

Now sitting on his own in Jack's, a male-dominated but friendly bar just off William Street, Martin imagined the night Dickie was about to enjoy.

The barn they'd been visiting for a while at the top of Sherriff's Mountain, and where fuck-head Kelly had tortured and killed the Brit, had been used too much. It was time to get rid of it. They'd known

Dickie would feed the intel to the Brits, and with the approval of the sympathetic farmer – who never asked questions but gratefully took cash – they'd booby-trapped its every entrance and more.

It was a major deathtrap. The place would go up like Hiroshima – or near to! They'd left a large concealed speaker with a repeating recording of loud shouting as men apparently heaved and hauled about some sort of bulky equipment. The Brits, most likely tipped off by Dickie if Father Connolly's information was correct, would hear that alright and likely storm in… and then it would blow. Even if they failed to score many Brit casualties, just the fact that they'd turned up would confirm Tricky Dickie was a lying, money-grubbing fucker of a grass who deserved to be severely punished.

Chapter 37

Patrick Gillispie and Brian Monaghan were delighted at the success of their recent mission. They'd spent several weeks ensuring they were well prepared both mentally and physically. It'd been a particularly hot early morning when they'd planted a 200lb bomb hidden in a drain pipe at the ornamental gates of Glencairn House the British Ambassador's house in South Dublin.

The two men idly watched the gates from a safe distance, leaning on the iron wrought railings of a local Nazareth House primary school. Their target was an ex-senior liaison officer between the British Foreign Office and MI5. A British spy.

In silence, they smiled as they saw small groups of carefree children say their goodbyes and run excitedly through the school gates to begin their day. A few younger kids seemed more reluctant to leave but were soon coaxed and gently pushed on their way. Eventually, all the pupils were inside, allowing some parents to stand by the gates in the hope to catch up on any gossip. A number of young mothers began to push their prams off, unaware of the two composed and unruffled bombers who followed from behind, making their way to detonate the killing device.

When they reached their old battered landrover they began to watch as a white Rover P6 drew closer to the point of detonation. Brian began to count slowly "One, two, three." With his finger on the button, he pressed it hard, and up went all 200lb of explosives.

The noise and vibrations were staggering as burning metal, debris, and soil flew high up into the sky. Screams from the bystanders waiting at a bus stop and young mothers filled the air as a blast of rapid hot flames engulfed and danced over the target and its immediate vicinity.

In silence, Brian turned the Landrover's engine on and drove slowly away.

* * *

Now back in West Belfast, Patrick was sitting in The Shamrock, the evening news on in the background. He watched his twin yap, yap, yapping. He concentrated on her mouth, idly wondering how she managed to talk so much and so quickly. He'd never known anyone like it. At his deadpan expression and obvious lack of interest, Dolores thumped him hard and painfully. He rubbed his dead arm as she hissed, "Are you fucking listening to me, Patrick? Have you heard anything I've said?"

He hadn't, not a word, but quickly nodded and told her reassuringly, "Course I have, love!"

Dolores scoffed and crossed her arms angrily. "You haven't heard anything, Patrick! Don't you understand what I'm telling you… There's something up with that one! I've been in her flat, for Christ sake, haven't you noticed? I bet you haven't; you're far too busy getting her into bed! Listen to me! There's nothing there to tell us a thing about her. Not a single thing that's personal. It's not natural."

Counting each item off on her fingers, Dolores continued, "There are no letters, no bills, no cheque books, no bank statements, no ID! There's nothing! I think she's a Brit, a fuckin' agent!"

At such a ridiculous suggestion, Patrick raised his head and laughed like he hadn't in years. At his sister's shocked expression, he laughed some more. After picking up his pint of Guinness and taking a good swill, he spluttered, "Jesus, Dolores, are you fucking serious? What an imagination you've got!"

Dolores was livid. She'd been waiting weeks for this opportunity to get him on his own. She worried about him. He was her twin. He was her ying, and she his yang – although sometimes he didn't see it that way. There was a stubborn independence instilled in him, but then he was a man.

"I'm not making this up, Patrick!" she hissed in frustration. "I'm telling you, there's something not right with her. I don't trust her."

Patrick could see she wasn't joking as she tilted up her long Grecian nose and set her jaw, challenging him to respond. Her expressive brown eyes were expectant.

He sighed deeply and wiped some Guinness off his mouth with his sleeve. "Okay, D. I'll go and see Brona later. It's been a while since I last did; I'm not even sure she'll talk to me. So you might not need to worry in any case."

Dolores was happy with his suggestion and agreed. The twins sat and finished their drinks, making small talk as they watched the punters passing in and out of the bar.

* * *

Alice had recently overheard a couple in The Shamrock mention Patrick Gillispie's name. *Bloody cheek, the way he'd just dropped her!* Command weren't pleased with her lack of progress in getting more intel, and the pressure was beginning to mount. They'd even suggested she be pulled back from the operation, but she'd pleaded for one more month. That should give her time to prepare for her solo attack on The Shamrock, if nothing else.

The buzzer in the shop went off, and she looked at the TV screen monitoring the entrance. Speak of the devil; there he was: Patrick Gillispie. It was getting late, and she was about to close. She shouted through the grilled door before switching off the outside lights, "We're closed!"

That'd teach him!

Outside, Patrick squinted as he looked through the barred windows, using his hands to block out the street light. "I see you in there, Brona. Come on now, love, let me in!" He banged the door hard and determinedly.

Inside, Alice waited. She really was tired and didn't feel like entertaining him this late. But she'd no real choice. She buzzed the door open and watched him enter.
She turned her back on him and switched off the last of the lights as she made her way to the back of the shop and storeroom. He followed her towards the bottom of the staircase, where he grabbed her arm and turned her round to face him. His eyes softened as he looked at her.

"Hey, you. Don't be angry with me. I'd things to do, places to go. Sorry."

Sulking like a disappointed child, she screwed up her face in a pout. To her surprise, he was suddenly on her, snatching her blouse off with one hand, sending buttons flying around the storeroom. She tried to remember her training, pushing him away, but he was too strong and seemed to predict her every move. She felt his teeth nibbling her lips and tongue as he hungrily kissed her. Once again, she tried to fight him off, but he had her locked in his arms.

His kissing was hard and passionate. She felt herself submit and instinctively began to respond, forgetting who or where she was. Lust took over as they fought to get each other's clothes off. They couldn't get enough bare flesh. The shock of it, touching and combining. The sensation consumed them and sent electricity through their veins. His hardness pressed against her, and she shivered. As her bra came off, he felt the tip of her erect nipples in between his fingers and lowered his mouth to take them, one at a time, between his teeth. His tongue played with each of them in turn as he moaned, eating her little bite by bite.

Alice gasped and stretched her head back in ecstasy. It'd been years, *years,* since she'd felt so alive, wanted and aroused. She couldn't control herself when he lowered himself to his knees, lifted her skirt and pushed her legs apart to remove her panties. Up he went, inside her with his tongue, tickling her, teasing her. She heard him moan,

"Sweet Jesus, Brona, you're delicious," but she couldn't speak as her body reached for its climax. He licked and sucked and played and tickled. His fingers joined his tongue as she became more and more wet. She'd never felt anything like it. She was lost and out of control.

Patrick Gillispie was in control, concentrating on her, continuing to use just two of his fingers. He looked up at her and smiled as he climbed up to her breasts again and teased her nipples, then set her off in an uncontrolled climax with rapid movements of his fingers.

It'd been far too long since she'd felt this release. She whined like an animal as her whole body shook uncontrollably. She couldn't believe how easily he'd made her do that! Her heart felt as if it could burst, and she was sweating. She felt so *light*. He went to touch her nipples again, but she pushed him away, using what strength she'd left. She couldn't take any more; he was killing her!

"No! Enough! What have you done to me!" she wailed, leaning heavily against the wall, oblivious to the nakedness of her breasts and her skirt up above her waist.

Patrick placed a hand to each side of her head. His eyes were knowing. He was good. Always had been, always would be. She'd obviously enjoyed it, he thought, as he studied her flushed face and heaving chest.

Without warning, he felt a huge slap across his head as she cried out angrily, pushing him off. Picking up her clothes, she yelped.

"You fucker! You think you can just walk in here, without a word of explanation, and fuck me!" Brona was, in truth, more furious with herself than with him. She couldn't believe she'd given in to his intimate exploration of her body. She felt humiliated by the speed with which she'd reacted.

Women! Patrick thought.

His hardness waned as he watched her open the flat door, at first fumbling to find her key that had fallen onto the storeroom floor. He followed her up the narrow steps as Alice stormed off to the bathroom to calm herself and get dressed. He looked around. There were shelves of books everywhere, all sorts of subjects: novels, biographies, history. It was like a library in here. His thoughts returned to what his twin had told him earlier, and he looked towards the bathroom to make sure Brona wasn't on her way back before lifting a number of the books and leafing through them to see if anything was hidden inside. He'd hoped a piece of paper or a photograph would fall from between the pages. But no, nothing. He continued to search until he glanced up and saw her standing by the bathroom door, watching him. She appeared extremely angry.

"What are you looking for?" she asked disdainfully, walking towards him and grabbing a book from his hands.

Her attitude was ever so slightly beginning to piss him off. "Nothing in particular," he replied, turning his back on her. "Just having a wee nosy."

Alice just wanted him to leave.

"I think you'd better go."

Patrick moved towards her, and she stood still. He looked into her eyes and saw her shame. He gently lifted a lock of hair from her face and tucked it behind her ear.

"Brona, what happened just now was beautiful. It was beautiful for me and clearly beautiful for you. Why don't you try and relax? Pour me a drink, and let's go fuck!"

She looked into his brazen eyes. *Christ.* He was beginning to get to her. He radiated so much confidence that she found she couldn't ignore his suggestion and found herself frantically responding to him once more as he roughly pulled her towards him and kissed her deeply.

* * *

Meanwhile, back at The Shamrock, where they were having a lock-in, Dolores was getting intoxicated. She was feeling lonely and had her eye on a fella at the bar who'd caught her staring. Just as she was about to wander in his direction, she was violently pushed back against the bar when a stream of armed RUC men and British soldiers stormed in. A raid! They'd battered down the reinforced front door and now flew in from every direction: shouting abuse, pulling and pushing the punters up against the wall, spreading legs, hands and fingers, fingertip-searching them.

In the middle of drunkenly attempting to push the gatecrashers away, she thought, Thank fuck we got it all out! Moments later, she was smashed painfully across the head by the butt of a British Army rifle.

Chapter 38

Weeks before, Father Connolly had pleaded with Tommy O'Reilly to join him on a visit to one of his young parishioners who'd been arrested. The boy, Donal, was being held in one of the recently built blocks, H-block 6, in the newly named Her Majesty's Maze Prison (originally Long Kesh). The gaol had recently been labelled "one of the most secure prisons in Europe".

He'd hoped O'Reilly could talk some sense into the lad, given Tommy knew the youngster and his family very well. The Kyles lived in the Creggan estate, and Tommy had known Andy, Donal's father, all his life. Andy was a well-known senior Republican who'd shot and murdered a British soldier as he left Fort George in Derry on foot patrol. A few days after the shooting, he'd left a safe house, was put in the boot of a car and driven safely over the border.

Months later, he'd been told his mother was dying and, under cover of darkness, sneaked back home to say goodbye. Someone grassed on him, the Brits were waiting, and he was promptly taken into custody and imprisoned. He never got the chance to see his mother, who died just a few hours after his arrest.

Young Donal Kyle was the first prisoner to be sentenced under the British Government's new ruling of "criminalisation". The authorities now viewed all recently convicted men and women as no more than common criminals and had decreed they should be treated as such. Denied special-category status, the youngster refused from day one to wear the prison uniform, conform to prison rules or undertake any prison work. He told them they'd have to nail it to his back before he wore their uniform, choosing to wrap a bed sheet around his body instead. His actions marked the beginning of the Blanket Protest.

O'Reilly and Father Connolly made the long drive to the small town of Maze, southwest of Belfast. The eight newly constructed H-blocks had been built to house recently convicted men – most of them on trumped-up charges.

Kyle's father and the other long-established prisoners were allowed to retain their political status but were separated from the new arrivals in the H-blocks. They continued to be locked up in their 1940s pre-fab huts or "cages".

Andy Kyle from Cage 11 decided to get himself into a fight with a warden. He was taken to court, convicted and then returned to the gaol – as a common criminal. He was incarcerated in H-block 6 along with his son, all within the space of a few hours. He, too, refused to wear the prison uniform and joined Donal on the Blanket Protest.

On this particular visiting day, father and son were pleased to be able to walk handcuffed together to the visitors' block half a mile away, where they were taken through the many air-locked gates to see Father Connolly. It didn't matter to them that they were denied transport. They were glad of the exercise and fresh air.

As they walked, they talked in low voices, aware they were being observed from the prison's many watchtowers. The cameras in the control centre continued to roll, likely recording them. Their guards were only three feet away and clearly trying to listen to their conversation.

The visitors' room was large and low-ceilinged. Small wooden cubicles filled the room, each one containing a table and four chairs. The men waited for their names to be called out and to be allocated a cubicle. As soon as they heard their name and number, they spotted the priest standing at the far end of the room and smiled even more widely when they recognised his companion, Tommy O'Reilly. Visiting privileges consisted of four half-hour visits a month. Inmates like Donal, who were appealing their sentence, were allocated a daily fifteen-minute visit with their legal representatives. They knew these conversations were recorded and were they to digress from "*appeal talk*" to anything else, even the weather, their consultation would be quickly cut short.

Father and son decided today would be the last visit they'd have for the immediate future. From now on, they'd only attend Mass and wouldn't leave their cell for any other reason. They felt they had no choice but to make a stand for what they believed in. They strongly felt they warranted political status, given that they were at war with the British, and should be treated as PoWs.

And so they were using this visit as an opportunity to share their decision with their priest, who would pass the word. Just for today, rather than sporting just their blankets, they wore tattered and scuffed blue boilersuits purely for this visit.

Young Donal Kyle felt his hand being squeezed tightly by his father. This was quickly spotted by a warden who raged and roared, spitting in the older man's ear: "No touching, you fucking moron, you hear me?"

Andy nodded, his ear ringing.

The smell of alcohol from the warden's breath was overwhelming and stuck in his nostrils. The screws had five social clubs on-site. They were continually in fear of their lives and rarely left the compound. Instead, they drank in the staff clubs and were at their worse for dishing out beatings and abuse to the prisoners when they were still drunk or hungover after heavy bouts of drinking.

As their visitors approached and reached out to shake hands, the same angry voice screeched, "NO touching!"

"Don't worry, Father, Tommy. It's good to see you both. Quick, sit down, tell us all the news. We hear nothing here!" implored Andy.

The priest and Tommy looked at each other, both unsure what to say. They were gobsmacked to see the condition of the men. The boilersuits were much too large for them, both the Kyles were unshaven, and their hair was too long, dirty and uncombed. Their teeth were covered in slime, and their skin was grey and blotched with sores. It was embarrassing and sad to see these proud men deteriorate in such a way. Young Kyle noticed their discomfort and joked, "Me Da's driving me crazy, Father, with his snoring. Can you have a word before I kill him!"

The young man's act eased the atmosphere, and the priest and Tommy laughed, watching his father pretend to slap Donal over the head.

"I SAID, no touching!" bawled an angry voice in the background.

"Fucking wanker," Andy whispered under his breath, quickly followed by, "Sorry, Father."

The priest smiled, and they settled down to engage in some light conversation. It didn't last as the mood of the visit changed when Father Connolly looked towards Tommy, his eyes pleading for support, and said, "Tommy, will you tell these two to stop what they're doing with their protests and just put the uniform on? Think about it, boys; you could be back in the compound *together*. They've got education classes there, access to showers, they've got a canteen and even a TV!"

Tommy looked at Andy and Donal Kyle and knew immediately it would be useless to try to make them change their minds. The steely determination in their eyes said enough. He and the priest were wasting their time here. Instead of backing Father Connolly, he asked quietly, "Is there anything we can bring or do for you for next time?" Together they shook their heads, and then Donal told them about the latest decision – there'd be no more visits.

The news came as a complete shock. Tommy was astounded and looked gravely concerned. "Jesus, boys, are you absolutely sure? This is awful! C'mon, Andy."

Silence. He turned to the boy and pleaded, "Are you sure, Donal?"

It was Andy who answered. "It's decided, Tommy, and we're doing okay – aren't we, son?"

Instinctively Andy leaned forward to pat his son on the back but stopped midway as he remembered, *NO touching!*

Time was precious to the men, but no one knew what to say after this bombshell. A heavy silence descended on them, and the visit became awkward and uncomfortable.

In the end, Tommy could only ask, "I suppose there's nothing we can do to change your minds?"

Andy sighed wearily. He couldn't explain or expect these two to understand their reasons.

He thought of himself and Donal, the two of them together in a cell with no beds and only a pot to pee and shit in. It filled quickly, and in the end, they'd no choice but to throw its contents under the door or out the window. Sometimes the POs would throw it back over them. After that, they'd tried to put their shit in a corner, but the POs threw their blankets on it. It didn't take long for the small space to stink. Andy knew things would most likely get worse, but over his or Donal's dead body, were they going to give in and wear Her Majesty's prison uniform.

He smiled at his priest first, then at Tommy. The big man shook his head in despair.

* * *

Back in Creggan, Father McGuire was finally packing his bags. It'd taken much longer than he'd hoped to get things sorted in the Parish, but now he was off. He was going to visit his favourite sister in Mayo for a few weeks, and then who knew what? He wasn't going to think that far ahead. He'd been suffering from migraines more than usual and looked forward to some peace and quiet – he'd even considered getting himself a dog.

Job done, he looked around the blue and white bedroom with its heavy oak single bed. The last ten years had been the most difficult of his priesthood, and he'd often felt sad, lonely and beaten. He thought of Tina McLaughlin often but knew he'd done all he could to help her and the other women in Armagh Gaol.

He understood he'd always feel it wasn't enough, but these days, no one wanted to know, and that new upstart, Yeaman, avoided him like the plague. At least at times, Governor Johnston had listened. Father McGuire had been devastated when he'd said his last goodbyes to Tina and the others and knew he'd never forget the women. The girl just smiled and said nothing when he'd hugged her; he was sure she'd no idea who he was – another tragic ending.

That morning he'd presided over his last funeral Mass – another victim of The Troubles, Paul Kennedy. The young man had lain in a coma for months after being run over by an army Saracen. It'd been truly heartbreaking as he'd watched Paul's mother, sedated and unresponsive, sit through the Mass and stand dead-eyed at the grave as her young son was buried.

Talking with William Barter, the newspaper reporter after the funeral, he'd been surprised when Barter commented on Father Connolly's trips to the States.

"You do realise what he's *really* up to, Father, don't you?" Barter asked, rolling his eyes. "All these trips back and forth, raising funds for special projects. Have you ever read one of his NORAID speeches, Father McGuire – they're mighty impressive?"

He hadn't but knew the younger priest had the support of the Bishop. Perhaps he should have paid more attention.

"To be honest, Mr Barter, I don't care. I'm finished. By this afternoon, I'm gone."

Father McGuire had wanted no fuss when he shared the news of his retirement. He'd insisted the younger priests were discreet. He didn't want any accolades, parties or presentations, only to leave quietly on his own terms. The American was surprised and frustrated as he'd heard nothing about the priest's imminent departure.

"What? But, Father, you're needed here. From what I've seen and heard, you're a pillar of the community. You can't just leave. What about all those folk who look up to you… who need you? Jeez, Father, that's not fair!"

"Ssshhh! Please. Don't fuss!" Father McGuire snapped. William Barter couldn't believe it, but ever the newsman, an idea soon popped into his head – a *great* idea!

"Sorry, Father, it's your decision, of course." He looked at the fatigued and beaten priest and offered him his hand.

They shook, and then Barter asked pensively, "I don't suppose you'd allow me to interview you? To talk about your time here… How you feel Derry has changed, what you've experienced and what's next for you?"

Pointing his finger and shaking it as though the thought was just occurring to him, he asked excitedly, "It'd give you a chance to say goodbye – all in one go."

The priest looked surprised, but he thought about it. Yes, it wasn't a bad idea, although he'd need to run it by the Bishop.

"I'll consider it."

William Barter wasn't going to take no for an answer. He'd make it into an exclusive – that's what he'd do! There were plenty of readers out there who'd be interested to hear what a priest living in the very heart of this hellish conflict had to say – especially in the States.

Chapter 39

Caitlin continued to work at the photographer's and over the past few weeks had seen James Henderson driving by the shop in his Jaguar on several occasions. Last time she was sure he'd seen her while she was dressing the shop's front window.

She'd completely blown it with Seamus, who never returned. Martin dropped the odd hint here and there about Seamus's absence and was bold enough to ask her what went wrong. She told him she didn't want to talk about it, and, sensing her hurt, he'd said no more. Seamus never told Martin anything either, and he gave up enquiring.

Caitlin's next visit to Tina had proved to be an unmitigated disaster. She'd made the long journey to Armagh by bus and patiently waited in the circle with many of the other families, only to be told her sister wasn't well enough for visitors that day. She'd shouted her frustration at the wasted journey to the very same small, stout, round-faced prison officer as she met last time. She reminded Caitlin of a raven with her coal-coloured, gelled hair. Caitlin tried to pass her a food package for Tina as well as some craft materials, but the barrel-chested woman ignored her. In the end, Caitlin was calmed by another frequent visitor, who told her this was a regular occurrence for many of them, and she returned home sad and disillusioned.

The only good things in her life now were Anne and baby Sean. The christening had gone well, although, to Anne's horror, Porkie had insisted that Dickie be named as Sean's godfather.

Anne continued to live on her nerves. One dark evening there was a loud knock at the front door. She hissed in fury, "Fuck it, Porkie, if that's Dickie, I'll kill him. I've just got the baby to sleep!"

She stormed out of the chair without looking at her husband. He was already on his feet, his terrified heart beating like a trapped bird's wings. *This was it!* Finally, the waiting was over. Oddly, he felt a surge of relief.

He heard Anne talking and, in a matter of seconds, saw two men standing menacingly on the threshold. They wore dark green army trousers and jackets buttoned tightly up to their necks. They had dark scarves around their faces, wore dark caps and sunglasses. They were carrying pistols. The taller man spoke in a Derry accent.

"Mrs Ballantyne, you'd better stand back now, please. We need to take your husband on a wee ride."

Anne was terrified. She knew she couldn't do anything, given Sean was upstairs. She stood and watched as they grabbed Porkie by the scruff of his neck and dragged him along the hallway, throwing him violently down the steps and onto the pavement.

She screamed as she watched them kick him viciously in the stomach and head. Within seconds a wailing cry came from the small bedroom upstairs that was used as the nursery. Anne frantically looked around the street, hoping someone would help. Instead, in response to her screams, net curtains were slowly drawn back and faces appeared at windows. There was no question of anyone getting involved. The way they were dressed and acting, these men were obviously a punishment squad, and no one sane got in their way.

One of the masked men lifted Porkie easily and tied his hands behind his back, pushing him towards a car with its engine running. The other walked back to Anne and, in a rasping voice, warned her: "Say nothing to anyone, Mrs Ballantyne; your husband's done too much of that already!"

She knew then that Porkie was finished.

* * *

As soon as it was light, Anne dressed Sean and caught a bus to Creggan to see Father Connolly. The journey was long and frustrating as she'd forgotten to bring the baby's dummy, and, sensing her anxiety and turmoil, he became unsettled, not taking his bottle and screaming. It was only when the tears began to stream down her face that one of the women on the bus moved in next to her and took the baby. Within moments, with the woman's bent thumb in his mouth, Sean settled.

"Thank you," Anne sniffled.

As a mother and grandmother she'd seen it all so many times, young girls with young babies, always disappointed in love. "It's alright, love. Just settle yourself there for a minute. Where you off to?"

"St Mary's. I have to see Father Connolly," she replied, wiping her red and dribbling nose with a piece of used tissue.

"He's away, love. Off to America, I heard, just this morning."

Anne couldn't believe her fuckin' luck. *Christ.* She looked to see where else the bus was headed and decided she'd visit her mother instead. Thanking the kindly woman, she got off at the nearest stop to her mother's home.

* * *

That evening Caitlin locked up the shop and found Anne and baby Sean waiting for her outside. She ran over to her crying, red-eyed friend and hastily asked, "Jesus, Anne, what are you doing out here? Why didn't you come in! It's been dead in there for the last hour or so; I could have got away. What's happened? It's that fuckin' Porkie again, isn't it!"

Earlier, Anne had tried to explain to her mother what'd happened. She'd been livid that Anne hadn't told her before about Porkie's antics with Dickie. She, too, had willingly taken money off Porkie and wondered, did that mean she was a grass as well? Were they all in for it!

She'd never felt as furious with her daughter as she did at that moment. Liz had screamed her rage to the high heavens, scaring the life out of poor baby Sean and Anne's younger siblings scattered around the house.

"Jesus, Mammy, take it easy!" she yelled over the din of her squawling baby. In desperation, she implored, "Listen to me, please! You've got to help me! Don't you get it!"

But Liz wouldn't listen and instead ran upstairs to comfort her youngsters. She wanted Anne out of her sight and roared down the staircase for her to: "Fuck off and leave us be! All you've ever done is bring trouble to this house! Now leave!"

Anne went to Brooke Park and sat for hours by the pond, envying the couples who passed by. Most of them looked happy – at least to her. The hours dragged by until she knew Caitlin was due to finish work.

* * *

"You'll be alright, Anne," Caitlin said now as she hugged mother and baby."Let's get you both home to mine."

They finally made it to Caitlin's, where she ran to the gas meter and topped it up. As usual, the house was cold, too cold for a baby. They ended up sitting at the kitchen table next to the gas cooker with all its rings burning brightly for heat. The kettle boiled, and Caitlin made the tea as Anne changed the baby on her knee. Sean was quite content and gurgled, smiling up at his mother as she baby-talked to him.

Caitlin sat in her chair and sighed. She was concerned for her friend.

"Tell me everything," she requested as she passed her a red mug of tea and a few pieces of buttered toast.

Anne was starving. Caitlin took the clean baby and watched while her friend scoffed down a piece of toast and, at the same time, attempted to talk. "Jesus, Caitlin, I've known for ages that Porkie and Dickie were grasses! I even told Father Connolly, but he said not to say anything to anyone. And now the Provos have taken him!"

Caitlin was shocked beyond belief – she'd never imagined those two to be informers even though they were both thick as shit. She understood the priest's advice, but rumours were that he was more involved than most people realised.

"But, Anne, you should have told me. No wonder Porkie looked so awful; he must have been shitting himself?"

Anne nodded eagerly. "He was, Caitlin, but I couldn't say anything to him. I did try, but he wouldn't or couldn't tell me anything. I blame that fucker Dickie. I'm sure he put the pressure on. I'm so scared because I took money from him to get stuff for the baby!" Caitlin waited and watched as Anne slurped her tea before continuing her rant. "He said he'd won it all on the dogs at the Brandywell. What am I going to do? They'll kill him, and now Mammy's told me to fuck off, and she even threw me out!"

Anne started to cry, and baby Sean, sensing her distress, once more became agitated and began to wail. Caitlin stood and walked around the kitchen with him in her arms to try and comfort him.

Anne and her baby were practically all the family she'd left. Her parents had gone. Tina might as well be gone. Martin could only drop in and see her infrequently. Tommy was up to his eyeballs and had his own problems. As for Granny, Caitlin considered her a lost cause. She'd helped out once with mammy, after daddy had died, but had been conspicuous by her absence when her daughter was consumed by grief following Tina's trial. There was no one else for Caitlin, only the young mother and baby sitting in her kitchen.

"You'll stay here with me, Anne. For as long as you want. We can make Sean up a bed on the floor with the cushions from the sofa. I'll go and see Father Connolly." Anne had forgotten to tell her the priest was away.

"Ah, Caitlin, sure Father Connolly left for America this morning."

As ever, it wasn't long before Caitlin suggested she seek help from Tommy. They'd no choice. He'd know what to do to trace Porkie and check what was going to happen.

In the end, Anne didn't stay at Caitlin's place too long, just for the first night. Sean needed his cot and continued to be upset and unsettled – no doubt sensing her fear and anxiety. Caitlin was worried when Anne left the safety of her house.

"You know you can stay here as long as you want. Both of you," she said lovingly.

"I know, Caitlin, but I need to get Sean home. I'll be okay." Anne hugged and thanked her again before she began the walk to the bus stop. She wasn't at all sure that she was okay but felt the need to get herself and Sean back to their house in Shantallow and to keep the world out.

Later that evening, she held her baby tightly as she watched a patrol of British soldiers tear into and search her new house. Word was out, and none of her neighbours came anywhere near her – they knew. The message written in bold red paint on her front door as she arrived back home confirmed it: *Die, Grass.*

Chapter 40

Once Dickie heard the bomb blasts, the screeches and screams, and saw the tongues of fire spouting from the barn into the night sky, he knew. They'd set him up! *Fuck.* He had to get out of Derry and fast. They'd be coming for him!

With great stupidity, he went straight home. Unlocking the front door and walking into his living room, he realised it was too late for him to run. They were already there, armed, masked and waiting.

He put his arms up in surrender, but they were yanked down and wrenched around his back, his hands tied tightly together. A heavy hood of sacking was quickly placed over his head, and he was led out by the back door, down the path to a waiting vehicle.

He was hauled in, his body hitting the uneven floor hard. He tried to sit up, but from out of the blue, a foot caught him right between the balls. He howled like an alley cat, in excruciating pain!

"Fucking hell! Jesus, me balls!"

A voice he'd thought he'd never hear again exclaimed, "Dickie… is that you, Dickie?"

"Aye, it's me, you wanker! You've just kicked me in the fucking balls!"

Porkie followed the sound of Dickie's voice and scrambled his way across the moving floor towards him.

"We're dead, Dickie," Porkie snivelled. "We're dead. What're we going to do?"

Dickie didn't answer.

* * *

Liz and Emmett were each given a zipped backpack and told not to look inside until they took leave of their passengers. Liz didn't seem particularly bothered by such odd instructions, but Emmett's gut instinct told him this wasn't going to be anything like their usual run. Something weird was going on, and it made him more nervous than usual.

At 3 a.m., Liz and Emmett sat in his car, parked in an industrial plant in Pennyburn. The minutes passed until a white van drove speedily into the darkened plant and quickly flashed its lights.

They walked over and waited while a number of well-disguised men climbed out.

They nodded in acknowledgement, silently opened the back of the van and dragged out two dishevelled, hooded men. One of them attempted to run away but was quickly caught, kicked, forcefully dragged towards Emmett's Austin and pushed into the back seat next to the other man. With their mouths taped securely, their muffled screams were to no avail. Within minutes their captors were back in the van and had driven off.

Liz looked at Emmett. "Fuck me, that was a bit 007, wasn't it?"

He felt he needed to reassure her, even though he was far from happy about this job himself.

"We'll just do as we're told, and it'll all be fine," he said, hoping she would not detect his inward misgivings in the tremor of his voice. She looked at him for a moment in a rather peculiar way but remained quiet as they opened the backpacks and read their instructions under the car light and against the unrelenting mumblings of their two demanding rear-seated passengers.

* * *

As directed, Emmett carefully parked the car by a discreet safe house, and he and Liz took the two men out of the car and pushed them through the back door of the red-brick bungalow. Liz screamed at them to settle down and get onto the floor. The bigger of the two, clearly terrified, had wet himself and was quietly sobbing. The other one remained silent and compliant.

They were left alone as the hours passed. Dickie tried everything he could to get free and finally lost his temper, kicking Porkie, who'd made no effort to help. He was filled with fear. He'd soon be dead, and there was nothing he could do about it. Eventually, he'd no choice but to give up and do the only thing left. He prayed. Fuck, how he prayed.

After a few hours, Emmett and Liz returned to the room. They'd taken turns to sleep, but Emmett only closed his eyes, guiltily aware of what the two captives must be going through if he, their gaoler, felt like this. He stood in front of the prisoners and pulled off their hoods. They squinted and tried to shield their eyes from the bright daylight, their cable-tied hands making it impossible. The big man remained frozen still while the one with black hair frantically looked around the room. He caught his breath when he saw his kidnappers. Fucking hell, they were just youngsters! He immediately recognised the boy. It was the lad who'd worked on his car a while back. Emmett something… Yes, that was it.

Dickie screamed through his taped mouth, hoping to make himself known. Shaking violently and trying his best to explain, he watched the lad fumble something out of his parka pocket. Dear God, it was a handgun.

Emmett was frightened too. He knew he had to keep the screamer quiet and pressed the gun barrel under his chin.

"Stop fucking screaming, or I'll do you! Now, I'm going to take the tape off so you can drink. Be warned; I WILL shoot you if you utter a sound or make any sudden movements."

Dickie nodded, and Porkie watched and waited.

Liz and Emmett tore back the hardened sticky tape just enough to allow them to drink. Taking great care not to spill any, they poured the cloudy drugged water down the prisoners' gullets.

Dickie was about to try and say something when he saw Emmett warning him not to by pointing the gun at him again. But Dickie wasn't giving up – if he could only tell the lad who he was!

"Listen, Emmett. It is Emmett, isn't it?! It's me Dickie! Remember?!"

At hearing his name, Emmett panicked. His hand holding the pistol began to shake and wobble uncontrollably until he had no choice but to drop the gun to his side. He finally knew he was well over his head; this wasn't what he'd agreed with Mickey. This was way off the line, a different league altogether! He stepped back against the wall and slid down, his head falling into his hands in distress. Liz had been watching him all night. She'd seen and sensed his fear as they'd read their orders earlier in the car. It was a shame. She'd grown fond of him, but she'd have to report back that he didn't have the guts to continue; he could become a liability. This whole operation had suddenly become a solo op - it was up to her now to see it through.

At making such a decision, Liz had had enough and roughly pulled the tape back across Dickie's sodden mouth, cruelly hissing into the side of his head, "Shut your hole, ye arse head! Do you hear me? Shut it!" She then did the same for Porkie and replaced the dirty, dark hoods over her captive's heads. It shouldn't be long now…

Liz and Emmett watched without speaking as the drug took effect. Porkie seemed ready to let it take him, but Dickie didn't give up without a struggle. Emmett's heart was in his boots. This was the hardest thing he'd ever had to do, and he knew there was worse ahead – for the two prisoners and maybe for him if he disobeyed orders. He needed to catch himself on and looked over at Liz for any sign of understanding. She gave him nothing.

Liz was keen to move on and told him harshly, "It's noon. Come on, hurry it up!"

Emmett drove his Austin to the very end of the lengthy driveway alongside the back door of the house. He opened the boot, and he and

Liz struggled to lift the cumbersome fat man first and stow him inside. They were exhausted by the struggle, but luckily the second man was easier.

* * *

Emmett and Liz approached the border checkpoint to be met with a horrendous queue: security services were on high alert. Liz noticed Emmett appeared a little more relaxed and suggested under her breath that they put on an act. She leaned across to his ear and pretended to kiss him, whispering.

"Pretend I'm saying something dirty in your ear!" She joked.

In return, Emmett laugh naughtily, playing his part and knowing it was likely they were being watched. Emmett's pulse raced, and his heart beat fast and furious. He was praying there'd be no sound or movement from the car boot where the two men were stowed away under blankets.

As they drew nearer, they saw a number of vehicles had been pulled over and were being meticulously searched. Car seats were being pulled out, front bonnets were up, boots were opened, and their contents uncaringly and randomly scattered across the ground.

They were next. *Sweet Jesus. Fuck!*

A soldier waved a hand for them to come forward, and as before, Emmett awkwardly rolled down his window to produce his driver's licence. The Brits all looked the same to him, and he paid no attention while his document was examined. The soldier looked into the car and noticed Liz. Suddenly Emmett thought he heard a noise coming from the boot. His heart jolted, and his mouth filled with bile. The soldier said something, but in his efforts not to vomit, Emmett didn't hear.

Liz knew her partner was in trouble and elbowed him whilst giggling and flirting with the soldier, who laughed along with her. He leaned down and smiled at her through the window as his eyes scanned the inside of the Austin. He then walked to the back, opened the two rear doors and checked there too. Emmett grimaced and swallowed.

The soldier chuckled. "She's still going then!"

"Sorry?" Emmett replied, confused.

"The car, mate! Who'd you think I meant? She's still going, your pile-of-shite motor?"

Once more, Liz elbowed Emmett – hard.

"Remember, silly, we've met before!" she told him, eyes widening for him to take the hint and then rolling sideways towards the soldier.

She looked at the Brit and smiled flirtatiously, digging her hands into her pockets as she spoke. "Weren't you the one taking the piss out of Emmett's wheels a while back?"

"That's right, miss! Good memory. You should be doing this job 'stead of me."

Liz quickly leaned across Emmett and held out her hand. Somehow, on the engagement finger of her left hand, a small solitaire ring had appeared. It looked to Emmett like it had come out of a cracker. He knew better than to say a thing. "We're getting married," Liz was gushing. "Yer man here asked me last night, so we're away on our own for a night or two, see how we suit." She winked at the soldier, who visibly gulped before looking hard at Emmett. *Lucky man.*

The soldier glanced across to the other side of the checkpoint. There were too many cars already pulled over and waiting to be searched. He liked these two and found himself envying them, thinking of his own fiancée far away at home. *Miss you, babe.*

"Well, congrats to both of you. Look, I'm causing a bigger queue here. Off you go – and be good!"

"Thanks very much. You too!" Liz replied, beaming.

Emmett nodded his thanks, started the engine and took off.

"What a dickhead!" Liz crowed when they were out of earshot.

"That was a good trick with the ring," Emmett said, surprised she'd never mentioned it before.

"Oh, I'm full of good tricks. You've no idea," she told him, settling back in her seat.

Just a little further down the road, with a brief wave, they passed through an Irish customs post into the safety of the Irish Republic.

* * *

When the car reached their final destination, Ned's Point just outside Buncrana, Emmett and Liz found two middle-aged men waiting for them, standing next to a battered red Land Rover. They looked like farmers, dressed identically in long waxed black coats. One wore a flat tweed cap, the other a woollen hat pulled down at the sides. Neither of them cracked a smile but moved straight round to the boot.

Few words were exchanged as Emmett quickly opened up to help the men remove the limp, drugged bodies and toss them onto the mossy grass. One of the men groaned and began to kick out his legs when he hit the ground.

To Emmett's horror, the hooded body was kicked in the stomach, head and groin, with steel-capped boots. His attackers' faces remained dispassionate throughout, and Emmett remembered the slaughterhouse workers who sometimes came to the tea-stall near the garage, flecked with red up to their eyebrows. The things they must see, every minute of the day. The things these two men must have seen. And done. Emmett's head began to swim.

"All done. Thanks," said the man in the woolly hat. "We can manage by ourselves now. Off with yiz."

Emmett drove away, slowly and steadily. Liz was saying something, but he wasn't sure what. After a couple of miles, he stopped by a farm gate, scrambled out and was sick in the hedge, his guts heaving and wrenching. He couldn't get the two men's faces out of his mind, the desperation of the dark-haired one and the resignation of the other. When he returned to the car, shivering and finding it hard to breathe for the pounding of his heart, Liz was in the driver's seat.

"I didn't know you could drive," he said, taken aback.

Her grey eyes looked almost colourless when she told him, "There's a lot you don't know about me, Emmett. Now get in unless you want to walk back to Derry. We'll have to take the long way – can't risk bumping into our British pal again, can we?"

He'd not even thought of that, just like it would never have occurred to him to bring along a toy ring to help them masquerade as sweethearts. And it would always be a masquerade; he knew that now, aware that he had failed whatever test had been set for him. And thank God for it.

* * *

Emmett read in the *Derry Journal* two days later that a man's body had been washed up on the beach of Lough Swilly, not far from Ned's Point, by a lone dog walker who'd noticed it floating near the shore. The remains were later identified as John Ballantyne (aka Porkie), a married man and father of one from Shantallow, Derry. He'd been shot at point-blank range in the back of the head. His friend, Kevin Moore (aka Dickie), had been reported missing but had yet to be found.

Chapter 41

PIRA Volunteer Dolores Gillispie stared boldly at Detective Jonathan Black in an interview room in the depths of Hastings Street RUC police station in Belfast. She'd been held for something like ninety hours, hadn't eaten, had been physically assaulted by Black and even threatened with rape. In fact, she was beginning to get on his tits since she'd proved to be both stubborn and defiant, refusing to utter a single word so far. Black hadn't been able to track down her twin either, from the information they'd been given, but knew he was somewhere in town after an unexplained absence. They suspected Patrick Gillispie was behind the recent spate of bombings in England and the recent murder at the British Ambassador's residence in Dublin, hence the raid on The Shamrock. To their surprise, during the raid, they'd found nothing and no one of any real interest other than Dolores Gillispie. The only consolation was that a number of the uniformed lads had confiscated a load of spirits and beer – all well hidden now in the section house for later use.

Fortunately, the day before The Shamrock was raided, Dolores had managed to convince her very reluctant twin to take out the cache of weapons and explosives they'd stored under the floorboards and move them to a safe house.

Black had obtained the necessary faxed Interim Custody Order form from the Northern Irish Secretary of State and now kept Dolores locked in a dank, filthy cell with only a stinking, damp and stained mattress for comfort and a thin soiled blanket. When she fell asleep in the cell, he'd insist she be woken up for further questioning. She was the only female prisoner in the station. The rest of the cells were filled with male Loyalists who continually shouted all sorts of profanity and abuse. Black made sure they knew they'd a Republican bitch in their midst. But all his attempts to frighten her failed. She gave him nothing, and eventually, he'd no choice but to get her transferred to Armagh.

A Black Maria drove her through the high gates and along the walled lane that led to Armagh Women's Gaol. Dolores had been a guest here before a number of times and knew Maureen Molony well. She felt almost at home amongst her protective and loyal comrades. As soon as she appeared in the committal area and word reached the wings that she was back, the women shouted out a welcome. She was surprised to see a number of male screws in the gaol this time. Unlike many of the women, though, it didn't bother her. They couldn't get to her. She was Patrick Gillispie's twin, and that carried a lot of kudos.

Strip-searches were a chance to show how insensitive she could be. She'd grown so used to them she now turned each one into a novelty. This time she goaded a couple of male guards by shaking her boobs and strutting her ass. From their reactions – some of them laughed, and others struck her – she could see who was a hardened bastard and who wasn't. She imagined some of them were likely perverts who'd enjoy peeping into the women's cells.

After a couple of days, she was taken to cell 23 on A-Wing. Supper was due to be served at the end of the wing under the huge window. It was coming up to 7.30 p.m., and she was hungry. She hadn't eaten for days – everyone knew the stuff served up in the committal area was regularly tainted by the screws. Pushed roughly into her new cell by a couple of male screws, Dolores fell down heavily on top of an empty bed. She looked up at the bulky cell door as it slammed shut. Always appearing tough and unreachable took its toll mentally – she was knackered. She sighed as she looked across at the youngster who lay on the bed opposite hers. *Fuckin' hell!* She looked tiny and so young.

The girl sat up straight when she saw Dolores looking at her. She grinned, displaying a top row of food-caked teeth. She was as thin as a famine victim, her face little more than bone under skin. She had bright red hair that must have been her glory once.

"Christ, wee girl, what happened to you?" Dolores asked, shocked beyond belief.

Tina McLaughlin laughed manically

A complete looney, then. *Poor critter*. Who the fuck was she, and what was her story? Dolores wondered.

The cell door suddenly opened, and the OC entered. Maureen's eyes were bright with excitement. She admired Dolores, believing this was just the type of woman the movement needed – she'd already proved herself to be a true comrade time and time again.

The two women hugged and held each other tightly until Dolores pulled away and shook her head in Tina's direction. So as not to offend, she whispered, "What the fuck, Maureen? What happened to her… Who is she?"

The OC looked at the youngin', and her heart lurched. When they could, all the women tried in every way possible to bring the girl back to them, but she continued to spiral downhill fast. When they attempted to take her out of the cell, wash or feed her, she'd scream mercilessly. Week after week, but to no avail, the OC complained to the Governor and duty doctor about the youngin's rapid decline.

"You must've heard about her. Tina McLaughlin? Got caught up with that cretin Kelly who tried to blow up the hotel in Derry along with those shootings. Remember Bishop Hegarty who was shot?"

A lightbulb went on in Dolores's head. Jesus, yes!

"God, aye, I remember now. But what's happened to the poor thing?" she asked sadly, looking at Tina once more.

The OC sighed heavily and answered, "It's a long story. Come away and have some supper. I'll tell you all about it."

During supper, she also told the sorry tale of Bridget Barry's abuse. Dolores was horrified but not surprised. In turn, she updated the OC on the progress of Blanket Protests in the men's prisons. Maureen knew a lot about them already. She and an H-block OC had secretly communicated, and it'd been decided the Armagh women would start a "no work" protest the following Monday. The new Governor, Yeaman, was a complete hole. A waste of space, who seemed determined to antagonise the women as much as he could. Recruiting male screws had been his idea. It was humiliating for the women and a complete intrusion on their privacy, especially the strip-searching of remand prisoners when they first arrived or those coming back from Armagh court.

* * *

A few days later, Governor Yeaman stood outside the Chief Officer's room in the circle. A new shift of POs was called to attention and lined up for inspection. Once they were told which wings they'd be on that day, the Chief Officer introduced the Governor, saying there was something he wished to brief them on personally. Yeaman had had enough of the Republican women in his gaol, who'd begun to dress in black skirts and black jumpers in commemoration of their so-called martyrs. Enough was enough, and so he issued an order.

"Those who have been assigned to levels A2, B2, B3… I want you to search each and every cell. As normal, confiscate any contraband, but, more importantly, I want you to remove every single item of black clothing. I will not tolerate these women attempting to wear a *uniform* of any kind in my prison! Take the lot of them to the association room and keep them there until you've finished. No stone should be left unturned! Do you understand?"

Smyth and Drake were thrilled to hear such news. They'd only been questioned over the Barry incident once by Yeaman, who didn't seem particularly concerned by their evasive answers. A search? Fantastic! They loved a good search, and now there were male officers on-site; it added even more excitement. Fists would soon be flying!

Yeaman finished off by asking the Chief Officer to update him at the end of the day and then left the circle. Once he'd gone, the space filled with the buzz of conversation as the POs prepared themselves mentally for what would inevitably be a long and difficult shift.

Upstairs in her cell, Dolores was organising her few precious belongings that she'd managed to get from one of the visitors. She'd pinned up her favourite black and white photograph of Patrick and herself as children, displaying it on a cupboard door. There they stood, side by side, holding hands. She knew she hadn't been a particularly good-looking girl but thought Patrick looked gorgeous in his long black trousers, shirt and jumper. His hair was short and neatly styled back with Brylcreem – a real teenager. She loved this particular photograph. It always made her smile when she remembered exactly where they'd been at the time. They were with a fantastic Catholic foster family in West Belfast, who'd cared for them for nearly three years. It ended when the fires in Bombay Street, where they'd lived, were burned down by Loyalists as well as several other Catholic homes. Sadly, the host family had been forced to move to a caravan whilst repairs were carried out, and the foster mother became very ill. Once again, the Gillispies were returned to the children's home.

Seeing her smile, Tina pointed to the picture.

"Ah, that's me and Patrick, my twin." Dolores smiled sadly. "My brother, Tina. Do you have a brother?"

A vague memory reached the forefront of Tina's mind. *Martin…* It was too hard for her to respond.

Poor mite, Dolores thought, as she began to put some clothes away in the cupboard. Out of the blue, an almighty roar started up at the far end of the wing near the Chapel. Loud clanging noises were heard, the sound emanating from batons hitting the wrought-iron rail where clothes were drying contrary to prison rules. These were summarily thrown off and fell onto the suicide net between the floors. The screws barked out their orders and swore as, cell by cell, the women were hauled out and made to stand in a row along the catwalk.

"Out! All of you!" screamed Smyth and Drake as they jostled in and out. "Wait in line!"

As Smyth reached Dolores and Tina, she stopped and considered McLaughlin. This was another prime opportunity to take a hit at the dead brain! She strode into the cell with her baton high and ready but was quickly stopped by the girl's cellmate, who violently caught and squeezed her hand, hissing in a threatening manner, "If you so much as touch a hair of that girl's head, I will get you killed! You and every member of your fucking family will be shot on your doorstep."

Although everyone regarded Smyth as a bully, deep down, she was a coward. She knew Dolores Gillispie's reputation and that she could easily carry out such a threat. At that, she lowered her arm and, with a jerk of her head, ordered Tina out. She didn't touch Gillispie either when Dolores led Tina out onto the landing. The pathetic cell was now empty. Smyth looked around, taking in the photograph pinned on the cupboard and others that lay scattered on one bed. *Later.*

The complaining women were led to the lower floor, where they were lined up and roughly searched. The remainder of the PO's, including Smyth and Drake, stayed upstairs to comb through the cells.

Starting from one end of the wing, each cell, in turn, was systematically wrecked. Mattresses were lifted, torn open and tossed onto the floor. Cupboards and drawers were opened, and their contents emptied out. Personal letters were torn up, and posters ripped from the walls. Compacts of make-up were smashed, and sanitary towels ripped apart. Smyth and Drake did as much as they possibly could to destroy the women's tiny personal spaces and treasured belongings.

Smyth smiled when she arrived back at cell 23. She noticed Tina McLaughlin had very few possessions, but whatever she had, Smyth destroyed. As for Dolores Gillispie: Smyth duly removed any black clothing. About to leave, she remembered the photograph, pinned to the cupboard and others on the bed. She studied them for a moment and then began slowly shredding them into tiny, tiny pieces that she threw up in the air like confetti. *Payback.*

Downstairs the screws finished their body searches after finding very little but tobacco and sweets. They'd been ordered not to feed the women yet but made them line up and wait until the search was over.

Much later, when the prisoners returned to their cells and saw the devastation, their cries of anger reverberated throughout the wings. One by one, the POs callously pushed them back into their destroyed cells, ordered them to be quiet and quickly locked the cumbersome steel doors. Dolores immediately spotted the remnants of her precious photographs now shredded and scattered on the floor. Like a roaring lion, she howled with rage, terrifying the life out of the youngin' who jumped about screaming as long and as hard as her cellmate.

Chapter 42

Chief Constable Thomas Bonner stood at the back of his office, leaning against the wall with his hands tucked tightly behind his back. He was an ordinary-looking man, and there was nothing special about his dark thinning hair, aquiline nose, thin moustache and short sideburns. He'd a brawny body of medium height and a pot belly. Conceited and vain, he'd refused to go to the next size up in his uniform, resulting in the silver buttons of his green tunic continually opening under a tightly buckled belt that only further encouraged his gut to hang out and over the top of his sharply pressed trousers. On this particular day, he was livid.

From what he'd just shared with Charles Jones, they'd a problem and a serious one at that. Somehow – *and he would fucking find out how* – Roger Henderson had managed to discover his brother's death wasn't an accident and through an intermediary had located a witness to his killing. Thank fuck for their mole Mrs Parkes who'd overheard James Henderson on the phone!

"What do you suggest you do now?" Charles Jones had asked provocatively, at the same time picking some hard skin off the side of his scarred face. Jones's lack of concern infuriated Bonner.

"*Me*, what should *I* do?" he yelled. "This isn't all on me, Jones. You're up shit creek as much as I am!"

Jones eyed him with contempt. He didn't like the fat twat very much but needed him. However, if the RUC imbecile thought Jones was going to pick up *his* mess, he'd another think coming. He lay back in his chair and raised his hands, encouraging Bonner to chill.

"Relax, Chief Constable. Relax. But remember, it was your idea to get Shalham removed as Chief, not mine. You'd been needling me about it from the very beginning. You wanted him to fail and likely were disappointed that worthless bomb hadn't gone off! You wanted him to take full responsibility for the security fuck-up that day, and he did. He took it all and resigned – only for you to fill his shoes so fast, the man didn't get a chance to pack! You then proceeded to freeze him out by telling your officers not to acknowledge him."

Jones was *mostly* right; he couldn't deny it. Bonner hadn't been able to bear George Shalham. He couldn't stand the adoration the man had received from his staff, from the community, from everyone! Bonner's father had been a RUC Chief Constable, and for as long as he could remember Bonner dreamed of following in his dad's footsteps. Ultimately he'd no choice but to bring down his predecessor.

However, killing someone like Shalham was bound to have repercussions. When Jones told him he'd arranged for the murder and said he needed Bonner to cover it, he'd been caught between the devil and the deep blue sea. Bonner owed Jones. Not only had he enabled him to become CC, but he'd also been paying him protection money. The cash proved extremely handy, allowing Bonner's voluptuous mistress to remain happy in a cosy, quiet cottage on the outskirts of the city.

The policeman sighed unhappily and sat down in his seat. He was trying hard to think of a solution when after a while, Jones piped up and slyly suggested a way out.

"Well, you are the Chief Constable, Bonner. Think about it. Once you find the witness, bring him in. Lock him up!"

At such a ridiculous suggestion, Bonner could only laugh. "Are you serious, man? For Christ's sake! Lock them up for being a witness to a murder? I've never heard anything so preposterous."

Jones picked at a painful and stubborn hangnail and, without looking at Bonner, explained, "It's really quite simple. Set them up. Say they're in the Provos or blame them for something else and just send them on their merry way."

Bonner shook his head and laughed again. Whoever this witness was, they clearly weren't stupid. They'd approached Shalham directly rather than going through the normal police channels and obviously knew the potential danger they were in. Even the Hendersons had as yet no direct knowledge of a name and location.

"I need to find out who it is first, Charles. I can't just pick up any Tom, Dick or Harry!"

Jones was growing impatient. He yanked at the nail in anger. It hurt like hell and began to throb. Raising his voice, he ordered, "I don't care if it's fucking Mother Teresa, Bonner. Find whoever it is and deal with it."

* * *

Marleen and James sat together on a bench in the kitchen garden at Melrose. It was a clear night and warm. James told her about his day and how he was growing more and more concerned about the viability of the factory. Each word he spoke added further impetus to her desire to bring matters to a head. She looked at James's familiar handsome face. He did look worried and was obviously seriously concerned about Roger's health as well.

"Darling, I need to put an idea to you. May I?"

James didn't hesitate. "Of course, Marleen, absolutely."

Now that she had to say it out loud and for real, it was proving a little bit more difficult. She suddenly felt nervous. Maybe it wasn't such a good plan.

James noticed her hesitation and urged her to go on. "Marleen, you and I have very few secrets, so come on, out with it."

Taking a dramatic breath and holding it, she turned and grabbed his hands, squeezing them tight as she began to explain.

"Darling, we've been friends forever, and you know almost everything about me and my *ways*."

Understanding her meaning, he smiled as she carried on. "I'll be frank, James. It's like this: Mummy and Daddy have been putting pressure on me to get hitched and produce an heir to the family loot. A sprog."

James wasn't sure where this was heading but was prepared to listen anyway. Marleen laughed at his puzzled expression.

"It appears, dear James, I need to find myself a husband and donor. I wondered whether you'd be up for the job?"

Relief washed over her like rain. It felt good to get that on the table, and she felt sure, businessman that he was, James would see the many advantages to himself of agreeing to her plan.

He was flattered, shocked, flummoxed, even amused at the proposal. He'd never have thought her capable of it in a million years! He loved Marleen; of course, he did, but not like he had Caitlin. A tidal wave of loss swept over him. Caitlin – God, he missed her!

His mind began to wander until Marleen, sensing his uncertainty, quickly pulled him back and told him excitedly, "Think about it, James. You can have my money to do with as you like – within reason, of course!" She laughed and, as an afterthought, added, "Here's an idea: you could use it to save Rocola. All those jobs, James, security for so many people. There's millions in my trust; you could afford it."

He'd never really thought about her money before, but she was right: it could save Rocola. Marleen babbled on. His mind raced as he half-listened.

"We'd obviously have to come to an understanding. We'd have to produce a sprog or two, but after that, you'd live your life, I'd live mine. That way, we'd have the best of both worlds. You know I love you to bits!"

Marleen's enthusiasm was running away with her. She'd given this so much thought – it couldn't fail.

James watched her while she continued to babble, thinking of the years they'd known each other and how incredibly fond he was of her. To her credit, she'd never said a word about the night they'd spent together, and he was pretty sure now nothing had happened. In the cold light of day, it'd have been far too weird and awkward, no matter how drunk they were. *Like having sex with your sister or brother!* He grimaced.

Nevertheless, here she was, offering him a golden opportunity to save the business. His uncle was gravely ill, and by marrying Marleen, he could make Roger very happy *and* revive Rocola.

He took her hand, and once again, his thoughts spontaneously returned to Caitlin. Too late for that. Slowly he nodded his head.

Jumping up in excitement, Marleen screamed with joy. "Oh, James! Is that a yes? Tell me it's a yes!"

His head bobbed faster in acceptance of her offer, and he kissed her tenderly on the cheek. " Marleen, it's a yes. But remember, we've got a great deal to talk about first!"

"Yikes! I'm so happy!" she screeched. "Oh, darling, at last!"

* * *

Somehow, distracting the ever meddling Home Warden, she'd managed to sneak him into the nurses' digs at Altnagelvin Hospital after dark, and here he was, lying next to her in her single bed. She shared her room with another nurse whose name he couldn't remember: Mary, Maureen or May, something similar – he'd never met her. Fortunately for them, she was on duty that night.

Unusually he wasn't feeling up to it tonight, and instead, they were lying by the light of a single candle, talking. Lynn was a good girl, and Lemon liked her a lot, unlike the nag he had at home, whom he could never please. He shivered at the thought of Mel. She was always screaming, shouting and complaining about everything. He didn't know how their five kids put up with her. He tried his best not to be at home with her and the kids and kept away as much as he could.

He smiled proudly as he looked at the photographs displayed on Lynn's bedside table. He was in every single one of them. The two of them were always smiling. Like him, she loved motorbikes, and they'd taken lots of pictures at the Northwest TT series on the Causeway Coast the year before. They both looked like rock stars in their black leather jackets and pants complemented with Hell's Angels Belfast T-shirts.

Lynn was a person he knew he could trust, and he'd told her a lot about what he did for Charles Jones. He'd not told her absolutely *everything,* and fortunately for her, she'd been wise enough not to ask too many questions. Little did he know, though, that Lynn loved to gossip with her roommate, Moira.

Until recently, Lemon had really enjoyed working for Jones, although their relationship had become awkward and difficult after his failure to kill the Yankee reporter.

As instructed, he'd followed him from Belfast to Londonderry, but then it all went very wrong.

Barter left his flat knowing he was being followed. He'd noticed Lemon on his tail from the moment he'd left Belfast. As he walked down Lawrence Hill, he heard his pursuer's footsteps getting closer and closer. Eventually, they were too close for comfort. Barter suddenly stopped in his tracks, turned and challenged him.

"Hey, dude, if you don't stop fuckin' following me, I swear to God, I'll kill ya!'

Lemon was momentarily stunned and unsure what to do. He wasn't expecting this!

The Yank looked furious and unafraid as he moved in closer and sneered in Lemon's face. He pointed his finger angrily and said, "You tell that weasel of a boss of yours, I have photos *and* evidence! I know what you guys are up to – you and '*the kids*'! So don't try anything on with me, dude, not here, not now!"

Lemon knew then that he couldn't kill the cocky bastard. So instead, he moved closer, keeping threateningly silent, face almost touching face. He stared hard and long at the reporter. Rigid and still, neither man made a move until Barber pushed Lemon off, using both hands, and cried angrily: "Get lost, Lemon, and remember – it's one hell of a file I have, in a very safe place. If *anything, ANYTHING,* happens to me, you and that lizard you work for are toast! I'm talkin' serious grief!"

Jones was incensed when Lemon reported back to him later. He'd wrecked his hotel room in the process, screaming hysterically. "The fucker, the fucking fucker! I knew he was up to something!"

Lemon had never seen his boss so angry and left as soon as it was safe.

* * *

Ned, Roger Henderson's dog, was lying solemn and sad at the bottom of Roger's bed, head resting on his master's leg. Ned seemed to be aware that death was not too far away. Roger rubbed the dog's neck gently and then lay back on his pillow. He'd been delighted to hear about James's and Marleen's engagement, absolutely delighted. Although they hoped to have the wedding as soon as possible, Roger knew it was unlikely he'd make it.

Over the past few months, long-suppressed memories had begun to creep into the forefront of his mind. He wondered whether it was his fear of dying that was encouraging them to haunt him one final time.

Most mornings in the early hours, he'd wake, sweating and shaking, from a recurring dream that never seemed to fade. He relived the biggest mistake he'd ever made and one he'd bitterly regretted from the moment it happened. He'd accepted that the shame of it was something he'd have to live with until his dying breath. No matter what, he must protect James from ever finding out what a vile and evil man Roger Henderson truly was.

Chapter 43

It was late afternoon in Boston on a beautiful, crisp winter's day, and Seamus could hear his name being called out over the timber yard: "Seamus, you gotta call!"

Removing his thick gloves and hard hat, he walked across the yard to the steps leading up to McMannus's office.

Seamus had no idea who'd be calling him as he made his way up the open timber steps. The black phone sat on the desk with its receiver snaked out and waiting. Seamus placed his gloves inside his white, hard hat with its shamrock logo, lifted the phone and answered hesitantly.

"Hello."

The line hummed as he repeated himself. "Hello."

Nothing. As he was about to hang up, he heard a faint voice say, "Seamus. Is that you? It's me."

He sighed. "Hello, Caitlin."

He could almost feel the relief emanating from her down the line. "Ah, Seamus, I'm so glad to hear your voice."

"Yours too, Caitlin. How are you?"

"Awful. I feel so awful, Seamus. I've tried to get you so many times. Listen, I wouldn't hurt you for the world. I'm so sorry about..."

"I know, I know. It's just… I didn't need it. I didn't need to get hurt all over again.

You want to tell me who he is. Who *James* is?" he asked.

The only thing he could hear was the deep humming of the line across the Atlantic. "Caitlin, are you still there?"

"I'm here," she answered softly. She'd been afraid he'd ask but knew he deserved the truth.

"So tell me."

And she did. She told Seamus everything. How she and James had met, about their time together, how happy he'd made her, and then his cruel and dismissive treatment of her after the bomb scare. She told him she thought she'd gotten over him when Seamus came back to Derry but obviously, she hadn't. She'd never meant to mislead or hurt him.

As he listened to her describe the affair, he knew there was no chance in hell he'd ever match up to this guy in her eyes and felt a pang of sorrow. It was time for him to let go of his unrequited love for this woman and his involvement in the Cause. It was time to make a new life for himself in the States. This was fate at work.

He knew it would be their last call. But even if he couldn't make her happy, he wanted to give her some good advice.

"I think you need to talk to him, Caitlin," he suggested. "If you love him as much as you say you do, you need to help him understand that. Tell him the truth."

But she couldn't. She very much doubted James Henderson would believe anything she'd have to say.

"You deserve some happiness, Caitlin. You're young, beautiful and clever. You owe it to yourself. You've got nothing to lose, so talk to him, for your own sake, please."

The humming on the line seemed to last forever until she answered hesitantly, "Okay, Seamus. If you think I should talk to him, I will."

"Good girl," he answered, mustering as much confidence in his voice as he could.

He heard his boss call out his name in the yard below and looked down to see him waving for Seamus to join him.

"I have to go, Caitlin. Take care of yourself," he said, closing the call.

"Okay. 'Bye, Seamus. You too."

"Goodbye, Caitlin."

He hung up with a feeling of relief. He was glad he'd spoken to her and that the black cloud that'd been hovering over his head now seemed to have lifted. He felt better. Everything was tidier now. He knew where he stood and was free to do as he pleased. He smiled and waved down at his boss. Whistling and feeling light at heart, he made his way back down the steps to the yard.

Chapter 44

Now that Patrick had got what he wanted, finally shagging Brona Kelly, somehow he began to look at her in a different light. Given his twin's sudden incarceration in Armagh Gaol after the raid on The Shamrock, maybe there was something in what she'd been nagging him about for weeks. The last time he'd stayed at Brona's place, he'd paid more attention and saw Dolores was right. There wasn't anything personal in sight, absolutely nothing that could tell him anything about her life. As a precaution, he'd ordered Brian Monaghan to follow her. For the first couple of weeks, he reported very little, only that she did her work, helped with the prisoners' defence fund, and at night and weekends was either with Patrick or home alone.

There came the time however when Brian came across something he thought odd and immediately put a call in to Patrick. As a result, the following evening, they sat in their usual corner of The Shamrock as Brian explained his concerns.

"It was weird, Paddy. I saw her go up the stairs to her flat, but half an hour later she came down again. She was all wrapped up with a big heavy coat on and her hood right up over her face."

Patrick encouraged him to keep going with a wave of his hand. "And…?"

"Well, she got the bus into the city centre and sat in that all-night café right by City Hall. I'm standing across the street, freezing me nuts off, when fifteen minutes or so later, this fuckin' gorilla walks in. Never seen anything like it. He was huge, and all dressed up like an undertaker. Before I know it, her hood's down, and she doesn't look anything like the Brona you and I know. It was definitely a wig 'cause her hair was bright blonde and down to her waist. No make-up. Nothing like how she normally is! She obviously didn't want the goon to know what she really looked like, that's for sure."

Fuck it – D was right! Shit, she'd never let him forget this one. Patrick drank three mouthfuls of Guinness and listened as Brian continued with even worse news.

"So I'm standing there watching them. They're alright at the beginning, just talking like, but then she starts to get annoyed, waving her hands around and shouting until they're both standing up and mouthing off at each other. He's trying to tell her something, but she's going ballistic until she walks right out, leaving him sitting there like a tosser!"

Sounded like the Brona he knew, Patrick reflected. She'd been like a cat on a hot tin roof since he'd fucked her that first night. This was explaining a lot.

"What happened then?" he asked eagerly. Brian was enjoying the moment and pleased he could report something solid back to Paddy. He hadn't liked Brona Kelly – or whoever she was – from the beginning. He and Dolores, whom he secretly fancied like fuck had spent hours dissecting her, and he was thrilled they'd finally found something. He'd be well in with Dolores after this. He never called her "D". He'd tried once, and she'd thrown a pint over him.

"Well, I waited a few minutes and headed inside. I sat at a table right next to the phone, thinking he'd make a call. Thank God I was right, and he did." Brian would never forget how pleased he'd been when he'd managed to overhear the goon's conversation.

"So your man's all angsty and well angry. Whoever was on the other end of the phone fucking got it. You should have heard him!"

It was Brian's turn to take a good slug of his beer. Patrick did his best to keep his patience. "Go on."

"Well, the gist was, he was complaining like fuck about her but calling her Alice. That must be her real name. Basically, he was calling her a cunt and saying she was a psycho! He was mad angry at whoever was on the line for sending her his way. It went quiet for a while until he lost it again and told the caller to go to fuck. That was it."

Patrick sat staring into his pint glass, thinking before he asked, barely daring to hope, "I don't suppose you got the number he called, did you?

Brian had deliberately kept this nugget of information back.

"Course I did, 1471! It was for some guy called Dillon. Turns out he's a part-time electrician from Bangor."

He'd done some further investigating and held back for the briefest of moments as he watched his friend's confusion. Forcing his voice to keep calm, he whispered deliberately slowly for effect: "And, Paddy, he's a fuckin' part-time UDR man."

"Jesus Christ!" Patrick seethed. What the fuck was the woman up to?

Brian was well pleased with Paddy's reaction and had one final piece of news to share. "There's one more thing," he said, waiting.

"More?" Patrick asked in surprise. Brian had done really well on this, and he'd not forget.

"It's an interesting one, this. The big gorilla. I asked the waitress if she'd ever seen him before. Turns out he's there all the time. His name's something like 'Lemon'. I mean, Lemon? Would you believe it? He looked more like a fuckin' pumpkin!"

Upon hearing the name "Lemon", Patrick's brain almost exploded. He knew exactly who this man was. He knew all about Lemon and his "kids". They were the fuckers who were butchering Catholics in Belfast, and he was right at the top of their hit list. The evening couldn't get any better!

"Fuck me, Brian, that's some job you've done, mucker. You've no idea! I'll get us another drink – a proper drink. What are you having?"

Brian was pleased as punch at such praise. Most people assumed he was a thicko, and that suited him to a tee. Other than Paddy, and his wife Teresa, very few people knew he was a member of Mensa and lived for his crosswords.

* * *

Brona knew she'd fucked up and badly. She'd no one to blame but herself as she was the one who'd allowed Patrick Gillispie into her bed. It went against all the rules, and the fallout from her mistake was hitting her hard. He did things to her that she'd never experienced, not only screwing her silly but messing with her head. Since that first night when he'd suddenly turned up at the offy, after no word for months, he'd become very confident and would just come and go when it suited him. She hated herself for it but couldn't resist him. She was on her last legs with Det and about to be pulled out of her covert operation with just days to go before she hit The Shamrock.

They didn't believe she could bring any more to the table. The only solace was that she'd got rid of Dolores – at least for a while. Patrick was furious when he'd heard of his twin's interrogation and her being sent to Armagh gaol.

She'd overheard him telling Brian Monaghan, "*D was right to get the gear out.*"

Sitting in her flat, Alice looked around. Other than the books piled high against the walls and on the shelves, it was devoid of grace or warmth. She thought of her home as a child, filled with family photographs, pictures, flowers, the little womanly touches her mother was so good at. All of a sudden, Alice missed her dreadfully. It'd been such a long time since they'd spoken. Maybe it was time for her to quit this work and give up. She was exhausted, both physically and mentally.

* * *

Part-time UDR man Ian Dillon was on his way to carry out a small electrical job that'd come in at the very last moment. His boss told him he'd pay time and a half since the old diddy who'd rung was in a panic and needed to get the heating working again. She was freezing and therefore prepared to pay over the odds. Ian was tired and reluctant to do the job, but the money could go towards the planned holiday he'd promised his wife Elaine for the following year. She'd been at him for ages to book something for them and the baby.

He'd been feeling down since his last meeting with Alice and was missing the thrill of working with her. She was so organised. They'd tried a couple of stunts, him and the lads, but they'd back-fired big time, and on one occasion, they were almost caught. A witness was able to identify one of their cars from its registration, but fortunately, he'd reported it stolen that morning. All in all, they'd managed to wipe out a couple more Taigs, but the last attack had been much too close for comfort and frighteningly disorganised. Now they were lying low.

As for the phone call from Lemon – it scared the shite out of Ian when he heard the ferocity in the man's voice. The last person he wanted to make an enemy of was Lemon. They were at school together years ago, and he'd been pretty useful to Ian up until then. Lemon told him Alice went ballistic when told he couldn't get her *everything* she wanted within such a short time. She wouldn't listen when he'd tried to explain that some of the specialist ammo she was after wasn't that easy to find. It could take months to get that kind of stuff in. He'd only asked what her target was, but she went crazy and wild! Lemon finished their conversation by calling Alice every name under the sun, saying she was a psycho and that neither Ian nor the stupid cunt herself should ever call or come near him again!

Sighing and weary at the thought of that warning, Ian knocked on the bungalow door. It was a nice area this, he thought, as he looked around the empty cul-de-sac. He fidgeted with the baseball cap he wore, and cursing it, took it off and put it into the top pocket of the hated overalls they all wore, marked with the company logo. His manager had recently introduced the new dress code, and Ian and his co-workers felt they were walking advertisements. It'd become a standing joke.

Unbeknown to him, the elderly occupants of the house were both tied up and gagged in the bedroom at the back of their home, absolutely terrified.

He knocked again and found the door open. Without thinking and keen to get home, he walked through the door, calling out a greeting, and turned left through the living-room doorway. The shot went through his right eye. He never knew what hit him as brain matter and shreds of skull splashed and sprayed the diamond-patterned wallpaper behind.

Brian Monaghan put his handgun away and quickly removed his balaclava before rolling it up and putting it into the pocket of his jeans. He walked over to the corpse and removed the boots so he could take off the large overalls that fortunately had very little blood spray on them. He put them on over his own clothes and fished his hand into one of the bulky pockets. He smiled as he discovered a baseball cap and placed it on his head. Ian's tool box held the van keys, which Brian removed. Good job. He'd use the vehicle to get away. He silently stepped around Ian's shattered head, quietly opened the front door and left without giving the trussed up old couple he'd left behind a second thought.

* * *

Alice's handler was furious. He sat opposite the sergeant who'd vouched that she was fit to resume intelligence-gathering. Barely finishing his cigarette, he stubbed it out and quickly lit another, brushing off the ash that fell onto his favourite red tie.

"I fucking knew she'd screw it up. I told you, didn't I?" he screamed.

Sergeant Dury paid little or no attention. He understood these guys were under major pressure, and besides, the man had never told him Alice would screw up, though he wasn't going to say so. He was genuinely sorry she'd failed, but hey, it was the name of the game – some you win, some you lose. This time Alice Wallace had lost.

"I told her to come in. I warned her! She was to report back first thing, and what's she done? She's gone AWOL! We've searched the offy and her digs. We've even searched the fucking Shamrock! There's no sign of her. They've obviously got her – stupid cunt! I'll kill her myself!"

Dury knew the man didn't mean what he said and understood he simply didn't want to lose another agent.

"We've got to find her before it's too fucking late!" he cried as he sat down, his head falling into his nicotine-stained hands. "There's nothing else for it. I don't want to put the wind up him, but we'll have to put a tail on Gillispie."

Chapter 45

Father McGuire had long gone, and Father Connolly had been given temporary responsibility for the Parish of St Mary's, Creggan. There was just him and young Father Moore to pick up the daily visits to grieving sons, daughters, mothers, fathers, widows and widowers. Bitterness was creeping into every pore of the priest. The constant violence, the rioting, the funerals – the misery was unending. He was beginning to understand why Father McGuire had given up and retired.

When he'd visited the Maze H-block way back with Tommy O'Reilly, he'd genuinely hoped the big man would convince young Donal Kyle not to protest but to accept the new rules and regulations of the prison. Their efforts had failed beyond belief since Donal's determination to refuse to wear the uniform had become a catalyst for many others, and now there were hundreds of men following his lead.

They were confined virtually 24 hours a day to cells plastered with their own shit and swimming in urine. Their hair and beards were long, and other than for Mass on Sundays, they refused to leave their cells. Hell on earth.

He'd not been back to Boston for months and missed it. Officer Halloran – whom he'd kept in touch with - had retired to the suburbs of New York and started up a terrific charity enabling some of the bored teenagers of Creggan to get away and visit his city for a holiday. It was hardly surprising that the scheme was going down a treat!

A few weeks before, Tommy O'Reilly had asked Father Connolly to talk to Bishop Carlin about supporting his campaign to bring his niece Tina McLaughlin back home to Derry. He'd recently visited her in Armagh Gaol and was truly concerned by her mental and physical condition. Tommy told the priest the poor girl had lost most of her hair, her eczema was rampant, and her body covered with red and oozing sores – some of which were infected. She seemed unware of who or where she was but more worryingly still was mortally thin. He did not believe she was receiving proper medical attention. Tommy was especially concerned she would get caught up in the midst of the uneasy and dangerous conditions in the women's prison.

Father Connolly immediately wrote to the Bishop asking for help. Thankfully, he'd been quick to reply and suggested a way forward. They should first fully brief his secretary, Father Alex Breslin, about Tina's sad situation, and his secretary would summarise the situation to the Bishop, who would then make a decision.

Father Breslin was the young priest who'd been with Bishop Hegarty on the fateful day he was murdered at the City Hotel and had since proved himself invaluable to his replacement, given that the Bishop was under an incessant barrage of pressure and demands.

* * *

Father Breslin warmly welcomed his colleague Father Connolly when he arrived for the meeting at the Bishop's residence next to St Eugene's Cathedral in the heart of the Bogside. The two men already knew each other well. When Father Breslin had arrived in Derry – not too long before the incident at the City Hotel – Father Connolly had taken him under his wing and shown him the ropes.

Father Breslin knew the Bishop was fond of his gaunt-looking friend and that he particularly admired the work Connolly had been doing in Boston. There was, however, a big gap in Derry's pastoral care now that Father McGuire had gone into retirement.

Yet at the same time, if Father Connolly were promoted to a more senior position and asked to fill McGuire's shoes, they'd need to find someone else to take on the NORAID fundraising. The Bishop and his secretary had already spoken at great length about this, and His Excellency remained uncertain of the best way forward. Father Connolly had proved to be a natural and popular orator and had already raised a substantial sum in the States. It was money that was making a huge difference to good causes in the city.

Father Breslin looked at Connolly. He noticed his friend appeared extremely tired but still very handsome in his own craggy way. Since Kieran's shocking death, Father Breslin had felt lost and frightened, living in continual terror that their sexual relationship might be uncovered.

When he'd first read Father Connolly's letter requesting help for Tina McLaughlin, he'd been mortified. This was the same girl who'd been exposed as Kieran's accomplice, and perhaps, to Father Breslin's secret horror, also his lover. Together they'd tortured and murdered British soldiers. To this day, Alex couldn't believe his beautiful boy, whom he'd loved so much, could or would have been involved in anything so horrific. During Tina's trial, he'd deliberately kept away from any news reports and would walk out of the room if the case was being discussed by anybody, anywhere.

Ultimately, though, he'd no choice but to remain professional and acknowledge a fellow priest's request for help. And so here he was, being professional.

"Father, please, sit," he requested, waving Connolly to a chair. "Would you like some tea?"

Father Connolly nodded and watched in silence as his friend came out from behind his desk to carefully pour a little milk into the china cups set ready on a tray.

Handing over a cup and saucer and taking his own, Father Breslin returned to his seat before enquiring, "Tough week? You look wiped out."

Father Connolly sighed, shook his head and answered, "A nightmare, Father. An absolute nightmare."

The Bishop's aide told his friend, "No need to be formal here, Cathal. Remember, call me Alex, please."

Father Connolly always found it difficult to address other priests by their Christain names, but he'd been asked so many times it'd become embarrassing, and so he reluctantly agreed.

"Okay, Alex. We've had four funerals this week. One of a twenty-year-old, shot by a soldier from a sangar in Fort George. He was sitting on a bus, driving past the barracks in Pennyburn, when four shots were fired. Another man and a poor woman were also injured. He'd just got out of gaol. The shot hit him in the neck. No chance. His friend got his stomach literally blown out and is still in a bad way. Apparently, the soldier had had a breakdown. Turns out he was a cook, not even a trained marksman."

Alex nodded. He'd heard about the incident and thought it an outrage. "Awful, Cathal. Just awful. Who else?"

"John McMonagle, prostate. Old bugger held on for much longer than we thought. Sore death, but thank God he's out of pain now."

He thought about the fight John had put up in the end and hoped that, as they'd joked together, he'd been fast-tracked through the pearly gates.

"The other two, you know about. IRA booby-trap bomb meant for the security services went off too early."

Alex didn't comment. He paused to reflect and quietly said a small prayer to his favourite saint, the little flower St Theresa, for all their souls. Once finished, he said emphatically, "I have to thank you sincerely on behalf of the Bishop, Cathal. We're both fully aware of what you've had to endure these past months, but please believe me, the Bishop and I are here to support you."

Cathal thought this a good opportunity finally to mention Tina McLaughlin, who was his real reason for being there. He sat forward on the edge of his seat.

"Father Breslin… sorry, Alex." Taking a breath, he continued, "We need to talk about Tina McLaughlin."

Alex nodded. *Here goes.*

And then he finally heard the whole sordid tale of her grooming by Kieran, her life imprisonment while seriously ill and how desperate her family and their priest were for the Bishop's help. By the end, Alex Breslin was completely taken aback, shocked by the way things had turned out for the young girl. It was clear as day now that Kieran hadn't just manipulated and tricked *her* – he'd done the very same thing to *Alex*. What a fool he'd been – what a complete fool.

* * *

William Barter had never envisaged he'd stay in Derry so long and thought back to the day of his arrival when he'd landed himself in the midst of a bomb scare at the City Hotel. It seemed like an eternity ago. How times have changed, he thought, when he remembered how low and on his last legs he'd been on his arrival in Northern Ireland. He knew then that Derry was his last chance saloon and, ironically, coming here had been the making of him. Every day there was something significant to report and, selfishly, he found the high-adrenaline reporting a real buzz. In between calling, telexing or even faxing in his daily briefs, he'd begun to do some additional work on a number of exclusive features.

The piece on old Father McGuire had gone down extremely well, and he'd received a press award for it. The priest had proved to be a goldmine of information on the old IRA in the North dating back to the early fifties. His tales had helped present-day readers understand where The Troubles stemmed from. The accolades the article had received had opened up to the reporter the doors of the many Republican houses and social clubs in Derry. He'd been made to feel like an Honorary Derryman.

Out of nowhere and some time back, he'd received an unexpected phone call from an old college buddy, Dale Horn. They'd been close pals until Barter's divorce when Horn – most likely under pressure from his wife – backed off from the friendship. Barter understood;

after all, she was his ex-wife's best friend. But he was delighted to hear from Dale again.

After they'd said their hellos and indulged in some reminiscences, Barter instinctively knew there had to be more to this call than asking how he was. "You still in the CIA looking for them spies an' all?" he asked provocatively.

Horn laughed heartily at such a direct question. "You know me too well, Barter. But, hey, just so happens I'm in Belfast. D'you fancy catching up? I've been reading all these fantastic articles you've been writin'."

Although flattered, Barter was slightly confused to hear this. "Belfast! What the heck are you doing in Belfast?"

"This and that," Horn replied, treading carefully.

"Okay. Well, sure. When?" Barter asked.

And so they met for lunch in the Europa Hotel. At first, their conversation was light-hearted as they recalled their college days and then the pain in the ass of trying to please their wives and ex-wives! However, it didn't take long before Horn's tone changed as he grew more serious. He looked around the restaurant and said discreetly, "You wanna know why I'm really here, Barter?"

He'd been dying to ask. What *was* a CIA man doing in Belfast? He'd a fair idea but wasn't going to say.

"No, Dale. But I guess you're going to tell me."

"Well," Horn said, looking around the room and lowering his tone even more,

"We're monitoring the situation here in Northern Ireland. We're also watching the gun and ammo smuggling between the States and here – via NORAID. Have you *any* idea how much money is flowing out of the States to the Cause here? Things are pretty sensitive with the Brits right now – they're far from happy and putting all sorts of pressure on us."

Horn moved in closer to Barter and hissed, "The cocky fuckers are even threatening our trade deal if we don't put a stop to it!"

"Go on," Barter said, keeping Horn talking by sipping his coffee. It worked as the CIA man told him more.

"We've also got a list of known suspects… and that's where we need your help."

Barter practically choked on his coffee, spraying it over the table top. He shook his head at Horn reprovingly.

"*Me*? You want *me* to help the CIA!"

"Keep your voice down!" Horn whispered harshly. He grabbed hold of Barter's arm and yanked on it, muttering, "It's no big deal. We need your help. *I* need your help."

Barter was stunned, almost lost for words. "Jeez, Dale. How can I help the fuckin' CIA? I'm just a journalist, for Christ's sakes."

"That's how, Bill! It's that easy. You just keep doing what you're doing: investigating. We know you've all sorts of intel up your sleeve. Except we're asking that before going into print with it, you tell us first. Anything and everything, no matter how trivial it might seem. One thing high on our agenda is some creep Jones – Charles Jones. Ever heard of him?"

Bizarrely, Horn's timing couldn't have been more perfect since Barter's next planned exclusive, the one he'd been working on for months, was about the Belfast Loyalist. He'd been regularly attending ranting, xenophobic speeches and rallies for months. Luckily for him, the only one he'd missed was Newtownhamilton, where someone tried to wipe out his subject and the man's cronies.

Barter disliked the man's politics, but they were shared by many. Worse by far were the hints he'd received that, under orders from Jones, his goon Lemon and a band of Loyalist bandits had threatened, terrorised and murdered Catholics all over Belfast as well as carrying out a number of armed robberies in the city. Despite masterminding this ruthless regime, Jones somehow managed always to keep his hands clean.

That time in Derry, when Barter had confronted Lemon for tailing him, he'd been talking bullshit. He'd no file hidden in a safe place with instructions in the event of his death! In fact, at that particular time, he'd very little verified intel, but the threat had worked, and they'd left him alone ever since. What intrigued him most was why? It seemed they stopped at nothing when it came to dealing with anyone who they felt were a threat of any sort. Which had to mean there was something even worse they were covering up, something with the potential to cause major repercussions – political ones.

"Your country would be very grateful," Dale was saying, continuing to persuade when Barter was already sold on the deal. "Remember, speak to us first about your findings. And in exchange, maybe we can offer a few little exclusives of our own."

* * *

Father Breslin described to the Bishop what had happened in the briefing between the two priests. His Eminence vividly remembered Tina's trial and family history.

"Ah, yes, poor wee girl. I heard about it from Father McGuire. The father died first, neglected in custody, I believe, and then the mother killed herself."

At the mention of suicide, the Bishop quickly blessed himself and said a quick prayer for her soul before he enquired, "And the brother… what was his name? Mark, Mike… ah, no, Martin! He's back on the scene now, is he?"

Father Breslin explained, "There's him and the eldest sister, Caitlin, who works in a photographic shop on Strand Road. Poor girl just keeps herself to herself, apparently. Father Connolly doesn't know her that well."

The Bishop sighed and sat lost in thought for a while before making his decision. "I'll write a letter, a personal letter to the Governor and the Secretary of State. If they ignore me, we'll take it to the press. I know, that Yankee Barter… I like him! And Tommy O'Reilly has done so much for this city – no one knows the half of it – he deserves something back. Right! Let's do it now; let's help his family."

* * *

Tommy and Caitlin sat opposite Father Connolly in his usual café, the Rainbow. Given the priest's workload, it'd been some time since he'd come in on a Friday morning, and he was greeted warmly and served by Siobhan. The priest had called Tommy to say he'd some good news for them and suggested this meeting.

For the first time in a while, Tommy was excited. He looked at Caitlin, who sat beside him, smiling and sipping her tea. She looked like the weight of the world had been lifted off her shoulders once the priest had told them of his briefing with Father Breslin and the Bishop's decision.

Tommy had to pinch himself to believe what they'd just heard was true.

"So you're saying Bishop Carlin's going to write a personal letter to the Prison Governor and the Secretary of State himself, demanding Tina's release on medical grounds? And if they don't, he'll personally contact the national and international press, specifically Bill Barter. Knowing the Yank, he'll get us some serious coverage. He's already supporting the appeal. That's great, Father, just great!"

"Thank you, Father," Caitlin put in. "This is the best news we've had in ages."

Tommy was elated. It went well beyond what he'd hoped. At last!

Father Connolly tried to calm his friend.

"Now, Tommy, don't get your hopes up too much. It's a start, I'll admit, but you know how these things can go. Sometimes they'll agree to anything, just to pacify you and keep you quiet, and then there'll be nothing for months."

"But you know Bishop Carlin's like a dog with a bone when he sets his mind on something. One thing I've always said about him, he's a supporter of the people. There's no way he'll not get our Tina home now!" Tommy said jubilantly.

Chapter 46

For the first morning in an age, Caitlin woke up feeling relieved and hopeful. Now that her sister's fate was in safe hands, she felt she could turn to her own affairs and act on Seamus's advice. There was unfinished business still with James Henderson. It was up to her to approach him and set the record straight. It could be at the factory, or when he was out running – she knew his route – or maybe just a knock on the front door of the Hendersons' home Melrose.

Her usual morning bus had once again been hijacked, and the remaining service proved to be erratic and slow. The usual suspects stood at the bus stop, waiting patiently. It'd been a particularly testing week for the Creggan estate, and an air of sadness hung over it. Too many funerals, she thought, as she eyed yet another coffin on its way to St Mary's followed by the usual black saloons that carried the grieving families.

Some time later, she arrived at the photographer's and unlocked the heavy-duty steel roller door. Raymond had taken the day off, something to do with his wedding anniversary. The shop was bitterly cold when she walked through to the back office, throwing the keys on the desk and shivering. Caitlin quickly put the kettle on. It was going to be a busy day. She was expecting a number of couples to come by and collect their wedding portfolios.

Just before 11 o'clock, she heard the tinkling of the shop bell and quickly made her way to the counter. Doing her best to look pleasant and helpful, she came face to face with a very elegant young woman.

"Ah, good morning, miss. I need your help!" she announced in ringing English tones.

Caitlin instinctively disliked her on sight but forced a polite smile. Who on God's earth was this? She was simply beautiful and perfect.

Blonde and blow-dried, with false eyelashes and frosted pink lipstick. Her clothes were immaculate in the Jackie O style, with a baby pink swing coat that matched the A-line dress underneath. Her supremely enviable handbag was a matching shade of pink also.

"You see, I'm getting married – rather quickly but not for the usual reason!" She giggled wickedly as she removed her white kid gloves, finger by finger. "And I've been told this man… Burns, is it? Yes, Burns… that he's the best in town! Am I right?"

"You are, miss," the assistant confirmed, though with a distinct lack of warmth.

This shop girl was an absolute beauty herself, extremely tall for a woman, though rather too skinny and boyish for Marleen's taste. Still, skinny was so *in* at the moment that for a split second, she felt rather envious. She had to work hard to keep her figure. This lucky girl's skin was almost opaque, not a pimple or a blotch on it, and her long straight black hair was neatly tied back in a plait. But it was those pale blue eyes that made Marleen look at them that little bit too long… The girl really was something.

Aware that she was staring, she shook herself and laughed. "Ah, sorry, thoughts off on a tangent there." Looking around and gathering herself, she muttered: "Yes, right, where was I?"

The woman's affected manner made Caitlin nervous. *What on earth was someone like her doing here?*

"You were saying about Mr Burns. Yes, he's the best photographer in the city and very popular. How may I help?"

Marleen carefully placed the gloves in her Hermès leather handbag while she chattered on. "Well, it's simple, *really.* I'd like to book him, please, to photograph our wedding. If he's available."

"Of course. Let me just get the diary. Won't be a second," Caitlin responded with a half-hearted smile. She left the woman and made her way slowly behind the curtain that concealed the back office. She reached Raymond's desk and picked up the diary, but before she did anything with it, she pulled the office curtain back a little to peek at the marvel that stood waiting in the shop.

Marleen was humming to herself and looking around at some of the sample images. He really was quite good, she thought. Not ideal, but better than she'd expected of a provincial. Uncle Roger wasn't fit enough to travel, so she and James had agreed they'd have a small, intimate marriage ceremony here in Londonderry and the wedding breakfast at Melrose. When things settled down or, bless him, the old bugger died, they'd celebrate by having a grand London affair, either at the Savoy or the Ritz – she loved them both equally and wasn't particularly bothered which. She waited patiently for the shop girl – *Caitlin* according to her name tag – to return.

"What date do you have in mind?" the assistant asked as she reappeared.

"Well, actually, we thought perhaps Christmas Eve. Don't you think that's *sooooo* romantic?"

Caitlin couldn't disagree but thought it more than romantic; it was amazing! She hated this woman even more now. Not only was she stunningly beautiful, but she was also getting married on Christmas Eve – probably to some stinking rich, tall, dark and handsome man at that. *Lucky bitch.*

Marleen watched and waited. She finally coughed in an effort to regain Caitlin's attention.

"I-I'm sorry, I just need to check the date, miss. What's your name?"

"Miss Marleen Fry."

Caitlin quickly wrote it down and asked inquisitively, "And the venue for the wedding, Miss Fry. Where's that?"

"Ah yes, Well, first the ceremony at the Church of Ireland, Prehen - I didn't want a big fuss and hold it at St Columb's, and then the wedding breakfast at our house. Silly me, my fiancé's place that is!"

"And the address, miss?" Caitlin requested curtly.

"The address? Oh..." Marleen reached into her handbag to pull out a piece of white letter-headed notepaper. As Caitlin breathed in her sophisticated fragrance – one she didn't recognise – Marleen carefully recited the address.

"Melrose, Albert Park, Prehen, Londonderry BT47 QR3."

Marleen looked at the girl to check she'd got it all down and witnessed the poor girl's face suddenly going even paler than pure white. She thought maybe she was in a trance or about to have some sort of fit and could only think of waving her hand in front of Caitlin's face and crying out, "You poor thing, are you *quite* alright?"

Caitlin heard nothing for the echoing sound in her ears. She thought she might faint and attempted to pull herself together by slowly repeating the address and the date.

Marleen was beginning to feel hugely uncomfortable. The girl was acting strangely, very strangely.

"I have to go now, I'm afraid. Can you tell me if the date works, or do you need to speak to Mr Burns?"

"I'll speak to him and let you know, Miss Fry," Caitlin murmured, taking note of Marleen's telephone number.

"Thank you so much."

Although Marleen instinctively wanted to leave, she couldn't help but take one last glance at the girl who stood rigid, pale and clearly distressed behind the counter. In this place, nowadays, best not to ask, Marleen decided before departing. The only indication she'd ever been in the shop was the fading jingle of the bell, the aroma of Chanel No. 5 and Caitlin's ashen face.

The news that James was marrying someone else had cut her to the heart.

* * *

It took a while for her to recover enough to attend to the customers who followed Marleen Fry. Before she knew it, Tommy was glancing through the shop door, excitedly waving at her to see if it was all right for him to come in and talk.

She stood on the doorstep. Before she'd a chance to speak, he'd pushed himself right past her. His face was red and feverish with elation as he told her the latest news.

"You'll never believe it, love; Carlin's only gone and phoned the Secretary of State's office this morning and some judge high up in the Appeal Court! He's given them both a real dressing down. Followed the calls up with a letter too – a real stinker! Father Connolly says, unofficially, there's a really good chance it'll work. They'll definitely review Tina's case now. A fucking mistrial or something of the like, love. We'll get your sister home!"

He looked at his niece properly for the first time and noted her drained expression and sad eyes.

"Are you okay. . . you look like shit?" he asked nervously, grasping her close enough to stare into the abyss of her eyes. *Jesus, what'd happened now?*

But Caitlin pulled herself together.

"I'm fine, Tommy, I'm grand. Just shocked by the news."

She wasn't going to spoil her uncle's happiness. She wouldn't spoil it for the world, and so she hugged him, squeezing her eyes tight shut to stem the tears. She muttered into the shoulder of his well-worn, black donkey jacket.

"I'm happy, Tommy, really I am. It'll be lovely to have Tina back."

He released her and looked at her with a wide-open smile on his face. God love her, he thought. She's crying with happiness too. His own eyes filled as he looked to the sky and prayed. *Thank you, God, nearly there. Please don't let us down now!*

Chapter 47

Maureen Molony bent down close to Tina McLaughlin's ear and whispered gleefully, "Do you hear me, love? You're going home."

Tina lay flat and still on her iron-framed bed placed next to the metal radiator. It made little difference. Her cell remained cold and damp. The other women had done their best to make her comfortable, but she remained weak and uncommunicative, having not eaten for days. They tried hard to feed her by making her broth and light meals, but her swollen stomach resolutely refused to keep anything down.

Staring blankly at the OC, Tina's face carried a continual smile. All she cared about was what Kieran was telling her. He stood right behind Maureen, looking down with love and tenderness. As ever, he looked gorgeous with his heavy fringe, long, jet-black curly hair and swarthy skin. Those chocolate brown eyes with the long lashes that she loved and envied brimmed with tears. His hand swept his heavy fringe aside as he whispered, "*Honey, I'm here. Come now.*"

She was so pleased to see him but her mind and body felt tired and sore. The skin on her arms, raw from her continual scratching, hurt, and the inside of her mouth stung from the multiple mouth ulcers that never seemed to go away. "*I'm coming*," Tina said weakly as she watched him fade away.

Maureen couldn't hear clearly what the youngin' had said. "What was that, love?" But Tina remained quiet and soon fell back to sleep.

The OC sighed deeply. The past few weeks had been a nightmare. After their wing was searched and wrecked by the screws, they'd been refused access to the toilets and bathrooms and had been kept locked in their cells for two whole days. Eventually, they were served cold food. When their *pos* quickly filled up, they'd pressed the buzzers in their cells, continually screaming to be let out to empty them. Their pleas were ignored. In the end, they'd no choice. The full *pos* were emptied under the cell doors only for the fluid and filth to be brushed back inside by the screws. Surprisingly, it was the urine that smelled the worst. A number of the women in the lower cells resorted to emptying their waste through their barred cell windows. However, these were soon boarded up, making the cells even darker, damper and more foul-smelling.

* * *

To Caitlin's astonishment, the radiant young bride-to-be was not her only notable female caller that week. A few days later, a very *soignée* older woman pushed open the door to the shop just as Caitlin was preparing to grab her coat and pop out for lunch. Her boss was on-site at a wedding, and she wasn't busy. There was something foreign but also slightly familiar about this woman, though Caitlin couldn't quite place what it was. The woman's long black cashmere coat was remarkable and beautifully cut – one of the obvious benefits of money and privilege. She was beautiful, blonde and appeared to be in her early-fifties, with a prominent but gracefully shaped nose, intensely green eyes and full red lips. She wasn't small but rather petite and perfect. Her eyes wandered around the shop until she saw Caitlin standing gobsmacked behind the counter. Aware she could have such an effect on people, the woman smiled to herself.

She quickly walked towards the young sales girl, her hand outstretched to introduce herself.

"Catherine Henderson."

Hearing that name, Caitlin quivered. So this was why she looked familiar – her eyes were identical to James's. The woman waited until Caitlin realised her hand was still outstretched and quickly shook it. This had to be James's mother!

"Oh, sorry. Caitlin. Caitlin McLaughlin."

"I know who you are, Caitlin." The woman's voice sounded odd with a twang to it that again Caitlin couldn't place.

"*You do*?" she asked in surprise.

"I knew your Mother Majella. She and I were good friends. She was very kind to me when I truly needed help. She was someone I could trust."

She knew Caitlin's mother? This was baffling. How on God's earth would mammy know James's mother… Alarm bells were going off.

Another female customer entered the shop, the doorbell breaking the spell.

Catherine whispered quickly, "Caitlin, I don't suppose we could have a cup of tea and maybe a bite to eat? Are you due to have lunch?"

"Sure. Yes. Let me just see to this lady, and I'll be right with you."

To pass the time, Catherine picked up and tried to study an A5 shop brochure whilst secretively watching Caitlin, admiring her from a distance. The young woman was really remarkably good-looking.

As soon as Caitlin finished with her customer, she grabbed her coat and was ready to leave. Catherine looked at her and smiled, asking, "Where do you suggest?"

"There's a nice little café just down the road."

As the two women left the shop, it was raining hard, and, without warning, a bus whooshed past very close to them, its wheels spinning furiously through a deep pool of water that sprayed high and fast, soaking them both. They gaped down at their wet clothes in shock. Seconds later, they were screaming with laughter.

Almost immediately, an unspoken bond was formed between them as Catherine – still laughing and unworried about her beautiful coat – casually linked her arm through Caitlin's. Memories flooded back to Caitlin of her days with Anne and how they'd often link arms on their way to the factory.

Simultaneously the women tugged their coats tighter against the cold rain and, talking animatedly, walked in the direction of the Rainbow Café.

As usual, Siobhan took their order with a smile. Once they were settled, Catherine spoke first.

"I guess you're wondering why I've come to see you, Caitlin?"

She nodded. "I am. Totally intrigued."

"It's nothing to worry about, really. It's just I wanted to say how sorry I was to hear about your Mother, and of course, Patrick."

"Thank you," Caitlin acknowledged this.

They waited as Siobhan served them two mugs of steaming, strong tea. Catherine smiled and thanked her before continuing.

"As I said, I knew Majella. She looked after me when I was extremely ill and desperately needed a friend. I'm not sure if she ever told you, but she worked for us at Melrose at the time."

At this news, Caitlin sat up and listened carefully.

"We became fast friends, and I adored her. I always remember her as being full of fun with a little touch of craziness mixed in." Catherine laughed softly at the memories.

Caitlin was intrigued and sad at the same time. It was hard to imagine or remember her mother being carefree and fun, given how sadly her life had ended.

"It wasn't for very long, but she nursed me. I remember so clearly her vigour and, my goodness, how she never stopped talking! She was so much in love with your Father. She spoke about him all the time, and I could've listened to her all day – in fact, *I did!* Her energy and love of life gave me a sense of purpose when I most needed it. I was extremely unhappy at that time, shortly before my son was born."

Caitlin didn't know what to say as she watched a wave of remembered misery pass over the woman's face. Whatever had happened to her, it must have been a difficult and depressing time. They drank their tea in silence until Catherine Henderson asked quite innocently, "I don't suppose you know James?"

At the sound of his name, Caitlin's heart rate rocketed. She thought she'd choke.

"I… I… do, Mrs Henderson. We worked together for a while. I know him very well."

Caitlin hesitated. She thought her throat would tear apart when she admitted, "There's no one quite like James."

"You do?" Catherine asked in surprise. Misery returned to that striking, half-familiar face. "Oh, my, I haven't seen my son since he was tiny. I've written many, many letters, but not one was ever answered. So here I am."

She grasped Caitlin's hand over the table and pleaded with her desperately, "Tell me, Caitlin. What's he like? What's my son like?"

And so Caitlin told her. She told his mother everything. The release of finally being able to talk about her feelings for James Henderson to someone who understood was immeasurable. She explained about Tina, the bomb scare and the shootings at the hotel. She told Catherine about James's rejection of her and found that once she'd started, she couldn't stop. Heartfelt and desperate words flowed from way deep down inside her. In between bouts of tears and hiccups, she finally told his mother about James's forthcoming marriage at Christmas and how she'd found out.

More than an hour passed. Siobhan, the waitress, sensing the seriousness of the women's conversation, returned time and time again to refill their mugs and give them a few little cakes in an effort to comfort the crying girl. She knew all about Caitlin McLaughlin, and her heart ached for the poor mite.

Meanwhile, Catherine Henderson hung onto every word Caitlin shared. This only made her more determined to meet her son. Undoubtedly Roger and Joceyln had done a good job of raising him. One thing she was sure of was that this delightful young woman in front of her was still very much in love with him.

"Caitlin, I don't know my son well, and that's the reason I'm here, but from what I see and hear, you really do need to talk to him. To tell him everything. Why haven't you done so before? If he's kind and caring like you say, he's not going to turn you away. Not now. Enough time has passed. If he's planning to get married, it's imperative you tell him beforehand. You must!"

Caitlin shook her head in despair. "I couldn't, Mrs Henderson. I couldn't take such rejection again. I'd be humiliated. He humiliated me! You've no idea what it was like afterwards: the trial, Tina going to gaol for life, then Mammy… She hung herself! She died horribly, all alone. She gave up, and I feel so angry with her for that. I loved her, I needed her – and she left me!"

Catherine quickly stood up and moved around to sit next to her in the vinyl-covered booth. She opened her arms wide, and Caitlin fell into them, savouring the contact and the comforting smell of her perfume.

* * *

Tina's mental and physical health were deteriorating daily, and everyone who cared knew they were running out of time. They had to get her back to Derry fast. Their MP had insisted that an independent medical evaluation be carried out, and its findings only added impetus to the appeal to have her released. Tina McLaughlin had been severely neglected by the medical team at Armagh Gaol, especially by one of the local locums, Dr Graham Harris, whose handling of her case was severely censured. When her weight sank to five and a half stone, he attempted to force-feed her but immediately stopped when official notification was received that she would soon be released into the care of Gransha Hospital – to recuperate there and, hopefully, go home.

Eventually, it was officially confirmed she was being released. Her uncle met Caitlin at the shop to tell her the wonderful news.

"I can't believe it! Isn't it great?" he said, lit up with delight. "When the prison system and the courts dragged their feet, yer man contacted the press, TV and radio, at home and abroad. God bless him!

"Will you come with me to collect her?" he finished breathlessly.

"Absolutely, Tommy. When?"

"Friday."

Caitlin told him she'd be there and spent the rest of the week cleaning and warming Tina's old room for her, buying new bedsheets and curtains from the market and accepting a second-hand mattress and a baby blue fluffy rug from the McFaddens next door. The room looked much better and actually inviting. Tina would soon be back for good, and Caitlin intended to spoil her rotten.

* * *

It was just over a week before Christmas, and the wedding between James and his posh Englishwoman was imminent. In between making arrangements for Tina's release, working and regularly meeting Catherine, Caitlin was running out of time to contact him.

She was convinced she'd seen him just a few days ago, parked at the far end of the street from where the shop was situated, sitting in his distinctive car. She was so sure it was him she ran out of the shop, leaving a customer in mid-sentence, and dashed towards the Jaguar. Devastated, she watched as he started the engine and drove down the street towards her. She waved frantically for him to stop. Her heart nearly burst with sorrow when he drove past.

He'd turned and looked in her direction, though. She knew he'd seen her. For a split second, their eyes locked. To the end of her days, she'd never forget the look of despair and pain on his face. *Maybe, just maybe, James Henderson had not lost all feeling for her after all…*

* * *

Dolores Gillispie, confined in Armagh Gaol, planned everything secretly and carefully. The deed would be done the following Friday. She'd been assured the two women would be on duty that morning and, as normal, would come to work in the same small red Fiat 125, registration number FRZ 3487T.

She'd never forgive Smyth for wrecking her cell. The fat cow had fucked up big time by destroying the few photographs Dolores possessed. After that, she'd watched her prey carefully and learned all she could. The two women lived in Ballynahone Drive in Armagh City – locally known as "murder mile" since there'd been so many killings in the district.

* * *

Maureen Molony read the letter from Bridget Barry and chuckled. It was a lovely letter with lots of good news, albeit Bridget was exhausted from the numerous visits of her two extremely young grandchildren. But she was happy. Ironically, she'd found she missed the prison – or at least the women – and sent them all her love.

The OC kept a close eye on Smyth and Drake. Somehow they knew after the cell searches that they were being monitored by the hardened Republicans and decided to back off.

However, stories received from the remand prisoners told the OC that the pair's relentless cruelty was being focussed elsewhere.

Governor Yeaman insisted that for court appearances, all women were to be escorted from their cells, taken downstairs, strip-searched and dressed again. They were then led over to the court house a short distance away, where they'd spend no more than ten minutes for their short hearings. Very rarely did they have any contact with anyone apart from courtroom staff and their lawyer. Sometimes not even that. On their return to the gaol, they'd again be strip-searched. It wasn't a question of security; all the women knew that. This was a tactic to try and break the women's spirits, to degrade and humiliate them – anything that could bruise them mentally, particularly if the male screws were watching. The younger, inexperienced women found it particularly horrific and upsetting.

* * *

It was Friday morning, and Smyth and Drake were up early, dressed and full from a hearty breakfast before they left for the gaol. Governor Yeaman had turned out to be as callous and unfeeling as they were. A proper bastard, in fact. As a result, they adored him, and he regularly turned a blind eye to their cruelty – just let them get on with it.

Smyth knew she'd gone too far when she destroyed the Republican bitch's photographs, and this was confirmed one day when Dolores cornered her by the Chapel.

With no witnesses to overhear her, the inmate's venom and anger were clearly evident. Smyth nearly shit herself but wouldn't let her fear show when Gillispie spat out a warning.

"I got you, Smyth. Keep looking over that fat greasy shoulder of yours. I got you." Smyth just wiggled her fingers in a "give-me-more" gesture and told her to fuck off.

She told no one, but just to be safe, would secretly double-check beneath the Fiat for devices before starting any journey.

This particular morning she and Drake were both feeling light-hearted. They'd had a good evening out the night before with some girlfriends. Chatting and laughing, they got into the small car. After a few attempts, the engine started, and Drake confidently drove out of the driveway and along Cathedral Road on their way to the gaol.

Smyth lit up a Woodbine and sucked on it hard before holding in the fumes. She deliberately and slowly released a hazy cloud of smoke into the confined space of the small car. At this, Drake lost it. Smyth knew she hated smoking in her car!

"Ah, feck, don't you spread your damn smoke in here. You know rightly I hate it!"

Smyth only laughed. She so loved winding her girlfriend up.

"Okay, okay! Don't get your knickers in a twist!" She laughed again and awkwardly lowered the car window.

Drake cursed and sat in silent fury at a red light. Out of the blue, a lone darkly clad motorcyclist seized the moment and came up on their left-hand side and stopped. Without warning, a small rounded missile was thrown through the Fiat's open window, landing straight at Smyth's feet as the bike sped off. For a split second, the two women looked at each other. *Ah, fuck!*

* * *

Tommy and Caitlin made the journey to Armagh on Friday morning courtesy of the ever-agreeable Charlie McFadden. Tommy insisted on stopping to pay for petrol. There was a carefree mood in the air today, and, bless Charlie, he was glad to help out. His wife had been constantly nagging him to get off his arse and find a job. Even his son Emmett, who came and went, had started to throw his weight about. Charlie was just glad to be out of the house.

Caitlin's heart was racing, but she was feeling good. In fact, she was feeling *very* good. She and Catherine had met twice more since that lunchtime in the café and shared their woes. They'd talked in great detail about James. Catherine was keen that Caitlin get to see her son as soon as possible, and she'd agreed to seek a meeting as soon as she'd got Tina safely home.

She was determined they'd have a good Christmas together and swore she'd become Tina's mother, sister, friend and nurse until she no longer needed her. Finally, everything seemed to be falling into place, and there was hope with a capital H on the horizon.

They parked the car as close to the gaol as was allowed. After being searched, they walked through the security gates to the circle to wait for Tina just outside the Governor's office. It was 11.00 a.m.

The two men and Caitlin waited and waited until they grew impatient. It was now 11.45 a.m., and they'd expected to see Tina being escorted down the wide corridor towards them for at least the last half-hour.

They were surprised when instead, a man in a suit opened a nearby door and introduced himself as Governor Yeaman. He then presented them to a tall, balding priest, Father Mullan. The priest nodded but remained still and quiet, his face expressionless. Tommy knew he had to be Father McGuire's replacement and immediately decided the man was a bit of a cold fish.

Yeaman waved his arm, leading the small party into his office. "Please follow me."

They knew then something was very wrong.

The Governor took his time before he began. "Mr O'Reilly, I regret to inform you that inmate Tina McLaughlin was found dead in her cell this morning."

Charlie McFadden hung his head and pressed his hands to his eyes. This poor family…

Caitlin didn't move an inch. She couldn't. Her breathing faltered as she stared at the Governor, eyes spilling over with heavy, tired tears that seemed to flow from her endlessly. Tommy stood up and swayed. He had to hold onto the desk to keep his balance. He was the first to speak, his voice breaking with the effort of not giving way to the grief he felt.

"How did she die? What happened to her?"

Yeaman looked towards Father Mullan for support, hoping he'd answer on his behalf and take up the awkward conversation. Instead, the priest sat straight-backed, expressionless and silent.

He wasn't going to make this easy for Yeaman. He'd already seen in his brief time at the gaol just how badly the women were treated, and his complaints about the conditions had been ignored on numerous occasions. He had formally asked for a transfer.

Tommy grew angry at the lack of response.

"I'm asking you how this happened?" he bellowed as he sagged back into his chair.

Caitlin felt drained of happiness. All of it, every ounce, had been cruelly snatched away. She couldn't believe Tina was dead. *Sweet Jesus*, her little sister! What was she going to do now? She hadn't even had a proper chance to say sorry for letting her slide into the wrong hands.

She'd never be able to say sorry again and wasn't sure how she'd live with that.

Like a wild banshee, she wailed and wailed in the crowded office, terrifying all its occupants. The men had absolutely no idea what to do with her.

Chapter 48

William Barter was just finishing his interview with James Henderson – another exclusive. He'd been impressed by the young man's vision for Rocola, but even more so by the way he spoke about the employees, the city in general and his love for Derry – all in a soft Scottish lilt.

They were running behind as they sat in James's office, quickly finishing their tea. It was freezing outside, and Barter couldn't get warm. He'd just had a tour of the site and had noticed and been impressed by the way in which all the workers here were comfortable and friendly with their young employer, greeting him with natural good-humoured banter. Henderson had agreed that a few select employees could be interviewed too. Barter felt he was onto something, and potentially it'd be a great article. By the end of the interviews, he felt he'd sussed the young guy out and looked forward to putting the piece together.

Henderson's grumpy and particularly unattractive secretary interrupted their flow by knocking softly on the glass-panelled door. She stuck her head around it and spoke quietly.

"Mr Henderson, sir. Mr Jones has arrived." Without waiting for his response, she disappeared.

Shit! James thought. Apologising to the journalist, he explained, "Sorry, Bill, a last-minute thing. I'm due to see Charles Jones, worse luck. It wasn't planned when you and I fixed this, but unfortunately, today was the only time he could meet. Otherwise, you and I could have talked a little longer."

At the sound of Jones's name, Barter's ears had pricked up. "I don't suppose that'd be *the* Charles Jones from up Belfast way, docks and all?"

James nodded. "Indeed. One and the same."

"You know him well, do you?"

"I wouldn't say well. He's not what you'd call a friend of mine. There was a business association – one we're trying to put behind us."

It was evident the young man had issues with Jones, and so Barter took full advantage. "I've really enjoyed today, James, but I'd like to share some important information with you regarding Mr Jones. I understand he attended that meeting you had at the City Hotel a while back?"

Intrigued, James stood and eyed the journalist – where was this heading? Did Barter know what he and Roger had already worked out? He walked over to the window to look down onto the factory forecourt.

"Yes, he did."

Adrenaline began to flow through Barter as his excitement mounted. He knew he had to be careful what he said about Jones and how he said it.

"I'd like to tell you…"

He didn't get a chance to continue before the office door was flung open by Lemon, who stood transfixed by shock when he saw the Yank sitting in James Henderson's office.

James didn't miss the look exchanged between journalist and goon before Jones roughly pushed the big man aside so he could enter. He was too focused on opening his briefcase to notice that James had company. Eventually, he saw Barter and offered his hand as they exchanged names. The atmosphere in the room chilled when Barter stared into the fat man's emotionless eyes and only reluctantly accepted his pudgy paw.

"Mr Barter. Good to meet you finally," Jones said nonchalantly.

He immediately sank down in a chair and placed some papers in front of him in preparation for the meeting with James, who coughed loudly to gain the flabby man's attention. Jones chortled when he realised he was sitting in James's chair. "Silly me!"

He then scrutinised Barter and gave him a dismissive look. The journalist got the message. He was finished here anyway. Jones gave him the creeps. But he was keen to get James on his own again – even for just a second – and jerked his head towards the corridor.

"Must show my guest out. Be back soon, Charles," James said as he lightly took Barter by the elbow, leading him out of the office. Mrs Parkes stood on guard outside.

"Mrs Parkes, could you offer Mr Jones a hot drink, please?"

"Of course," she replied, eagerly entering his office.

Alone, Barter whispered quickly and rapidly to James as they walked down the corridor. "We need to meet up again soon. I have to talk to you about Jones!"

The journalist appeared worried.

"Okay, I'll call you. We'll definitely talk," James reassured him.

"Good, good," Barter replied with relief. "Please. And soon," he finished.

James watched the journalist make his way to the lift. He shook his head. *What the heck was going on*?

* * *

Back in James's office, Mrs Parkes took the orders for drinks and was about to leave when she turned to Charles Jones and whispered conspiratorially to him, "Mr Jones, I just wanted to say, I've been to all of your speeches in the Free Derry Church, and I think what you say is absolutely right! Myself and a few others from the WI are great fans!"

She blushed as she acknowledged his thanks and left. She and the other women made a point of seeing Charles Jones as often as they could and were so relieved when he'd survived the Newtownhamilton attack.

Jones laughed. "See, I've got some female fans, Lemon! Silly old biddies!"

The two men, who very rarely laughed together, were chuckling when James returned.

Taking his chair, he looked at Jones and had to suppress a surprised reaction. He hadn't seen him since he'd been injured at Newtonhamilton, and it was not a pretty sight. Jones was using a white monogrammed handkerchief to wipe an eye that continually wept. He'd asked for this meeting, refusing to tell James on the telephone what it was about but insisting they must see each other face to face.

"How are you, James?" he asked. *Not giving a fuck.*

"All good, thank you, Charles," James replied non-committally. He wasn't going to say anything he didn't need to.

Jones was buzzing. He hated this arrogant young Scottish gobshite and was looking forward to bringing him down.

"I'm sorry I didn't make it to your father's funeral," he said, shaking his head in an attempt to look sorrowful. "Terrible business."

James felt a wave of anger at the reminder. He'd agreed to today's meeting purely because he didn't wish the Belfast man to realise what they'd discovered. They were still looking to tie the matter up definitively and bring the witness *MG* to testify before a neutral party – if any such could be found in the Province. It wasn't easy, though, to confront this man, given what they believed him to be responsible for.

"However, there is a bit of an issue that I think you, and of course your kind and generous uncle, should be made aware of," Jones pontificated.

Here we go, James thought.

Just then, Mrs Parkes returned with the tea, poured it and added milk and sugar where necessary – three for young Mr Henderson, he loved his sugar – then carefully passed the cups and saucers around. Suspecting from the overwhelming silence that this was a volatile meeting, she quickly left.

Jones drank the tea that the stupid bitch had put too much milk in. It was cold. He swallowed it anyway and put the cup down, leaning forward across Henderson's desk.

"James, your father sold me his shares."

"What shares?" he asked quizzically. "I don't understand."

"Shares in this place," Jones answered gleefully, stretching out his arms as if to snatch up Rocola.

James knew his father didn't have any shares – he'd sold them years ago to Uncle Roger.

"I'm sorry to disappoint you, Charles, but my father no longer had any shares in this company."

Charles Jones laughed aloud. The Scottish upstart was clearly lying. He waited for James to fill the silence, and when he didn't, threw what looked like share certificates across the desk, growling, "See for yourself!"

Remaining calm, James reached out and took the pieces of flimsy gilt-edged paper. After James Snr's death, his uncle told him about one of his father's many scams. James Henderson Snr had defrauded a number of his debtors, it seemed, for quite substantial amounts of money.

From just one original Rocola share, he'd somehow got a number of fake copies made. In his desperation for funds, he'd used them as collateral for unsuspecting lenders.

These counterfeit shares that Jones had produced certainly looked good but were totally illegal and worthless. The look on Jones's face made James smile as he described his father's trick.

"And that's the shameful truth, I'm afraid. Father was a fraudster, and there's nothing either myself or my Uncle can do for you. I hope you didn't lend him too much."

Charles Jones couldn't remember the last time he'd been so angry. Sweat gathered on his forehead and began to slide down his patchwork cheek. Lemon, sensing his boss's anger, moved closer to him but was abruptly brushed away.

"Thirty-five thousand pounds," Jones answered with open fury. He wiped his useless leaking eye again.

"Thirty-five thousand, eh?" James repeated slowly and whistled. Good on the old man! It wasn't always comfortable having a fraudster for a father, but this monster before him had in all likelihood sent

James Snr to his death. It was some comfort to see his father striking back from beyond the grave.

"Unfortunately, Father is dead, Charles, and not even the long arm of the law nor his many other debtors can do anything about that. I'm sorry you've had this wasted journey. Now, if you'll excuse me, my fiancée is waiting. Our wedding's next week, and there's so much still to do."

Thank God the days of needing to invite Jones along to family events were over, he reflected, calling Mrs Parkes to see these visitors to the lift.

* * *

Marleen had been back and forth to London for her wedding dress fittings and, just as importantly, a little bit of last-minute *fun*! Her girlfriend Penelope needed some extra loving. She wasn't amused in the slightest by the upcoming marriage, whatever excuses her lover gave her, and Marleen felt she had to make it up to her. They'd both had a blast, visiting Ronnie Scott's and Annabel's, which they did night and day. They'd stayed up until dawn both nights, and it was wild. Exactly what they'd both needed.

Everything for the wedding was practically done and dusted, and for the first time in a while, James was glowing with contentment. Pleased to see it, Marleen assumed it was because of their wedding. She was wrong. He wasn't even thinking about the wedding but was still high on Jones getting stung for £35,000. He knew he shouldn't be proud of his father's criminal behaviour, but he was.

Roger laughed heartily when James described the scene, the expression on Jones's face, his body language as he left the office and how he'd been led out by Mrs Parkes, who looked particularly concerned by his changed demeanour.

"Uncle, you should have seen him. It was magic, pure magic!"

Roger was happy about the day's events but physically quite unwell. However, in celebration, he'd made a special effort to eat in the dining room. James topped up Marleen's glass first, then Roger's. Finally, his fiancée managed to broach the subject of the wedding.

"Well, boys, I've arranged everything, including the caterers, dress, music and photographs. It's all done!"

Roger and James could see her excitement and expectation of their approval. Roger duly delivered it.

"Well done, Marleen. I'm sure it'll be delightful. I can't wait! No problems, I assume?"

It'd been quite easy in the end, she reflected. She couldn't think of anything to complain about except one tiny issue.

"All good, Roger, although the photographer was hard to nail down. But it's sorted now."

James, about to put a forkful of wild salmon into his mouth, stopped halfway. He placed his fork down and looked at his fiancée.

"Photographer?" he asked, almost afraid to hear her answer. His heart raced. *Jesus, no*!

"Yes, Burns, the one on that main street." Marleen paused, trying to remember its name. "Ah, yes, Strand Road. You must know it? The girl there was particularly unhelpful. I don't know what I did to upset her – odd thing, really. Anyway, don't forget, James, rehearsal Thursday evening!"

Caitlin, he thought. *She knows*!

* * *

On the morning of the wedding rehearsal, James left Melrose to drive to Rocola and noted a black taxi passing him as he left the house. He looked into his mirror and saw that it'd slowed and turned into Melrose's drive. They weren't expecting guests, and he wondered who it could be. He'd call Roger when he got into Rocola, he decided.

Catherine Henderson sat in the back of the cab. She hadn't slept a wink but knew if she didn't face her demons once and for all now, she never would. The years of anger had lasted long enough.

She wondered why she hadn't heard from Caitlin, feeling instinctively that the young woman needed rescuing. Maybe just like her mother Majella, who'd rescued Catherine, she could do the same for the girl. There was a natural camaraderie between them, and they'd already become friends.

After having met Caitlin and listened to the story of her relationship with James, the purpose of Catherine's visit to the city had changed. Not only was she determined to meet both James and Roger, but she'd also make a point of assessing what James's bride-to-be was all about. She was going to make sure her son was doing the right thing, marrying the right woman. Not long ago, he had been in love with Caitlin, and his mother believed if that had been true love, as the girl's behaviour seemed to indicate, then it couldn't just disappear in a heartbeat. There was more to this wedding than met the eye.

The house hadn't changed much, though the rose garden, painstakingly laid out by Roger's late wife Jocelyn, was sad-looking and dormant on this cold December day.

Catherine's memory took her back to those carefree, summer days when she and her sister-in-law had marvelled at the hybrid tea roses in shades of crimson, yellow, pink and white. She'd loved spending time at Melrose when James Snr had been away in the army. Reflecting on the past, she recognised they'd married for all the wrong reasons, and it was clearly always destined for disaster and failure. As for Jocelyn, Catherine was extremely fond of her and still remembered the day she'd found out she couldn't carry children. It'd been a nightmare for the young woman, and there was nothing Catherine could say to pacify her.

She'd never seen anyone cry so much – for the babies she would never have or hold. It'd been heartbreaking. She often thought of poor Jocelyn.

The taxi came to a sudden stop outside the main entrance. Catherine paid but asked the driver to wait. She climbed out and rapped the lion-headed door knocker. She turned and looked over the lawn and gardens. It really was beautiful here. She could hear her heart beating loudly. Eventually, the door opened, and Mrs McGinty stood there in her striped wrap-over apron, shocked at the sight of a face she had not seen in decades.

The old woman couldn't believe her eyes and, for the first time in many years, took the Lord's name in vain.

"*Jesus Christ*! It's Mrs Henderson!"

"Hello, Mrs McGinty." Catherine smiled at her, and before she knew it, she was in the warm arms of the housekeeper, breathing in her long-forgotten sweet, honeysuckle smell. They held each other for what seemed like an eternity until Mrs McGinty waved the taxi driver away and pulled Catherine over the threshold of Melrose.

* * *

At the office, James completely forgot to call home to ask who was in the taxi he'd seen and only remembered at lunchtime. He dialled the Melrose number. He knew Mrs McGinty would be baking today on her own, and Marleen had gone to Belfast for a few last-minute wedding things – he hadn't paid much attention, to be honest. Once he found out Caitlin knew of his marriage, he'd driven to the beach at Lisfannon to think. Torn between his loyalty to Rocola and Marleen and the old feelings for Caitlin that seemed to have been revived, his head told him one thing, his heart another. In the end, he'd made the thirty-minute drive back to the city and found himself parked outside the shop once more. This time, he entered and walked to the far end, where he was met and greeted by the proprietor, Raymond

Burns. Burns knew James already: he'd been the official photographer at Rocola's doomed meeting in the City Hotel. Thinking the customer was here to talk about his forthcoming wedding, Burns was mildly surprised when instead he was asked if his assistant was available.

"Caitlin? Why, no. She's off today. Family stuff."

More problems, James thought, and grimaced. "Ah, okay. Never mind."

The surprised shopkeeper considered him, suddenly interested, and asked: "That's it?"

"Yes. That's it. Thank you," James muttered as he quickly made his way out.

* * *

He rolled his eyes as the phone rang unanswered in Melrose and hung up, thinking his uncle was likely asleep and Mrs McGinty too busy. He'd find out later who the visitor had been.

He grunted, looked at the vacant space outside his office and thought of Caitlin whilst remembering how wonderful they'd been together. They'd worked so hard over those months before the ill-fated conference. They'd been so happy. He knew then he desperately needed to see her and soon. But how? He couldn't go near her house after his last visit when he'd been practically hijacked at gunpoint – or could he? He didn't know, but somehow, he had to find a way and soon. He had things to say to her, very important things.

Chapter 49

The return journey from Armagh was nothing like their emotionally charged early-morning trip. The miles seemed longer, silent and sad. When they reached Blamfield Street, Mrs McFadden, clad in her usual curlers and pinny, was waiting patiently by her front window and saw the red car drive up.

Charlie had called her earlier and shared the sad news. She ran as fast as she could down the concrete path as the weary group climbed out and stood on the pavement – unsure what to do next.

"Come here, love! Come here!" Mrs McFadden cried out as she ran to Caitlin, enveloping her in her arms.

The men looked at each other and shrugged. With a sigh, Charlie invited Tommy in for a beer. Mrs McFadden nodded vigorously and mouthed for him to go ahead as she led Caitlin to her front door.

"Do you have your keys, love?" she asked kindly.

Caitlin nodded and fished for them in her bag, hands shaking as she attempted to enter. Her neighbour gently took the keys away and murmured encouragingly as she unlocked the front door, "Let's get you inside, love, and make you a nice cup of tea. Leave everything to me."

* * *

Anne had called to see Caitlin as soon as she'd heard the news and, after comforting her friend, had carefully asked her if she'd talk to Martin on her behalf. She wanted to make sure that she and baby Sean would be safe after Porkie's ultimate betrayal. Caitlin promised she would as soon as Martin put in an appearance. She knew he would even though it was unsafe for him to visit Blamfield Street with the security services monitoring it.

Martin must have entered a house in the street behind and climbed over the yard wall. He tapped on the back door an hour later after Anne's departure and crushed Caitlin to him when she opened it. Her brother refused to come straight in, saying he had to have a smoke first. Caitlin didn't allow it in the house, so she stood outside in the yard with him.

"They'll kill you one day, you know?" she said with a small smile as she looked at her brother's pack of cigarettes.

"Bugger that!" he replied rebelliously, taking a deep drag on one to prove his point.

He made her laugh, and she was glad he was here. She knew he'd been up to something and that he couldn't stay long. They'd grown closer than they'd ever been, with both of them feeling crushingly sad about the dissolution of their family.

As if sensing her guilt, Martin looked at her tenderly and said, "You shouldn't feel bad about Tina, Caitlin. I know you do. But I was the one who filled her head with ideas about the Provos and the Cause. I just never thought…" He looked down at his feet and dragged his heel back and forth across the stone in an attempt to force out some stubborn weeds.

"It was all my fault. I even knew Kelly. I met him during the time he was leading her on. Did you know that?" His eyes welled up with tears of shame as he ran his hand over his mouth.

Caitlin was stunned. *Bloody hell!*

"You did?" she asked in disbelief. The skin crawled on her arms and neck as he looked at her. Her heart ached for her brother as she watched a slow, silent tear run down his cheek. She never thought she'd see Martin McLaughlin cry. She moved towards him, but he gently held her back as he explained angrily: "We knew he was a live wire, and I warned him not to break ranks. We knew he was likely a queer too, so I missed what he was at, Caitlin. I missed his game with Tina. And all the time, he was using her, treating her lower than shite. Christ, I should have put a bullet in him when I had the chance!"

He broke down then and fell to his hunkers, put his head in his hands and cried despairingly. Caitlin wrapped one arm around him and let him weep. Let him release the tension and guilt that had obviously been eating him up.

In time, he stopped and looked at her. "Sorry." His eyes were watery, red and already swollen.

"Don't be sorry, Martin. I know you loved her."

He shuddered and groaned aloud. "Another bloody useless death! I don't know anymore, Caitlin; it's all getting out of hand. I never expected the killing and stuff to go on for so long."

Caitlin found she'd nothing to say to that. He was the one who knew about killing after all.

"Anyways, forget about me. What about you? I heard Anne was here earlier."

Martin hadn't seen her since the Shipquay Street bombing.
He finished his cigarette, preparing to go indoors. Before he could, she touched him gently on the arm and said warily, "Talking of Anne, there's something I need to ask you."

Instantaneously he knew what she was going to ask – he'd been expecting it.
"About Porkie and Dickie?"

Caitlin nodded as Martin leaned close to her ear and muttered, "We know about her and what she did. Tell her she's okay. She's got nothing to worry about. Now, no further mention of it again, Caitlin, okay?"

"Okay. Thanks, Martin. I'll tell her."

Harris and the Governor had released Tina's remains almost straight away. A few hours later there was a knocking on the front door, and Caitlin hurried down the hallway to answer it. Through the glass pane, she could see car headlights. It was the hearse bringing Tina home.

She gestured for Martin to stay out of sight in the yard.

"Jesus Christ, here we go again," he whispered sadly.

* * *

Two days later, Caitlin looked down at the newly dug grave and watched as her sibling's small pale wooden coffin was lowered deeper and deeper into the sodden Derry soil. Heavy grey clouds in the sky looked ready to unload their contents at any moment. Too many funerals. Caitlin thought of Martin, who couldn't attend – he'd to get out and head back to America. However, they were good, and he assured her he'd keep in touch this time.

Tommy was struggling with his emotions. He stood beside Caitlin feeling weak, tired and broken, with an almighty hangover that wasn't helping. He felt sick in the stomach *and* the heart.

Caitlin looked towards Anne, standing in the crowd of mourners opposite. She gave her a gentle nod in acknowledgement. She'd been told that she and baby Sean were safe; the Provos knew what she'd done.

But for today, she'd stand alongside the remaining McLaughlin family, looking down at the familiar sodden grave in the impending Derry rain.

Chapter 50

Alice Wallace didn't know what else to do but hide out in the open. She found herself sitting in the diner next to Belfast City Hall, where she'd had the disastrous meeting with Lemon.

She re-read the headlined article in the previous night's edition of the Belfast Telegraph. "**Part-time UDR Man Murdered**". Ian Dillon had been shot dead while responding to a bogus job. She'd become paranoid, thinking it just too much of a coincidence that she'd met Lemon, whom Ian had recommended as someone to help her get explosives, and then within days, her friend had been murdered.

She believed everyone was watching her, although at least she wasn't on her own. There were lots of people in the diner and outside on the main street. She should've reported back to base this morning but couldn't. She'd failed – again – and was absolutely gutted. She couldn't face the wrath of her handler. She really had no idea what to do next, and for the first time that she could remember during her army service, she was frightened.

* * *

The OC watched Dolores pack the small number of belongings she had. Her few bits fitted neatly into a single plastic bag. Dolores was looking forward to seeing Patrick and finding out what he'd been up to. He'd be waiting outside today to take her home.

"I'll probably see you again soon, Maureen," Dolores told her friend, half-smiling. "You know they'll never leave me be."

"I know," the OC said. "We're all on their radar now. Just be careful."

Dolores lifted her coat, put it on and looked at the vacant bed in her cell. She shook her head sadly, thinking of the youngin's death. *Unbelievable.*

"I know," Maureen said and moved aside to let Dolores pass. They walked side by side along the catwalk until they reached the wrought-iron staircase in the middle of the wing.

"I'll be seeing you then," Maureen said, hugging her tight.

"See you," she replied.

Oddly, she'd miss this place. She'd miss these strong, united women though she looked forward to breathing the clean air of freedom. Black hadn't been able to charge her with anything, and so she'd been released.

Outside as promised, Patrick waited for his sister. He'd missed her. His first concern was to tell her what they'd discovered about Brona Kelly. Unwrapping a cigarette pack, thinking he'd get one in before he drove them back, he watched his twin exit by the main gates. Her searching eyes found him, and she began to run towards his car, exclaiming, "Yes! There you are!"

He hugged her tight, took her plastic bag and carelessly threw it into the back seat, shouting, "Hurry up, D! I'm freezing!"

Dolores jumped into the front, shivering. She looked at the grey Victorian façade of the gaol and smiled, thinking of all her friends inside. *Keep strong.*

* * *

On the drive back, Patrick kept the conversation light, filling his sister in on what was happening at home. It wasn't long until Dolores brought up Brona's name. He told her everything and waited.

"Told ya!" she bragged, delighted she'd been proved right.

"I knew you'd say that!" Patrick answered, laughing and adding wickedly, "She wasn't a bad fuck for a Brit!"

Dolores squealed, "Ah, Patrick! Yuck! Too much!"

She looked out of the car window at the passing countryside. God, it was beautiful. She couldn't count the different shades of green in the fields, trees and hills. She smiled. The song was right; there were forty shades, and all of them beautiful. She felt elated by her brother's news.

"Do you know where she is?" Dolores asked.

Patrick nodded. "Brian's been tracking her. She's been sitting in some diner near the City Hall all day."

"Are we going straight there?"

He'd decided to leave the Brit to Dolores – she deserved it.

"No, we'll pick up Brian, and you two can go together. This one's yours – just be careful. Make sure you bring her straight back to The Shamrock. I'll wait there."

Dolores couldn't be more pleased at being handed such a responsibility and looked forward to dealing with the British spy herself. "Thanks, Patrick."

They drove on in comfortable silence, ignorant of an unmarked car following them from a distance.

As soon as they reached The Shamrock, they found Brian Monaghan waiting dutifully. He was looking forward to working with Dolores again and walked towards the oncoming car.

"Good to see you, Dolores. How you doing?" he asked casually as he opened the passenger door. Dolores looked at the big man.

"I'm good, Brian. How's the family?" She knew he had a crush on her, so she continually reminded him he'd a wife and family at home – she liked the man but wasn't going there. She'd been hurt badly before by a married man and swore she'd never go there again.

* * *

Inside The Shamrock, Dolores knocked back a couple of quick shots in the backroom and kissed her brother goodbye. She was dying to get moving and sort the Brit out once and for all.

"Come on, Brian. We'll go in your car. Let's do this!" she shouted excitedly.

The traffic into town was heavy, but eventually they reached the diner where Brian parked his car directly outside on the double yellow lines. He put the hazard lights on, stepped out and casually glanced through the diner window. His eyes searched until he found Brona Kelly, aka Alice, in the far corner of the room on the phone. Fortunately, there weren't too many other people inside.

He climbed back into the car and told Dolores where their target was. She took a deep breath, released it loudly and climbed out.

"Good luck," he said quietly.

She looked down into the car, smiled and told him, "Won't be long."

* * *

"Is that you, pet?" Alice's mother asked down the line. "Alice?"

She'd called her mother because she had to. She'd no one else to call. No one left alive.

"Yes, Mum, it's me," she answered softly. "How are you?"

"Ooooh, Alice, it's so lovely to hear your voice! I've been so worried."

"I know, Mum, and I'm sorry. I can't explain over the phone, but you've been on my mind these past few days."

Sylvia Wallace immediately knew something was very wrong. She could tell by her daughter's voice, and alarm bells began going off in her head. She knew more about Alice's job than she'd let on but never discussed it with her child. Now it was clear she was in trouble.

"What is it, Alice? Tell me, please."

"Nothing, Mum. I'm just missing you."

Alice tucked herself into the corner next to the payphone and listened to the concern mounting in her mum's voice. "You don't sound yourself, love."

"I'm alright. Honest. Just feeling a bit low, that's all."

Alice listened to her mother's reassurance for a few minutes and turned to look across the diner. Her heart nearly stopped when she saw Dolores Gillispie walking purposefully in her direction, face twisted with hatred and anger.

Alice, shocked beyond belief, let the handset drop with her mother still talking on the line. She looked around for an escape route but found herself trapped. Picking up the handset and with her eyes locked on Dolores, she cried down it in a terrified voice: "Mum, listen, I have to go! I love you, Mum! I love you so much…"

The grey handset was violently pulled from her hand and raised high before Dolores crashed it into the side of Alice's head.

Dolores screamed into her bleeding face, "Come with me, bitch!"

The next thing she knew, Alice was being dragged painfully by the hair out of the diner towards a parked car driven by a huge, dark-dressed man. No one from the diner moved an inch or said anything as they watched the woman's abduction. It wasn't any of their business, and, besides, most of them knew who Dolores Gillispie was.

Inside the car, Dolores sat stony-faced and quiet as a lamb. Earlier, they'd agreed it would be better to remain silent as a means of instilling more fear in the woman. They'd do all the talking when they got back to The Shamrock.

* * *

Patrick felt unusually worried. He'd seen how wound up and excited his sister was and hoped she'd kept to their plan. Sometimes she could be way too impetuous. They'd been gone well over an hour and should have been back by now. He picked up the newspaper and read the piece on the part-time UDR man's murder in Bangor. Brian had done a neat job there. There wasn't any way the security services could trace it back – he was a pro. Patrick was well satisfied with their plans for the next on their list: James Carroll, aka "Lemon".

He soon heard a car engine stop at the back and rushed to the door to watch Brian, Dolores, and Alice climb out.

* * *

Alice wasn't shocked to see Patrick Gillispie as his sister roughly pushed her in at the bar's back entrance; she was afraid. No, she was petrified. The couple's silence on the journey had unsettled her greatly. She was shoved forward again and thrown down onto a single red plastic chair. She watched Dolores grin as she reached for a small reel of blue nylon rope, cut a piece off, then painfully wrenched Alice's arms behind the chair, binding her hands tightly together.

As before, everyone remained quiet until Dolores was confident Alice was secure. She looked at her brother and asked nonchalantly, "You staying for this?"

Patrick shook his head and walked across to Alice. He leaned down, hawked and spat in her face, his thick saliva landing on her lowered eyelids and upper cheekbone. She frantically shook her head to get the stuff off her and screamed with fury and fear.

"You cowardly bastard! They'll get you. You fucking dickhead!"

Patrick smirked and walked towards the door leading to the bar. He stopped when he reached his sister's side, kissed her lightly on the cheek and murmured, "She's all yours."

Alice began to scream with rage until she was swiftly stopped by Brian, who struck her face and head with the back of his huge hand. His thick, gold Irish Claddagh ring caught her exactly where the phone had cut her head earlier. She rolled and shook her head to get rid of the ringing in her ears.

Dolores tutted and told him off.

"Now, now, Brian, remember she's a lady. Men don't hit ladies!"

He looked amused – Dolores was on form tonight. He loved her like this. "Apologies, Dolores. Apologies, miss," he said, looking from one woman to the other.

Dolores opened the green felt bag that lay on a small beer-stained table and pulled out the same revolver Brian had used to kill Ian Dillon.

Weighing the gun in her hand, in a voice as cold as ice, she leaned over and said maliciously, "I'm going to kill you now, Brona, or should I call you Alice?"

Dolores cocked the loaded weapon and placed it in the very centre of Alice Wallace's forehead.

Alice looked right back and then closed her eyes. A vivid memory of Graham and her laughing and drinking wine on a picnic they'd once shared suddenly returned. They'd been so carefree and young, free from worry, free from heartache. They'd just made love after he'd proposed. Alice smiled at the memory. Dolores Gillispie smiled too and fired off a single round.

As the loud pop of the shot sounded through The Shamrock, other than one or two people making eye contact, not a single patron openly acknowledged the familiar *crack* but continued to drink, talk and laugh – *business as usual.*

Outside, three plain-clothes army operatives also heard the shot and leapt from their car and ran as fast as they could towards The Shamrock's newly repaired extra thick security door. Like wallies, they stood for a moment, wondering how the fuck they were going to get in, but soon realised they'd no choice but to retreat back to their car and call for assistance.

Chapter 51

Chief Constable Bonner had no option but to charge Charles Jones and his hoodlum Lemon for the crimes detailed in William Barter's exclusive in the *Irish News* and syndicated by the remaining Irish, as well as the international press. The stories of brutal and bloody sectarian murders, money laundering, armed robbery, intimidation, anti-Catholic propaganda, and so much more were reported for days. Jones's photograph was prominent in the major newspapers, local and Irish TV news. The only way Bonner could save his ally was to immediately dismiss the claims made by the journalist that Jones was somehow behind the fatal shooting of Bishop Hegarty. The RUC Chief Constable maintained throughout numerous statements that Kieran Kelly was a lone gunman and bomber, far more likely to be behind the killing than someone as socially prominent as Charles Jones, Esq.

Bonner knew Jones and Morris were behind the murder of the Bishop and many others, but there still wasn't sufficient evidence to indict the Belfast man. Morris and Kelly were the perfect fall guys for the City Hotel events. The Chief Constable also knew his public denials were shallow and superficial. However, fortunately for him, through his gritty perseverance, they seemed to stick, and the murder charges against Jones were eventually dropped.

How Barter found so much solid evidence for all the other charges against Jones and Lemon, he'd never know. Bonner had to raise his hat to him; the journalist had done one hell of a job – so much so that even the Chief Constable couldn't sweep the other charges against Jones under the carpet. He'd done all he could but couldn't save him from the inevitable. Fortunately for Barter, as promised, he'd shared all his information first with his CIA friend and vice versa, Dale – to Barter's delight – was able to reciprocate. The CIA information was dynamite…

The Honorable Justice Matthew Dodds looked down upon Charles Jones, standing next to James Carroll in the dock at Belfast High Court. A number of Lemon's fellow villains or "*kids*" stood next to their leader, heads held high and defiant. None of them, including Lemon, would say a word against Jones. They knew it was wisest not to, given his continual threats to their families. They also knew he'd soon find someone else to fill their shoes.

Unsurprisingly Jones had arranged for Dodds to fill in for the original judge in this case. Apparently his colleague was ill with some nasty disease, but Dodds didn't ask too many questions. He knew Jones had set it up and was glad he'd another chance to repay his benefactor for the introduction to Boodle's. He loved the club and had already leveraged it by making some bloody good connections… To their delight, he and Mrs D had even been introduced to some junior royals!

The judge paid close attention to the mass of evidence, listened especially to the American journalist who – page after page – related his findings from interviews, photographs and recordings. He'd spent months collating evidence from witnesses, snitches and people with grudges against Jones in an attempt to prove the crimes. Once he'd assembled the evidence, he'd shared it with the CIA and had then taken it straight to a senior contact in the RUC based in Newtownabbey outside Belfast. Dale Horn had told him the man was neutral and fair-minded and had been proved right. It wasn't long before Charles Jones found himself under arrest.

His lawyers had done their best to represent him, but even so, the evidence was damning. All Judge Dodds had to do now was to pass sentence – guilty on all counts.

In a bid to quieten the babbling court, he coughed loudly and began summing up. This was his favourite time in court – when he was the centre of attention. He felt he was on-stage. It was his moment. The courtroom soon became as silent as the grave as it awaited the sentence.

"Charles Anthony Jones, you have been found guilty by this court of the following…" Dodds read out the long list of crimes.

Once he'd finished the list, he completed his statement by calculatingly and sombrely looking at Jones and passing sentence.

"… I therefore sentence you to three years..."

He coughed again, this time for real. Slowly and deliberately, he wiped his nose before continuing: "…three years' suspended sentence."

The public gallery was filled mainly with Jones's fans and followers, who clapped, cheered and heckled. They unfurled, waved and swayed their huge Union Jack flags, their King Billy and Orange Lodge banners, high in the air. In the remainder of the gallery were primarily family members and victims of Lemon and his "kids", who'd been shot, tortured or otherwise butchered. Some screamed and shouted in fury; others remained unmoved and still, clearly in shock.

At the pandemonium, Dodds angrily cried out, over and over: "Silence! Silence! Silence in my court!"

Jones looked over his shoulder at the public gallery and rebelliously raised one fist high in the air, clenched it for victory and yelled, "*No surrender!*"

Meanwhile, Lemon stood rigid and waited. His heart raced. He knew what was coming. The cries from the public gallery eased and eventually stopped in response to Dodds's cries for silence.

The judge read from a piece of paper.

"James Carroll, you have been found guilty of eleven counts of murder."

Once again, the long list of charges was repeated until eventually, Dodds closed with:

"I therefore sentence you to life – without parole." Lemon gasped and gripped the wooden dock tightly. *Fuck.*

He looked at Jones, but the disfigured man simply raised his eyebrows and shrugged. *Sorry, pal, you're on your own.* Dodds continued to sentence the others, and they too were sent down for life – no parole.

They were quickly taken down, but their insolent cries were heard all around the courtroom. “No surrender! No surrender!”

Jones looked up at Judge Dodds and gave a smile of complicity.

Up to now, the press and media had been ruthless in their summing up of Charles Jones. Their condemnation had seriously damaged him, both personally and professionally. He’d already lost a number of large, fruitful contracts in Belfast and would soon be feeling the pinch. Most of his money had gone into the upkeep of the UVF. He didn’t mind. They were doing such a good job. Anyway, he had other plans up his sleeve.

* * *

William Barter sat pinned to his seat. He couldn’t believe it. He couldn’t believe what he’d just witnessed. It was a farce! The judge *had* to be on Jones’s payroll. The man was found guilty, for crying out loud! Three years, three fucking years, and the paltry sentence was suspended at that! He watched as Jones clumsily climbed down from the dock to make his way over to his lawyers. They congratulated each other with hard pats on the back and numerous handshakes. Jones spotted the stunned journalist and walked his way.

“Mr Barter. Well, as you see, I’m still here,” he said triumphantly, holding up his arms like a victorious heavyweight.

“You are, Mr Jones. I see that,” Barter replied, feeling disheartened.

Jones’s smile was too wide. There was something chilling in his harsh whisper as he moved closer to say, “Will you give up now, Mr Barter?”

Repulsed, he drew back, looked the murderer square in the eye, and said firmly: “*Never.*”

Charles Jones chortled and mockingly applauded him while walking backwards for a few steps. He smiled mischievously then and turned towards his waiting legal team.

Later that evening, the journalist was preparing a briefing for Langley, complemented by a large gin and tonic. His fingers speeded over his Brother typewriter as he transferred his fury at the judge's findings into words:

> *It is evident that in this case, there was an egregious breach of justice stemming from obvious collusion between the court, Charles Jones and the cabal that is the Ulster Security Services. However, without more proven and documented evidence, any rectification of this situation will not be forthcoming.*
>
> *Across this province – on a daily basis – disreputable, scandalous and officially sanctioned kangaroo courts are being used to violate and disregard fundamental human rights, thereby, unsurprisingly, adding impetus to the Republican terrorists' war against the British Government...*

Chapter 52

Mrs Mac, as Catherine fondly called Melrose's housekeeper Mrs McGinty, prepared some tea and placed two warm, buttered scones on a plate in front of her. At the thought of food, Catherine's tummy turned. She was so nervous.

She looked around the kitchen. Everything here seemed to be exactly the same, from the eight-seater, solid oak farmhouse table positioned in the very centre of the functional stone-flagged floor to the copper pots and pans of all sizes hanging from a grille attached to the ceiling. An old pitch-black stove filled the inside of an arched fireplace, sending a wave of heat across the room. A double Belfast sink with a worktop on either side sat under a long rectangular window that looked over a stairwell leading down to the second cellar kitchen. Mrs Mac had obviously been baking. The smell in the room was mouthwatering.

The housekeeper sat down beside her surprise visitor, whom she was delighted to see after all these years, and poured her a cup of tea from a well-used red-and-white-striped teapot.

"And how are you keeping, Mrs Henderson?" she asked warmly.

"Nervous, Mrs Mac, extremely nervous," Catherine answered shyly.

"Ah, don't be nervous, love. What have you to be nervous about? This is your home too. I'm sorry you can't see Mr Henderson, but he's in bed. He's really not well. Not well at all. Between me and you, love, I'm not sure he'll make this wedding." Mrs Mac added dramatically: "You know about that, I suppose?"

"Yes. I've been told. I'd heard Roger wasn't well too, but I do need to talk to him. I've written so many times, Mrs Mac."

The old woman nodded. She'd seen the numerous airmail letters that had been ignored, discarded or returned to sender. Life must go on, she thought, and now Mr Henderson's health was getting worse. It was time. Time to get it all out in the open.

She thought back to that fateful night so many moons ago and its far-reaching consequences.

* * *

Melrose was at its best, dressed up with fairy lights strung across the garden on a beautiful clear summer evening. A number of guests had arrived already whilst Roger remained upstairs in the middle of another major row with his wife, Jocelyn. He'd had enough of her ranting and ran down the staircase to meet his sister-in-law Catherine, who stood at the bottom. He was extremely fond of her. She was a breath of fresh air, a tonic compared to the forever sulking, miserable woman upstairs.

Catherine was petite with a childish sense of humour. She was sweet, funny and kind. Her heart-shaped face had rosebud lips that were always smiling. Tonight she looked particularly beautiful in a long dark navy chiffon dress that clung perfectly to her boyish body. Her shoulder-length dark-blonde hair was simply pulled back and held by a large coral clasp. She was too good for his brother, and Roger knew the bastard had already hurt the poor girl over and over.

He gently took her arm and led her to a bar set up in a corner next to the Adam fireplace in Melrose's dining room. He ordered two large gin and tonics and looked around his favourite room.

The atmosphere in here was already vibrant, and clearly everyone was having a good time. It was still early in the evening, and a fading orange sun shone through the tall, sash windows.

He caught sight of Police Inspector George Shalham, his long-time friend, who smiled at him from across the room and raised his glass in salute.

Catherine was on fine form, and their conversation was merry until, after a short time, a bell rang to announce dinner. Roger noticed his wife had joined the party and was sitting at the bottom of the long, linen-draped table. He caught her eye and smiled, hoping for a positive response, but in return received nothing but a cold hard look.

At the end of the evening, the host and hostess escorted their guests out. After James and Jocelyn had said their goodnights, Roger and Catherine were left alone in the drawing-room.

All night Catherine had watched and felt sorry for him. She was convinced most of his guests had sensed the difficult atmosphere between the couple and witnessed his efforts to converse with Jocelyn, who had been borderline rude, ignoring him.

Treading carefully, Catherine took a moment before she asked, "Are you okay, Roger?"

"It's that obvious, is it?" he answered dejectedly.

"I'm afraid so," she answered truthfully. "She's not getting any better, is she?"

Roger shook his head sorrowfully. Feeling lost and dejected, he reached for the poker and stabbed at the open fire before turning to look at her.

"I don't know what to do, Catherine. I just don't know what to do!"

She rushed to him as his whole body convulsed with sobs. She held his hand and rubbed his shoulders before tenderly embracing him.

It felt like an age since he'd received any love or affection from a woman, and he returned her embrace. His sobs subsided as he looked into her beautiful, anxious face so full of understanding. She really was very lovely.

And then he kissed her. At first, she responded a little, but soon his natural desires swamped him. His kisses grew hungrier and more demanding. This was wrong! He was going too far, she thought, as she tried to push him off. But to no avail. He roughly threw her down onto a large sheepskin rug and forcefully pushed her onto her stomach. Her attempts to scream were violently smothered as he forced her into the soft rug.

He attempted to get his hand under her chiffon dress, struggling frenziedly to unwind the twisted fabric in search of her knickers. Finally, he grasped them and tore them away with one hand, discarding them across the room. Within seconds, he'd unzipped his trousers and pulled them down enough to push himself into her.

She fought back, but he was hurting her, hurting her so much. She couldn't stop him. Her eyes screwed up in pain at her failing attempts to get him off. It made no difference. He was riding her, deeply and painfully, oblivious to her thumping fists. In the end, sore and exhausted, she gave up and stopped dead. He released a feral moan. It was all over in a matter of minutes.

* * *

Christ! Oh, Christ! What have I done! Roger Henderson's mind screamed. Mortified, he looked down at the dishevelled woman who lay motionless beneath him. Climbing up onto his knees, he saw her pained and bewildered face turn away from him in burning shame. He immediately climbed up and quickly fixed his clothes, weeping with humiliation and remorse.

"I'm so sorry, Catherine. Dear God! I'm so sorry!"

He offered her his hand, but she ignored it. Instead, with great dignity, Catherine Henderson pulled down her torn dress and grabbed her discarded shoes and hair clasp, looking around for her underwear. As soon as she saw her ripped panties, she curled them up in her hand and, with her head hanging low, quietly left the room.

Mrs McGinty, who'd been on her way to fetch the last of the wine glasses, gasped as she saw how distressed and unkempt Catherine Henderson looked as she came out of the drawing-room. *What on earth!* She quickly ran to hide in a darkened corner under the huge staircase. The housekeeper blessed herself as she watched the weeping woman walk upstairs. Almost immediately, she noticed her tousled and dishevelled employer standing, still and white-faced, at the drawing-room door, his pained eyes staring after his sister-in-law. *What on God's earth?* Then she knew. *Mr Henderson! What have you done to the poor child? The poor, poor child.*

* * *

In Melrose's kitchen many years later, Mrs Mac asked Catherine Henderson,

"What are we going to do with you, Cass, eh?"

Catherine had loved it when Mrs Mac called her Cass. It'd been such a long time since she'd heard it.

"I have to see James. I have to talk to my son, get to know him. A day hasn't gone by that I haven't regretted leaving him."

The housekeeper sighed. What a mess all around, but a mess that needed to be sorted and no better time than now.

"And are you going to confront Mr Henderson?" she asked.

"Confront, Mrs Mac? I don't understand." Catherine pretended she didn't know what the housekeeper meant.

Mrs McGinty had never spoken to anyone about what she'd witnessed in the hallway. Her heart broke that night at the sight of Cass, desolate and clearly violated. Perhaps against her better judgement, she'd also felt sorry for Roger Henderson, who, clearly repentant, thereafter retreated deep into his work and was rarely at home. He was never the same man again.

Soon after the incident, Catherine desperately wanted to leave Melrose, but at her husband's insistence, she'd no choice but to stay. Time and time again, he told her they couldn't afford to go anywhere else, and even if they could, it was better for them to stay put at this comfortable and socially desirable address.

As the weeks and months passed, James Snr watched his wife become increasingly poorly, depressed and withdrawn. Eventually, the only person she'd let near her was a young Londonderry girl who'd been recommended by Mrs Mac, Majella O'Reilly. Majella was full of life and jests and never stopped talking. Catherine enjoyed listening to her as they sewed together upstairs. Majella knew something bad had happened to the sad young woman who constantly stayed in her bedroom. She never asked – it was none of her business. But with the energy of the young, Majella blabbed on and talked enthusiastically about her dreams of a life with her fiancé Patrick. Her good humour, laughter and enthusiasm soon gave Catherine comfort and hope for the future until her pregnancy began to show.

Her husband returned to his unit once she'd no choice but to tell him she was expecting. Having spent six difficult months living with just Jocelyn and Roger, Catherine gave birth to a 9lb 2oz boy. James Henderson Jnr.

Mrs Mac, Majella, and surprisingly Jocelyn took great joy in caring for both mother and baby. The arrival of James Jnr seemed to lift Jocelyn out of her depression and give her the strength to channel all her thwarted love into this child.

Catherine tried her best to love the infant but found it too difficult. Eventually, she announced to her husband their marriage was over, and she was leaving for South Africa *without* her son.

Carefully placing her teacup down on the table, Catherine repeated her question. "Why would I confront Mr Henderson, Mrs Mac?"

She refilled their cups and replaced the pot on the tray. She knew she needed to tread exceedingly carefully here. She took Cass's hands and held them tight. Looking her in the eye, Mrs McGinty explained what she knew.

"I know what happened, my love. I saw you afterwards on your way back up the stairs."

Catherine shook her head, trying to understand until relief washed over her like a cloudburst. She had always feared Roger Henderson was too well respected and admired in Londonderry for her story ever to be believed. And now, Mrs Mac had confirmed it all. She'd been there!

Too choked to respond, Catherine nodded numbly. At last, she wasn't on her own.

Her dark secret had been hidden for so many years, and she hated herself for her rejection of her baby boy. After the years and months of living with the enormous guilt of abandoning him, burying the memories of how he'd been conceived, she'd finally understood it wasn't James's fault. It wasn't *her* fault! She'd blamed him unfairly when he was a baby, and now it was only fair her son should learn the truth. Although she was thankful that Jocelyn cared so much for James and recognised Roger had provided well for him, the boy had been gone too long from his mother's life. She was here to make amends for deserting him and to finally say sorry. The guilt she carried for that was killing her. She'd felt wretched and so miserable for too long. It was time for Roger to accept his role too.

"It's been too long, Mrs Mac. I can't live with myself any longer. I need to see Roger and for us both to tell James the truth."

Mrs Mac hesitated. "I don't know, love. The shock of seeing you could kill him, honestly. As I say, I'm not even sure he'll last till Saturday for the wedding. It'll be a miracle if he does. There's a rehearsal tonight, but no one's expecting him to go. Young James wants him to rest as much as possible."

"I'm not here to cause a scene, Mrs Mac. Just to talk," Catherine answered meekly.

The housekeeper was torn. She got up and walked around the kitchen, suddenly noticing the smell of burning. Remembering her baking shortbread, she rushed to grab her oven gloves and opened the smoke-filled oven to bring out a tray of black burned lumps.

"Ock, dear. What a shame," the woman said as she opened the kitchen pedal bin and dumped the contents of the tray straight into it.

Catherine said nothing but waited. She watched as the old woman threw the hot tray into the sink and looked out of the basement window, thinking. Moments later, she grunted. She'd made her decision. *Cass was right. Young James needed to know the truth, and it was only right that she speak to Mr Henderson first.*

"I'll go see how he is. If he agrees, then that's okay. Give me a minute."

Catherine sat impassive and still in the warm kitchen awaiting her return. Time seemed to slow down until the housekeeper returned and nodded.

"Come with me, pet."

Upstairs, Roger Henderson felt his heart palpitating through the fine bedclothes. He'd thought about this moment for years and finally welcomed it. He wasn't for this planet much longer. His bedroom door swung open, and he looked at Catherine Henderson for the first time in over twenty years.

Mrs McGinty led Cass over to a red velvet, two-seater couch set next to Roger's bed and, with an encouraging smile, quietly closed the double doors behind her.

Catherine was shocked by Roger's appearance and knew Mrs Mac was spot on. The old man's death mask was already making its way through. He looked old and, to her chagrin, heartbreakingly vulnerable. His voice was hoarse and threadlike when he greeted her.

"Hello, Catherine."

"Roger," she answered tightly.

This was so awkward. Not at all what she'd expected. Not at all what she'd darkly imagined. She'd seen herself rushing at him, hitting him over and over again, screaming at him in fury. Instead, what she saw in the bed was a sick, sad, dying old man with his dog lying solemnly at the bottom of the bed watching her.

Her eyes betrayed her, and Roger knew what she was thinking.

"Not what you imagined, Catherine?"

"No," she answered unhappily.

A hacking cough overtook him, and he struggled to find his breath. He pointed frantically at a glass of water on the bedside table. She rushed to the glass and helped him drink from it, propping up the back of his balding head. His face contorted in agony at the sharp, stabbing pains in his chest. His mind was reeling. Nothing could be said before the wedding, nothing! Eventually, he waved to say he'd had enough, and she gently laid him back on his fluffed up pillows.

"I'm very sorry, Catherine. I never meant to hurt you. I'm so ashamed," he said, his eyes begging forgiveness.

She ignored his apology and answered with as much steel in her voice as she could muster, "We need to tell James the truth."

He nodded sympathetically. "Yes."

She hadn't expected this either and couldn't find the right words. Another racking cough hit him again until he asked sheepishly, "Catherine, could it wait until after the wedding? I promise I'll tell him everything then. He's getting married to the most beautiful girl and is happy. I'll tell him afterwards. *Please?"*

She blanched. She didn't want to wait, not a single minute more.

"*Please*?" he repeated tentatively.

White-hot anger seared through her. *What right did he have to ask anything of her!* She glared at him in silence until her anger ebbed away.

Her silence panicked him.

"Please, Catherine, wait! Wait until after the wedding!"

Roger's face darkened as yet another spasm of coughing overtook him. His body shook and contorted with pain.

All the time, Mrs McGinty had been standing quietly outside her employer's bedroom. As soon as she heard his cries, she opened the door and ran through to help.

"Mr Henderson! Mr Henderson! It's okay. Slow now, like the doctor said. Take it easy. Try some water!"

Roger pushed the glass away defiantly until eventually his coughing lessened, and Mrs Mac looked across the large bed at Catherine.

"You'd better go, Cass. Just for a while until I get him settled. We'll sort this out, I promise. Why don't you go to the rehearsal tonight – take a peek? It's at Prehen, Church of Ireland, not too far. But be careful."

Catherine pondered this idea as she made her way out of the bedroom. She looked back to see Mrs Mac lowering Roger onto his pillows and tucking him in. She waved at Catherine, implying that she

should wait. Before she closed the double doors, both women looked back at the weary body on the bed. Roger appeared to be asleep.
"Before you go, I'm just thinking there's something else. James's fiancée Marleen and her bridesmaid are staying at the Beech Hill Hotel. You know that fancy place out near the hospital?" Catherine knew exactly where the hotel was. She'd been there many times in the past.

"Well, Marleen and whatever her name is, are there now. Mind her, though; she's a funny one, that bridesmaid. Bit snooty and a know-it-all too."

Mrs Mac thought a bit before adding, "I like Marleen, she's a good one, but there's definitely something not quite right about that friend of hers! It's annoying me, and I can't put me finger on it… Anyway, forget it for now. Why don't you go there before the rehearsal and see for yourself?"

Alarm bells began to ring in Catherine's head as she pondered over what Mrs Mac meant, but it was a bloody good idea. She'd go and suss out the two of them– after all, she'd nothing else to do. A taxi was ordered, and soon Catherine Henderson was on her way to the Beech Hill Hotel.

Chapter 53

"Mr Henderson! Mr Henderson! You have to come quick! I've had to call an ambulance. They're here for him, Mr Henderson!"

"Calm down, Mrs Mac," James shouted down the phone.

Mrs Parkes heard the noise through the glass door and ran into his office to see what was going on. She watched her boss use his shoulder to hold the phone against his ear whilst attempting to put on his coat, ready to leave. She ran to him and helped him put it on properly.

"What's happened? Tell me that again!" James listened as the housekeeper explained. Mrs Mac said nothing about Catherine's visit, only that Roger had taken a bad coughing fit and was struggling to breathe. It was serious.

"I'm on my way, Mrs Mac. I'll go straight to the hospital." James placed the phone back on its cradle and looked at Mrs Parkes fearfully. "It's Uncle; he's bad. I have to go!"

"Of course, Mr Henderson, of course. Off you go now, leave everything here to me!"

On his way to the hospital, James was stopped numerous times at several army checkpoints. Another series of bomb scares had blocked the main arterial roads that led to Craigavon Bridge and the hospital. He could hear his breath rising and falling in his throat. *Please, God, let him be okay.*

* * *

Caitlin wasn't surprised to find herself sitting on a chair next to a bed in Ward 8 of Altnagelvin Hospital, where Tommy O'Reilly had just been moved from A&E. They'd been waiting hours, but it didn't matter. She was just glad her uncle was finally being looked after. She'd noticed the derision on the face of the grim-faced doctor when he smelled the whiskey sweat coating Tommy's skin.

For days after Tina's funeral, Tommy had gone for it and had drunk far too much. Ultimately the stresses and strains of the past weeks and months caught up with him, and he'd collapsed in Caitlin's living room early that morning after sleeping on the sofa the night before. Martin was long gone, and so here she was facing trouble – again. She'd already called her cousin Kathy, Tommy's daughter, who worked on the ambulance crew at the hospital and who was on her way.

* * *

Upon reaching the hospital, the cold air struck James as he left the Jag as quickly as he could. He ran straight to the signed A&E area next to the Grand Hall on the ground floor. There was a queue at the reception desk and no sign of his uncle or Mrs Mac in the waiting crowd. The heat of the place was stifling, and he quickly removed his woollen suit jacket and loosened his silk tie. He ran his hands through his hair. It left his fingers wet with sweat. He kept looking around until eventually, it was his turn. He was met by a dour-faced nurse who barely acknowledged his presence. She looked back at him and snapped, "Yes."

"I'm looking for Roger Henderson. He was brought in by ambulance," James answered impatiently, staring into her cold, uncaring eyes. Upon hearing the Henderson name, Nurse Elizabeth Blood's demeanour changed entirely, and her eyes lit up, taking in the gorgeous man who stood before her.

"Ah, yes, Mr Henderson. We've sent him upstairs to Ward Six."

Using her pen as a guide, she promptly and efficiently gave James directions on a hospital plan whilst breathing in his aftershave.

"Through the double doors and the lifts are just there on the left, sir." About to ask if there was anything else he needed, she noticed he was already running towards them. Nurse Blood muttered to herself. She looked at the next in the queue and barked, "Next!"

* * *

Kathy O'Reilly rushed into the open ward, eyes searching for her dad and her cousin. She saw Caitlin at the far end, right next to the large window that overlooked the housing estate. She hastily made her way over, and Caitlin stood to greet her. "Hello, love."

"Hey. How is he? What did they say?" Kathy asked anxiously.

"Don't know anything yet. They're observing. I think he just overdid it, Kathy," Caitlin said quietly. Kathy already knew what she meant.

"I know, I've been telling him. He's taking on far too much. How long have you been here?"

"Since early morning," Caitlin answered, feeling suddenly exhausted. She looked at Tommy, who, oblivious to all and sundry, was sleeping deeply and peacefully.

Kathy smirked. "He looks so innocent when he's like that, doesn't he? I could kill him at times!"

"I know," Caitlin answered, her own smile full of love for the big man.

Her cousin removed her coat. She was on duty later that evening and happy to sit and wait to find out what the doctors had to say.

"You want to go on, love, go home and rest?" she suggested kindly.

"I'm okay, Kathy. Half-day closing, I've nowhere to be. I'll sit with you for a while."

* * *

Mrs Mac was in the corridor outside the private room where the hospital had placed Roger Henderson. She looked through the small square glass window on the door and sighed as she saw the forlorn body wrapped up tight in white and green cotton bedclothes. The patient was on oxygen and attached to a drip. She was never so glad to see young James as she was when she saw him running through the ward door.

"Over here!" she shouted from the bottom of the corridor. James ran to her and grasped her arms. "Is he alive, Mrs Mac? Is he?"

"He's alright, James. Calm now. He'll be okay." The woman's words didn't seem to compute as he copied Mrs Mac and looked through the window at the sad figure lying motionless on the hospital bed.

"He looks so helpless," James said to no one in particular.

"He was lucky," Mrs Mac said.

James looked at her for the first time. She still wore her flour-dusted apron under a double-breasted coat. She'd clearly had a fright; her hair was ruffled, eyes red and puffy. She looked exhausted. Mrs Mac felt him looking at her, smiled and squeezed his cold hand as he told her, "What a day, Mrs Mac."

The housekeeper shook her head, thinking: You, young James Henderson, have no idea!

* * *

It was dark by 4 p.m on the late December evening when Kathy finally managed to persuade her cousin to leave the hospital. Tommy remained fast asleep, and Kathy assured her as soon as she'd any news, she'd do the usual and ring the McFaddens.

"Off you go now, Caitlin, please. I'll call as soon as I've news. Sure, look at him; he's out cold. He'll likely go through to tomorrow!"

Caitlin looked at Tommy. Kathy was right. He was sleeping like a baby with not a care in the world. Kathy had been checking his obs since she arrived, and everything was A-OK.

"Thanks for everything, Caitlin. I'm sorry I didn't make the funeral. Never seem to get a moment off work here."

"Don't worry, Kathy. Your Daddy's been amazing, but he's well upset."

"Lots going on, Caitlin. More than I think we all know. Leave him to me now for a while."

The young women hugged, Caitlin towering over her petite cousin. She wearily buttoned her coat and made her way to the lift, wondering how long it would take to get home and hoping there would be a bus at the stop.

* * *

Mrs Mac had – at James's insistence – left a few hours back. Roger had opened his eyes now and then and mumbled some nonsense, calling for Catherine, James's mother. Obviously delirious. James paid no heed. He saw it was dark outside now, aware he'd the rehearsal later that evening. As if reading his thoughts, a grim-faced doctor entered the room.

"Mr Henderson?" he asked. James returned his nod and said hello.

The doctor's tone fell somewhere between sulky and bored.

"Mr Henderson, as you know, your Uncle is very unwell. I propose that he remain here at least for the next twenty-four hours so we can follow up on some tests and keep him under observation."

"Do you know what's wrong exactly?" James asked.

The doctor almost smirked. *What wasn't!* He was tired and just wanted to go home. He'd been on call for almost twenty-four hours and needed to sleep.

"We can't be definite, not yet anyway. His lungs are well below capacity, and we won't know more until we get the results."

"Can he go home tomorrow?" James asked hopefully. He couldn't get married without his uncle, couldn't contemplate it.

The doctor answered, "I really don't think so, Mr Henderson. As I said, your Uncle is a very ill man."

His pager rang out. "Excuse me; I have to dash. Please go home. Call in the morning if you wish." At that, the white-coated man was gone.

James sat for a moment and looked at his uncle. He couldn't imagine life without him. Roger was his mentor, his teacher, his friend. He was more of a father than James's real one had ever been. He began to cry, quietly and softly. The thought of his real father only added to his misery. Tommy O'Reilly had so far not produced the mysterious MG who had witnessed James Snr's murder.

As if sensing his pain, Roger opened his eyes and ran them over James. *His son.*

James's head hung low, and he was sobbing softly whilst grasping Roger's hand. Roger squeezed back as tightly as he could and closed his eyes again. James felt the soft pressure and looked up. After a while, he knew he had to leave. After kissing his uncle on the forehead, he left the room and made his way to the lift. He daren't miss the rehearsal.

* * *

Caitlin pressed the button for the lift and waited. Unusually the indicator light soon flashed. She remembered how long she'd had to wait on the night she'd visited her dying father. She remembered the crimson-headed mop that the cleaner used to wipe the hospital's bloodied floor following the bomb in a tea shop and all the poor victims who'd arrived here that night. She remembered everything. There was no one else in the mirrored lift, and she was glad. She walked to the very back and leaned heavily against the glass. Groaning, she placed both hands inside her coat pockets and closed her eyes. Christ, she was tired.

Just two floors below, James Henderson pressed the button for the lift and waited. It didn't take long, and soon the doors opened. He looked inside and saw a lone girl. Her long black hair was loose and hung around her face, and she was leaning against the mirrored glass with her head back and eyes closed. Upon hearing his footsteps, her eyes slowly opened then widened when she heard his familiar Scottish lilt.

"Hello, Caitlin."

Time stopped for them both.

"Hello, James."

Chapter 54

Catherine sat in the lounge area of the Beech Hill Hotel, waiting and hoping to spot Marleen Fry and her chief bridesmaid. It was tea-time, and from Mrs Mac's description, it shouldn't be hard to find them. She walked through to the bar. Two smartly dressed young women were just arriving, giggling as they made their way to a table set in front of a blazing fire. The cosy space was decorated with garlands of holly, red berries and small white fairy lights.

Their chatter and laughter soon dominated the room whilst the barman stood still, watching them. He wiped dry and shone a number of wine glasses while glowering at the spectacle. Typical, he thought. Typical bloody English – loud and brazen.

The women were so unalike, Catherine thought, hoping Marleen was the blonde Grecian goddess. The other one reminded her of a shire horse. She barked her order from the depths of a black leather winged chair.

"I say, Mr Barman!" The man promptly turned away, putting the wine glasses at the far end of the bar in an attempt to ignore her.

She cried out again, pompously and rudely, and snapped her fingers.

"I say, could we have two *large* gin and tonics, as soon as!"

Penelope didn't wait for the barman's response but turned to her friend and whispered naughtily in her ear. Upon hearing what she said, Marleen nearly burst out of her dress, laughing outrageously. The women were well on their way to tipsy already after a long lunch. She'd better pull herself together, Marleen thought. They'd the rehearsal in a while. She hiccuped, and Penelope screamed with laughter.

A number of residents tutted, folded their papers and made to leave. The barman was cross as the duo had already upset a number of other guests earlier. He couldn't say anything. His hands were tied. She was marrying a Henderson, for fuck's sake.

Catherine moved closer so she could hear what the pair were saying. Something wasn't quite right about their behaviour; it seemed odd, off-key in some way. Mrs Mac was onto something. What she did hear was enough to cause Catherine great concern. Marleen was whispering to the other girl, like a mother comforting her child.

"I told you, Pen, it's okay. It'll all work out for the best. James and I have an understanding. For obvious reasons, I need a man in my life, and he needs my money. It's as simple as that. It'll be fine, I promise. Just leave it to me."

Finishing her drink and handing the empty glass to the barman with a smile, Catherine quickly made her way over to the chortling pair.

"Excuse me, darlings do you have a second?" she asked, in an exaggerated English accent. She sounded ridiculous in her own ears, but it worked on them.

"Oh, hello!" Penelope cried enthusiastically and loudly. "How frightfully reassuring to meet another Brit in this dreary, god-forsaken place!" She waved her arm around, indicating the hotel.

Marleen hit her hard on the arm and whispered harshly, "Don't be so rude, Pen! Remember, Londonderry is going to be my home so behave!"

Catherine couldn't agree more. She took an instant dislike to the horsey girl, who fell forward, sniggered close to Marleen's lovely face and kissed her on the mouth. Pen hated it when Marleen told her off.

"I'll get you back later," she whispered impishly.

Catherine hesitated. *There was definitely something not right here!*

"I apologise for my dear friend," Marleen said deliberately loudly, allowing the barman and few remaining guests to hear.

"Not to worry. May I?" Catherine asked, pointing to an empty sofa.

"Yes. Absolutely. Please do," Marleen replied, encouraging her to sit.

The barman made his way over and asked, "Mrs Henderson, can I get you another?"

"Ah, no, I think I've had enough. Thank you," Catherine answered politely. He nodded and walked back to the bar.

"*Mrs Henderson*?" Marleen asked inquisitively, raising her eyebrows. "I don't suppose you're any connection to the Hendersons of Rocola?"

Catherine had to tread very carefully here. "Actually, I am, but a *very* long time ago."

"You are?" Marleen asked in surprise. There hadn't been *any* other Hendersons on their guest list, nor did she know of any other family members around. "How?"

Catherine smiled at her enthusiasm. "Ah, my dear, that would be telling tales! Definitely a conversation for another time. I believe you're getting married this weekend? How exciting. I love weddings!"

Quickly swerving away from the difficult topic of the Hendersons, Catherine encouraged the bride to tell her about her forthcoming wedding. Time passed quickly until Marleen realised she should drink some water since she was feeling particularly tipsy. She looked at her Cartier watch and swore.

"I'm so sorry, but we've got a rehearsal in half an hour. We really must go! It was lovely to meet you."

"You too," Catherine said, getting up to leave and asking the barman to order her a taxi. "Bye now, and best of luck!"

"Thank you!" Marleen shouted after her.

After a few glasses of water, she prepared to leave too and looked across at her girlfriend, who had by now passed out in her chair. Her head had fallen back, allowing her prominent chin to stick out and her mouth to open. Drool had settled on one side of her red, boozy face. She was a truly sorry sight. Marleen grunted and elbowed her lover hard to wake her. At first, scatty Pen hadn't a clue where she was until she heard Marleen hiss in her ear about hurrying up or they'd be late for the rehearsal.

Oh, God, Marleen's wedding rehearsal! Pen doubted she'd be able to bear it.

* * *

Catherine managed to get a cab to take her on the fifteen-minute journey to the church. She'd passed by the place so many times in her previous life but had never stepped inside. Unlike her ex-husband, who'd been a devout Presbyterian, she'd didn't have much faith. She was the first to arrive, so she decided to spend some time reading the few gravestones she could make out by the illuminated entrance.

She heard a number of cars draw up and quietly moved inside to some pews at the back. It was a pretty church and rather small. It was the perfect setting for a wedding; intimate and traditional. The florists had been hard at work today, and the whole place smelled of hothouse roses and stephanotis. She felt herself becoming a little emotional. It was hard to believe her son was of an age when he could marry.

Loud voices echoed through the church as a number of people entered. First came a rather young-looking vicar casually dressed in blue jeans and a grey jumper with his white collar clearly visible underneath. He seemed to be particularly frustrated and slightly agitated, only half-listening to the handsome young man who was following him and trying to introduce himself.

"My apologies, Vicar. I'm Timothy Armstrong, the best man. Just call me Tim." He put out his hand, but it was ignored.

Timothy Armstrong was an old pal of James's from his Oxford days. He was a good sort, and though James hadn't seen him for some time, they'd always managed to keep in touch. Tim felt rather flattered when he'd been asked to be best man. He knew Marleen particularly well from their jaunts in London but knew Penelope even better and decided he wouldn't mention the rumours in town about the two of them. It was, after all, almost the man's wedding day.

"I've just spoken to James, and he's running late," he said to the sulky vicar.

"His Uncle was rushed to hospital earlier, so why don't I stand in for him? I'm sure I'll do!"

Reverend Andrew Ward wasn't enamoured of the best man's suggestion. He was particularly meticulous about marriage preparation and found it extremely rude when the participants were late – no matter what the excuse.

"I don't suppose I have much choice, Mr Armstrong, although I have to say, I'm not one bit happy about it. Marriage is marriage, and young people these days don't seem to take it seriously anymore."

Tim caught his arm and pulled him along.

"Ah, don't fret, Vicar. James will be here soon, I'm sure of it! Piece of cake."

"Tim! Tim! Where's James?" Catherine heard Marleen shout from the open church door. "What's happened? Is he okay? Oh my God, what's happened!"

Tim sighed at such drama and attempted to reassure her.

"He's fine, Marleen. Perfectly fine. His Uncle has apparently been taken ill and is in hospital. James is running late, that's all. He says he'll do his best to be here as soon as. If not, he suggested I fill in."

He watched Marleen crash her way up the aisle, followed by what looked like an already very hungover Penelope. *This was going to be some evening.*

Catherine stayed put. She didn't make a sound but kept her head down as if in prayer. No one noticed her. She was torn by guilt that Roger Henderson was suffering. Had she caused it? And now she'd lost her chance to talk to James and wasn't sure what to do next. What a mess.

Reverend Armstrong was determined to get the rehearsal done and dusted even though there was no groom yet and so rushed through it rather perfunctorily. By the time they'd finished, there was still no sign of James, and they all made their way to the exit to leave. Marleen was furious with her absent groom, and Penelope was keen to get the hell out and back to the warmth and distraction of the hotel bar. They quickly said their goodbyes whilst Tim and the clergyman remained behind.

"Thank you, Vicar," Tim said, not looking forward to going back to the hotel on his own. He'd been hoping to catch up with James, but given that his uncle was poorly, it was highly unlikely.

Reproaching himself for his sharpness earlier, the vicar offered the young man a hot drink in the vestry next door. Tim accepted willingly, and as they made their way out, Reverend Armstrong finally noticed Catherine huddled at the back of the church. He told Tim to wait for a second and made his way over to her.

"I'm sorry, but I have to lock up now."

Catherine looked at him, and he saw a raw sadness in her lacklustre eyes. She seemed so despondent he couldn't bring himself to shoo her out but whispered, "Take your time, no hurry. I'll come back later."

Catherine smiled her thanks as he gingerly touched her hand and told her to take care.

* * *

It was too much. Caitlin could hardly believe it. Fate, after deserting her for so long, had finally smiled her way. As if in answer to her prayers, James Henderson stood in front of her, his face drawn and pale.

Both of them remained motionless and dumbfounded. As if to break the stalemate, the lift doors started to close. Caitlin quickly placed her finger on the button to keep them ajar and asked quietly, "Going down?"

"Yes. Yes, please. Sorry," James stuttered. "I... I'm just... You're the last person I expected to see tonight, Caitlin."

The sound of her name on his lips hurt like hell. “And you,” she said woefully and waited. Nothing happened.

“Better press Ground,” Caitlin said, “otherwise, we’ll be here all night.”

She was bowled over, amazed and thrilled to see him. James, who rarely became flustered, had so much to say he didn’t know how or where to begin. He knew he had to get this right. It’d be his only chance. It was Caitlin who once again broke the ice. Worried by his appearance, she said, “You look tired, James. Everything alright? Have you been visiting someone?”

“Uncle Roger. He had a turn of some sort. He’s not been well. Not since…” He paused. “Well, you know.”

She knew and whispered, “I’d heard.”

It was awkward when the lift reached the ground floor, and the two of them stepped out. He held the door open for her as they entered A&E which, as usual, was hectic, hot and noisy. James was overdue at the church and by now running extremely late. Nevertheless, he wasn’t going to let this golden opportunity pass him by.

They looked at each other. Like one of those corny moments from a romantic movie, neither of them knew what to say but stood shifting their feet awkwardly. They were pushed aside by a running team of doctors, shouting to them to get out of the way as they pushed a trolley towards the lifts.

James looked around in frustration and said, “Caitlin, I have to go. I have something to do, and I’m already really late. Is there *any* way we can meet later? I can’t emphasise enough how very much I need to talk to you. I’ve been into the shop. Did your boss tell you?”

“I haven’t been at work lately,” she said, sorrowfully remembering Tina. He obviously hadn’t heard.

“Ah, yes, of course. Family stuff. He told me.”

“A little more than family stuff, James. Tina’s dead.”

His heart almost stopped. He didn’t know. He’d been so busy he’d not had a chance to read or listen to the news for days.

"Ah, Caitlin. I'm sorry. I hadn't seen that."

"It's a long story," she told him sadly.

Out of the blue and without warning, she found herself asking the dreaded question outright. "I hear you're getting married?"

"Yes," he answered miserably. "Tomorrow."

She eyed him. He didn't look like a man on the eve of his wedding. He looked wretched, and she candidly told him so. "You don't look too happy about it, James. In fact, you look miserable."

At this, he grabbed her hands and pulled her through A&E. Outside, he found a dark corner where he kissed her full on the lips. She didn't waver as her body and senses, starved too long for the nectar of James Henderson, drank him in.

* * *

Eventually, James made it to the church. He knew he was late, but he had to try. As he ran up the path that led to the lighted building, he'd thought he'd gotten away with it. Instead, breathless and rushed, he ran through the door to see no one except for a solitary woman sitting on a pew at the very back.

"Shit!" he hissed. He'd turned to leave when he heard the woman call his name.

"James!"

He hesitated, unsure if he'd heard right, but she called out again.

"James, please." He slowly and carefully made his way towards the woman until he recognised her. She hadn't changed too much from the odd photograph he'd seen over the years. And here she was, the mother who'd abandoned him and his father so many years ago. Sweet Jesus, what a night this was turning out to be.

He rebuffed Catherine's cries as he turned on his heel to leave. He wasn't having this, not tonight. He was too happy having finally spoken to Caitlin and wasn't going to let this neglectful parent ruin it for him. He was seeing her later at the Rainbow Café, which opened late on a Friday night.

Catherine ran after him, crying, "James, wait, please. Let me explain."

He ignored her and made his way to the Jag. While he was fumbling for his keys, she caught up with him and gripped him tightly by the arm. He pushed her away in fury.

"Don't you come near me, Mother." He couldn't find the fucking keys. She grabbed him again.

"No, *you* listen to me, James Henderson!" she screamed. He had to listen. He had to!

"I have to tell you the truth. The absolute truth!"

What the fuck was she talking about? What truth? He knew the truth; his father had told him it numerous times. *ALL* the fucking time. How she'd run away, abandoned them, and then nothing from her for years until her recent letters. He didn't care. His life was better without her. No, he wouldn't listen to her, not tonight nor any other.

He looked at her with scorn. She was crying. In a cold, furious voice, he told her, "I have nothing to say to you, nor do I wish to hear anything further from you."

For yet another time that day, this wasn't what she'd imagined. She didn't want to upset him, not on the eve of his wedding, but she had to say something, had to say anything she could to get his attention, and so she used the only weapon in her arsenal.

"I've met Caitlin. I know about you two."

At the mention of that name, he froze. *What the fuck!*

"Caitlin?"

"Yes. I know everything."

Catherine guardedly told him, "I'll explain how, James, but first, I need to tell you the *real* truth about why I left Ireland. Please. It won't take much of your time. Come back inside."

She gently tugged his arm, hoping she could stir him to follow her.

James had no choice. He'd listen to what she had to say, but not for long. All he cared about now was talking to Caitlin. *Only Caitlin.*

Once inside the church, he and his mother sat down next to each other. Catherine half expected the vicar to return and throw them out, but fortunately, there was no sign of him or Tim. James's body language and expression were still hostile. She understood she had to make this opportunity count and began to speak.

"I didn't leave Ireland of my own accord; I left because I was desperately unhappy with my circumstances here. I didn't run away with anyone. I went on my own to Southampton first, then by ship to Cape Town."

She waited for him to respond, but he remained resolutely silent.

"I'm not quite sure what your Father told you, but this is very, very difficult for me to say." She paused and closed her eyes. "Roger is your biological father, James. I'm sorry."

He couldn't fully comprehend this. What was the woman saying? He shook his head and flinched. Catherine thought it best to keep quiet.

His face paled. "*What*?" he asked in shock and bewilderment. He couldn't believe this was happening. "How?"

She knew then she couldn't tell him the whole truth, it would kill the relationship between him and Roger forever, and so she lied. "Your father and I were very unhappy for a long time. It happened just once. Just once, James, you must believe me."

Minutes passed as he took it all in. His mind reeled. It made perfect sense. He thought of his relationship with James Snr over the years, the undercurrent of awkwardness, the way he'd been so difficult and argumentative. If he were honest with himself, they'd never been really close or comfortable in each other's company. James had known for a long time that he loved Roger more as a father and had always been a disappointment to James Snr. All that time Roger and Jocelyn had cared for him like parents, it had been true of one of them. Poor Jocelyn!

"Did Aunt Jocelyn know?" he asked brusquely.

"No," Catherine replied. "She knew nothing about who'd fathered you."

James shook his head and grunted. He stood up. "I don't know what to say. I don't know what you expect of me or what you want me to do."

Catherine remained seated and looked up at him as he towered over her. The likeness to Roger was remarkable, and she was surprised no one, but she had noticed it. At the thought of him, she asked, "How is Roger now?"

"He's very ill. Have you seen him today?" he asked curiously.

"Yes. At the house," she answered sorrowfully. "I had to talk to him, James. I had to tell him I was going to see you. It was only fair."

"But why now? Why the day before my wedding?" he cried out in frustration. He opened his arms, encompassing the church decorated in wedding flowers.

She drew in a breath. *This was so God-damn' difficult and painful.*

"James, I've tried for months, years even, to contact you, but there were never any answers to my letters."

Suddenly he remembered the one he'd left on the hall table. She was right. He hadn't answered it or even read it. And it'd disappeared. He quickly changed the subject.

"And Caitlin? Why on *God's* earth have you been talking to her?" he snapped.

"I didn't know you knew each other when I first met her. I knew her Mother well," Catherine said nervously. Now he was intrigued. He remembered Majella McLaughlin. Well – at least from the first and only time he'd met her. Catherine could see his confusion and tried to explain.

"She helped look after me during my pregnancy with you, and we became close. I just wanted to meet Caitlin and give her my condolences."

James grudgingly sat back down. It seemed there were unsuspected links between his family and Caitlin's. How strange.

"And Caitlin – do you love her, James?" his mother asked.

Her directness surprised him. "Why? What did she say?" he asked hurriedly.

Catherine could see how he flushed at the mention of Caitlin's name. He was smitten, and the girl was too. So why was he about to marry the English girl? She attempted to take his hands, but he pulled back as if burned.

"She obviously cares a great deal for you, James. A great deal. And I can see you care for her."

He wasn't going to answer this, not in a million years. It was none of her business. He was torn between anger and the need to know everything.

Catherine could see he wasn't going to say any more and told him, "James, this is one of the most important steps you'll ever take, so please believe this from one who knows: it's vitally important that you choose the right person to spend your life with. Be very careful. Happiness is delicate and precious. Believe me."

"James! A bit late, aren't you?" his best man suddenly hollered from the door to the church. "I saw your car outside."

James stood up and looked down at his mother, noticing belatedly that she was a beautiful woman. She felt desperate as she waited to see what would happen next. Tim rushed over and looked quizzically at his friend and then Catherine. He sensed something was up as he waited to be introduced.

James mumbled, "Tim, this is Catherine. My Mother."

Christ, this has been some evening, Tim thought in surprise. *That's one for the books!* In all the years he'd known James, he'd never once talked about his mother.

Tim put his hand out politely. "Mrs Henderson. Good to meet you."

"And you," she said, looking at James. An awkward silence fell.

Tim asked, "Will we see you tomorrow, Mrs Henderson?"

Catherine answered quickly, "No, I'm afraid not. I'm flying back to South Africa then."

James turned his head in surprise. "You are?"

"I have to."

Timothy Armstrong wasn't stupid and knew when to make himself absent. He noticed the vicar entering the church and, pretending he needed to ask him something, took his leave.

Mother and son looked at each other. Feeling drained by the events of the day, Catherine picked up her bag from the pew and apologised to her son.

"I'm sorry it turned out like this and sorry too that Roger is so ill. I never meant to cause an upset. I just wanted to see my son. I'm sorry, James, I'm so sorry for everything." He could see the tears welling in her green eyes as she looked up at him. They were very like his own.

His anger ebbed. He could see she was genuine and knew he couldn't let her leave – at least not like this. He still had unanswered questions.

"Please stay. We need to finish this conversation. I have to go and meet Caitlin now, and I'm late. Will you stay for a few extra days? Marleen and I are not due to go on honeymoon until Tuesday. Just a short time. We have to talk again."

Catherine didn't hesitate. Her heart soared. "Of course, if that's what you want. But remember: think carefully, James, about what's going to make you truly happy."

He knew she was right. Together the small group left the church to be locked up by the vicar, and James offered Catherine a lift back to her hotel, which wasn't far from where he was to meet Caitlin.

Chapter 55

Inside the Rainbow Café, she waited. James was late; she'd been here half an hour already. She looked out of the window, decorated with spray-can snow and adorned with a string of flashing multi-coloured Christmas lights. It was a beautiful clear and frosty evening. The café was near empty. A familiar car pulled up right outside, and she saw James climb out. Her heart hammered so hard she was sure she could hear it, and her throat constricted.

She watched him as he entered, eyes searching for her. Her stomach swooped.

"Ah, Caitlin, I'm so sorry. You wouldn't believe the evening I've had!" he cried as he hurried over and kissed her on the cheek. He looked flustered, and she quickly grew concerned for him.

"Come and sit down. Get warm. I'll order you a drink. What would you like?"

"Coffee, please. A strong one."

Siobhan took their order. As soon as she'd gone, Caitlin asked, "What's happened, James? Is it Roger?"

"Ah, no, he's stable, thank God. You know what, I'm not sure if this is good news or bad!"

He leaned across the table and took her hand. "It's my Mother, Caitlin. She turned up at the church for the wedding rehearsal. I was late, so I didn't see Marleen, just my Mother."

Caitlin waited in silence for him to continue. "She told me you've met. I have to admit, I was surprised. I never knew she and your Mother were friends."

"Neither did I, James! I was as shocked as you were," Caitlin admitted. "What else did she say?"

"That Roger Henderson is my real Father."

Hearing himself say it, the revelation hit him like a train.

"Jesus, Caitlin, all these years and I'd no idea!" He grasped her hands. "But it explains it all; it makes sense. I always had a suspicion about the uneasiness between Father and me."

He chuckled nervously. "I'm not even sure what to call Roger now!"

The drinks were delivered.

"I don't know what to say." Caitlin seemed dazed. "You have to remember, James, Mr Henderson clearly loves you very much. You can't be too angry with him. Especially now he's so unwell."

James nodded. "I know, but it's all a huge shock." He gulped his coffee; it was good.

"Listen, Caitlin, no more secrets. I've had enough of them. I love you, Caitlin McLaughlin, I *really* do! I've missed you so much. Have you *any* idea how many times I've driven past that shop, hoping for a glance of you?" His words were music to her ears until reality hit home as she waited for the "but". Here it came.

"But, Caitlin – I have to marry Marleen. It's the only way to save the factory. She's agreed to give us the money to keep going and save the workforce. I can't let those women and their families down. I can't let Rocola close, not after everything we've been through. Roger is depending on me. I don't think he has much time left," he told her sadly.

Nothing he said surprised her. She'd suspected he was marrying for money, but she needed to hear him say it.

"Don't you love her at all?" she asked fearfully.

"Who, Marleen? Of course not, my love. Not in the way I love you. She's a good friend, Caitlin, and always has been. She's a lesbian, for Christ's sake. At least, most of the time. That's the problem – her parents don't know."

Stunned and exasperated, Caitlin cried, "She's what?"

James smirked at her shocked expression. "I've known it for years, Caitlin. She's tremendous fun, rackety, and always out to enjoy herself.

You have to understand, she's from one of the wealthiest and best-connected families in England and must produce an heir for them. It's a business arrangement between us, that's all. Purely and simply business."

He knew this sounded cold and calculating and hoped she'd understand. "It's only you I love, Caitlin. It'll always be you. No one else. Not ever."

"I love you too, James." There! She'd finally said it out loud. "I can't stop thinking about you. But first, you have to talk to Roger. If he's as ill as you say, do it soon. Be kind to him and make him happy. I'm sure he'll be relieved and at peace that it's finally out in the open."

As for James marrying Marleen… A business deal, he'd called it. Loud, blaring alarm bells were going off in Caitlin's head. She was glad she'd heard him say he loved her and was glad she'd told him her feelings too. But was she prepared to sit and wait for him or, as he'd highly likely suggest, be his bit on the side? She had her own life to live too. There was no one left in Derry for her anymore; everyone was gone. She knew Tommy would be alright; Kathy would look out for him.

Her head knew it was time for her to move on, with or without James Henderson. The idea of him marrying someone else and them living in the same place as her was too much for Caitlin to bear. She couldn't tolerate the pain.

She looked at him imploringly and told him, "James, I'm going to Belfast then London tomorrow. I can't stay here any longer and wait for you. You're getting *married*. It'd be too much for me, too painful here. The past months have been hell on earth every day, wondering where you are, how you were, if I'd ever see you again. I can't keep doing that. So *please* come with me. Let's try and build a new life together, away from all these Troubles – the blood, the pain, the grief. Let's try and build a new beginning, just the two of us. *Please.*"

He couldn't speak. She was asking too much, but he loved her like he'd never loved anyone. His gut ached. He couldn't imagine his life without seeing her, talking and laughing with her, and making love to her. Somehow he'd managed to drag his way through ever since he'd stupidly and cruelly rejected her for something that wasn't her fault. But he understood he wasn't being fair to her.

"I love you, Caitlin. Only you," he repeated.

She knew what he was really saying with those words. He'd made his choice. But still, she gave him an ultimatum.

"My train leaves tomorrow afternoon, James, three o'clock from the Waterside station. Go to Mr Henderson, tell him you know, make him happy. I'll wait for now, but I'm getting on that train tomorrow, James, with or without you."

He couldn't say that at three o'clock the next day, he was due to marry Marleen Fry.

* * *

They talked for as long as they could before Siobhan had to close up. He'd called Caitlin a taxi from the payphone first, and now they waited for it outside. He opened his arms wide to give her a hug. Laughing, he squeezed her as hard as he could and moaned until she looked up at him and then, without warning, ardently kissed her. It felt like the most natural thing in the world. She couldn't be happier or sadder, all at the same time. It'd been such an age since she'd felt so wanted and loved, and yet she felt she was likely to lose him. Eventually, they parted, James making no promises as he blew a kiss at her through the taxi window.

* * *

On the morning of his wedding, James attempted to eat a small piece of toast. He felt ill, deflated. Outside it was a beautiful start to the day as the sun shone brightly on Melrose's frost-swathed glistening lawn.

Inside, the house was lavishly decorated with giant black and white ceramic vases filled with white tea roses and hydrangeas. The reception would be held here after the ceremony. Garlands of green foliage and white heather were woven through the spindles of the staircase from top to bottom. It could only be described as a spectacular sight.

As James prepared to leave for the hospital to visit Roger, he felt a wave of sadness as he stood by the stairwell, remembering as a child watching his father and uncle walk down it, handsome and proud in black tie before another dinner or dance where they'd be at the centre of things, popular and welcome wherever they went. The Henderson brothers. His father and uncle, uncle and father.

Surprisingly, when he reached the hospital and entered the private room, he found Roger upright and alert.

"Hello, you. Please sit with me," Roger said weakly, patting the bed.

"How are you, James? I'm so happy for you. I want you to know that. You and Marleen will be very happy together, I'm sure. I'm only sorry I can't be there today."

Roger stared at him in mute appeal, and James's heart sank. He understood he should tell Roger about what had happened between him and Catherine, that he now knew his real parentage but didn't know where to begin or whether he had the courage.

"I know, but let's be honest – it's all about Marleen's money and saving Rocola."

Roger was mildly surprised and saddened by his nephew's bluntness but knew he was ultimately right. His thin hand reached for the oxygen mask, and he inhaled deeply.

He winced as he attempted to speak. "Well, since you're being so honest about saving Rocola, I want you to have it. It's all yours now."

James sat with his head slumped and his hands on his knees before he said, gently, "I'm not sure I want it, Uncle."

Roger attempted to reach out to him. Maddened by such a disappointing response, he insisted, "But it's my wedding gift to you, James. I'll hear no more about this. It's too late; it's done!"

Suddenly he felt light-headed and woozy as the room started to spin. He fought to control his senses, to keep calm, attempted to smile and cheer up his son, but couldn't. Sharp pains seared his pounding heart. "You must take it, son; it's yours. All I've ever wanted is for you to have it." *Son!* He'd called James *son!*

He noticed the colour draining from his father's face. He was clearly in trouble. The young man rushed to find a nurse. Roger lay back, ignoring the pain. It was done, the gift handed over and acknowledgement made of his much-loved child. It was time for him to rest.

* * *

Tommy was released soon after Caitlin had left the hospital and was now in Kathy's care. She'd telephoned and told Caitlin he'd be okay, but only if he looked after himself. Caitlin explained that she was going away for a few days over Christmas and said she'd be in touch very soon. She'd decided explaining why she was leaving would be too much at the moment. She'd write to her uncle later.

She was an hour early when she arrived on the platform, yearning for James to appear. All night she'd heard his voice telling her he loved her and no one else nor ever would. To pass the time, a fellow male passenger attempted to chat her up, but she politely rejected his advances by moving away along the platform.

* * *

"I assure you, Mr Henderson, your Uncle's condition is not likely to change anytime soon. Please leave him in our hands. Go, for goodness' sake, young man, you're getting married!" Sister Moira Gallagher pleaded with him. "Mr Henderson's told me all about it, and he'll be angry with himself if you don't make it – no matter the bride!"

The sister turned to look at the doorway of Roger Henderson's private room as she heard a voice ask, "Sorry to interrupt MG, have you got a moment please?" MG shook her head and told the young nurse she'd be with her shortly. Looking expectantly at James, Moira half-hoped he'd heard the nurse using her pet name, MG, but he hadn't as she watched him whispering to her patient whilst squeezing his hand.

She sighed and made her decision. Given the old man was so ill and that the younger Henderson was about to get married, she'd thought it best to say nothing for now. The right time would present itself.

"Are you absolutely sure?" James asked, picking up his waxed raincoat.

"Of course I am! He's just had a bad reaction to the medication, that's all. We need to give him time *and* rest. You've been here too long. Now, quickly, go. You can't be late for your own wedding!"

James thanked the smiling young sister and left the hospital to make his way back to Melrose, where Tim Armstrong was waiting. By now, he was growing seriously worried at James's long absence and was relieved when he saw the sleek Jag make its way up the driveway. Already dressed in his morning suit, he ran outside as the groom climbed out of the car, calling, "Christ, James, where've you been? I thought you'd done a runner!"

Bless him, Tim always was a bit of a panicker, James thought with a sigh. "Sorry, Tim, had to see Roger and got held up. All okay?"

Phew! Tim thought. He'd a feeling something was up with his friend. It seemed more than just last-minute jitters or the worry of his uncle's condition. Something was definitely amiss. He wondered whether James had found out the truth about Marleen and Penelope...

"Still time for a quick drink, James, come on," Tim said as he led the way inside. James glanced at his watch. It was nearly 2 p.m.

The men talked in the library briefly, and then James ran upstairs to dress. He then looked at himself in his tailor-made morning suit reflected in the walnut mirror and fought with his emotions. He threw himself down on the bed. Rocola was now his. It was all he'd ever wanted, but he wanted Caitlin too. Why couldn't he have both?

* * *

The station's double-faced wall clock read 2.40 p.m. The train had already arrived and was in the middle of being prepared for the scenic journey back to Belfast Central Station for her connection to the airport. Caitlin looked around anxiously for James and prayed as she watched the other passengers board ahead of her. She'd brought with her just one small battered suitcase containing all she'd cared to preserve from her old life.

* * *

Meanwhile, Marleen was on her way to the church with Penelope, her Matron of Dishonour, sitting beside her, tightly holding her hand. Her father's and mother's flight that morning had been delayed, and they were running late. Marleen was bitterly disappointed and could not help feeling it was a bad omen. This whole match had been made to please them, and now the big day was certainly not going the way she'd hoped and dreamed. She still hadn't forgiven James for missing the wedding rehearsal. What else could possibly go wrong?

As the bride's car arrived at the church, Marleen noticed Tim Armstrong running wildly down the road towards them. He was waving and shouting, and it wasn't until they got closer that his arm gestures and shouts alerted the chauffer to continue driving slowly around the block.

"What's going on?" Marleen screamed.

At the same time, at the Waterside station, Caitlin McLaughlin stepped onto the train headed for Belfast Central.

To be continued

IS REVIEWING STONES CORNER DARKNESS IMPORTANT?

Book reviews are much more important than you may think, especially to self-published authors. At times, self-publishing can still be considered a free-for-all - anyone can do it just stick your book on Amazon and hope for the best ☹

Nonetheless, I've worked extremely hard to make my work professional and enjoyable for readers and having seen the reviews for *Turmoil* so far, I might be just doing that!

Book reviews can take many forms, either brief or long, including a critique or comment on style etc – it doesn't matter either way, it's a review and that's what matters.

The benefits of a review to both you *and* me include:

Saves Time, Decreases Risk to Readers

- Book reviews make books a known quantity. They decrease the risk that a particular book will not be what you had in mind.
- Book reviews help you become familiar with what a book is about, give you an idea of how you might react to it and determine whether this book will be the right book for you!
- Book reviews save you time, prepare you for what you will find and offer you a greater chance of connecting with a particular book, even before you read the first page!

Greater Visibility, Greater Chance of the Stones Corner Series Getting Found!

- Book reviews give books greater visibility and a greater chance of getting found by more readers.
- On some websites, books with more book reviews are more likely to be shown to prospective readers and buyers than books with few or no book reviews.
- Book reviews will also help amplify a book's reach among book clubs, bookstores, blogging communities and other opportunities to gain attention from new readers.

Reviews can open doors to new and bigger audiences for the author.

So please, take a few moments to leave a review for *Turmoil and Darkness* on either:

https://www.goodreads.com/

or

https://www.amazon.co.uk/

ACKNOWLEDGMENTS

In memory of Daddy, Charles, Brian and Frank sorely missed and much loved, and for all the victims of The Troubles Everywhere.

John, thank you for the bottomless cups of tea and loving support, Lynn Curtis for your endless guidance, and thank you to my girls and grandchildren for just being you!

Lightning Source UK Ltd.
Milton Keynes UK
UKHW021314020922
408223UK00002B/313

9 781914 225598